OVER
THE
LINE

OVER
THE
LINE

Book Four in the BODYGUARDS Series

CINDY GERARD

ST. MARTIN'S

For Mom and Petey.
I miss you guys.

And for friends—who
make life special and
just a little bit crazy.

RANGERS LEAD THE WAY.

OVER
THE
LINE

Prologue

Saturday, June 17th, Reliant Astrodome, Houston, Texas

Sixty-eight thousand screaming, swearing, and hard-drinking World Wrestling Alliance fans rocked the dome to various chants of "Death Mask! Death Mask!" and "Bull! Bull! Bull!"

Jase didn't exactly get it. But then, he didn't exactly care. He wasn't a headliner like Death Mask or The Bull. In fact, he'd barely made the roster. What he was, was filler. Half of a warm-up match—veteran Bruiser Cahill versus the rookie, ex–U.S. Army Ranger Jason "Plowboy" Wilson—for a crowd that thrived on mayhem and muscle and blood.

Jase could give them all three. Although at the moment, he was a little shorter on one commodity than the others. His nose gushed blood like a gas pump.

"For chrissake, take it easy, will ya?" he muttered as Cahill—280 pounds of steroid-pumped flesh and nasty body hair—locked him in a half nelson and tried to bury his ass on the stinking mat.

"W'sa matter, *hero*?" Cahill mocked. His breath was rank and his BO even ranker, adding insult to injury as he cranked the nelson tighter. "You bite off more than you could chew when you decided to take me on? Fuck. You ex–Army Ranger types are all alike. Think you're tough. You're just a pansy-ass pussy punk."

Ho-kay. That did it. The fun and games were officially over. Jase had been putting up with Cahill's shit for close to ten minutes now. He was willing to play the patsy— hell, a buck was a buck and this gig kept his belly full— but insult the Army? Insult the Rangers? Screw that.

Cahill might outweigh him by a hundred pounds, but the fact was most of Cahill's muscle was in his head. Jase was smarter. He was faster. And he outmeaned the WWA veteran by half.

"You just couldn't keep your mouth shut, could you, Cahill?" Jase muttered, knowing that what he was about to do would probably cost him his paycheck. He didn't give a shit. Putting this asshole in his place would be worth it.

One hard kick for momentum, a hard chomp on Cahill's forearm, and Jase was off the mat and riding Bruiser's back like an organ-grinder's monkey.

The crowd roared and booed and hurled cups of warm, foaming beer at the ring. Cahill bellowed and stumbled to his feet. Jase clung like Velcro, locked one forearm around Cahill's throat and the other over his mouth and nose so the old boy couldn't breathe.

Bruiser lurched around the ring, trying to shake Jase off. He clawed wildly at Jase's hands, but Jase had sealed them tighter than a wrestling promoter's wallet. Out of breath, Bruiser dropped to his knees again; Jase used the downward momentum to flip Bruiser to his back, wrestle him into a cradle, and pin him. It was all over in less than thirty seconds.

Over. Done. New *champeen* of the who-gives-a-shit-let's-get-to-the-main-event match.

"I'm gonna fuckin' kill you!" Bruiser screamed with a feral growl as he staggered to his feet to the taunts of the irate crowd who'd laid out hard-earned money and side bets with chumps stupid enough to play the odds that Bruiser wouldn't win.

Score one for the chumps.

"Kill you, you little bastard!" Bruiser roared again.

Jase ducked between the ropes and jumped out of the ring onto the arena floor. "Promises, promises," he muttered, dodging a flying cup as he headed for the backstage locker room, beer mixing with the blood that dripped down his face.

In one way or another, Jase had been half-ass trying to kill himself since he'd DX'd out of Ranger Bat six months ago. And he'd gone at it with some pretty good ammo; this counterfeit WWA gig was his latest attempt. Which meant he highly doubted that Bruiser Cahill could accomplish what he himself hadn't been able to do.

When he swung open the locker-room door, his Army duffel hit him square in the chest. He caught it, then looked up from the blood dripping from his nose and into the eyes of Clem Lamont, the promoter for the Houston event.

Lamont looked like he'd been chewing nails and one had stuck in his throat. His normally pasty-white face was fire-engine red. His bloodshot gray eyes bulged. A vein in the center of his Cro-Magnon forehead throbbed like a bitch.

"You stupid shit!" Lamont roared.

Jase held up a hand, not up to putting a helluva lot of effort into supplication or apology. "Yeah, yeah, I know. I was supposed to lose."

"You're the biggest loser I know, asshole. And you just proved it. You're through. Finished! You'll never get another gig in this business."

"My life is over," Jase said in a bored monotone. "However will I live with my dreams shattered?"

"You know your problem?" Lamont rolled a shoulder, all jerky and irritated beneath the raw silk of his royal blue suit coat. "You're a smart-ass. I was grooming you, kid. Grooming! I went out on a limb when I hired you. A no-name. No-brain."

Lamont had the last part right. Jase had been a no-brain for ever thinking he was cut out for this sideshow. "I'll just shower and get out of your hair."

"You'll just leave, goddammit! To hell with the shower. Boys." Lamont stepped aside as the backstage security crew—Mutt, Jeff, and Leon, three cement blocks on legs, knuckles dragging on the floor—came ambling toward Jase, fists clenched, jaws tight, smiles nonexistent.

"Your shit's in the bag," Lamont added, and walked away, shaking his head.

"And the check's in the mail, right?"

Lamont flipped Jase the bird over his shoulder. If he had anything else to say, Jase didn't hear it. But he got the message just the same as Mutt and Leon each grabbed one of his arms and *assisted* him outside.

Jase leaned back against the building as Jeff slammed the alley door shut behind him. He told himself good riddance and breathed in air that wasn't scented of blood, sweat, and beer. Instead, car exhaust, Texas dust, and the pungent scent of the downside of a hundred-plus-degree city day filled his lungs. Still, it was an improvement.

An hour later, he was flat on his back on a cheap motel bed staring at the ceiling. A neon light blinked on and off through the grimy window. A cockroach crawled across the cracked wall.

Other than the cockroach, he was alone—a not so nice place for a man who was a far cry from a loner.

And he was damn weary of the solitude. He was also very alert, suddenly, of the most acute stab of honest emotion he'd let himself feel in six empty months: shame.

He was so ashamed.

This was what he'd become. A loser. A brawler. A phony gladiator who couldn't even throw a fight he'd been paid to lose.

How had that happened? How had an apple-pie-and-ice-cream farm boy from Clear Creek, Iowa, who'd been raised on responsibility and spoon-fed integrity, come to this? How had a boy who'd dreamed of becoming a cop become a joke? How had a veteran of Afghanistan and Iraq, a decorated U.S. Army Ranger—*Hooah!*—fallen this far from grace?

And how much further could he actually fall?

He covered his eyes with a forearm. Heaved a deep breath. Okay, yeah, so he'd sworn off the booze several months ago after he'd come to facedown in a gutter, robbed of everything but his humility. But he was still as shiftless and aimless as a drunk with a case of Mad Dog. The thing was, booze hadn't been his answer. It had only dulled the pain. Jase didn't want it dull. He'd needed to feel it. Feel something, anyway.

He dragged his sorry self out of bed. Stared at his bruised and bloodied face in a smoky mirror. And almost buckled under the wave of disgust that swamped him.

His eyes were supposed to be blue, but they looked

mud-gray and gritty with strain, his color pasty from lack of sleep. The ringing in his ears was a constant, steady annoyance—one of the only constants in his life these days. A constant reminder that his dream job considered him a nightmare.

"Sorry, son. We're damn proud of what you've done for our country. Damn proud. And we'd love to have you on the force, but—"

But Jase couldn't pass the Atlanta police department hearing test. Couldn't pass *any* police department hearing test.

"So far, civilian life hasn't worked out real well for you, has it, chump?" he muttered, dragging a hand over his buzz-cut blond hair.

Nope. Not working out so great.

On a weary grunt, he ambled toward the shower to wash off the blood and the beer and the sweat. He twisted the faucet, let the water get good and hot. Then he stood beneath it and let it scald his skin and drown out the scent of mold.

Not only was he a man without a purpose; he was a warrior without a war. And he was still trying to figure out where that left him.

He hadn't been able to stay in the Army; that was for certain. Not with his hearing loss. Not with Sara still at Benning and probably married to Debrowski by now.

Sara. God, he loved her. And he'd told her so. After she'd healed. After several months had passed from the day she'd buried her husband. A husband Jase had fought alongside in Iraq. A husband who'd come home safe and whole, then taken his own life—but not before he'd tried to take Sara's, too.

"I love you, Jase. I will always love you for being here for the boys and me. But I'm not in love with you. I'm so, so sorry."

She'd had tears in her eyes when she'd said it. Tears of pity. Tears of regret.

Jase lifted his face into the shower spray, ignored the sting as the hot water shot needles of pain into a fresh, raw cut on his cheekbone.

He'd had to get away. Away from Benning, where there was a chance he'd run into Sara every day. Reupping hadn't been an option. The doc had made that clear. He sure as hell couldn't go back to Iraq, even as an independent contractor. His concentration was for shit. And his hearing—well. He'd have gotten someone killed for certain—and the sad truth was, it probably wouldn't have been him.

He twisted off the faucet and stepped out of the shower onto mildewed tile. *What a pathetic loser,* he thought, reaching for a dingy "white" towel. He wondered if No missed it. Missed the battalion. Missed his squad.

"Hell no," Jase muttered aloud. Nolan miss the Army? Not in this lifetime.

Nolan—*No-man*—Garrett was married to the woman of his dreams, raising babies and doing legitimate security work with his brothers and sister in sunny West Palm Beach, Florida.

Jase dug around in his duffel until he found a clean pair of boxers. Stepping into them, he thought of his former squad leader. Nolan Garrett was the man. If Jase had ever looked up to anyone other than his big brother, Jeremy, and his father, it was No.

As it always did, thinking of Jeremy brought a sharp ache of loss. He had died way too young. And Jase had started drinking too young because of it—disappointing his father in more ways than one. Disappointing a lot of people.

Back in Jase's heavy-drinking days in the Rangers, No

had had to bail him out of more tight spots than he could count. He remembered a night in West Palm in a dive named Nirvana where No had backed down a pack of bad-guy biker types with nothing more than a pool cue and a feral scowl.

"Too bad No can't get you out of *this* fix," Jase muttered, thinking about the mess his life had become in the months since.

He froze with his white T-shirt halfway over his head. Then slowly tugged it down over his bruised ribs as his heart rate ratcheted up a couple of beats.

Too bad No can't get you out of this fix.

The words echoed around in the spot where his brain was supposed to be. *Maybe . . . hell*, he thought as a kernel of an idea took root. Maybe he could. Maybe Nolan Garrett could do exactly that.

Four hours later, Jase was on a flight to West Palm Beach, experiencing a swell of excitement that he hadn't felt in a very long time. The next afternoon, short on sleep but long on hope, he stood in the reception area of E.D.E.N. Securities, Inc., the firm Nolan ran with his brothers, Ethan and Dallas, and their sister, Eve.

"Who should I say is here to see him?" A cute brunette, who smelled like heaven and introduced herself as Kimmie, sat behind a reception desk smiling up at Jase when he asked if he could see Nolan.

"Just tell him Plowboy's here," Jase said, then glanced to the right when he heard a door open down the hall.

No, looking all professional and businesslike in a pair of classy charcoal slacks and white linen shirt, stepped out an office door.

When he spotted Jase, he did a double take.

"Jesus H. Christ," No said, with a trademark grin that Jase had seen reduce a woman to drools. "Would you look what high tide washed in."

Jase's former squad leader walked down the hall toward him, a curious look on his face. "Guess the rumors are true. Nobody's killed you yet."

Jase grinned and accepted the hand No offered. "Not for lack of trying."

No laughed. "That I can believe. Great to see you, man. What brings you to the Sunshine State?"

This was the hard part. But Jase hadn't cut it as a Ranger by being soft. He cleared his throat and went airborne.

"That job offer you made me six months ago . . . the one I was stupid enough to turn down. Don't suppose it's still open."

If he was surprised, No didn't show it. What he did show was exactly what Jase needed to see. Understanding, stark and simple. Brotherhood from one warrior for another. Acceptance from a man who knew where the other had been.

But most of all, he saw relief—not some hackneyed attempt to muster up enthusiasm.

"It's still open," No said. "And your timing couldn't be better. We're spread so thin we're turning work away."

Now for the really hard part. "Um . . . well, there's something you need to know. Before . . . well, before you make your decision. My hearing . . . it's . . . well . . . spent too much time a little too close to the heavy fire, you know."

"How bad?" No asked, looking more concerned than wary. He understood. Hearing was a common casualty in the military.

"Twenty percent loss in the right. A little less in the left."

"Well, hell," No said, a slow grin forming, "my wife's got one hundred percent loss when she doesn't want to hear the word 'no.' Doesn't seem to keep her from getting the job done. Can't see any reason you can't get it done, either."

He extended his hand. "Welcome aboard, man."

And just that easy, just that fast, Jason "Plowboy" Wilson stepped out of the land of the lost and back to the land of the living.

1

Three weeks later, Sunday, July 9th, South Florida Fairgrounds, Sound Advice Amphitheatre, West Palm Beach

She was a bustier-wearing, hard-living, tabloid-headlining, top-of-her-game rock star. And as of tonight, Jason Wilson was responsible for keeping her alive.

Lord Jesus God, what had No gotten him into?

Arms crossed over his chest, legs set wide, Jase stood well back in the wings, watching Sweet Baby Jane gyrate to a hard and heavy rock beat, then strut her stuff across the stage on needle-sharp heels, gearing up to close the first of three West Palm Beach bookings.

Sweet mercy, did the woman have stuff to strut.

No wonder they called her sold-out tour Fire and Soul.

Sweet Baby Jane was the flesh-and-blood component of both the fire and the soul.

A wild, thick tangle of long blond hair streaked with shots of chestnut bounced on top of her head. Her lips were painted fireball red. She had a face made for magazine covers and, from where Jase was standing, put the wet in wet dreams. And her body—whoa. That was someplace he wasn't going to go within a Baghdad mile of.

She wasn't any bigger than a bug, her waist so small he figured one of his headbands would fit around it. Best guess, without those heels she'd probably top out at a little over five feet.

It was more than obvious that she was in great shape. Fighting shape. All slim limbs, toned muscle, and steady agility, she moved tirelessly and sometimes frenetically all the hell over the outdoor stage, her skin covered in a glittering sheen of perspiration.

Wet, he thought again. *Very. Wet. Dreams.*

He shook off the thought, tuned back into her performance. She had a set of pipes; he'd give her that. Although why she wanted to belt out that rock crap when she could groove on a sweet country ballad was beyond him. So was the reason she wanted to wear all that makeup and those skimpy, outrageous clothes—not to mention she seemed to have a thing for tattoos. Small ones—one on her neck, another on her biceps, and one just above her right breast. Probably more he couldn't see, all with some deep, mystical meaning known only to her, no doubt. Babes, he'd learned, were like that.

Then there was the pierced belly button. For some reason, he actually found that a little scary.

But he wasn't here to critique her choice of music—or her wardrobe or her body art. Or, for that matter, to wonder what she saw in Derek McCoy, the bleached-blond pretty-boy drummer with the ostrich-skin pants painted on so tight they announced to the world that he dressed to the left.

To each his own. Jase was here to provide security, not judge the rock world's best bad girl and her bed partners as reported by *Entertainer Magazine* and half a dozen other rags.

And he was here to prove himself. If not in No's eyes, in his own. He had a lot of proving to do.

Who'd a thunk it? Plowboy Wilson, country boy with a capital C, *a personal securities specialist to a rock star.* And not just any rock star. According to her file, she was big business, big draw, and major star power.

She was also in a little bit of trouble. Trouble of the crazed-stalker-fan variety.

Jase scanned the sea of fans rocking to the music and crowding the stage. What a mob. Seemed big venues had many things in common—whether it was the WWA drawing the crowd or Sweet Baby Jane. The scent of beer, weed, BO, and about a hundred or so different perfumes and colognes hung in the charged air like smoke.

House security was doing a good job keeping the crowd from mobbing the stage, but since Jase was officially on the payroll as of tonight, he was ready to move in if things got out of control.

The only thing out of control right now, though, was Sweet Baby Jane. Damn, she was a sight. And though she was a mite of a thing, onstage and in person she projected a much bigger presence than on TV or in print. Sure, he'd known who she was. He wasn't a rocker, but he didn't live *under* a rock, either.

She was "the next big thing," the current decade's answer to what you get when you cross Janis Joplin, Joss Stone, and Madonna.

And No trusted *him* to protect her. He shook his head, still bowled over by that vote of confidence. Never figured he'd see *that* on his résumé.

"Max Cogan is an old friend of Dad's," No had informed him at staffing yesterday, explaining about a call from a new client. "They served in 'Nam together."

Ethan, Dallas, and Eve had also joined them at morning staffing, where they doled out assignments and briefed one another on their current clients.

"Anyway, Max manages Janey Perkins—"

"Wait, wait, wait," Eve interrupted her brother, her blue eyes wide with excitement. "Dad is friends with rocker Sweet Baby Jane's manager? Holy shit. Do you suppose I could get her autograph?"

Three sets of eyes—all blue like Eve's—turned on the little sister whom no one in the group would ever mistake for a ditsy blonde.

Jase had heard stories about Eve Garrett—Eve Mc-Clain now—from No. Some of them made his short hairs curl. She was sharp and she was shrewd, and behind those cover-girl looks and misty blue eyes, she could hold her own with a Ranger chalk if she had to.

She had to be tough to keep up with the Garrett brothers, all of whom Jase respected. Hell. More than respected. He liked them. Admired them. They were heroes. Veterans. All ex–special ops, like Jase, which, in a way, made them all brothers. Sure, one gene pool had given the Garrett men their tall, dark good looks and another had given Jase a fairer complexion and a little less height, so it was obvious there was no blood relationship, but they were brothers, just the same.

And he was grateful as hell that all four Garretts—Eve, who'd once been a Secret Service agent, included—had given him a thumbs-up when Nolan had introduced him to them three weeks ago and they'd welcomed him to the firm.

Their father, Wes, a Vietnam veteran, had founded E.D.E.N. Securities, Inc., after he'd retired from the West Palm PD. Now, under the Garrett siblings' capable hands, E.D.E.N. had expanded and built on Wes's principles of integrity, trust, and excellence.

Jase was impressed as hell. He'd spent the past weeks familiarizing himself with company protocol, done some job shadowing, and sketched out a plant security plan that had been implemented. But he'd been itching for his first hard assignment. He'd do anything. Night security. Surveillance. Hell, he'd clean the head if they wanted him to, but that day at staffing, he'd been ready for something other than paperwork.

"I was just asking," Eve had said with a roll of her eyes when her brothers' "give us a break" stares told her what they thought of that idea of meeting the star.

"Cogan wants us to head up all aspects of security for Janey. Or Baby. Or Sweet. Or whatever the hell she wants to be called," No had finished with a frown.

Then he'd tossed a file folder across the conference table toward Jase. "The tour moves from Miami to West Palm tonight and E.D.E.N.'s been tagged to provide personal and ongoing security for the star. This one's yours, Plowboy."

Jase had blinked. Stared at the folder. Looked around the table to see if anyone was laughing, like No had just pulled a big joke or something. No one was.

He picked up the folder. Squinted at his boss. "No shit?"

That *had* made them laugh.

"No shit," No confirmed with a grin. "Read the file. It's a six-month contract, subject to renewal. Pack a bag and head over to the fairgrounds. You're about to break your cherry big-time."

And that had made *Jase* laugh. A nervous, thanks-for-the-vote-of-confidence laugh.

He wasn't laughing now. Sweet Baby Jane rock star was a tornado. A firestorm. He was going to have to pull out all the stops to keep up with her.

"Whatever it takes," No had said.

Looked like it was going to take an army, Jase thought as she skipped across the stage, then leaped gracefully up onto a speaker. Fist in the air, she belted out the last notes to a hard-living, hard-drinking song about life and love on the road.

Yeah. It was going to take an army all right. An army of one.

The booze from the free bar flowed like a fountain. Janey avoided it and greedily gulped bottled water while around her everyone helped themselves to their alcohol of choice and a steaming buffet filled with local Cuban cuisine that ranged from black beans to plantains. Max Cogan, her manager and ever the promoter, schmoozed with the press, the local radio jocks, and their sponsors.

She was always dry after a concert. Dry and ready for some time to wind down alone. But the show was never officially over until the after-concert party wound down. Fans with backstage passes shoved concert programs under her nose and the noses of her band members and backup singers, then flushed red when they scored a much-coveted autograph.

As usual, her drummer, Derek McCoy, was eating it up with a spoon and making his usual and tiresome post-concert play for her.

"You were hot tonight, babe." Slinging his arm over her shoulders and pulling her close, Derek made a big show of nuzzling her neck like it was something he had

a right to do—which he sure as hell didn't. If you believed the tabloids, however, Derek was her on-again, off-
again love interest. Derek would like nothing more than
to make those stories true.

Wasn't going to happen.

He smelled like booze and smoke and the expensive
leather of the black vest he wore over his bare chest. Twin
nipple rings peeked out with winking diamonds whenever he moved. From the corner of her eye, Janey caught
a glimpse of Chris Ramsey's video recorder catching all
the action. Janey gritted her teeth, not for the first time
wishing she'd never let Max talk her into letting the free-
lance videographer tape the tour for an MTV documentary. The last image she wanted preserved for posterity
was one of her and Derek in a clinch.

"What do you say we put a cap on the night in my
room?" Derek continued, not taking Janey's hint when
she pushed against his side. "We can make the night even
hotter."

Janey squirmed out from under Derek's imprisoning
arm. For the sake of the gathered crowd, she forced a
smile rather than snarl at him. "Okay, we've gone over
this before, but for clarity's sake, what part of 'when hell
freezes over' isn't registering with you?" she asked
sweetly so only Derek could hear.

How a man with such a swaggering ego could affect
the look of a pouty little brat she'd never know.

"You know, one of these days, I'm going to quit
askin'," Derek warned through a smile that held more
venom than regret.

She waggled her almost empty bottle of water at him.
"This is me—living for the day you keep that promise."

She was beyond caring that she'd dealt his massive ego
another blow. Derek was becoming a pest—one she really didn't have time to deal with.

"'Fraid you can't handle my brand of action?" he taunted with a sneer.

She couldn't help it. She laughed. Derek considered himself God's gift, and it royally pissed him off that she wasn't interested in unwrapping his "package." "If that's what you want to think, you just run with it."

She turned to walk away, but he grabbed her arm, jerked her up tight against him, and pressed his mouth to her ear. "You're a cock tease, you know that? Sometimes I wonder why I even bother. But there's one thing I do know. One of these days, you're going to be sorry for stringing me along. Very, very sorry."

Janey dealt with the little shot of unease that zipped through her blood by turning it into outrage. She glared from his hand where it wrapped in a bruising grip around her upper arm to the ugly anger in his eyes. "You are very close to crossing a line here, Derek. Get your hand off my arm and walk away and I'll chalk up your little tirade to the booze and a bad day. . . .

"Now," she ordered when several seconds passed and he still hadn't let go of her.

"Fuck it," he swore, and released her with a flourish. "No skin off my ass." And finally, he walked away.

After a deep breath, Janey finished her water and grabbed another bottle, her attention suddenly riveted on a clean-cut, all-American-boy type approaching her.

Just what the doctor ordered. A diversion from that nasty little scene with Derek. And what a diversion. He was not the prototype of her usual fan, who preferred grunge to gleam. This boy practically shined.

His hair—a sun-bleached brown—was buzz-cut, his black T-shirt and jeans pin-neat and free of holes. Not a scrap of leather, a piercing, or a soul patch in sight. His complexion was apple-pie and wholesome. She'd guess him at about five nine, five ten. And while it was obvious he'd spent hours pumping weights and bulking up the impressive muscles that strained the seams of his black T-shirt, she'd bet tonight's gate receipts that those baby blues hadn't witnessed half the things most rocker fans his age had seen.

Innocence. Something about him flat-out shouted it.

She couldn't resist smiling at him as he came within a yard of her. And when he actually blushed, she felt a curious surge of protective instinct. All that naïveté was refreshing. And kind of cute. So was he—in a baby-face, beach-boy-with-a-body kind of way.

For the first time ever, she considered the merits of a one-night stand. *That's* how hot he was.

And that's how deprived you are, she told herself with a self-effacing smile. *Ah, the downside of celibacy.*

Oh well. A little harmless flirting couldn't hurt.

"Hi, sweetie." She was still jazzed on the residual adrenaline that always gave her a buzz during and after a solid performance. Plus, she was a little revved up from her face-off with Derek. "You a member of the fan club? And does your momma know you're out this late?" she added with a teasing grin.

He smiled then. All slow and amused and lazy. And something amazing happened to his face. It transitioned from Babe in Toyland to just plain babe. Twin dimples dented his clean-shaven cheeks. The Michael Douglas cleft in his chin widened. And though he couldn't have been much more than seventeen, he suddenly looked a whole lot older—and just a little more naughty than he might be nice.

The fleeting notion of groping a groupie raised its ugly head again. Especially when she got a whiff of him. Clean. Mostly he just smelled clean. It was a turn-on of epic proportions.

She gave herself a mental head slap while a hundred conversations from the gathered crowd buzzed around them. *Can we say statutory rape?*

"Actually," he said, in a voice that was gruff and gravelly and way outdistanced the youthful picture he made, "I'm on the payroll."

She brushed a fall of damp hair behind her ear, ran the cool water bottle over her forehead. "Yeah?"

"Yeah. Yours."

She did a double take. Looked him up and down.

"Jason Wilson, ma'am." He offered his hand. "I'm your new securities specialist."

Janey blinked. Then blinked again as a wave of disbelief rose inside her like a helium balloon. She pushed out a laugh.

"That's a joke, right?"

He tilted his head, shrugged. "No, ma'am. No joke."

"Oh, for the love of . . . Max!" she yelled, and, grabbing Jason's hand, tugged him across the room in her manager's direction.

"Yo, what's up?" Max Coogan turned, cigarette in one hand, gin in the other, still smiling over something a local sponsor had said. He sobered abruptly when he saw her face. "What? What's wrong?"

"By any chance, have you met my new *bodyguard*?"

Max's brows rose as he glanced from Janey to the "bodyguard" in question. He managed an uneasy smile. "Problem?"

"*Problem?*" She couldn't believe this. "Yeah, there's a problem. While he plays bodyguard for *me* . . . who's gonna babysit *him*?"

Janey rode the hotel elevator in silence, tuning out Max and her new "bodyguard's" conversation as they ascended to the Breakers' penthouse suite.

She mentally shook her head and thought back to the conversation that had landed her in this position in the first place. It had been Monday night, after the third and last Miami concert.

"Things are getting out of control, snooks," Max had said, slumping in the backseat beside her as the limo crept away from the back entrance of the concert hall. He'd tugged at his ripped jacket sleeve, then given up on setting it right, with a disgusted grunt.

As usual after a concert these days, hundreds of fans had crowded next to the stretch, screaming her name, some of them crying, some of them stoned, all of them hoping for a glimpse of their rock idol behind the bullet-proof smoked-glass windows.

"And I'm getting too old for this shit," he'd added wearily.

"*I'm* getting too old for it." The adrenaline rush that always followed a performance had started to let her down.

"Seriously, Janey. I can't take care of you like I used to. Sweet Baby Jane is no longer one among a pack of rockers with a broadening fan base. You're a megastar. A supernova. You've evolved into a monster machine. If I'm with you, then I'm letting the business end slide. You can't afford for me to do that. Not with the numbers you're racking up."

As she had that night in the back of the stretch, she really looked at her manager. Max's dark brown hair was tied back at his nape with a leather thong and was relatively free of gray. His face was only slightly lined by years of wheeling and dealing for the record industry's hottest properties until he'd dropped them all and signed on exclusively as her full-time manager.

From that day six years ago, Max Cogan had been at

her side whenever she was out in public and often when
she was in private. He was her rock. Her anchor. Her
sounding board. She might act tough and unshakable for
the public, but she couldn't imagine facing these kinds of
mobs without him. Neither could she imagine facing
those hours when she was alone.

Especially not lately. The past few days she'd been experiencing an extreme and almost paranoid feeling that
she was being watched.

But she didn't need a bodyguard. She'd told Max as
much that hot Miami night. "If you need help with the
business, then hire someone on that end."

Max had shaken his head, looked sad. "I need help on
this end, sweetie. Someone we can trust. Someone who
can handle your day-to-day needs."

That's when the light had dawned. "You're talking
more security."

Looking guilty, he'd nodded. "Yeah. I'm talking more
security."

"*Not* the old twenty-four-seven-bodyguard discussion," she'd said with a groan.

"Yep. That old discussion."

Janey had sagged back against the seat. "Just up the
number of rent-a-thugs so you don't have to run all the interference yourself."

Then as now, she couldn't wait to take a shower. Her
own sweat plus cigarette smoke from the after-concert
party clung to her clothes and hair, making her half-sick.

"We can do that, yeah, but it still won't be enough. I
want around-the-clock protection for you—and I don't
want to see a new face in every city and have to wonder if
I can count on the guy.

"Now wait before you shoot me down," Max had interjected when she'd geared up to protest in earnest. "I know

you don't want a personal bodyguard. I know that. But what you don't seem to realize is that you've run out of room. We can't dodge this particular bullet any longer. Between the press and the crazies out there, I'm wearing out, snooks. I can't deal with these mobs anymore. I need to turn the reins over to someone who can actually protect you if you need protecting. Someone who can oversee your security issues as well as be there for you to count on."

Like Max had always been there for her to count on during her six-year "overnight" rise to success. That's what this had really come down to. If Janey caved on the bodyguard issue, she gave in to the idea that she'd lose Max. Lose that constant, steady smile, that quick wit and warm shoulder.

She glanced at him now as the elevator hit the Breakers' penthouse level. The strain and fatigue on his face was telling. At first glance, in his faded designer jeans and silk designer jacket, Max didn't look a day over fifty. That was if you didn't look at his eyes. His eyes were tired, which meant he was tired, and that gave Janey a twinge of guilt.

It had given her more than a twinge in Miami that night. Maybe that's why she'd known she was going to cave. Max did need to slow down, and she was being selfish hanging on to his expert hand-holding.

And then there was the issue of the ever-present invisible monkey she felt riding her shoulder at the oddest moments lately. Like when she was alone in her hotel room and she suddenly didn't feel alone anymore—and not in a Casper the Friendly Ghost sort of way.

Maybe she *was* getting paranoid. Or could it be she'd simply grown so self-involved that she suspected she was constantly being watched?

Turned out she'd had good reason. When Max had taken her hand in the back of the limo that night, she'd found exactly how good.

She remembered that moment right down to the look on his face and the sweat on his palm.

"Janey." Max had squeezed her hand tight. "I've been putting off telling you this. But it's time you knew." He'd waited for her to look at him. "Edwin Grimm was released from prison last week."

As the elevator hit their floor, Janey's heart took a deep dive—just as it had that night.

Max had just given her the answer to why she felt she was being watched. Somewhere in the back of her mind, she'd been marking off the months and years on an internal calendar. Somewhere in the back of her mind, she'd known it was time for Grimm to be released. Her subconscious had already figured out that her worst nightmare could be coming back to haunt her.

Despite the warm Florida night, she'd shivered. Yeah. There could be a damn good reason she'd been certain someone was watching her.

Someone was.

"Hire the bodyguard," she'd told Max, shocking him when he'd been about to lay out another set of arguments. "Just hire the damn bodyguard."

So what does he bring her? she thought with a shake of her head as the elevator door opened and said "bodyguard" stepped out of the cab, then motioned her to follow?

A baby.

Oh yeah. She felt *damn* safe now.

2

"It's a gene thing," Jase explained to his new, and so far not so nice, assignment. It was one thirty in the morning. They were in the living area of a plush penthouse suite at the Breakers—him and Ms. Indignant and Max Cogan, who had suggested they take this discussion away from the party. "My dad's fifty-something. Looks like he's thirty."

"Look, I'm sorry," the hotshot rock star said. Barefoot now but still wearing that skimpy black leather bustier and almost skirt, she paced back and forth in front of the sofa where he and Max sat behind a brushed chrome coffee table holding an arrangement of brilliant exotic flowers. An almost sickeningly sweet scent filled the air. Gardenia maybe? Hell, he didn't know a rose from a weed, but his mom liked gardenias. She had a candle or something that smelled like this.

"I didn't mean to insult you," Janey continued, casting an impatient glance his way. "It's just . . . I'm used to Max is all. I rely on his . . ."

"Suave sophistication?" Max suggested with a broad grin.

That finally got a smile out of her. It was gone all too fast.

"His maturity," she clarified with a pointed look.

"I served three tours in the Middle East, ma'am," Jase said simply. "Afghanistan and Iraq. You tend to grow up in a hurry over there."

He would not get fired. Not before he even got started. Not without a fight. He couldn't let No down.

His client—and that appeared to be dangerously up in the flower-scented air at the moment—narrowed her eyes, considered him carefully. "How old are you?"

He gave her his best badass look. "Old enough."

And then he took a chance. "Pardon me for being blunt, ma'am, but if I were to judge you by the package you're wrapped in, I'd figure you were a spoiled, high-maintenance diva who makes decisions based on some crackpot psychic's advice or . . . or on a mood ring or something. Or that you let your minions do your real thinking for you.

"But I don't take things at face value," he continued when she stopped her pacing and locked those dark brown eyes on him.

"See, I figure that someone who's built a career as successful as yours," he added, now that he had her undivided attention, "well . . . I figure there's a lot more to you than meets the eye. And I figure I'd be a fool to think otherwise. Ma'am," he added when it looked like she might be trying to decide if she'd just been insulted or manipulated.

In any event, some of the wind let down out of Miss High-and-Mighty's sails—*Thank you, Jesus.*

Beside him, he could see Max Cogan fighting to cover a grin.

No such luck with his rocker. She was still scowling. But she had stopped pacing long enough to walk to the bar and open another bottle of water. Jase took the opportunity to dig a deeper toehold.

"You tell me what you need from me, Miss Perkins, and I'll deliver," he assured her. "And my looks? People tend to underestimate me. You'd be surprised how many times that actually works *to* my advantage." Although this, obviously, wasn't one of those times.

It was up to her now. He'd done his worst. She could take him at his word or screw it. He didn't want to let E.D.E.N. down, but he'd be damned if he'd beg for the job.

"Okay, fine," she said after a long, grudging silence. "Just . . . fine," she repeated on a weary sigh, and headed for one of the three bedrooms in the suite. "We'll give it a try. I'm going to bed."

The door swung shut behind her with a bang.

And Jase breathed his first breath of relief since she'd dragged him across the room by the hand like a naughty little kid. He felt like he'd just dodged an RPG.

"Well played," Max said, and clapped a hand on his shoulder. "She's a little tense. A lot tired. The tour's been a pisser. We've been on the road for three months straight. And she has to deal with the Grimm creep being on the loose again. Give her some time. She'll be fine with this.

"In the meantime, looks like you're in for now," Max said, and stood. He handed Jase a folder. "If you want to stay in, you'd best memorize her schedule. Besides arranging security for all appearances and events and providing personal protection, it's up to you to keep her on task. And to keep her happy and free of additional stress. Any schedule changes, you'll hear them directly from me. Until then . . . consider this timetable," he jabbed his finger on the schedule stapled to the top of the folder, "carved in stone."

Max walked to the door of a second bedroom, then paused with his hand on the door handle. "I'd trust Wes Garrett with my life. Because of that I trust his kids. If they say you're up to the job, then I'm counting on that to be true."

"I'm up to it, sir."

"She means the world to me," Cogan added after a long look. "Grimm . . . he almost killed her once. Don't let him get anywhere near her again."

And that left Jase flipping through the contents of the folder—and wondering what the hell he'd gotten into. According to his list of duties, he wasn't only a body-guard. He was a fucking butler.

Janey lay back on the hotel bed, clutched the phone in her hand, and stared at the ceiling. She'd already di-aled the number once—then hung up before it ever rang.

Juvenile. Childish. But then that was how she always felt when she thought about her mother.

Her mother. Janey ran her nails absently across the re-ceiver. She hadn't seen her mother in nearly two years. Hadn't talked to her for over a year. And Janey honestly didn't know why she felt the need to talk to her tonight. It was late. Close to 2:00 a.m.

And yet . . . she drew a deep breath, hit redial, put the phone to her ear, and waited. And waited while it rang and rang. She almost hung up again . . . then she heard the sound of a connection and a gravelly mumbled, "Who the hell is calling at this hour?"

Her heart stumbled. Her throat closed up. Her fingers clutched tighter around the receiver.

"Who's there?" Alice Perkins growled in an angry, gritty slur.

"Mom? Hi. It's . . . me. Janey."

Silence, then, "Janey? God, girl, you got no sense of time? I was asleep."

Janey's heart sank.

What? You expected that after a year you might get something like, "Hi, sweetie. Oh, it's so good to hear from you"?

No. She hadn't expected that. At least the adult in her who knew the score hadn't—the child, however, well, the child was still waiting for some sign that her mother loved her.

"Sorry, Mom." This was a mistake. She wished she'd never given in to the impulse to make the call. "I was just . . . just wondering how you are, was all."

"Tired. That's how I am," Alice grumbled.

Janey closed her eyes as silence settled, then jumped with surprise when her mother spoke again.

"So . . . where are you?"

"Florida. West Palm Beach, to be exact. I had a concert here tonight. Two more before we leave on Friday."

More silence.

"Um . . . other than tired, how are you, Mom?" Janey prompted. "You've been getting the money I send, right?"

"Every month." Somehow Alice made it sound like a complaint. "I've told you before. You don't need to do that."

"I want to, Mom."

"Yeah, well, I don't need it. I'm getting by."

For as long as Janey could remember, her mother had never worked. There weren't too many job opportunities for a woman who looked at life through the bottom of a bottle of Jim Beam. Janey doubted very much that without the cash she sent her mother would get by at all.

"See you in the papers now and then."

"Yeah," Janey said, feeling a little too much pride, a little too much warmth, knowing that her mother might actually follow her career. "I get my share of press these days."

"Embarrassing, is what it is," Alice groused. "You look like a slut with all that makeup, wearing them short skirts that barely cover your ass."

Janey closed her eyes, deflated.

"So what else did you want?" her mother asked after a protracted drought of words.

What did she want? Good question. Something. Some little something to tell her that her mother was happy to hear from her. That she missed her.

"Nothing," Janey said, grounding herself back in reality. She'd never gotten much from her mother other than the back of her hand. There was no reason to think time and distance would change that. "Look. I'm sorry I bothered you. Go on back to bed. Good-bye, Mom."

"Yeah. Good . . . good-bye."

The line went dead.

It was a long time before Janey set the receiver on the cradle and went to sleep.

Alice Perkins, on the other hand, was dead to the world half an hour later.

But first, she stared at the phone. Then she stared across the bedroom to the picture she'd cut out of the paper last week of Janey singing her heart out on a big concert stage.

The girl had become something. In spite of her drunk of a mother, she'd made something of herself. When the first wave of guilt and regret rolled over her, Alice headed for her kitchen and the bottle of Beam.

Her hands were shaking as she poured the first shot. "Hurry, hurry, hurry," she whispered, begging the whiskey to dull the pain of her failures that latched on with a brutal fist and twisted.

She was a joke as a human being. A horror of a mother. She didn't deserve Janey. Never had. And so she pushed her away.

Alice's reflection stared back at her from the window over the sink. Stringy brown hair. Sallow complexion. Old, faded eyes. She'd been pretty once. Not pretty like Janey, but pretty enough.

Now look at her. She was used up and worn-out. A drunk. How had this happened to her? She'd had such big plans. She was going to be something . . . someone important. She hadn't meant to be an unwed mother with a baby to feed and bills to pay. She hadn't intended to become a drunk.

And she hadn't intended to survive by the knife of deceit, trickery, and threats.

God, what a mess she'd made. Of everything.

"I'm sorry, Janey," she mumbled. "I'm so, so sorry."

Then as she had almost every night of her adult life, she passed out. This time, instead of at a seedy bar or under a sweaty body that reeked of booze and bad decisions, it was with her head on the kitchen table, her hair wet from the pool of tears she hadn't wanted to shed and that the Beam hadn't been able to stop.

*T*he next night, Monday, July 10th, 2:00 a.m., Blue Heron Boulevard, West Palm Beach

Edwin Grimm lay on his back on a queen-sized bed in an upscale hotel that cost him three hundred plus a night. Compared to his six-by-six cell and his lumpy cot at the correctional facility in San Luis Obispo, California, it was a bed fit for a king.

Freedom was not free. Neither was the skill of the high-priced hooker he'd sent packing after he'd gotten his rocks off a few minutes ago. She'd been blond like Janey. Petite. Pretty. The similarities ended there.

But he'd needed some relief, so he'd made do. And he'd already repented for giving in to the demon lust. He'd found Jesus in prison and Jesus forgave. Now he could just lie here and relive seeing Janey again.

His ears were still ringing. The concert tonight had been one loud, wild blast of a ride—just like the night before. God, he'd missed it. These past three years, he'd missed the rush of rocking to Janey's beat. Groovin' on that smoky, sultry voice.

Watching her incredible body.

She'd learned some new moves while he'd been in stir. He stared at the program he'd sprung for to the tune of twelve bucks. Pocket change now that he had access to his bank accounts again. There was a great head shot on the cover. She looked so fine. Back in the joint, he'd liked to lie at night, quiet like this, and look at her pictures. He'd found them in magazines in the prison library, ripped them out, and taped them with care onto the scarred metal bed frame above him. Some were old and dog-eared at the corners. Some were ripped and taped together. Bastard guards. Couldn't leave a man's private possessions alone.

Private possessions. Like he'd really had any in that hellhole. Just those pictures of Sweet Baby Jane. And his memories of how she had smelled, how huge her deep brown eyes had gotten when he'd paid his little visit to her house three years ago. If only he'd had time to touch her. It would have all been worth it.

He worked his hand down inside his briefs and thumbed his cock. Despite the hooker's expert manipulations, thinking about Janey got him rock hard again.

It had been a damn long time since that night. Damn long years of his life wasted. Just because he'd wanted to see her. Smell her. Touch her. She hadn't understood.

She would soon. This time, he'd make her understand. He just had to deal with some bothersome obstacles first.

He rolled to his side, laid the program with a full-length centerfold photo of his Janey on the pillow beside him. Touched a blunt index finger to her face, eased it along the curve of her breast. He could still hear her sing. Could almost smell her now. Could come just staring at those ripe, vixen lips.

Vixen. He liked that word, he thought, slowly working his dick. Female fox. That's what it meant. He'd looked it up in the prison library after some slick Nancy-boy reporter had called Janey that. A vixen.

That dumb-fuck reporter had been right about that one thing, but he didn't know anything else about Janey. Edwin knew. He knew everything. He wished someone would have asked him tonight at the concert. *Hey, Edwin,* he wished they'd say, *what do you know about Sweet Baby Jane?*

He'd tell 'em. He'd tell 'em that she was as sweet as her name even though they dressed her up like a slut. He'd tell 'em that she'd grown up without a daddy in a dozen low-rent trailers all up and down the state of Mississippi where her momma drank like a fish and washed other people's clothes along with doing a little back work to make ends meet—most often they didn't. He'd tell 'em that Janey was loyal. That she took care of her mom even though she'd never been a mom to her.

Yeah, he knew everything about her, even before she made it big. And oh, had that little girl made it big. Even bigger than when his high-priced gutless wonder of a lawyer had let the Los Angeles D.A. whip his ass on their defense case three years ago and he'd ended up in San Luis Obispo.

Yeah, Janey coulda been a runaway. Coulda been a street whore like her bitch of a mother. But she was too good. Too sweet. Too smart. She'd gone to school. She'd worked summers bussing tables until she'd hitched a ride to one of them amusement parks and tried out for a singing job when she was sweet sixteen.

That was where it all started for her. Singing her little heart out on a stage to entertain snot-nosed brats. One of those brats had been there with her granddaddy. Granddaddy the record producer.

Yeah. One mighty smart record producer. Jack Swingle had seen talent. Real talent. And now Janey was a star.

As big as they got.

God, he'd missed her. He'd be seeing her again soon, though. Was in the process of clearing the way.

Edwin imagined Janey riding him hard and finished himself off with a deep, guttural grunt.

"I'm coming for you, honey," he whispered, then grinned at his little joke since, technically, he'd already come.

Oh, he had so much more he wanted to give her. So much he wanted to say to her. So much he had to make up for.

This time Janey would understand how he felt about her because this time he was going to make sure she knew what he was capable of doing for her.

He picked up the phone. Made an important call.

*S*ame night, U.S. Highway 45 truck stop, Tupelo, Mississippi

"Does it . . . bother you?"

The voice on the other end of his cell phone was hushed, shaken, and, if Alex didn't miss his guess, something else.

The slight tremor, the rise in pitch, told him there was also some vicarious excitement going on here. A thrill provoked by the kill. No doubt about it: He was dealing with a very sick fuck. But then, most of his clients were.

He stood in the wide hallway on a cracked gray tile floor between the minimart and the men's john, glaring at a bank of banged-up metal lockers. "Last I knew, you weren't paying me to be bothered. You're paying me to do a job. It's done and I want the rest of my money."

This was the first job Alex had ever done for this client. The cash was good. The method of payment wasn't. Half up-front, the balance after the completion of the job. But first, the client insisted on this little blow-by-blow account. Alex had to put up with these annoying questions as the scent of diesel, grease, grits, and smoke clung to his shirt like a cheap whore.

"There has to have been a time . . . a time when it bothered you. Death . . . it's so final. So . . . irreversible. And yet . . ."

An outside door opened, letting in a suffocating, muggy heat along with the cush and squeal of air brakes and the grind of shifting gears as an eighteen-wheeler pulled into the truck plaza.

"And yet what?" Alex growled, way past impatient.

"You really feel no guilt? No sense of wrong?"

He grunted out a chuckle. "No pity for someone's dearly departed?"

"There's no need to laugh. This is difficult enough."

That did it. "Difficult for who? I was the one who had to wait. Sit in the dark and the rain in this mosquito-infested swamp town. I took the risk. I pulled the trigger."

In this case the "trigger" hadn't been his Sig but a 1979 Pontiac. *Had* to be a '79 Pontiac Lemans. Green. His client had even told him where to find one. Like he said. A real sick fuck.

No one would find the car now. He'd driven it off an embankment. The Lemans was lost somewhere outside of town, stuck at the bottom of the Tombigbee River, sunk hood deep in silt.

Christ. Alex didn't know why he was wasting his time talking. He'd never have contact with this joker again. Yet . . . something about this particular client provoked a sort of morbid fascination. It took all kinds. But this was a first for Alex.

Disgusted and feeling mean with it, he decided to employ the old axiom and give the client what they wanted. "You want to hear about the crunch of bones and spray of blood when she hit the windshield?" Alex asked in a hushed voice so no one passing by could hear him. "How her skull cracked like a ripe melon? Want me to tell you how her body crumpled, then slid off the hood before I ran over it?

"How about her eyes? You want me to describe how they widened in shock, then surprise, just before I plowed into her?"

"No. Please. That's . . . not necessary."

Alex had figured the gory details would put an end to the questions. He wanted his payment. And he was weary of the chitchat. Patience was a virtue that was far overrated.

But then, so was virtue as a concept.

"Just tell me the damn locker number and the combination," he demanded. "Let's get this over with."

Finally he got what he needed.

Alex located the locker, spun the dial, and opened it up. It was a damn good thing the envelope was there. After counting out the bills, he pocketed them, wiped the locker clean of prints, and headed outside.

"Pleasure doing business with you."

"Wait. Don't hang up. I have another job for you."

Alex shoved out the door of the truck stop and walked from stale, poorly conditioned air into what felt like swamp water. Now this *was* interesting. "Lotta people must have pissed you off, huh?"

"Do you want the work or not?"

Head down, he dodged a trucker walking a mongrel dog and headed for his car. "You got the money. I've got the means." He was, after all, a businessman.

Five minutes later, he had the next target, the details of the job, and a nicely negotiated price. All was well in his world.

Yet as he drove through the thickness of the southern night, a sharp, unexpected memory of his first kill surfaced with the clarity of a newscast. It had been almost ten years ago now. After the first gulf war. After he'd left the force. Yeah, that first professional job had been a rush, a real power trip. And yeah, he'd felt a trace—but just a trace—of guilt at the time. That was a long time ago.

Now a kill was a kill. Now there was just power in the process. And in the cat-and-mouse game of evading the law he used to uphold.

There was one other major perk. The money stockpiling in his Grand Cayman bank account went a long way toward making up for the occasional pang of guilt . . . and the recurring nightmares.

3

Tuesday, July 11th, 3:00 p.m. Backstage dressing room, West Palm Beach

"Ms. Perkins?"

Janey was perched on the edge of the sofa in her dressing room, studying the blocking for a new number they'd added for tonight's concert when Jason Wilson poked his head into the room.

"What's up?" She glanced up from her notes, trying to mask her impatience. It was almost time for sound check, and she still hadn't worked this number through in her mind. One look at Wilson's face, however, had her forgetting all about the concert.

"Problem?"

"Sorry to interrupt, but the police are here. They need to talk to you."

She stood abruptly, tossed her notes aside. "Police?"

Before she could ask him another question, Wilson opened the door wide, and two uniformed officers entered the room. She was barely aware of Wilson making introductions. All that registered were the dour and grim expressions on both men's faces.

"What? What's happened?" Her heartbeat ricocheted around in her ears as she looked from one to the other. "Oh God. Is it Max? Did something happen to Max?"

"Max?" The taller of the two shot a glance at Wilson.

"Max Cogan. Her manager," Wilson supplied.

At some point, Wilson had ended up right beside her. Janey wasn't sure how that had happened, but she was suddenly glad for his steady presence. Max had had a meeting across town this afternoon. All she could think was that he'd had an accident. Or that the recurrent indigestion he'd been fighting had actually been his heart, and he'd had an attack.

"No. This has nothing to do with your manager."

The relief was almost as crushing as her concern. So much so that she must have wobbled. Wilson's fingers wrapped around her arm and steadied her.

"Thank God." She smiled, feeling foolish. "Sorry about that. I'm a little wired. Big show tonight." She lifted a shoulder. "So, what can I do for you? Oh—hey, this isn't about the damage the band did to the hotel in Denver a couple of weeks ago, is it? We covered that. At least, we were supposed to."

"Ma'am," the officer who she thought introduced himself as Richards interrupted. "It's not about Denver. I'm afraid we have some bad news for you."

Again, she was aware on a peripheral level of Wilson's strong, steady support beside her. And once again, she searched for a plausible reason for their concern.

Then it came to her. "Grimm? Is this about Edwin Grimm?"

Officer Richards shook his head. "Your mother," he said, his eyes kind and sad. "I'm sorry to have to tell you this, but she's dead."

Her mother.

Dead.

Janey stared in numb silence. Numb but for the sharp, tight knot twisting in her chest. Numb but for the rush of blood pulsing at her temples, blurring her vision.

She shook her head. Wilson's hands on her shoulders now felt strong and warm and real in a moment that had otherwise lost all semblance of reality. "Dead? My mother is . . . dead? Are you . . . sure?"

"I'm sorry, Ms. Perkins, but yes. The Tupelo police identified her body. They didn't want to deliver the news by phone so they contacted us and asked that we inform you."

"How?" she finally managed to ask, still caught somewhere between disbelief, denial, and bewilderment.

"According to the report, she was killed by a hit and run driver. There's an ongoing investigation, of course, but that's what appears to have happened, ma'am."

"Ms. Perkins." It was Wilson's voice that penetrated the fog again. "Come on. Let's sit you down."

She let him lead her to the sofa.

"I'll leave a number for the Tupelo police. When you're up to it, you can call them. They can fill you in on the details." She heard Officer Richards's voice as her mind spun back to the phone call she'd just had with her mother.

"I just talked to her," she said aloud.

She was vaguely aware of the shifting of feet. Someone cleared his throat. "We're very sorry for your loss, Ms. Perkins."

She nodded as they left the room, closing the door behind them.

"I just talked to her," she repeated, lifting her head and meeting the concern in Jason Wilson's baby blue eyes.

"Do you want me to call Max?" he asked gently.

Already, he knew her so well. Knew that she needed Max. Max who was always there for her. Who she wanted to be here for her now.

And yet, she shook her head. "No. I don't . . . um . . . I don't want Max to know about this. Not yet. He'll insist we cancel tonight's concert."

Wilson was quiet for a while. "It's not my place to say so, but if he did cancel, he'd be making the right call."

Wilson meant well. But suddenly she couldn't handle the compassion in his voice, the tenderness in his eyes.

"Max is not to know about this," she insisted and dug deep to stiffen her backbone. "Got it?"

He looked at her long and hard. "You're the boss."

She made herself smile. "Yeah. There is that."

"Is there anything I can do for you?" he asked after several moments passed.

"Yeah. You can give me a little time alone, okay? I . . . I need to . . ." What did she need to do? She didn't know. She didn't have a clue. "I just need to be alone for a while."

She figured it went against his better judgment and his macho gene to leave her, but in the end, he nodded. "I'll be right outside the door. You need something . . . a shoulder maybe . . . just let me know."

"Sure." She compressed her lips. "I will. Thanks."

Then she closed her eyes and waited for what seemed like an eternity for the sound of the door to close behind him.

Only then did she let the tears that had been building fall. Only then, did she give herself permission to mourn for a mother she had never really known.

◆ ◆ ◆

Smoke from Max's cigarette curled up behind Janey's dressing-table mirror. It made her think of fog rising from a boggy river bottom on a cool October morning. And it made her shiver. She'd seen a lot of foggy mornings from a lot of shabby little Mississippi backwater river towns. As Brenda Jane Perkins she'd known a lot of cold mornings. Scared and hungry mornings. And the news the West Palm PD officers had brought her earlier today made her remember them far too clearly.

She lifted her chin. Determined to get past it. And to remember that where she was now was a long way from Mississippi. Remember that at twenty-seven, with five platinum CDs and a portfolio that would make Martha Stewart blink, she was a long way from scared and skinny little Brenda Jane.

"Didn't I ask you to put that thing out?" She glared into the dressing-table mirror, meeting Max Cogan's passively curious expression.

The conversation of the other occupants of the dressing room stalled into shocked silence.

They didn't call her *Sweet* for nothing. She could talk trash with the best of them, belt out a song in what *Rolling Stone* magazine had labeled a velvet hammer of a voice, but she only played the role of diva for the paparazzi. Never with her inner circle.

And she'd just snapped at Max.

After a considering look, Max slowly roused his long, lanky frame from a deep slouch on the cushy red leather sofa.

"How about you-all give Janey a little room?" Max suggested to the entourage lounging and languishing and helping themselves to the open bar that Janey never touched.

Nobody questioned Max's quiet request. Not Neal Sanders, a carryover friend from her summers singing at amusement parks. Not Christine Ramsey, who was still busy videotaping her chronicle of Janey's Fire and Soul tour for her documentary. Not Derek, who had backed off—at least for tonight if the busty brunette he had in tow was any indication. No one, from the rest of the band members to the backup singers, said a thing for several long seconds.

Finally, looking uncomfortable, they all mumbled quiet versions of "break a leg" and shuffled out of the room.

Janey caught a glimpse of Baby Blue—as she'd started thinking of Jason Wilson—standing outside her dressing room as the door closed behind them. *Vigilant as hell,* she thought sourly.

Great. Now she was complaining about a man who was just doing his job. It wasn't his fault she needed a body-guard. Or that since he'd come on the scene she some-times found herself thinking about sex—or her lack of it.

She turned back to the dressing-table mirror—and saw that Max was pointedly meeting her gaze. With a grand flourish he dropped his half-smoked cigarette into a mug of stale, cold coffee.

"Okay, snooks. It's out. It's just you and me now. You wanna tell me what's got your tail in a knot?"

Janey went back to work on her stage face, painting on black eyeliner with a heavy hand covered in sheer silver diamond net that crawled up to her elbow. The same glit-tery mesh matched her thigh-high stockings. And the hand that applied the makeup was shaking.

The shaking ticked her off. It reminded her of that wretched little girl she used to be. The one who had got-ten cross with Max, who didn't deserve her anger, and added guilt to the mix. The one who still had a need for her mother. A knot of pain twisted in her gut.

"It's a big gig," she hedged, and lined her lips with a fire-red lipstick pencil. "Last I knew, the headliner was allowed to be a little nervous."

Max grunted, folded his big, long-fingered hands together between splayed knees, and frowned at her through tired brown eyes. "Look—sweetie, if it's Grimm, relax. Wilson's got it covered."

"It's not Grimm." She'd be damned if she'd let that wacko control her life again.

Outside the paper-thin walls of the backstage dressing room, she could hear the rumble of the sold-out crowd. The opening band had done a good job warming them up for her. A few would already be stoned. Many were slowly working up a nice buzz on eight-dollar-a-cup beer. Most were here for a good time and a good hard rock concert beneath a blanket of Florida stars. All of them were here to see her—Sweet Baby Jane—Horizon recording label's top-grossing star for six years running.

"Janey?"

She met Max's concerned gaze in the mirror again, then looked away, pushing herself to her feet. She walked across the dressing room on four-inch silver platform boots that rose to just above her knees and elevated her to a whopping five five. Inspected her stage costume—what there was of it—in the full-length wall mirror.

Her mother had been right. She looked like a slut. Hell, there was more covering her arms than the rest of her. She was exposed from her shoulders to the top of her breasts, where a black leather band cinched tight, leaving her bare to the micromini leather and white lace skirt riding high on her thighs and low on her hips. So low, she could see the tail of the clef note she'd had tattooed low on the left side of her abdomen right after she'd signed her first recording contract eight years ago.

Since then, she'd added three more tattoos—all kanji, all with meanings and reasons known only to her. The one on her neck, just below her left ear, was the kanji equivalent of *Naughty Girl*. That one was for the paparazzi. The other two—*Mad Power,* two inches square, on her right biceps, and *Soul,* the size of a postage stamp, etched above her right breast—were for her.

Of course, no one would take notice of any of them tonight; they'd be more interested in the interlocking silver hearts hanging from her pierced navel on a thin diamond-studded chain.

Image, she told herself with a slow blink of her eyes, and brushed a fall of the hair she'd straightened for tonight back into the spiky nest swept up on the left side of her head. It was all about image. The more outrageous, the more attention. The more attention, the more album and concert sales.

That's what the industry was about these days, she thought, no longer surprised by the bitterness she sometimes felt. It sure as hell wasn't about the music.

"Snooks?" Max rose and walked up behind her. He moved a little slower lately. It was one of the few giveaways that he'd turned sixty-two last month.

"Truth now," he pushed when she remained silent. "What's bothering you? You've been as jumpy as a Jack Russell pup since sound check."

She flinched when she felt his hands settle on her bare shoulders; her muscles tightened at his paternal touch when normally they would have relaxed.

"Whoa, whoa. You're shaking." His bushy brown eyebrows drew into a scowl. "Okay. What'd that little bastard Derek do this time?"

"Derek has nothing to do with this." For once, that was actually true.

"If it's not Derek then . . . oh, hell—you're not letting that Bible-thumper get to you."

Six months or so ago, popular hellfire and brimstone TV evangelist Samuel Black had begun referencing Janey and her "ilk" and her music as the downfall of American morality in his sermons. His wife, Tonya, a Tammy Faye Baker wannabe—although only God knew why—had even organized a handful of his followers to show up at Janey's concerts recently, demonstrating against moral decay and rock and roll, and selling cookies to support their summer youth camp. Had to love it.

Or not.

Okay, yeah, it bothered her that Black's group had singled her out, but then so did the paparazzi who wouldn't give her a moment's peace. But neither the news media nor the fundamentalist Holy Roller was at the top of her list tonight.

"Janey?"

"No." She shook her head. "No, it's not Black."

Hands on her shoulders, Max turned her around to face him. "You're okay with Wilson and the new security setup, right? He came highly recommended, kiddo."

Actually, she had made peace with that. She'd been wrong to judge Wilson on looks alone. And he'd impressed the hell out of her when he'd made his case the night before last. And she'd been glad he'd been here for her today. Besides, it wasn't his fault that when she looked at him the emphasis was on "body," not "guard." "I'm fine with it. Max. . . . Look. It's nothing," she lied. "Just let it go."

"I would, but your drawl is thicker than syrup and I only hear it these days when you're upset."

The absolute bafflement and open concern in Max's voice finally did it.

She hadn't wanted him to find out about this tonight.

Not before the concert. She wanted to be strong. She wanted to be tough.

So much for what she wanted. She was about to wimp out. And she hated that. Really, really hated it.

"The police were here earlier. While you were talking to the suits at the label."

"Police?" The concern in Max's tone switched to alarm.

"She's . . . she's dead, Max." Finally, Janey met his eyes. "My mom. She's dead."

Shocked silence swelled into the room. Outside, the muffled rumble of the partying crowd reverberated off the walls.

"Oh . . . oh, sweetheart." Max folded her into his arms when he'd fully absorbed the news. "I don't know what to say. Lord. What . . . what happened?"

She soaked in the familiar comforting scent of him. Leather and spice and smoke. She shook her head, needing his familiar support more than she should. "There was an accident. Hit-and-run. It . . . it happened last night. It took them this long to identify the body and to locate me."

A chill ran through her as she thought about it—and about that indefinable something that had compelled her to call her mother the night before she died. A phone call Janey had been putting off for over a year.

Max let out a slow, deep breath. "I am so, so sorry, kid."

"Yeah. Hey. Look." She pulled abruptly away, knowing that if she let herself lean into all that caring and concern much longer, she'd fold. Worse, she'd cry. She couldn't cry now. She had a show to do. "It's . . . it's okay, you know. It's not like we were close or anything.

"It's okay," Janey repeated, working her damnedest to convince both of them that she was tough. She blew it by jumping like a rabbit when a knuckle rap on her door and the anticipated cue of, "Five minutes, Ms. Perkins," told her she was due onstage.

"We're canceling tonight," Max said without hesitation. "You don't need to do the show. Not now. Not after this news."

He was not your typical manager, Max Cogan. With Max, Janey came first, not the money.

She kissed his cheek, then used her fingertips to wipe off the lipstick she had left behind. "I do. I do need to do it."

She pulled herself together and left her dressing room despite Max's worried frown. Baby Blue was there waiting outside the door. Gorgeous and vigilant in full bodyguard mode with his scowl fierce and eyes watchful. Until he saw her face and watchfulness transitioned to concern.

He took her arm. Held her gaze. "You doing okay, Ms. Perkins?"

He really was concerned. She felt as well as saw it. Was as touched by it as she was surprised again that he would be so sensitive.

For some reason she found herself wanting to reassure him. It was that beautiful baby face, she supposed. And maybe some deeply buried mothering instinct coming into play—which actually made her smile, because mothering was the last thought that usually came to mind when she thought about Jason Wilson.

"Right as rain," she assured him, and flashed him her brightest smile.

"Glad to hear that, ma'am. How about you go on out there and knock their socks off?"

Her mood suddenly brightened. "How about I kick a little ass instead?"

He grinned. "That'll work."

He took her arm and, along with two additional rent-a-muscle-men plus three members of the Amphitheater's security staff, escorted her to the stage, where her band had already launched into her opening number.

The sky was midnight dark; the crowd was on its feet, chanting her name. Electricity crackled in the air.

It was showtime.

And Sweet Baby Jane never missed a show.

L *ater that night, after the concert*
"Do you think she liked me?"

Derek McCoy drew deep on a hit of prime Colombian, held it in his lungs, then passed the joint to the girl. He made quick work of stripping off his clothes and lay back on the king-sized bed of the suite Her Highness, Miss Cock Tease Perkins, had sprung for.

"Quit worrying about impressing her and start impressing me, darlin'," he drawled, working to curb his temper as she passed the joint back to him. "Lose the threads. I promised you I'd get you backstage to meet her and I did. Now it's time to pay up. Show me those big tits you're so proud of. And then I want to see your head in my lap."

Tammy, or Tansy or Tara or whatever the hell her name was, whipped her crop top over her head, unself-consciously displaying her firm, full teenage breasts. God, he loved his life. All the pussy and weed he wanted. All the head he could handle.

Yeah, he thought as she went down on her knees between his thighs and took him in her mouth.

He fuckin' loved his life.

He jerked to a sitting position when she started working him over, cupped her head in his hands, and guided her in a fast and frenzied rhythm, pretending it was Janey kneeling and supplicant and kowtowing to him.

Yeah, he loved his life. But he hated Janey Perkins with a passion.

The bitch. She shut him down. Over and over again, she fuckin' shut him down. Women didn't turn Derek Mc-Coy away. Women fought to get into his pants.

But not Janey Perkins. Hell no. To her, he was nothing but a lapdog. Licking her feet. Scrambling for the scraps she tossed him. Begging her to throw him a bone.

"Harder," he growled, knotting his hands in the hair of the girl who was a poor substitute for the woman he wanted to bring to her knees.

More. He wanted her more than on her knees. He wanted to make sure she got what she really deserved.

As the girl finished him off, he clenched his teeth, came with a groan, and fell back on the bed.

Yeah. He wanted Janey Perkins to get everything she deserved. And someday, someday soon, he'd be dancing on her grave when she got it.

*T*hursday, July 13th, Tupelo
       "You doing all right, snooks?"

Janey pinched out a smile to reassure Max that she was holding up, thankful as always, for his support. As of three days ago, he was the only parental figure left in her life—even if on a surrogate basis. Not that her mother had ever been stellar in the role.

Guilt—for the bitterness she felt—settled heavy and deep. Alice Perkins was dead. She hadn't been much of a mother, but she deserved someone to grieve for her. Janey appeared to be the only candidate. And yet her eyes were dry. Partly due to shock. Partly due to fatigue. Mostly because she'd lost her mother a long, long time ago.

Baby Blue sat stoic and watchful in the front seat of the Lincoln Town Car that drove them from the cemetery back to the funeral home. Outside, through the Lincoln's tinted windows, Janey caught glimpses of the press with their zoom lenses aimed at the vehicle. The Lincoln actually had to stop in the middle of the highway when a slew of photographers blocked their way.

"Damn jackals," Max sputtered. "Bastards can't even let you bury your mother in private."

It was the cost of being who she was.

One of the costs, anyway.

Fanatics like Edward Grimm were another.

And now this. The news of her mother's death had compounded the feeling that someone was watching her. And not just the paparazzi who dogged her like a bad aftertaste. Just knowing that Grimm was on the loose had her constantly fighting the urge to look over her shoulder. The feeling had intensified since her Gulfstream had landed last night.

Or, she thought pragmatically, maybe it was the questions that had surfaced and lingered since the hit-and-run. Neither a car nor a driver had been found. No one had confessed. No one had seen anything. Aside from the obvious horror of knowing her mother had died that way, something didn't feel right about it.

Janey had plucked a single red rose from her mother's funeral spray. Or maybe, she thought, inhaling the bud's subtle, clean fragrance, it was more of a sense of being out of sync, out of place. She was back in Mississippi. Back in Tupelo, one of the many Mississippi towns where she'd spent her childhood. And where she'd never wanted to return.

"I called her," she said quietly, then lifted her head when she felt Max's concerned gaze on her face. "The night before she died . . . I . . . I don't know why I did it. She was just . . . on my mind, you know?"

Max squeezed her hand. "It's good. It's good you got to talk to her."

Yeah. Good to hear her mother grumble about being woken up and dress her down about her makeup and clothes.

And now she was gone. Janey lifted a hand to finger the Celtic cross she'd found among her mother's things that morning.

"I've never seen you wear that before," Max said.

Janey looked down at the cross. "I gave it to her. I was thirteen or something. Saw it in Wal-Mart or Kmart or someplace like that. Fell in love with it. Just a piece of cheap discount-store jewelry, but I thought it was beautiful. I bought it for her with my babysitting money one Christmas."

She let go of the necklace and stared without seeing out the window. "I never saw her wear it." The cross felt heavy and cool yet, for some reason she didn't understand, comforting lying against her skin. "Wouldn't have dreamed she'd kept it all these years."

"I'm sure it was special to her."

Tears stung Janey's eyes as guilt outdistanced both the sense of displacement and the paranoia. "I should have known her better."

Max covered her hand with his. "She didn't exactly make that easy for you now, did she?"

Janey roused herself from her thoughts, tuned into what Max was saying. Comfort. He was offering comfort . . . and absolution. No. Her mother hadn't made it easy to know her. Or to love her.

And no matter how many times Janey told herself that alcoholism was a disease, a warring faction in her mind and heart told her that her mother had had a choice.

She'd chosen the booze.

And that had left a fatherless little girl wanting for a mother, too.

*J*ase flanked Janey on one side, Max the other; all three of them stared in stupefied silence as they stood in the middle of Alice Perkins's living room—or what was left of it.

"Jesus," Jase muttered, surveying the destruction, and watched for a sign that Janey Perkins, who had buried her mother not more than thirty minutes ago, was going down for the count.

The entire house had been ransacked. End tables and lamps lay drunkenly across the tile floor, smashed and broken. Chairs were overturned. Cushions slashed. House-plants had been upset; the fetid scent of damp potting soil permeated the air. Even her mother's clothes had been strewn all over the bedroom. Shards of pottery and shattered glass were scattered all over the kitchen floor.

Her face chalk-white against the black of her funeral dress, Janey reached out, unaware that she was doing it. Jase grabbed her hand to steady her. Her fingers were ice-cold. Shock. Against her throat, below the delicate strokes of her tattoo, he could see her heartbeat knocking out of control.

And as he had several times today, Jase resisted an unexpected urge to offer her more than a steadying hand.

"Why would anyone do this?" Her voice was as shaky as her hand.

"I'm afraid it's all too frequent an occurrence, Baby— pardon me. I mean, Ms. Perkins."

The uniformed officer who'd been the first to respond to Max's 911 call was a young, scrubbed-faced freshman cop. Officer Rodman of the rapidly blinking blue eyes, steel-wool cap of carrot-red hair, and nervous shoulder jerk was obviously also a fan. His face flushed as red as his hair. He smelled of gun oil and Mississippi heat.

"You'd be surprised how many break-ins coincide with obituary listings in the newspaper," Rodman continued.

"That's just sick." Max scrubbed a hand over his face as he surveyed the damage.

"Yes, sir," the officer agreed with a slow southern drawl. "There's a criminal element even here in Mississippi that preys on these types of situations. They scan the papers, know the house is empty during the funeral services, and figure they've got easy pickins."

The officer waited for that information to settle, then pulled a notebook out of the breast pocket of his uniform shirt with another jerk of his shoulder. "Can you tell me if there's anything missing?"

Janey hesitated, clearly still grappling with the devastation. Hell, Jase was having trouble grasping it. It looked like a lot more than a break-in. It looked like someone had been good and pissed.

"I have no idea," Janey said, responding to the officer. "I've . . . this is the first time I've been to my mother's . . . to her house."

"Well," Rodman said, glancing around, "it's obvious they weren't going for the bigger items. TVs are still here. So's the DVD player, the stereo system. Would she have kept cash in the house, do you think? Jewelry?"

"I . . . I don't know. I don't know anything about what she might have kept in the house."

For that matter, it was obvious by the way she looked around, kind of lost and uncertain, that she didn't know much of anything about the way her mother had lived. Jase found that a little sad. And he could see in Janey's eyes that she did, too.

"Officer Rodman," Max intervened, steering the young policeman toward the door. "You must understand. Ms. Perkins has had a difficult day. She's just buried her mother. And now this. Is it possible these questions could wait? Perhaps until tomorrow?"

Rodman nodded, his face flushing red again. "Sure thing.

"Listen," he added with another jerk of his shoulder, "I wish I could let you stay for a while, but we need to get Forensics in here and—"

"Just give her a minute, okay?" Jase said.

Rodman looked uncomfortable, but finally nodded. "Just for a minute, but don't disturb anything."

"Yes. Yes, of course," Max chimed in. "We understand. Let me give you my card. You can reach Ms. Perkins through me or Wilson here, if you have more questions."

Jase had questions. A lot of questions. But he kept them to himself, watching, with a growing concern that he hadn't expected to feel for a bad-girl rocker who suddenly looked as fragile and breakable as a piece of delicate handblown glass.

4

The sense of violation was crippling. So was the sense of doom. Janey stood in numb silence, vaguely aware of Max talking to the officer, of Baby Blue's quiet vigilance behind her, and thought, *This was where my mother lived.*

The small two-bedroom ranch was Alice's home—but it had never been Janey's. She'd never lived in anything remotely this nice as a child. And yet even in the shambles of the break-in, Janey could see the house was modestly furnished—just like the house itself was modest. Small.

She didn't understand. Given the amount of money she'd been sending her mother the last few years, Alice Perkins should have been living like a queen. Another knot of emotion Janey didn't entirely understand balled up inside her.

She heard Baby Blue's voice in the background, reaching her through a hollow tunnel as he asked the officer some questions. She walked numbly across the living room, skirting an overturned end table to get to an open window and the fresh air scented of summer roses and lilies that she suddenly needed. She glanced jerkily around the house, unable to shake the sensation of being caught in the crosshairs of a rifle scope.

Perfect. Now her paranoia came with details.

Outside, a soft, hot Mississippi breeze rustled the trees in this quiet suburban neighborhood. She could hear the shouts of children playing in their yards, smell suppers cooking on grills nestled on patios opening onto neatly manicured lawns.

It was the kind of neighborhood she'd dreamed of living in when she was a little girl. Quiet and clean.

Safe.

Her reality, however, had never been any of those things. Her reality had leaned more toward rusted-out trailer houses with weedy dirt yards where mangy dogs fought rats for the garbage rotting in overflowing trash cans. And where crack houses flourished every four blocks.

Instead of flower scents, she remembered the scent of stale, spilled beer or, if her mother had scored a "visitor," the whiskey that had been her drink of choice.

"Come on, snooks."

She started when Max's voice and bracing hand on her arm brought her back to the moment.

"Let's get you out of here. If the local Barneys want to talk to you again, they've got mine and Jase's cell numbers."

She didn't argue. More than anxious to leave, she let Max guide her out the door as Wilson dealt with the throng of reporters lurking like gnats and yapping like dogs and help her into the waiting Lincoln they'd rented at the airport. An hour later they were airborne in her private jet.

Janey closed her eyes, let her head fall back against the plush leather headrest, and steadied herself by breathing deep of perfectly conditioned air. Alice Perkins was dead. She'd died a violent, solitary death outside a run-down bar—probably at the hands of someone whose blood alcohol level had rivaled that of the woman whose life had been taken.

Liver disease. Suicide. Janey had always thought that was how it would end for her mother. That was the call she'd always anticipated. But this. This was just one more grievous insult to a sad and wasted life that could have been so much more.

She wished she could cry. She wished she could feel something . . . something more than empty . . . as if someone had used a rusty knife to carve a gaping hole in her chest.

How a hole could have a presence she didn't know. But the weight of it stayed with her—along with a persistent, nagging sense that someone was watching every move she made.

*F*riday, July 14th, Atlantic City Hilton, New Jersey "You're not going to believe what happened." Chris Ramsey wedged the phone between her shoulder and ear and rummaged through her suitcase for her green silk blouse. She liked the way it looked with her red hair. Liked the new short and sassy cut she'd gotten before joining Sweet Baby Jane's Fire and Soul tour.

Quincy Taylor, Chris's longtime lover, an independent movie producer, was sitting poolside back in California.

"Babe, I'd believe damn near anything you told me after some of the tape you've sent. This documentary is going to make you the most sought-after videographer in L.A."

Which was exactly what Chris was shooting for when she'd wangled her way into Sweet Baby Jane's inner circle. She'd begged. She'd bribed. She'd called in favors. And it was all paying off. Janey Perkins's mother—a drunk, from what Chris had been able to dig up—was dead, the victim of a hit-and-run. This kind of drama was going to be the power boost that propelled Chris's career to that A-list level.

Quickly, sparing little detail, she filled Quincy in on Alice Perkins's death. "And on top of that, Edwin Grimm—the guy who was convicted of stalking her three years ago? He's been released from prison. They've hired a full-time bodyguard to protect her because of it."

"Holy shit."

Almost giddy with the scent of success, Chris laughed and flopped to her back on the hotel bed. "I'm so high, if you were here right now, I swear I'd take you on a ride you'd never forget."

Quincy groaned, which made her laugh. "You're killing me here, babe."

"Speaking of killing," she rolled to her side, propped herself up on an elbow, "wouldn't it be something if Sweet Baby Jane ended up dead, too, before this was all over?"

Quincy made a sound of agreement. "Yeah. Wouldn't that be something? This Grimm character—you thinking he's going to come after her again?"

Chris smiled. "He almost killed her once."

"The world loves a dead artist, I always say. Think of the bucks you'd make off this documentary then."

"Way ahead of you there, pal."

"Going to be interesting to wait this out, see what unfolds, huh?"

"You know me, Quin. I'm not the waiting kind."

"Say what? What are you up to?"

Chris laughed at the shock in Quincy's voice. He had her pegged. She'd been known to "help things along" from time to time to elevate the drama level of a story. "Nothing. I'm up to nothing. Don't mind me, okay? Too many late nights. Love you, babe. I've got to go."

She headed for the shower after she hung up with Quincy, who would be shocked if he knew how much Chris thought about Janey Perkins's demise. Thought about it so much, in fact, that sometimes it scared her. She'd even caught herself plotting ways to facilitate Janey's death.

She'd never actually do it, of course—but it wasn't against the law to think about it, right?

"The world loves a dead artist."

The play this film would get if Sweet Baby Jane suddenly turned up dead would make Chris a fortune.

She lathered up her hair, thinking that she'd been chasing the dream of megasuccess for the last ten of her thirty-one years. Near misses. Always, the best she came up with were near misses. She'd watched competitors upstage and outgun her time and time again. And she hated—absolutely hated—that her career was going nowhere.

But . . . if a famous star whom Chris just happened to be filming ended up getting whacked. Well. An almost orgasmic shiver eddied through her. Hell, she could end up optioning her footage for millions.

She dried her hair, then got dressed for the meet she'd set up for later tonight. Had to be tonight, because Janey Perkins would return to the tour here in Atlantic City tomorrow.

"Yeah. It would sure be something if Janey Perkins ended up dead," Chris said aloud, and headed out the door for her appointment.

Okay. Dead might be going a little too far—but a close call . . . well, that was something she might be able to make happen. And she knew just whose buttons to push to do it.

*S*aturday, July 15th, two days after the funeral, Gold's Gym, Atlantic City

Janey felt the impact from her ankle to her hip as she aimed a hard kick that landed her heel dead center in her opponent's midsection. When he doubled over, she pivoted and clipped Bryce Jennings behind the ear with her calf, dropping him like a stone.

The gym's trainer fell to the mat with a thudding grunt. "Mother of God. Who've you been taking lessons from? Bruce Lee?"

Sweat dripped into her eyes and down the small of her back. The hair she'd drawn into a loose tail on top of her head was drenched and falling into her face; her breath came fast and deep. She was revved and she was rockin'. And she'd gotten carried away. "Sorry. Didn't mean to drop you so hard."

To his credit, Bryce laughed as he rolled to a sitting position. "The hell you didn't."

Janey conceded with a guilty smile, *Okay*. She'd put her all into that kick. She'd needed contact. She'd needed crunch. She'd been more than edgy lately, and poor Bryce had just borne the brunt of her excess tension. "Well . . . I'm still sorry. I should have pulled the kick."

"Hey—you took me clean. You're out of my league, Ms. Perkins. Who *did* you train with?"

"Actually, she's self-taught." Max entered the closed workout room along with Baby Blue—who was, in part, responsible for her need to let off steam—on his heels.

Max's voice bounced off the walls of the cavernous room that had been reserved and emptied to protect Janey's privacy.

"And I pity the fool who catches her on a bad day," Max added in his best Mr. T voice.

Bryce lifted his hand. "Pity me then," he said, and let Max tug him to his feet.

Janey bent over to snag a towel off the mat—only to find Wilson had already picked it up. He held it out to her, his eyes meeting hers for the briefest of moments. He smelled of summer heat and sunshine, and clean. He always smelled so damn clean. And he looked better in worn jeans and black T-shirts than any man had a right to look.

"Thanks," she said, both surprised and—and what? Aware? Intrigued? Or maybe just puzzled by the vibrations she picked up from him from time to time. Vibrations that sometimes made her think he might be feeling some of the same physical heat that she was.

Which was just plain stupid, she conceded, wiping her face and neck. Just like her fascination with him was stupid.

Rent-a-hunks were a dime a dozen. He was one of hundreds she'd dealt with on many tours. Maybe she was struggling with all this physical awareness because unlike the others, he was going to be around for the duration. A part of her life.

Max had already started extricating himself from her daily routine, and Wilson was taking up the slack. Professionally, competently. Quietly leaving her to herself. Where she had plenty of time to study him. And speculate. And fantasize, which was something new for her since she was, as Max liked to remind her, too grounded in reality for her own good.

But with Wilson, it was like constantly staring at the cover of an intriguing book—but never being offered the opportunity to open it up. Look inside. See if there was substance to match the beautifully designed packaging.

You spend way too much time looking at that package, she told herself, dragging the towel over her chest and, in the process, feeling the burn in her muscles when she stretched. She'd needed this. Needed the physical outlet. She just wished the workout had burned off a little more tension.

And she wished she could quit thinking about her mother's death. Just like she wished she could shake the untenable sensation of being watched. And she wasn't referring to the way Baby Blue's gaze made a quick survey of her in her damp workout clothes before he averted his gaze to Max. Always in the back of her mind was the reality of Edwin Grimm.

"Shake a leg, snooks," Max said, clapping his hands together. "We've got to move."

Janey groaned. "Is the hour up already?"

"'Fraid so. Time to lock and load. Traffic's a bitch, and judging from the size of the mob waiting by the back door, word leaked out that you're here. We'll be cutting the photo session close."

"How does that happen?" she sputtered, and headed for the shower. "How does that *always* happen?"

No matter where she went, no matter how secretive and careful they were, someone always found her. The fans she could handle. She loved her fans. But not the press. They were relentless.

Her hair was still wet as, dressed in a pumpkin-colored leather hip-hugger mini, a gold halter top, and the Celtic cross she never went anywhere without now, she braved the crowd waiting in the sweltering heat on the south side of the building. Max and Wilson helped her run the gauntlet to the car that had been hired to take her to the beach, where a photo shoot was set up on the boardwalk for a spread in *Vogue*.

She smiled and waved to her fans, then dove into the backseat beside Max. It all felt so surreal sometimes. So surreal that she often wondered if she were living someone else's life. She had her very own $30-million jet and a layout in *Vogue,* for God's sake.

And sometimes, she thought absently as she stared at the hard, clean lines of Baby Blue's profile as he vigilantly scanned the mob outside the car for trouble, she wondered what it would feel like to work off a bit of her tension with her bodyguard.

Sunday morning, July 16th, Atlantic City Hilton
Jase rapped a knuckle on his charge's closed bedroom door the morning after another sold-out concert. "Wakie wakie. Chow's here."

As of today, he was alone in the suite with the superstar. Max had made the move into a separate suite of his own so he could get some work done.

Jase was a little nervous about the new arrangement. It was bound to make for a lot of up-close and personal day-to-day contact, and as unlikely as it seemed, he'd been picking up some pretty hot vibes from the rocker lately.

At least he thought he was picking up something. Wishful thinking? Hell no. Just . . . a gut feeling was all. And probably a crock. By her standards, he was an aw-shucks country clod. She was a star. And he was delusional.

In the meantime, he'd showered and dressed—thinking the five-star hotels the small entourage frequented were whopping steps up from the housing at Bat and the fleabag motels he was used to—by the time breakfast arrived.

He'd risen around seven and, according to his bodyguard slash butler duty roster, ordered room service—bacon, eggs, hash, and coffee for him, fruit and chai latte for her. According to the folder, it was her standard breakfast. Once a week she indulged in crème brûlée oatmeal.

And wasn't that damn special?

Actually, it was. So far, the God's honest truth was that the woman had surprised the hell out of him, he admitted, glancing toward her closed bedroom door. He'd expected spoiled. He'd expected demanding. And he'd expected to be disgusted—regardless of the package she came wrapped in.

Instead of spoiled, demanding, and disgusting, he'd seen the grace and strength with which she'd handled her mother's death. She'd been steady under some pretty heavy fire, there. And she didn't obsess or boo-hoo or "poor me" about Grimm—even though she had good reason to. The creep had to be a constant source of concern for her.

Jase had watched her after several concert dates now, kept expecting her to join in on the decadence. But she always left the booze alone, opting for water instead. Now and then he caught a whiff of weed at one of those gatherings, but she never smoked any of it. And she never disappeared to the head for a hit of something to keep her high.

He'd seen dope-induced skinnies before. She was slim, but she wasn't wasted. She was fit and fine. And she worked hard at it—the proof was in the way she'd laid out that trainer the other day.

So yeah, so far she was a huge surprise. And every surprise so far was going to make his job easier. He'd been envisioning tailing her from club to club during the next six months, fighting off crowds, keeping her out of trouble. He'd also figured he'd have to put up with Derek Mc-Coy sniffing around, but Jase was beginning to wonder if the tabloids had missed the mark on that one. Oh, McCoy had the hots for her all right—but Janey never gave him much more than a cursory glance.

So, unless she was on her good behavior for Jase's sake—which he highly doubted—they both just might live through this without too many complications. Well, except the obvious ones he'd been hired to handle.

When fifteen minutes had passed and she still hadn't shown, he walked back to her bedroom door and knocked again.

"Miss Perkins. You wanted to get up early so you could get a run in this morning." She'd decided that instead of working out—which she did five days a week, even on the road—at the local gym, she wanted to jog on the beach this morning.

"Miss Perkins?"

Nothing.

Jase stared at the door, drew a deep breath, and bit the bullet he'd been trying to dodge. He was going to have to go in there.

He inched open the door.

"Miss Perkins?"

Nothing.

On a heavy breath, he poked his head inside.

And damn near swallowed his tongue.

She was still asleep all right . . . and the tabloids had missed a particular juicy tidbit. Sweet Baby Jane slept in the nude. And apparently, she was a restless sleeper.

She'd kicked off the covers. Left nothing to the imagination. She lay on her back, all slim curves and small, fine breasts bare to the world, berry-pink nipples puckered tight. Her left leg was bent, knee elevated, her heel dug into the bedding.

The right leg—sweet Christ—the right leg was positioned to give him a clear view that answered another popular tabloid question. Sweet Baby Jane was a natural blonde.

And that wasn't all. He swallowed thickly, then glanced up to make certain she was asleep. Her eyes were closed, her hair splayed wildly on the pillow, one hand flung up over her head.

The other hand—sweet, sweet, *sweet* Christ—the other lay low over her abdomen where a tattoo of a clef note tucked low toward that spot where her fingertips, wet and glistening, curved into that silky nest of pale blond curls.

Lord Jesus God, give me strength.

His brain finally engaged, and he backed out of the room. Shut the door behind him.

Heart hammering, he leaned back against it. Wiped an unsteady hand over his face. Let out a serrated breath that had been stuck in his chest since he'd opened that damn door.

It couldn't have been more than a second, maybe two, that he'd stood there. Hell, it had taken that long to bumble past the shock.

Never should have opened that door.

Never should have looked.

He wasn't a voyeur. Wasn't a freaking Peeping Tom. And he could have lived forever without the image of all that sultry, sexy woman heat lying there, obviously drifting on the downside of a little self-gratification, indelibly burned into his brain.

But he had opened it. And he had looked.

And he would never forget what he had seen.

He was in some deep shit here.

Okay. Deep breath. Get a grip. It never happened.

He spun around. Pounded hard on the door.

"Miss Perkins!" he all but bellowed through the ornate wood. "Miss Perkins!" he repeated, rapping until he thought his knuckles would bleed.

"What? What—who?"

Weak with relief that he'd finally roused her, he toned things down a bit.

"You wanted me to wake you up," he reminded her.

"Mission accomplished," she sputtered. "For God's sake, did you have to break the door down?"

Umm . . . yeah.

"Next time, I'll ring down for a wake-up call."

"Hell, next time *I'll* request the wake-up call," Jase muttered, his face still flaming, his mind still filled with the erotic image of her wanton and naked on that bed.

Yeah. He was in some seriously deep shit. Hell. He was the *mayor* of Shitville.

5

She opened the door five minutes later.
   Jase chanced a glance up, relieved to see she was dressed. Well, sort of. She'd evidently showered, because her hair was damp and she smelled like every fresh, cleansing scent known to God. She'd wrapped up in a short jade-green silk kimono that did very little to camouflage all the fine lines and slim damp curves beneath it. Not to mention the slight sway of her breasts and the tight pucker of delicate little nipples that he now knew were the palest, prettiest pink.

   "Morning," she said, joining him at the breakfast table.

   "Morning," he mumbled back, and kept his nose in a file folder that outlined her schedule for the next few days.

   She didn't have much to say. That was fine by him. Chitchat, thank you, Jesus, didn't appear to be in the job description. And the truth was, he didn't think he could look at her again without flaming red.

Didn't seem to be able to help himself, though. He glanced up at her over his coffee. Her face was scrubbed clean of makeup, her hair smoothed free of the rat's nest of a do she usually wore. Instead, she'd tied it back into a loose soft, fluffy tail at her nape. Her hair like this made him think of that stuff his mom used to use to decorate their Christmas trees. Angel hair—that was it. Very full. Very fine. All soft and a little curly this morning and sort of out of control.

No. This Janey Perkins wasn't even a close second to the glitzy rocker the public was used to seeing.

Or the centerfold material he'd just ogled like a damn pervert.

Feeling guilty about that and trying not to stare, he watched her dig into her chow. She thought *he* looked like a kid? Right now she looked all of twelve . . . and as she ate her fruit, he realized it wasn't just her fresh-scrubbed face that lent the impression of youth. It was the way she carried herself. Without her makeup and high-end boutique clothes, she'd transformed from personality to person. And this person, though steady and serene, was far from the controlling, commanding rocker who'd threatened to boot his ass out the door a few nights ago.

"Be back in five," she said after finishing her fruit. "And we'll have that run."

Yeah. They'd run. And maybe he could run off that picture he kept seeing in his mind's eye. The one of her wet fingers and feathery curls.

Whoa, whoa, wait," Jase said when she came scooting out of her bedroom wearing a skimpy

black leather and silver bikini and enough bling to choke
a horse.

*Lord Jesus God. This morning is just one trial after
another.*

"Pardon me, ma'am, but you're not really planning to
go out in public like that?"

Hot. It was very hot in here, he thought, doing his
damnedest not to ogle all that smooth sleek skin and those
amazing curves. And that low-riding tattoo of a clef note.
But hell. He was human. He was male. It was against the
laws of nature for him not to notice how totally rockin' she
was. But it was against company rules for him to do anything about it. Not to mention his personal code of honor.

Which he'd shattered all to hell when he'd let himself
stare at her naked in bed.

He should apologize for that. He *needed* to apologize
for that. Told himself he was about to when she challenged
him.

"What's the matter with the way I'm dressed?" She
looked down at herself, reacting, no doubt, to his scowl.

Besides the black, almost–bathing suit, she was wearing that clunky Celtic cross around her neck. The thick
silver and leather bands she wore on her forearms and
around her wrists fairly shouted that whips and chains
couldn't be too far from reach.

The glittery silver-threaded do-rag she'd wrapped
around her head was a nice subtle touch. So was the silver
link chain circling her bare hips that hooked on to a silver
hoop complete with a twinkling diamond. The hoop hung
from her pierced navel. And unlike her fresh-from-the-
shower rain forest and sunshine scent, she smelled—
Hooah—she smelled like sin on a silver platter. Something
floral and musky and designed, no doubt, to grab a man
by the gonads and squeeze him into a stranglehold.

Jesus.

"Nothing's wrong—if you want to draw your usual crowd, ma'am. But we're talking public beach here. I'm good, but I can't control a mob, and that's what you're going to get, decked out like that."

No shit, Sherlock. Besides her "look at me, I'm a rock star" getup, there was that world-class body to deal with. Wouldn't be anyone missing that. Strong, firm legs. Slim hips. Tiny waist. Not much of a rack, but mighty fine, just the same.

And she has the prettiest diamond-tight little pink nipples.

"And you suggest—what?" She gave him a look.

He cleared his throat and tried not to think about racks and nipples and natural blondes. And about the way she smelled, which was almost too good to bear.

"Well, for starters, you could lose the bling, ma'am. Go for a tank top. Gym shorts. Running shoes. No glitzy designer labels, if you own such an animal. And if you've got a ball cap and a pair of dark glasses—a pair without rhinestones," he clarified with a glance at the ones propped on top of her head, "that would be swell."

For some reason, she found that amusing. "*Swell*, huh?" Grinning, she crossed her arms beneath her breasts and slung her weight on one hip. "You know, it occurs to me that you've been on the payroll for several days now and I know nothing about you. Where you from, Wilson?"

It was where he was *going*, not where he was from, that was at issue here. To hell, for certain. Out the door, maybe.

"Iowa, ma'am."

"Ahhh. Iowa." She drew out "Iowa" in that slow, smoky southern drawl of hers—the drawl he'd heard break through a couple of times when her guard had been down and she'd been talking with Max. Jase knew she was born and raised in Mississippi—he'd read the folder—and this was mint julep and magnolia up close and personal.

"Figures," she added, as if that explained everything.

He was used to it. A lot of people thought that his Iowa upbringing explained a lot of things. Like why he looked like Opie Taylor's distant cousin.

"Are you always this polite?"

He hadn't been ten minutes ago.

"Yes, ma'am," he lied.

"All those homegrown midwestern values, right?"

If only she knew. "I suppose so, yes, ma'am."

"Okay. Let's stop with the 'ma'am' crap, all right?" She headed back for her bedroom without the fuss he'd expected. "Makes me feel like a nun or something."

As fuckin' if.

No one would *ever* mistake her for a nun. A sinner, maybe, but not a sister. Not if they saw her in that skimpy suit. And got a whiff of her. And definitely not if they got a rear view of her walking away, he thought as he stood in the middle of the hotel suite and watched her tight little ass disappear behind her bedroom door.

And lest we not forget, *not* if they saw her sprawled and naked and sated in her bed.

He scrubbed a hand over his face and walked over to the window. Stared at the surf washing against the beach several stories below while a boner the size and consistency of a railroad spike changed the shape of his shorts.

"What took you so long?" he muttered, pressing the heel of his hand against his dick.

Okay. Time-out. *Time-fucking-out.*

This was *not* happening.

Talk about unprofessional.

And talk about left field. Where in the hell was this coming from? Sure, she was a hot property, but hell, that didn't mean she was the kind of property that made *him* hot.

Sara. Sweet, vulnerable, reserved. Now that was a woman to get worked up over. Lord knew he had. But a rock star? So she was a surprise. She'd still probably done or been done by jerk-offs from here to the West Coast and back again.

No. Thank. You.

It did not compute. And yet, there was proof in his pants that it did.

He needed to figure this out.

The best way to do that was to treat it like an op.

Analyze. Assess. Act.

Analyze: Okay. He'd been running in the muck too long. After Sara—well. There hadn't been any women after Sara. There'd been booze and bar fights and bawling in his beer. And then there'd just been the brawling. The WWA. He hadn't been with a woman for a while was all. And he didn't count the girls prancing around the ring in their skimpy bikinis and silicone implants holding signs announcing the round numbers. They'd been available and attainable and a total turnoff.

He wasn't a saint. He'd had his days of cheap thrills and one-night stands. Hell, when you were going off to war and you didn't know if you were coming back, you took it when and where you could get it and told yourself it was the least you deserved.

He'd been a kid then. And stupid with it.

He was older now. Liked to think that he was smarter. Too smart to blow a great job over an unexpected testosterone rush. One that had come out of the blue and reminded him that his heart might still be broken, but his equipment worked just fine.

Assess: No damage done. Not yet. Not ever. Now that he had an idea where this was all coming from, he just needed a plan to keep it from happening again.

Piece of cake.

Act: Focus on the job. Take care of his duties. Keep the big head on his shoulders and the little one in his pants and remember what was at stake here. Potentially a woman's life—at least her well-being. All he had to do was review the info on Edwin Grimm, the pervert who had gone to prison for stalking Miss Perkins—and from this point on, she was Miss Perkins to him—three years ago. Grimm had done his time. He was out on the streets again. And possibly on the prowl.

That was what Jase needed to act on. That and the constant assaults on her privacy from the press and the fanatics who thought of her as their personal property to idolize and fantasize about and were potential threats because of it.

A door opened and closed behind him, her amazing scent preceding her into the room. Okay. So he just wouldn't breathe the rest of the day, he decided, and squared his shoulders.

When he turned, he found a toned-down version of the siren who had knocked him for a loop. *Thank you, Jesus.*

She'd ditched all the silver and gold—even the cross. Her T-shirt was white; her shorts were tan; her ball cap was red. She looked like an ice-cream cone with a cherry on top.

Yummy.

"Better," he said, tamping back the thought of munching on damn near everything he saw. "Guess there's nothing to be done about the tattoos."

"Actually," she said with a thoughtful look, "I think I can fix that. Be right back."

When she came back into the living area, she'd tied a small red scarf around her neck, effectively covering the tattoo there.

"Help me with this, would you?" She handed him a roll of gauze. "You can play doctor. We'll pretend I have an owie."

At the thought of playing doctor with her, the part of his anatomy that hadn't yet figured out there wasn't a snow cone's chance in hell of that ever happening twitched to life again.

Another part—the part that was trying to deal with the stupid part—did some mental ass kicking as he wound the gauze around her upper arm and over the tattoo. Unfortunately, both parts realized at the same time that he'd never been this close to her before. At least not without a slew of reporters or fans or crew around.

Aside from the softness of her skin, there were a lot of other sensual firsts happening. Like getting drunk on the incredible scent of her. Some amazing mix of floral and musk and . . . hell, he didn't know. Something intrinsically female. Undeniably sexual.

And her hair. Up close like this, he could see how truly fine it was. Fine and thick and fired through with a hundred shades of silver and gold and chestnut where it hung in feathery little waves midway down her back.

"How ya doin' there, Doc?"

His gaze snapped from her hair to her face. She'd turned her head, was looking up at him over her shoulder, and he was hit with another jolt of awareness. Of the color of her eyes. The depth and the complexities. "Brown" was too mundane. Cinnamon, mocha, sorrel, gold . . . hell, and shades he didn't know the names of.

He wondered if her eyes went smoky when she came.

"Umm . . . problem?"

The puzzlement in her tone finally jarred him into action and out of dangerous territory.

"Nope. I think I've got it." He quickly tucked the end of the gauze under the band of the fake bandage he'd made. Just as quickly backed away.

Way the hell away. He snagged his black cap with the

U.S. Army logo and gave her what he hoped came across as a "pass the muster" once-over.

"So we're set?"

"Your hair," he said, then cleared his throat when the words came out sounding like a croak. "It's a dead give-away."

No one had hair like hers—although he was certain many women, from fans to supermodels, had tried to get that look.

He watched as she gamely whipped off her ball cap, scooped the streaked golden mass together at her nape, then twisted. With little effort and some magical thing that beautiful women were probably born knowing how to do, she managed to tuck it all up and under that red ball cap.

"Work for you?" Hands on hips, she grinned up at him.

Too many things were working for him. And on him. He needed air that wasn't saturated with the scent of her. And some distance. And he was having some major second thoughts about confessing.

"Let's do this."

"Yes, sir," she replied with a sharp salute.

"Sorry." Now was not the time to forget who was boss. "When you're ready, we can go, if you like, ma'am."

She grinned and headed for the door. "Don't worry about it. And I asked you to quit calling me ma'am."

"Sorry, ma'—Miss Perkins," Jase corrected, following her.

"Okay, let's take this a little further. We're going to be spending a lot of time together, right? Don't you think it's time we ditch the formalities? How about we go for 'Janey'?" she suggested as they waited for the elevator to take them to the lobby.

"I'd prefer 'Miss Perkins,' if you don't mind."

She glanced up at him. He couldn't see her eyes behind

her dark glasses, but he had a feeling she was laughing at him again.

"Have it your way, sugar."

Fine. Let her laugh.

"And I think it's time we figure out what I should call you."

" 'Wilson' would be fine."

She smiled—a wicked glint in her eyes. " 'Iowa' it is then."

He hadn't intended to smile back. The superior look she shot him told him she knew it and figured she'd scored a point in whatever game she thought she was playing.

Okay. So she was competitive. He'd seen that the day she'd laid the poor schlep of a trainer out flat. Competitive was cool. He liked competition. He liked a challenge. The problem was, *she* just might be easy to like and *like* under these circumstances could be just as dangerous as lust. He couldn't afford either. He was going to keep this professional and impersonal if it killed him.

And as they walked out one of the back entrances of the hotel, crossed the boardwalk, and hit the beach, he decided it just might.

Her ass looked as good in those loose running shorts as it had in that leather bikini bottom.

6

"Amazing," Janey said aloud when they slipped out one of the Atlantic City Hilton's ocean-side doors and right past the paparazzi who had been lying in wait on the off chance she would make an appearance. "They didn't recognize me."

"That was the plan," Wilson said without a trace of "I told you so" in his voice.

Okay, so he'd been right, Janey thought as they crossed the boardwalk and she set a steady pace alongside him on the Atlantic City beach sand. She was so used to perpetuating crowd reaction she'd forgotten how to dress with subtlety. Early on, the orders had come from the suits at the label. They'd wanted buzz—as much as she could create—and outrageous fashion statements were the most direct route. They'd wanted the hype and the stir it caused when she'd started to become notable.

Now she was. And she'd forgotten how to dress so that she didn't draw attention to herself. It felt kind of nice to blend for a change instead of standing out. One thing she'd never forgotten was how much she missed anonymity.

Right now, she missed Max. He'd been the grown-up in her day-to-day life. Now *she* was the adult in this party of two—her and Baby Blue—and she wasn't certain she liked the shift of power.

Oh well. It was done. Time to suck it up. Just like she'd sucked up over the news about Grimm being on the loose again. That didn't mean she didn't think about him. Or about her mother. But she wasn't going to dwell on any of that today.

The sun was big and bright and hot as a firebrand. The breeze off the Atlantic was a wonderful mix of salt and suntan lotion and sea spray. Her running shoes sank into damp sand, working her thighs to the max.

And beside her was the diversion she needed to keep at bay thoughts of crazed stalkers and dead mothers who never gave a damn—and yet Janey had loved her anyway.

Baby Blue was a mass of fluid muscle and powerful strides, holding himself back, she suspected, to keep pace with her. She supposed she could count this, at least, as a plus. She loved to run and Max had never been one to break a sweat, so she rarely got to run outside.

She wouldn't mind a little conversation, though.

"You like to run, Iowa?"

"Wouldn't say 'like' is exactly the word."

"Clocked your share of miles in the military, huh?"

"Most often humping a hundred pounds of gear and firepower, ma'am. Sorry," he added when he realized he'd slipped again.

Obviously it was going to take some work to break him of that habit.

"Army? Navy?" she asked when he fell silent beside her.

"Army," he said. "Rangers."

"Whoa. Rangers. That's pretty heavy duty."

"It's all heavy duty these days."

Yeah. She supposed it was. But she knew he was downplaying his service. She was like any other concerned citizen in today's world. She read. She understood the difference between regular army and special ops—at least she understood that the criteria were tougher and the washout rate was high.

"How long you been out?"

"Come again?"

He bent his head down closer to hers and for the first time since she'd met him he smelled something other than squeaky clean. Oh, that amazing clean scent was still there, but today it was competing with the scent of physical heat and healthy male sweat. It was all very . . . well, arousing.

And she was very . . . well, certifiable, she thought with a self-deprecating shake of her head.

"How long have you been out of the service?" she repeated, competing with the roar of the surf, the cry of the gulls, and the squeals of the children playing tag with the tide.

"Six months."

"Decided not to make it a career?"

"No, ma'am."

She pushed out a laugh. "You are really getting on my nerves with that 'ma'am' stuff."

From the corner of her eye she caught the barest hint of a smile. "Sorry."

"Yeah," she said, and poured on the speed. "I can see that."

It was kind of hard to be irritated with him, Janey thought as they kept a steady pace along the long stretch of beach. Baby Blue—though not a baby after all—was determined to do the job. And he was determined to keep things professional between them.

Professional was fine. It was also comforting, and she had to admit, she felt a sense of peace with him around since she'd found out that Grimm was back on the scene. So yeah. Professional was fine.

Stiff and stodgy, however, was another issue. Max had not only been her personal manager; he was her friend. Her confidant. Her comic relief when things got too crazy. She missed that.

Maybe, she thought, as the two of them skirted a sand castle a little girl had made with a little pink plastic pail and her mother's guiding hands, she needed to iron some of the starch out of that stiff neck of Wilson's and get him to play well with others. Specifically with her.

He was such a hottie, she admitted again. And the main reason she'd woken up this morning in the throes of an erotic dream. A *major* erotic dream that she'd had to play to its conclusion after she woke up.

Whew. At least it had served to unleash some of her tension. Although just being aware of his muscled body pumping away beside her got her juices flowing again.

If it weren't for that damnable ache low in her belly, it would be laughable. She could see the tabloid headline now: Rock Star Lusts After Hunky Bodyguard. How clichéd was that?

It was somewhat gratifying to know she wasn't the only one he affected that way. As they made their way down the beach, Wilson was turning his share of flirty female heads.

"They think you're hot," she pointed out, which had his head whipping her way.

He didn't exactly stumble, but he did misstep.

"Excuse me?"

She grinned and hitched her chin toward a trio of high-school girls who were well into ogle mode and making no bones about it. "The little beach bunnies. They're flirting."

He grunted . . . and turned beet red. "And they would be all of fifteen. Does the term 'jailbait' mean anything to you?"

Janey chuckled. Bait was exactly what she was doing. It wasn't nice to bait the bodyguard, but it sure was fun—especially since he was giving her so much trouble with her previously dormant libido.

"You got a girlfriend, Wilson?"

"No, ma'—" He cut himself off mid-"ma'am." "No. No girlfriend."

She wasn't sure why that little tidbit of information pleased her. Like hell she wasn't. The thought of him getting it on with some little sweet thing actually made her a little jealous.

Talk about juvenile.

She concentrated on her run. On the freedom of it. She owed him for that.

"It's really great not being the one attracting the attention," she told him. "I'd forgotten what it felt like to move freely without turning heads. You might be worth keeping around after all."

"I'll sleep easier tonight knowing that."

She chuckled. "You make me laugh, Iowa."

"We aim to please."

Sure we do.

"How you holding up?" she asked after they'd run another quarter of a mile. "Got another mile in you?"

The look he gave her said, *You've got to be kidding!* "I just broke a sweat."

Boy, had he. He'd stripped off his T-shirt a quarter mile back and stuffed it in the waist of his running shorts, showing off his incredible physique.

"Ripped." "Buff." Pick an adjective. He was calendar material—and he didn't exactly look seventeen anymore. Not with that American eagle tattooed across the breadth of his chest. It was an amazing piece of work. About a hundred times the needle work of all four of her pieces put together and ten times the color.

Ouch. But then, he'd been a Ranger. They were supposed to eat glass for breakfast and nails for lunch.

Maybe knowing his military background had altered her perception of him, she thought as they made their way at a steady clip down the sand. Maybe she'd just had an opportunity to finally study him in depth without security issues pulling first priority.

At first glance he *had* looked like a baby. But when she looked, really looked, at his eyes—framed not only by character and experience lines but also by the thickest sun-kissed lashes—she'd seen the measure of his maturity. Yeah. If a boy wasn't a man when he went to Afghanistan or Iraq, he would be when he got back. If he lived through the experience, that is.

Jason Wilson had. And she suspected it had changed him. There was a look that came over him sometimes that was almost scary. Like now when a group of kids came running toward them and he went on full alert. His jaw hardened. His muscles bunched and the fingers he wrapped around her upper arm to steer her in a wide path around them made it clear he was in complete control. And capable of doing things to ensure her protection that gave her both confidence and pause.

What had he seen? What had he done?

She wondered if she'd ever ask him. Wondered if he'd tell her if she did.

When the group didn't veer but kept running in a straight line past them down the beach, he let her go. But he didn't drop his guard.

They'd passed the last lifeguard tower and were running out of beach. They had to either turn around and head back or stop and cool off. Frankly, she needed to cool off. As much from the good workout as from some genuinely intriguing thoughts about her bodyguard. She hadn't been around this much beefcake in a long, long time.

Not that beefcake was her thing. In her experience, beefcake always came with ego and ego equated asshole and she could live just fine without that kind of fly in her ointment. Been there. Hated that.

Nope. She was just fine on her own. While the gossip rags loved to pair her up with Derek—yeah, *that* was gonna happen—she'd been celibate for over two years. She hadn't met anyone who had given her a reason not to keep it that way. Or to stick her neck and her heart out the way she had with Kevin—hard lessons learned were often the most valuable.

Celibacy had certain rewards—and, of course, certain consequences. Her reaction to Jason Wilson seemed to be one of the latter. Not to mention confusing.

She barely knew him. In the interest of keeping it simple, she decided, it was probably best not to change that. And to quit baiting him.

"I'm going in," Janey said, deciding she'd take advantage of the opportunity to enjoy her freedom and to cool off in the process. She tossed her dark glasses and cap onto the sand. "How about you?"

He shook his head, watched her walk backward into the surf. Again, she couldn't see his eyes behind his dark glasses, but she got the impression that he was suffering her impulsive decision in disapproving silence.

The guy really was too much.

"You always this vigilant, Iowa?" Standing knee-deep in the water, she had to shout to be heard above the roar and rush of the surf as a wave slapped her hard around her thighs.

"Don't go out too far," he said.

"Guess that answers *that* question." He did *not* return her grin. Big surprise.

"There are riptide warnings posted at the lifeguard stations."

"Noted." Ignoring his dark scowl, she turned toward open water and, holding her breath, made a shallow dive.

Thanks to her kindergarten teacher, she was a strong swimmer. Her mother never had it together enough to enroll her in the summer Red Cross swim classes, but Mrs. Buttons had taken a special interest in Janey. She'd seen to it that Janey got to her lessons.

And thanks to those lessons Janey had great breath control. She could hold a note forever, and that particular ability, along with her range, was one of the things that had gotten the attention of talent scout Lee Haversham and landed her the gig at Dollywood where Jack Swingle had discovered her.

She pushed herself farther under the water, relishing the tug and pull of the warm Atlantic. The freedom of absolute solitude.

And then freedom turned to terror when she felt a hard bump against her hip.

What the hell?

There hadn't been anyone within fifty feet of her when she'd gone into the water. She felt another bump along with the slam of her heart as a hard pressure at her waist dragged her through the water.

"What the hell do you think you're doing!" a winded

voice growled in her ear when she broke the surface. "I told you not to go out too far!"

Gasping for air, Janey shoved her wet hair out of her eyes. And found herself pressed belly to belly and hauled up tight against her bodyguard. "Jesus. I . . . thought you were a shark."

He shook his head, sending water in a spray around them as the surf slapped against their bodies and rocked them closer together.

"You scared the hell out of me!"

"Guess that makes us even. I thought you'd drowned!"

Another wave hit and she lifted her hands to his shoulders to keep from going under.

"Drowned? For God's sake. I wasn't going to drown."

"Damn right you weren't. No way in hell was I going to lose a client the first week on the job."

She didn't know who was angrier. Her or him. Didn't know whose heart was beating faster, either. But she did know she wasn't the only one aware of the rocking motion of the surf bumping and locking their bodies together. The bunchy muscles of his thigh wedged between hers. The unmistakable thickness of a very healthy erection pressed against her belly.

At the moment, she was too ticked off to dwell on it.

"Fool woman," he sputtered, abruptly shifting her weight so she was cinched up beside him and well away from whatever was happening down there.

"Macho man," she fired back as he trudged his way toward shore, dragging her with him.

Woman doesn't have the sense God gave a rock," Jase sputtered under his breath when they reached the hotel half an hour later. It had been a long, quiet jog back to the Hilton.

She was pissed. He was pissed. It had made for a damn pissy trip back.

He couldn't wait to hit the shower to wash away the sand and the salt and the sweat. And the memory of her compact little body hitched up against his in the water.

A hard-on. Lord Jesus God, he'd gotten another hard-on. And she had to have felt it.

She stood beside him in the hallway, her arms crossed over her breasts, her foot tapping with impatience as he slipped the key card in the slot. He opened the door to the suite—and shifted from pissed to red alert when he saw what was waiting inside.

Jesus. Jesus Christ.

"Don't." He clutched her arm, blocking her way when she would have shot around him. Then he shut the door. "You don't want to go in there."

Like rain washing down a windowpane, all the color bled from her face. Wide brown eyes met his—frightened and far too wise. She let him steady her with a hand on her arm.

"It's him, isn't it? Grimm was here," she said so softly that if he hadn't read her lips, he would have missed it.

Between setting up security ahead of the tour's next stop in New York City and seeing to details for the next two days, Jase had read everything he could get his hands on about Edwin Grimm. And yeah, it looked like the creep had left his standard calling card.

A heart-shaped crystal bowl sat on the carpet just inside the door. Inside the bowl was a red velvet cloth. On the cloth were two bloody hearts, each no larger than a robin's egg.

7

Between the Atlantic City cops, the hotel security, the backup singers and band members who all showed up, the next hour turned into a world-class cluster fuck. And it royally torqued Jase off.

"Okay, that's it, people." With a hard look he took the arm of Lakesha Jones and herded the backup singer toward the door. "Let's everyone just hustle on back to whatever it was you were doing, all right? Party's over."

Lakesha had heard via Christine Ramsey—a videographer or some such thing who was taping this leg of Janey's tour—that the police had been called to Janey's suite. Ramsey had just happened to stop by—a coincidence that had all of Jase's "got a bad feeling" vibes revved—to see if she could film a little downtime, star style, when hotel security had arrived followed by Atlantic

City police. Not only was Jase having a hard time buying that the videographer had just happened by, but he hadn't been able to catch Ramsey, a sharp-featured, thin redhead, before she'd whipped out her cell phone and given Lakesha a call.

Of course, Lakesha had called the other backup singer, Tess Brewer, who'd called someone else, and the next thing Jase knew, the whole damn entourage had made an appearance, from the band members, to the rest of the singers, to Neal Sanders, whom Jase had met at a postconcert party and disliked on the spot. And who smelled like he'd drunk his breakfast *and* lunch.

Max was notably absent.

Janey was still notably shaken, although she was doing her damnedest to show a brave face.

Just like the day the police had told her about her mother's death, Jase was out of his comfort zone on this one. He was here to provide security, not a shoulder to lean on. Yet every time he caught sight of her wide, haunted eyes, he fought an unprecedented urge to pull her into his arms and promise her that everything was going to be all right.

Neither playing out the little fantasy that had been cooking in the back of his mind since finding her naked in bed this morning nor playing nursemaid was in the job description, he reminded himself and let out a breath through puffed cheeks when the last lookie-loo was finally gone. That done, he dealt with any remaining questions from the police, then hustled his charge up to the new suite the hotel had offered up so the original suite could be preserved as a crime scene.

When he shut the door behind them and turned to her, he felt another sharp stab of compassion. She was still wearing her damp shorts and top. He tried to focus on her wet, straggly hair, far too aware of the way that tight, tiny shirt molded to her breasts. Hell, he didn't even have to imagine her little nipples puckered up tight as berries beneath it anymore. He'd seen them. Still saw them, no matter how many times he'd tried to banish the image from his mind.

"Why don't you go and shower?" he suggested as much for his sake as for hers. It wasn't just the air-conditioning that was making her shiver. Shock was setting in. "Warm up. Then we need to talk about this."

Her gaze cut to his and he could see the hesitation there. She was still wearing her brave, tough-girl face, but he knew better. Grimm's visit had shaken her. And with damn good reason. The pervert had almost succeeded in killing her once. Looked like he'd come back to finish the job. But not before he played with her a little first.

"The police did a thorough search of the hotel," Jase assured her. "He's gone. Was probably long gone before we ever got back from the beach."

She nodded . . . and stood there.

And in that moment he saw her for who she was, what she was. A woman as scared as any kid would be and trying not to show it. And she looked even more like a kid— a lost, hunted kid—than she had at the breakfast table.

"Come on," he said, instead of making her ask, because he could see from her eyes that she never would. "How about I go in ahead and take a peek around for good measure?"

Hell. He could be professional and not be a jerk about it. He could save her the humiliation. Just like he'd decided he'd save her the humiliation of knowing he'd seen her naked in bed this morning.

She sort of wilted with relief before sucking it up again. "It's okay. You don't have to do that. I'm fine."

Tough. She was one tough cookie. She was also a long way from fine, but he wasn't going to tell her that.

"Just doin' my job."

Because that's all it was. End of story. He wasn't going soft in the head over a hard rocker who'd most likely find a reason to razz him about his homespun down-on-the-farm upbringing by sundown.

He led the way into her bedroom, where the house-keeping staff had resettled her personal things. Not that she'd have asked them to do it for her. He'd been surprised to find her original bedroom as neat as a pin. She'd picked up after herself after changing her leather for lay-man clothes. Interesting. And unexpected.

He'd figured she'd have minions to do the work for her minions. Come to think of it, he'd expected a large, tightly clinging entourage shadowing her every move. Making her feel important. Making her feel loved.

But the lady traveled light. Other than the road crew who handled the stage setup and hauled the equipment in a convoy of semis, the only others on hand were her band, her backup singers, that Sanders guy—Jase still hadn't figured out what he did—the videographer, and Max. Who, come to think of it, hadn't answered his page or returned the message Jase had left on his cell phone.

"All clear," he said, turning around to reassure her and damn near knocking her over before realizing she'd been tailgating.

"Whoa." He grabbed her by the shoulders to steady her—took one look in her eyes and decided the hell with it. It wouldn't hurt him to give her what she needed.

"Hey. It's okay now," he said softly, and pulled her into his arms. And felt her body just sort of give and sway into his.

It didn't feel wrong. It didn't feel stupid. It didn't feel sexual. At least not at first.

It simply felt like the right thing to do. So he did it. She needed steadying. He had a broad shoulder. She obviously needed one, and Max wasn't here to offer it. So he'd stand in. No big deal.

And as they stood there—her slight and trembling and leaning into his embrace—he couldn't help but think of Sara.

She'd been broken and weak and in need of someone else's strength after Will had killed himself. But not before he'd shot her, too.

Jase hadn't expected to fall in love with Sara. He'd just wanted to help. That was all he wanted to do now. But try as he might to remain detached, that wasn't the way his mother had raised him. He could almost hear her voice.

The girl is hurting, Jase. You can do something about it.

That was why he'd helped Sara. And he'd fallen in love.

Now he was helping Janey.

Different circumstances. Different results.

With Sara he'd been acting on emotions.

With Janey—well, it was just different was all.

That was his story and he was sticking to it.

He made a clumsy attempt to pat her back. Amazed all over again by how tiny she was. How, in spite of the salt and surf scent clinging to her hair, she still smelled amazing. And, unfortunately, he was also way too aware that her cheek was resting against his bare chest. Her breasts pressed against his upper abs. Things had happened so fast, he hadn't thought to put his shirt back on.

Big, big oversight on his part.

Lord Jesus God. Her breath was hot. Majorly hot where it fanned his nipple, and he did a little puckering of his own as an unbidden image of her mouth cruising across his skin came to mind.

He cleared his throat because it suddenly felt like his heart had swollen to the size of a frag grenade and lodged dead center behind his Adam's apple—just before it had pumped all the blood in his body to his groin.

"How you doing down there?" he asked because he had to say something. And he had to put some distance between them before she noticed all that tightening going on beneath her fingertips.

She sniffed. Lifted her head. "I'm doing."

When she pulled away, he let out a breath of relief because, Jesus, things had somehow gotten very intense all of a sudden. He almost swallowed back a much-needed breath when she tipped her head and looked up at him.

Aw, God. She looked so little and so lost and so vulnerable. Like Sara.

Only, one more time, she was nothing like Sara. And he'd do damn well to remember it.

It was hard to remember anything, though, when Janey looked at him that way. The only thing he had a real good bead on was that she was a woman. All woman. The kind a lot of guys would do crazy things for.

Like risk their lives. Risk their jobs.

She had a mouth made for French kisses. Long ones. Deep ones. Wet ones. She'd taste of salt right now. Salt and sex and a little bit of fear.

He was wondering what she'd do, what she'd say, if he took a taste. If he just lowered his mouth, opened over hers, tasted her with his tongue.

And he almost did it. God*damn* he almost did it. But then his brain finally engaged and reminded him with a swift kick what was at stake here: her life.

Dumb ass.

He was such a dumb ass.

"Sorry about that." He heard her voice through a distant ringing in his ears. "I don't usually . . . you know . . . let things get to me."

He believed her. And that made her little meltdown all the more poignant.

Poignant. Shit. Listen to him. He was going all soft in

the head. And he was falling into the same downward spiral he had with Sara.

What was it with him, anyway? Just because a woman needed saving didn't mean she needed anything else from him.

And just because he had a sudden case of testosterone-induced insanity didn't mean he had to take up residence in the loony bin. And that's where he was headed if he didn't straighten up and fly right. He wasn't so far from needing saving himself, and he'd do well to remember that.

"Yeah, well," he groped for and miraculously grasped the thread of their conversation, "I don't usually play big brother, so don't get used to it, okay?"

He'd wanted her to smile. Thank you, God, she did.

"Big brother? Thought never crossed my mind. Now *little* brother, maybe."

Good. Great. Let's just ramp up this fraternal image.

And let's keep her shored up. He liked it better when she was spunky. It was a helluva lot safer because she was usually a helluva lot farther away.

"So. You want me to wait here in the bedroom while you shower?"

"No. It's okay. My Weak-kneed–Wilda moment has passed. Go take your own shower. I'm fine."

He headed for the door, couldn't get out of there fast enough.

"Hey . . . Iowa."

He stopped reluctantly, turned with even more reluctance, and looked at her.

Jesus, look at her.

"Yeah?" he finally managed around that lump that wouldn't go away as her brown eyes met his and held.

"Thanks."

They stood that way for a little too long. Let their gazes cling a little too intensely.

"That Bryce guy—at the gym," he said, dredging up the memory from God knew where. "He's a lousy kickboxer."

She tilted her head, gave it a confused little shake at his total disconnect from the current conversation. "Is that how you say 'you're welcome' in Iowa?"

"No, ma'am. That's an offer. If you ever want to work off a little tension, I'll be happy to kick your ass. You won't be thanking me then . . . ma'am."

And he left, shutting the door behind him. Feeling like he'd just escaped a major disaster.

He leaned back against the door. Wiped a hand down his face. Wiped the picture of her standing there with a grateful little smile and a body he'd give his right nut to know in every possible way.

How had he ever managed to conjure up a big-brother image in the first place? No matter how many times he told himself he wasn't going to be ruled by testosterone, he did not want to be her brother. Not in this lifetime. Not in a million lifetimes.

He'd like to meet the man with a beating heart and working equipment who could look at her and think brotherly thoughts. She was tiny, delicate, and as hot as a desert night.

In damp clothes and scraggly hair and no makeup.

And flat on her back, stunningly naked and floating on a rush from her own hand. He wanted it to be his hand pleasuring her. His mouth. His . . .

Jesus, there he went again. He so should have gotten laid before he took this gig. He should have gotten himself a soft, willing woman and screwed his brains out. To hell with love and commitment and all those things he believed a man ought to feel for a woman he took to bed.

"Shit," he muttered; then he reviewed analysis, assessment, and action all the way to the shower. "Shit, shit, shit."

• • •

F or the record," Janey said, fresh from her shower,
"I really don't let down like that."

And she didn't, Janey acknowledged to herself as she
lifted her wet hair out from under the gold chain that held
her mother's cross.

Dressed in short blue sweatshorts and a yellow skinny
T, she sank down into a wing chair in the living area of
the suite, tucked her bare feet up under her hip, and
worked a pick through her damp hair.

In her own defense, her whole life had turned upside
down in the past week. Starting with Grimm's release from
prison. She absently fingered the Celtic cross, her last link
with her mother. Alice Perkins was gone, her death still a
mystery—just like her life, Janey thought sadly.

Then there was Max's sudden departure from her
day-to-day life. And Baby Blue's unsettling insurgence
into both her life and her dreams. Now this. Grimm was
definitely back. No denying that now. And a nightmare
she'd never wanted to relive had hacked its way back into
her life again.

All right, fine. Just deal with it. She'd had her little moment of weakness. It was over. And she wouldn't let
Grimm or anything else get to her again.

Her bodyguard sat across from her on the sofa, poring
through a file folder. Full of information on Edwin
Grimm, she'd guess.

At least Jason Wilson provided a different type of diversion. She wished she had a folder on *him* so she could
get a bead on what made him tick. She wasn't used to
underestimating men. She'd underestimated him, though.

He kept surprising her. The erection at the beach had
been a helluva surprise. And she wasn't yet sure what to

think about that. Just like she wasn't quite sure how to handle the battalion of butterflies that, despite the gravity of her situation and her determination to keep things on a professional level between them, had started taking flight in her stomach.

Oh yeah. She'd been trying to ignore them, but they attacked at the oddest times.

Like when she looked at him. Or when he touched her—like he had just before her shower. All that strength, but his hands had been gentle. His muscled chest had been a refuge. And yet the scent of him—all sweaty and salty and warm and male—hadn't felt one bit comforting in the final windup.

Unsettling, yes. Comforting, well, no.

He hadn't intended the embrace to be sexual. She knew he hadn't. But somehow that was what it had become. When he'd looked down at her, those incredible blue eyes so intense and searching . . . well. For a minute there, she'd thought he was going to kiss her.

And she was pretty sure she would have let him.

Pretty sure? Who was she kidding? She'd have latched onto those amazing lips like a Hoover.

She'd thought about that a lot during her shower. And finally chalked things up to the high anxiety of her situation. It was as good an explanation as any. And it worked to steady her.

The butterflies were settled now, too. At least they were until he glanced up at her and little wing beats tickled her from within. He'd showered, too. And that clean, masculine scent she had begun to associate with him reached out and put a touch on every erogenous zone in her body.

8

"Miss Perkins?"

Janey blinked, tuned back into their conversation, and realized that Wilson had been talking to her.

"S . . . sorry, what?"

"I said I believed you the first time," he said, and went back to his reading.

She drew a total blank, mostly because she had become completely transfixed by his face. By the beauty of it. By the contrasts. Gentle blue eyes and soft, sensuous lips juxtaposed intriguing angles and hard planes. Fascinating.

And she was staring. So was he—like he was wondering what the hell was wrong with her.

She'd missed something. "You believed *what* the first time?"

"That you don't usually let things shake you."

"Oh. Oh yeah," she said, feeling foolish because she'd completely spaced out of their conversation.

Because he was gorgeous? Had amazing muscles? And incredible baby-blue eyes? And the sexiest smile?

What are you, sixteen? This was so high-school.

She had a problem. A much bigger problem than renegade hormones. And the name on the folder he was reading was finally enough to sober her up. "Grimm's a real whack job, isn't he?"

He grunted in agreement. "In spades."

"I wasn't ready for him the first go-round," she said, staring at the fingers on her left hand as she plucked absently at a thread on the upholstered chair. "I was totally unprepared."

"I'm thinking there's no way to prepare for a loose screw like Grimm."

"And yet I fool myself into believing that I have," she said with a self-effacing smile.

He frowned, then got her meaning. "The kickboxing?"

She nodded. "If I ever meet that bastard face-to-face again, I'm looking forward to the opportunity to kick his nuts up through the roof of his mouth."

He blinked, then blanched. "Oo-yeah. That'll send a message, all right. In the meantime, I'll live with the hope that I never land on your bad side."

He had a way of making her laugh. So she did. Which made him smile.

Which sent the butterfly squadron in flight again when their eyes met and held for another one of those searching, assessing moments.

A red flush stained his cheeks just before he looked away, and Janey experienced an "Ah" moment.

Having some trouble with this attraction thing, too, aren't you, Baby Blue?

She still wasn't sure what she thought about that.

Or what to make of it. Or more to the point, what to do about it. Although some very interesting images came to mind.

"Tell me about Grimm," he said, shuffling the sheaf of papers, then setting them aside.

Nothing like a cold, hard slap of reality to jar a girl out of an erotic daydream.

"Can't imagine that everything you need to know isn't in that stack of reading material." She nodded toward the folder he'd tossed on the coffee table.

"I want to hear about him from your perspective."

She looked toward the window showcasing a blue-green view of the Atlantic and a sun so bright she could almost smell the heat through the glass. She didn't want to think about Grimm, let alone talk about him. But ignoring him wasn't going to make him go away.

"Okay. Where to start. I guess . . . at first he was just a regular fan. He showed up at my concerts—always front-row. Always smiling. Sometimes with roses. Sometimes with a stuffed animal or something."

"A love-struck groupie," he concluded with a dark look.

"It seemed very . . . sweet at first. But then it got creepy. He'd be at every concert no matter where we played. I was thinking, man, this guy needs to get a life. And he started sending letters. Sometimes e-mails. Those weren't so sweet."

"Explicit?"

She nodded. Felt her stomach turn.

"The next time he made an appearance, Max had security remove him from the building. Grimm went berserk. From then on, we were on the lookout for him. As far as I know, he never made it into another concert. And then . . . well, then the hearts started arriving."

She hated Grimm for that almost as much as for the terror he'd put her through. Hated him for ruthlessly killing something small and innocent and defenseless just to make some sick impression on her.

"According to the file, he comes from money."

"Money. Yeah, lots of it, apparently. I was told that his parents died in a car accident. When he was seventeen, I think. They were investors, savers—anyway, that's what I was told."

"So after he broke into your place, he had the means to hire a high-ticket lawyer who got him off with three years served."

Another sick feeling rolled through her. "And now he's out."

"And has access to enough cash to go wherever he wants," Baby Blue concluded. "And to grease a few palms, considering he got into the suite today."

Despite the sky full of sunshine warming the beach below, Janey felt chilled. "How long do you think it will take the police to come up with something?"

He leaned back on the sofa, his strong legs splayed wide, his bare feet flat on the tile floor, and stretched his arms above his head. "They'll question the staff and eventually hit on something to tie him to today. When they do, they'll put him away again."

"*If* they can find him." Rising and walking toward the bank of windows, she hugged her arms around her waist.

"They didn't find him before. Not until he . . ." She trailed off. It was still hard to talk about finding Edwin Grimm in her house that night three years ago.

His eyes had been wild. His voice eerily soft as he'd told her what he was going to do to make sure they were together forever.

She'd run. She'd hidden. She'd managed to trigger the silent alarm. The police had arrived just as he'd kicked his way through the bedroom door that she'd barricaded with a full chest of drawers. To this day, she didn't know where she'd found the strength to move it.

"He's not going to get to you again."

She started, pulled out of the terror of that night by the steady, true cadence of Wilson's voice.

"He's not going to get to you again," he repeated when she turned.

She realized that she was shaking—saw that he hadn't missed that fact. "Yeah. That's what they said the last time."

"Hey."

His hard tone snapped her gaze to his.

"This time is nothing like the last time. This time, he has to get past me. And that just isn't going to happen. Got it?"

She assessed the determination in the blue gaze that held hers. Stared at him long and hard. At this American-pie Iowa boy who had earned the right to be regarded as a man in the cold mountains of Afghanistan and the burning deserts of Iraq.

"Yeah," she said, giving him his due. Even more. Believing him. "I've got it."

Because she couldn't take one more second of a tension that was as thick as sludge, Janey made sure it went away. "Guess maybe I'm glad you're on the payroll after all."

He grunted. Grinned. Shook his head.

"What's funny?"

"The 'guess' and the 'maybe' part of your endorsement. Your unqualified confidence just makes me all gooey inside."

His sense of humor pretty much did the same for her. She couldn't help but wonder what could have happened between them if they'd met under different circumstances.

Which was a ridiculous thought because they never would have met. Different circles, different styles.

He was pure country. She was rock and roll. And yet here they were. Sharing a suite. Sharing a life, for all practical purposes, and sharing a common goal: keeping her alive.

"Yeah, well, I don't often give endorsements, so consider the source."

"I have. I am." He rose from the sofa with a long, indulgent stretch that delineated the impressive breadth of his chest beneath his T-shirt.

And the butterflies revved up their engines again.

It had been so long since she'd had a man affect her this way—with fluttery heartbeats and tingling fingers, not to mention with X-rated thoughts the likes of which the tabloids would figure were status quo but she found, well, shocking.

His cell phone rang then, giving her a much-needed opportunity to regroup. But when he glanced at her mid-conversation, his jaw as hard as the Italian tile on the floor, a sense of foreboding had the bottom of her stomach dropping again.

W hat?" Janey asked when he'd snapped his cell phone shut.

"That was the detective from the Atlantic City PD. He just got a call from Officer Rodman."

"From Tupelo?" She fought a heightening sense of alarm that tried to grab her by the throat when he nodded.

"They found a car. Sunk in the Tombigbee just outside of town." He wiped a hand over his jaw. "An old Pontiac—probably stolen. They're still running the plates. Anyway, seems a fisherman hooked a propeller on the roof, got stuck, and when he went into the river to cut himself loose, there was this car."

Okay. So this wasn't real news, she told herself, working hard to dodge an escalating sense of doom, despite the fierce scowl on his face. "I imagine there are all sorts of junk cars stuck on that riverbed."

"I imagine so," he agreed, his eyes hard. "Only this one wasn't junk. Hadn't been submerged long enough to get rusty."

Janey felt her blood run cold as she waited, knowing that what came next would land as heavily as a hammer.

"They found a piece of cloth stuck in a headlight. They've been able to match it to the dress your mother was wearing the night she was run down."

Cold changed to hot like a switch had been flipped. From her ears to her fingertips, she suddenly felt hot.

"And they've found a witness."

She touched her fingertips to the cross. It was warm from lying against her chest. "Someone saw what happened that night?"

"Some guy in a parked car outside the bar was playing patty-cake with a woman who wasn't his wife. He was reluctant to come forward until now, but apparently his conscience finally got the best of him."

Like anxiety was getting the best of her. Her heart kicked out several fast, hard beats. "So . . . so he saw the accident?"

He gave her another long, searching look, like he was hesitant to tell her the rest of the news.

She braced herself, a sixth sense making her just as hesitant to hear it.

"It was dark and he couldn't see the person driving, but the witness stated that whoever was behind the wheel had to have seen your mother, that they had plenty of time to break or swerve to miss her. Instead, the driver of the car accelerated and deliberately headed straight toward her when she crossed the street."

Janey's mouth was so dry and her heart was suddenly beating so fast she could hardly get the words out. "Some . . . someone intentionally k- . . . killed her?"

He shoved his hands into his back hip pockets, nodded. "It's pretty much looking that way, yeah."

She dragged a hand through her hair, aware on some peripheral level that it was shaking. That *she* was shaking. "Why? Why would someone want to kill my mother?"

The look on his face had her pushing herself back against the sofa—like someone riding in the passenger seat of a car going too fast, and instinct made them press their feet against the floorboard as if they could put on the brakes and stop a wreck from happening.

But nothing was going to stop this.

"There's something else. I didn't tell you this before," he said slowly. "Grimm left a message with his 'gifts' today."

She closed her eyes. "Something tells me you don't want to share it any more than I want to hear it."

He puffed out his cheeks, clearly reluctant, confirming her suspicion.

"Let's have it," she said, bracing herself.

She watched his face, waited in horrified silence until he reluctantly told her what Grimm had written.

" 'We're both orphans now.' "

. . . and the silence became a white-hot roar of noise.

She took it like a soldier. It was the biggest compliment Jase could give anyone. Yeah. Janey Perkins knew how to take a punch. All the while looking like a small, fragile doll.

Jase walked over to the fully stocked bar, grabbed a Coke and a bottle of water. He twisted the top off the water and handed it to her.

She accepted the bottle without a word, sat quietly for a moment, then rose and walked over to the window, absently touching her fingers to the cross she'd put on again after her shower and had pretty much always worn since she'd found it at her mother's.

And she said nothing.

It didn't seem to matter that prior to starting this assignment Jase had crammed in several hours of online research on "Sweet Baby Jane the Rock Star" in her spike heels and black leather and badass pout. Each time he saw her like this—her face scrubbed clean and her hair pulled back in a thick, shiny tail like a thirteen-year-old would wear—all he could think of was innocence. It was not the image she portrayed to the general public.

Living the life she lived, exposed to some of the fastest crowds, the highest thrills, how could she possibly be innocent? And what that had to do with the price of an RPG in Iraq he didn't know.

In the meantime, she had to be quaking inside over this latest bit of news. But she'd sucked it up. Just like she'd sucked it up during her mother's funeral. And when her mother's house had been broken into. Taken it in stoic silence. And Jase's admiration factor kicked up another notch.

It had to be hard enough to think your mother was the victim of a hit-and-run accident. But to find out she was intentionally run down. Murdered. All of this on the heels of a burglary and a convicted stalker's impromptu "visit" to her hotel room.

Jase could think of any number of things he'd like to do to the pervert if he ever got his hands on Grimm. Things he'd learned from the Taliban in Afghanistan and from the fedayeen in Iraq, where barbarism was king and human life held no more value than the price of a spent rifle shell. Sometimes, when he was aching cold on a godforsaken mountainside north of Karbāla' or rotting in a hellish hot sand bunker outside of Tikrit, the only thing that had separated him from the bad guys was a very loose grip on sanity.

Seeing what Grimm was doing to Janey—well, Jase felt a little too close to a savage side of himself that he'd discovered over there and wasn't very proud to know existed.

He didn't want to think about any of it now. Yet the memory of one night in Ramadi surfaced without warning. The night patrol. The crack of a door against a mud hut wall. The burst of firepower.

He swallowed, unable to erase the grisly image of the severed head. The lifeless eyes of what had once been an Italian journalist, the violated body on the other side of the room.

"Would he have done that?"

Her tentative question brought his head up and his attention back to the here and now.

"Grimm," she clarified, turning away from the window to look at him with eyes that looked a lot hunted and a little wild. "Would he have gone that far? Did he . . . do you think he killed my mother? In some . . . some sick attempt to . . . be closer to me?"

"We don't know that Grimm had anything to do with your mother's death."

She looked up at him and his heart damn near broke for her. "We're both orphans now? *We're both orphans now?*" Her voice rose on a note of hysteria.

She checked herself. Gathered her composure. "My God. He practically confessed."

"Whoa, wait," Jase cautioned, battling the urge to go to her and offer that shoulder again. "You're making a huge leap of logic here. He could have read it in the papers, heard about it on the news."

And yet. Jase had been thinking the same thing—not that he wasn't covering all of his bases. He'd called No back in West Palm after he'd showered. Asked him to run background checks on everyone from Max Cogan, to Derek McCoy, to Christine Ramsey. Neal Sanders and the rest of the band and backup singers weren't off the hook, either. No was running checks on them, too. Any one of them had access to Janey's suite. Of course, the hearts were 100 percent Grimm's MO, but even so, Jase wanted them checked out.

All he could do on those counts was wait. Right now, however, he had to stop Janey from taking the direction in which she was going. He saw in her eyes what she was doing to herself. Heaping on the self-blame with a shovel the size of a tank.

"Edwin Grimm's obsession is not your fault."

"Isn't it?" She shouldered past him. But she had no place to go. She stopped in the middle of the suite, spun back around, knotted her fists in her hair, and appealed to him with guilt-filled eyes.

"Every time I take the stage, isn't that what I'm asking? For people to be so obsessed with my music and my image that they become my fans? My *fanatics*? Fanatics who might resort to murder to get my attention?"

"Don't do that," he said so harshly that she flinched. "Don't get caught up in the blame game. Even if—and that's a big if—Grimm is responsible, your mother's death is not your fault."

He wasn't sure why he felt the need to set her straight. Maybe it was the haunted look in her eyes. Maybe it was because he'd been where she was now—questioning his motives, questioning his calls. Men were dead because of him. In the name of freedom. In the name of good.

Sometimes even in the name of God. But the end result was the same. Men were dead.

"You can't hold yourself accountable for the actions of creeps like Edwin Grimm. You've got millions of fans who do exactly what fans do. They buy your music. They come to your concerts. They don't blur the line. The Grimms of the world are born waiting for a chance to dive off the deep end. They don't need to be coaxed or co-erced. They've spent their lives looking for a reason. You just happened to be the one to provide his. And let me repeat—there is nothing but conjecture to tie him to your mother's death."

She wasn't buying it. He understood.

Dead was dead.

"Janey." He forgot about his determination to call her Miss Perkins as once again he found himself resisting the urge to reach for her and hold her together until she sorted this out. "It's not your fault," he insisted.

She blinked back tears, shook her head. He saw the transition on her face, recognized the exact moment when she decided she needed to move on. Still heaping on the guilt, no doubt, but dealing with it.

"The police have to be looking at him as a suspect, though, right?"

Despite the way Janey was beating herself up over the possibility, Jase hoped Alice Perkins's death could be pinned on Edwin Grimm. The sonofabitch would never see the light of day again. If they got real lucky, the death penalty would come into play.

But Jase knew better than to assume. "Yeah. I'm certain they are. Right now, he's probably on the suspect list, but the witness's report has just taken the investigation to a new level. We're no longer looking at negligent or ve-hicular homicide. We're looking at murder. And we need to give the police time to retool their investigation."

"And in the meantime?"

"In the meantime, I think you should consider canceling the rest of your tour dates."

She didn't even think about it. "I'll tell you the same thing I told Max. It's not going to happen. Besides tonight's final booking here in Atlantic City, there's only the Garden and the Boston gig before we take a two-week hiatus anyway."

He'd figured that would be her response. Just like he'd figured that without Max to support his argument, he didn't have a Humvee's chance against an IED of making her see reason.

And that brought up another question.

Where the hell was Max? And why hadn't he answered his cell?

9

Despite the cool, dark interior of the heavily air-conditioned bar, Max Cogan felt a trickle of sweat slide down his back beneath his shirt. His brow was damp. His hands were shaking.

And the damnable tightness in his chest just wouldn't leave him the hell alone.

He fished a pack of antacids out of his slacks pocket, popped a couple in his mouth. Elbows on the bar, he huddled back over his gin and tonic and lit a cigarette. Gin always tasted good on a hot day. Nothing tasted good now.

Where the hell is Meyers?

He was doing this on purpose. Making Max wait. Making him sweat. Bastard knew exactly what he was doing. And Max couldn't do anything but take it.

He checked his watch. All of five minutes had passed since the last time he'd looked.

The tightness in his chest had intensified to an ache when a hard clap on his back damn near knocked him off the bar stool.

"Cogan," Herb Meyers said in a jovial, good-ole-boy greeting. "Sorry to keep you waiting, partner."

Max closed his eyes, gripped his glass with both hands. He drew a settling breath and lied between his teeth. "It's okay. I haven't been here that long myself."

Just long enough to know he had a message on his cell phone from Jason Wilson that he needed to return but couldn't deal with until he got past this meeting with Meyers.

Max forced himself to look at Meyers. Made himself smile at the droopy-eyed, bulldog-jowled man who used to be his bookie but was now a lieutenant in the organization. Meyers's barrel belly strained the buttons on a limp white shirt and folded over a pair of baggie brown Bermudas. He smelled of sour sweat and casinos.

Herb Meyers looked like a schlep. Red, ruddy face beneath a Friar Tuck pate, fat, freckled arms, and an embarrassment of grayish-red hair curling out of every visible orifice.

Yeah. He looked the part of a chump. A patsy. And he owned Max Cogan right down to his tighty whities.

"Me," Herb said conversationally, after motioning the bartender to bring him a draw, "I like sitting lakeside in my own backyard. Sweet breeze off Superior. Shaded under an umbrella. Give me Chicago and leave the Jersey shore to the gamblers. Too damned hot in July. And bars . . . bars just ain't my thing. Even hoity-toity ones like this."

"To each his own," Max said, and drained his glass. He rattled the ice and slid it across polished mahogany toward the bartender, who promptly refilled it.

"Speaking of own," Herb said, twisting sideways in his chair and looking directly at Max, "guess you could say you own the corner on bad luck lately, huh, partner?"

Max shook another smoke out of his pack. "I'm on a little downward streak, yeah."

Herb grunted. "You're on a mud slide, Maxie. Like one of them big ones out in California that wipes out everything in its path."

Max could feel Herb's beady eyes bore into the side of his face and knew what was coming next.

"I just need a little more time, Herb. Things will turn around. You know I'm good for the money."

Herb managed to look sad. "That's an old song, partner. And this is the second time in two weeks we've had this conversation. Me and my backers are growing a mite weary of hearing it."

A sharp pain stabbed Max right beneath his sternum. He breathed deep. Dug for the antacids again.

"But here's the deal, Maxie. You've been a good customer over the years. That's why they flew me out here to have this little face-to-face. To let you know we understand. That we're willing to work with you."

Work *with* him? So why did he feel like he was about to get worked over?

"You've got forty-eight hours, Max. That's a four and an eight. You come up with the two hundred K by then, okay, buddy?"

Jesus.

Max chased the antacid with a stiff hit from his gin. "You've got me by the balls here, Herb. I can't get you that much money that soon."

Herb sucked the foam off his draw, then wiped the mustache off his mouth with the back of his hand. He snagged a beefy handful of peanuts from a communal bowl. "How much can you come up with?"

"Thirty, maybe forty K." Max stared at his glass, waited for the fallout.

Herb chomped noisily on the nuts, then finally swallowed. "Not good, Maxie. Not good," he said, after downing another deep draw on his beer.

No. It was not good.

"That little girl . . . that client of yours. What's her name? Janey. Janey, right?"

Max could suddenly hear his heart beat in his ears. Feel every pump like a sledgehammer on his chest. "She's got nothing to do with this."

"Word is, she's big-ticket. Really raking in the coin," Herb continued as if he hadn't heard Max. "I'm thinking she might be a good place to look for that money you can't find."

"You leave her out of this," Max ground out as panic paired with the pain in his chest to make him dizzy.

"Let's get something straight here, Maxie." Herb's chum smile disappeared. A sneer that had earned him the nickname Herb the Hatchet morphed his face from bulldog sad to pit bull mean. "You ain't callin' the shots on account of you got nothing for collateral. Nothing but that girl."

Max felt his blood gel in his veins, smelled his own sweat. "Look. I screwed up. I know it. But you want retribution, you take it out on me."

He hadn't realized he'd raised his voice until the bartender shot him a questioning look. He turned to face Herb. "You take it out on me," he repeated in a low, strained voice.

"Whoa, whoa, whoa, buddy." Herb offered up another one of his good-ole-boy smiles. "Have you heard me say anything about retribution? Course not. We just want our money, but we're getting into that blood-out-of-a-turnip area here, Maxie. Can't be done."

He clamped his beefy hand on Max's shoulder, squeezed until it hurt. "We ain't gonna hurt you. And that pretty little blonde?" He shook his head. "I understand she's like a daughter to you, right? Must be hard for her, what with her momma getting killed and all."

Max locked his gaze onto Herb's. And froze statue still. Jesus. They wouldn't have killed Alice Perkins. Would they?

"Be a damn shame if something was to happen to little Janey now, too, wouldn't it?" Herb went on, his eyes on Max as he hoisted his beer.

"So help me God, if you hurt her—"

"Hey. No cause to get excited. I was just making conversation."

"I don't have the money." Max pleaded with his eyes, not for himself but for Janey.

"She does," Herb said with a long, meaningful look. "She does."

"Forty-eight hours, Max," he repeated. Then he finished his beer and walked out of the bar.

Max breathed past the pain in his chest.

Jesus.

Jesus. What the hell was he going to do?

He sat for another half an hour, downed another gin and smoked his last two cigarettes before he was calm enough to get up from the bar stool.

Outside, under the blinding July sun, he told himself he'd figure something out. Get a loan. Hit up a friend.

Who was he kidding? He didn't have any friends with that kind of cash. And the only way he'd get any money out of a bank was if he robbed it. His credit was for shit.

Janey. God. He couldn't ask her. Couldn't bear to have her know about his gambling problem.

His cell phone vibrated in his pocket, startling him.

He dug it out, fumbled with the flip cover when he saw Wilson's name on the digital readout.

"Yeah."

"I've been trying to reach you," the kid said.

"I've been busy, okay?" he snapped for no particular reason except that he felt guilty for being out of touch and his control was pushed to the limit.

"You might want to get back to the hotel, sir," Wilson said. "There's been an incident."

Janey.

The bastards. The bastards had already gone after Janey. He gripped the phone in both hands, a film of sweat suddenly covering his body. "Is Janey okay?"

"She's fine. A little shaken but fine."

Christ. Oh, thank you, Jesus Christ. She's okay.

The sweat on his body turned cold and clammy as Wilson filled him in.

Grimm. This wasn't about Meyers and his muscle but Grimm. Grimm had gotten into Janey's room. The bastard had gotten close to her!

But she was safe. She was fine. Max pulled himself together—then literally felt himself falling apart when Wilson told him the rest.

Alice Perkins had not been a random victim of a hit-and-run. Alice Perkins had been murdered.

Meyers's words came back to haunt him.

"Must be hard for her, what with her momma getting killed and all. . . . Be a damn shame if something was to happen to little Janey now, too, wouldn't it? . . ."

He couldn't believe it. But what else could he think? Had Meyers and his "bosses" ordered a hit on Janey's mother? Why else would Meyers have brought it up?

Because he wanted Max to know they meant business. Because they wanted Max to understand that they wouldn't have any qualms about hurting Janey if he didn't come up with the money.

Wilson was still talking when Max hung up.

He started walking. He had to think. He had to think of something fast.

*M*idmorning Monday, July 17th, TriBeCa, New York City

"Move it or lose it."

Jase stood away from the setup for the photo shoot, close to the catering table, where fruits and cheeses and everything from milk to freshly ground coffee waited for anyone who might want to nibble. He wasn't close enough to Janey to hear her whispered warning to Derek McCoy but could read her lips. Out of necessity, Jase had gotten better at that over the past months.

Just like during the past few days he'd gotten better at reading Derek McCoy and the rest of the entourage on the tour.

They'd made the quick flight from Atlantic City to the Big Apple this morning while the road crew had torn down the set after the concert last night and driven the semis with the set and sound equipment here. Another sold-out concert was on tap for tonight at Madison Square Garden, but at the moment, Janey was in the middle of a photo shoot for a new album cover.

Janey being Janey—not nearly the spotlight hound Jase had pegged her for—had insisted on including the band on the cover.

Jase suspected she was now having second thoughts— at least where McCoy was concerned. He glared at McCoy, who had positioned himself directly behind Janey—apparently for the sole purpose of taking liberties with his hands. Hands that were currently clutching her low on one bare hip and high on her bare rib cage, just below her left breast.

The guy was a frickin' weasel. And in the background, Chris Ramsey was filming it all for posterity, a pleased smirk on her face.

"I said move it," Janey warned McCoy again.

Jase shifted from one foot to the other, stalling an itch to add a little of his own suggestions to the mix. But in a very short time he'd learned not to underestimate Janey Perkins.

A weaker woman would have fallen apart yesterday. Janey had had some bad moments, yeah, but then she'd put them behind her. She'd let it go. And today, you'd never know she was being stalked by a sicko who might have murdered her mother.

Janey was tough and she was strong. And short of McCoy getting flat-out abusive, Jase was going to let her handle the creep in her own good time.

That didn't mean he liked seeing McCoy paw at her. Still, he watched, and he waited, his jaw clenched, his entire body coiled tight in anticipation of a reason to move in and flatten the asshole.

The photographer was going for a film noir look. The background was stark white. Everyone was dressed in black—which seemed to suit these leather-loving headbangers just fine, Jase thought without an ounce of charity.

Okay. That was a bit harsh. As far as he'd been able to figure, McCoy was the only true asshole in the lot. With his bleached-blond hair, sleeveless vests, bare chest, chains, and engineer boots, McCoy preened and pranced and generally made it known he thought he was God's gift.

Jase thought of him more as God's joke—especially when Janey put the hammer down and stomped the hell out of his instep with a four-inch spike heel.

"Fuck me!" McCoy howled, stumbled, and landed flat on his pansy ass, knocking the carefully choreographed tangle of legs, limbs, and leather into a tailspin.

"What the hell'd you do that for?"

"Oh," Janey said innocently, tucking a fall of hair behind her ear. "Was that your foot?"

For the first time since the shoot began, Jase relaxed. He crossed his arms over his chest and somehow managed not to grin too broadly when Russ Bryant, the band's lead guitarist, grabbed the back of McCoy's vest and hoisted him to his feet.

"It's not like she didn't warn you, mate."

Jase thought he could like Bryant but was still working his way past the guy's full body suit. He had to have spent years collecting all those tattoos. The tall, rangy, and very bald Aussie played a mean guitar, though. He was quiet, quick with a smile, and pretty much kept to his own business. Cam Logan, keyboard, was much the same—although Jase could have done without the yard of black hair that was always flying around his face like a cobweb.

"Be nice if you could keep your hands to yourself long enough to get this done, McCoy." The photographer—some high-ticket guy who'd been flown in from L.A. because Janey's schedule didn't have room for her to go to him— was checking his light meter and repositioning umbrellas. "But hey, I'm getting paid by the hour, so what do I care?"

The rest of the band members, Avery Blanchard, rhythm guitar, Eric Holmes, synthesizer, and JoJo Starbuck, bass, grumbled good-naturedly.

"We'd like to get in a few sets of handball before the concert, so give it up, McCoy. Get used to the rejection."

"That wasn't rejection. That was foreplay, right, Janey?" McCoy joked, trying to reclaim some of his macho.

"Yeah, I'm all atwitter." Janey flashed McCoy a warning glare when it looked like he was going to tailgate her again.

"JoJo," she said, "why don't you move in right here?" She made room directly behind her, edging out McCoy, and sending him into a surly pout.

The guy was a piece of crap.

"How's Cara?" she asked as JoJo got in position.

Jase had heard JoJo talk about his wife and the baby on the way.

"Wondering if it's too late to back out," the guitarist said with a laugh that showed a wide gap between his front teeth—both of which were gold. "I'm thinking she's about eight months too late."

"Baby's doing okay?"

"Better than okay. Ultrasound showed him with a guitar in his hand."

Even Eric Holmes, who rarely showed any emotion, smiled. All the boys, it seemed, were excited about the procreation of one of their members. All but McCoy, who rolled his eyes to show he was bored by the conversation.

A strobe flashed. "Fantastic!" The photographer beamed. "A real Kodak moment. You guys almost looked like normal folks in that one. Now let's get this done for real, shall we?"

This time Jase had to smile. *Normal folks?* Between the excessive tattoos, the body piercings, the leathers, the Mohawks, the soul patches, and the makeup— most of it on the men—"normal" wouldn't come within a transport bird of this motley crew.

Two hours later, they called it a wrap—Chris Ramsey, however, kept on shooting. Something about her still didn't feel right. Jase had felt something off about her the first time they'd been introduced. Chris Ramsey was too much, well, everything. Too professional. Too intense. Too pleased, sometimes, to see friction and tension. Like it all fit into some master plan or something. He'd figure it out eventually.

The door opened again, and Neal Sanders ambled into the rented studio, helped himself to a table loaded with drinks and food while Max talked with the photographer and Chris shot more video.

Jase still didn't have a bead on Sanders, either. He'd asked Janey about him on the quick flight from Atlantic City. They'd been sitting beside each other in the butter-soft, gray leather seats of her Gulfstream.

She'd given him a closed look, then a dismissive, "Creative consultant and old friend, so you can quit staring at him like you're trying to decide if he's an ax murderer."

To which Jase had responded, "Actually, I was thinking gigolo."

She'd barked out a laugh. Shaken her head. "You're a laugh a minute, Iowa," and she'd gone back to listening to a CD of demos, searching for new material for her next album.

Okay. So that was exactly the reaction Jase had wanted from her about Sanders. Dismissive and ludicrous. Which meant there wasn't an ounce of fact in his little bit of fiction about them possibly being an item. For reasons he didn't want to explore, he'd been relieved as hell.

He could have been right, though. Since the tabloids had missed the mark on McCoy being Janey's love interest, for all he'd known Sanders could have been her boy toy. He sure as hell didn't seem to be taking up anything but space in the overall scheme of things. Taking up space and drinking complimentary booze and acting like he was someone everyone ought to get excited about.

"Don't try to figure that relationship out," Lakesha Jones had advised Jase later when they had both been standing by the jet's galley, stretching their legs.

"Pardon me?" He'd thought he'd heard her right, but

the cabin pressure and the hum of the engines played hell with his hearing.

"I heard you ask Janey about Neal," she'd clarified. "They go way back. Friends in school. Performed together at one of those amusement parks during the summer."

Jase had had an opportunity to talk to the ebony-skinned backup singer a couple of times and enjoyed her quick smile and straightforward take on things.

"Ah. So he's just a tagalong."

"In my book, yeah. In Janey's, however, he's a friend. And Janey's as loyal as they come."

"But what does he *do*?" Jase had asked. He hadn't added, *Besides mooch.*

"He's a songwriter. A wannabe performer."

"He writes material for Janey?"

Lakesha had shrugged. "Tries to. So far he hasn't hit the mark."

"And this would be in *how* many years?"

"Never said he was any good at it." She'd smiled and headed back to her seat.

Jase watched Sanders now, thinking the guy had no class. The exact opposite of Janey was true, however, when she hugged Sanders hello.

A teenage girl who'd been helping as a cater waiter and who was obviously a fan and clearly starstruck sidled up to Janey.

"Could I have your autograph?" the girl gushed and babbled and dropped all pretense of being cool.

"For chrissake. They just come out of the woodwork, don't they," Sanders sputtered with a glare at the girl before mumbling under his breath, "Another goddamn cheerleader."

The girl—who probably *was* a cheerleader—blanched and fell silent.

"I think she's sweet," Janey said, giving the embarrassed girl a reassuring hug.

"That's because you're a Pollyanna," Sanders said with a grunt. "I need to take a piss."

And with that charming announcement, he went looking for the head.

No class, Jase thought again, wishing he could be the man to teach Sanders some.

"Everything okay?"

Jase nodded at Max, whom Jase had seen sneak in a few minutes ago. "Fine. We're about to leave for the Garden and sound check."

"You've got security set up?"

Because Jase knew the incident in Atlantic City had shaken Max, he didn't take the question as an insult. "Everything's taken care of, sir. And so you know, I called the Garretts back at E.D.E.N. They're tracking Edwin Grimm's financial transactions. He's not using a credit card, but if he hits another ATM, we'll know where and when. He's not going to get the jump next time."

Max nodded, but not for the first time Jase wondered if there was more than concern about Grimm and the new information about Alice Perkins's death bothering him. Not that it wasn't enough, but Max had impressed him as a roll-with-the-punches type of guy. He'd been as spooky as a ghost since yesterday.

"Pardon my asking, but are you all right, sir?" Jase asked.

Max seemed to visibly get ahold of himself. "Fit and fine," he said with a forced smile. "I'll be off then. Just wanted to check to make sure the photographer got what he wanted."

Jase stopped him with a slight move in his direction. "I'm not going to let anything happen to her," he said, sensing that Max was more shaken than he wanted to let on.

Max nodded and squeezed Jase's arm. "I'm counting on it. Oh," he said before he walked away, "and you can count on a little additional distraction tonight. Almost forgot. I just found out that the Reverend Samuel Black, our favorite televangelist, has dispatched a contingent of his local supporters to picket the concert tonight. And the missus has rallied her cookie squad again. They're already camped out in front of the Garden and are bound to be a bit disruptive."

Jase grunted, didn't bother to tell Max that he already had it covered. "Just so their cookies are as good as the Palm Beach bunch."

When Sanders sauntered out of the restroom, a surly scowl on his face, Jase made a mental note to have the crew back at E.D.E.N. put a rush on his background check.

He didn't like that guy.

10

Six thirty that night, arriving at the Garden

"We're thirty seconds and counting." In the back-seat of the limo with Janey, Jase spoke into his walkie-talkie as they rounded the corner and headed for the back entrance of the Garden. "What's it looking like there, Mike?"

"The usual." Jase had been working with Mike Smith, Garden security for this gig. "Hundred or so die-hards milling around hoping for a look and thirty or so picketers with 'Jesus Save Us from Sweet Baby Jane' signs."

Jase swore under his breath. The Reverend Black's contingent must have opted out of the cookie business to-night. "Okay. Keep it tight. You should have a visual of us by now."

"Got ya," Mike answered, and in the background Jase could hear the swell of screams. The crowd had spotted them, too. "We're ready."

"What about you?" Jase turned to Janey. "You ready to run another gauntlet?"

She sat silently beside him, staring with unseeing eyes out the tinted window. "As I'll ever be."

"No stopping in the crowd tonight, okay? No signing autographs. No shaking hands."

She turned her head. Looked at him. "They're fans," she pointed out.

"We don't know what they are," he countered as the limo pulled to a stop and Mike stepped forward and opened the door.

Jase stepped out first, checked to make sure the boisterous crowd was contained, then turned and took Janey's hand to help her. When she stepped out of the limo, the throng erupted. They stood ten deep on either side of the barricades of sawhorses and orange cones set up in a ten-foot-wide path leading from the limo's back door to the Garden entrance.

"Janey! Janey! Janey!"

The cheer rose up in a deafening roar. Fans of all ages and sizes pushed against the barricades, hands reaching, bodies pressing.

"Jesus," Jase sputtered, then tucked Janey under his arm and headed for the building's entrance.

"Mike!" He had to yell to be heard above the roar that was now mixed with the noxious chant from the Reverend Black's contingent of, "Sister of Sin. Satan's spawn," that spewed into the night like sewage.

"Move 'em back, Mike!" Jase shouted just as a barricade rattled over.

It was like a dam broke. Instead of water spilling over the break, bodies poured through the opening.

Jase swept Janey up into his arms and shouldered toward the door—but not before one of Black's pious disciples got to her.

"Whore!" a woman spit, her eyes blazing brimstone and damnation. "Tainted blood! You're nothing but—"

"Fuck!" Jase swore, and shoved her aside, but not before she managed to throw something . . . aw hell. Blood poured over his shoulder where he'd ducked to protect Janey, and ran down his arm.

With a roar, he charged headlong toward the door, knocking down anyone who was stupid enough to get in his way.

Finally, he made it inside, then fell back against the door when Mike managed to close it behind them. Just before it closed, Jase swore he saw Chris Ramsey in the crowd, grinning.

He didn't have time to think about that now. His heart was hammering. So was Janey's. He could feel it drumming against his chest. Feel her horror in the grip of her fingers on his arms.

"It's okay," he said, lowering his head to hers. "You're okay."

"Yeah. Yeah," she said with a little nod. "I'm fine. Wet. But fine."

He looked down then . . . and saw that he hadn't managed to block all of the blood. Her pale face was splattered with it. Her arms speckled as well.

"Christ. I'm sorry."

She gave him a game smile. "Not your fault. Besides, I always wondered what it felt like to be in a bloodbath. Now I know.

"Hey," she said when Jase just looked at her. "It's okay. Welcome to my world."

He shook his head. *Tough*, he thought again. "You're one tough cookie, you know that?"

"Speaking of cookies, I liked it a lot better when they showed up with them."

"Black just made it to my list," he said. Tomorrow, he was calling No. He wanted this bastard checked out—if for no other reason than to see if he could find any dirt on him. Paybacks, he thought as the stickiness of the blood that had hit him sucked onto his skin through his shirt, were hell.

"Um . . . you could put me down now, you know."

Oh. Yeah. He'd forgotten he was still holding her. Or maybe not.

"I could," he agreed and headed for her dressing room.

He felt her gaze on his face as he carried her down the hall. She didn't say anything. Neither did he.

And he didn't put her down until he'd set her safely inside and locked the door.

S ame day, Peoria, Illinois, 10:30 p.m.
It was because people made his job so easy that Alex was so good at it. That and his patience.

He didn't even have to use his pick kit tonight. The back door hadn't been locked. What was it with these small-town yokels? They had no fear or they were just plain stupid. Or both.

He'd waited until the husband left for his bowling league half an hour ago, watched the house until the bathroom light went on five minutes later, then let himself in the back door of the white ranch house on Englert Lane.

Kathy Wallace was lying back in the tub, a scented candle burning on the counter, music playing from a sound system in the den, bubbles bouncing and popping and floating like foam.

By the time she spotted him in the doorway, it was too late to save herself. She just didn't know it yet.

"Don't scream," Alex ordered, shoving the business end of his Sig dead center between her eyes.

She was too terrified to scream.

And he was too focused to care much if she did. This wasn't going to take long.

He glanced around the bathroom until he found what he was looking for.

"What . . . whatever you want . . . just . . . just t- . . . take it." She covered her ample breasts with an arm, her brown eyes wide and pleading behind a pair of wire-rim glasses.

Alex plugged the handheld hair dryer into a socket. He flipped it on and, looking into those huge, horrified eyes, dropped it into the tub.

It was over with barely a splash and a sizzle.

Simple.

Neat.

And tomorrow, the coroner would rule Kathy Wallace's death an accidental electrocution.

She might have been a pretty woman once, Alex thought as he took a moment to make sure she was gone. But she'd let herself go. An extra twenty or thirty pounds, by the looks of it. She wasn't going to need that diet book sitting on the edge of the tub anymore.

Satisfied that she was dead, Alex slipped out of the bathroom and out the back door. Then he walked through the dark streets and the three blocks to the car he'd paid thirteen hundred cash for and would abandon at the airport.

"It's done," he said into his cell phone, half an hour later.

He'd set the terms for payment for these last four jobs. He already had all of his money. There would be no more half before and half after crap. He'd proven he was capable of delivering and he'd be damned if he was going to sit through anymore blow-by-blows so his client could get off on the gore.

"And it will look like another accident?"

"Just like the others."

"Good. Fine. I've got another . . . assignment."

Another one? Whatever.

And while Alex had to admit he was curious as to why he'd been paid to off a middle-aged barfly from Mississippi and a pudgy preschool teacher from Illinois, it was no skin off his ass. The other three—same thing. They were average Joannes. Hardly his usual hits, but hell, he'd never seen South Dakota before. Lots of grass. Flat as hell.

That was where the Richards woman had met with an "accidental" death two days ago due to carbon monoxide poisoning. Poor soul had slipped on a patch of oil in her garage—after she'd turned on her car and, unfortunately, left the garage door shut. People were probably still wondering what she was doing out in her garage in her bare feet at two in the morning. Any bruises on her body would be attributed to the fall.

Tampa had been just plain hot the next day. It was a little more difficult taking care of Lana Fredrickson there. Or it would have been if it hadn't been for the impressive open staircase in her two-level condo. The fatal fall from the second floor had broken her neck.

And Texas. Hell. They could leave that place to the cactus. It was a stroke of luck that Mrs. Smith had just had a new pool installed in her backyard for her grandchildren. Too bad about her drowning. Well, not too bad for Alex.

He'd take that kind of easy money any day. A job was a job. He was for hire.

And a hundred K was a hundred K.

*T*uesday, *July 18th, New York City, the morning after the Madison Square Garden concert*

"Okay, if we're going to do this," Jase cast a dark look between Max and Janey, "we're going to do it my way."

Other than the incident with Black's pious perverts before the concert, the Garden party had gone off without a hitch. Once inside, Jase had called for doubled security, positioned a 24-7 guard at the door to Janey's suite, and never let her out of his sight.

The Jersey contingent of Bible-thumpers hadn't raised any more Cain. Grimm hadn't shown his perverted face, either—at least he hadn't been spotted.

That didn't mean Jase was happy about how exposed Janey was onstage each time she performed. But short of locking her up, his hands were tied. She insisted that the shows would go on.

Now they had to deal with this new development. The bank at Tupelo had contacted Max earlier this morning. It seems that Alice Perkins had a lockbox. As the only survivor, Janey was entitled to the contents. The hitch was, she could only access the lockbox in person. Which meant she had to return to Tupelo.

"And what's your way?" Janey asked from the table by the window in the hotel suite where she was autographing a stack of eight-by-ten glossies.

"No limo. No private jet. We take a cab—just you and me—to LaGuardia. Then we fly commercial back to Tupelo. Jeans, T-shirts, no bling. No attention. No fuss."

"I don't like it," Max said, looking uneasy. "Makes her too accessible."

"Pardon me for being blunt, sir, but you people are so used to traveling like royalty, you forget how the 'real' folk live. And dress. No one's going to recognize her if they aren't expecting her. Especially if she's traveling with me." Jase stood with his feet planted wide, his palms stuffed in the back pockets of his jeans, and gave his best farm-boy face to drive home his point.

"I still don't like it. And I don't think you should go," Max said.

Janey hadn't intended to go at first. Jase hadn't been all that surprised by her reaction to the news. She'd been estranged from her mother. She'd had it rough as a kid. Jase could sympathize but not relate. His family was loving and close.

And they had expectations. Especially after Jeremy died.

Ones Jase hadn't fulfilled. Which was why his last visit home had been so short. His mother had cried when he left. His father . . . well, his father had been, as usual, disappointed and working damn hard to hide it. Which made Jase feel that much more guilty.

"Janey?" Max prompted again, jarring Jase out of his little side trip into guilt and Janey out of her funk.

"I'm not going to hide out the rest of my life, Max. I'm not going to let him do that to me. I'm going. I need to get this done if I want to put it behind me."

Jase waited for Max's reluctant nod, then started making arrangements for a flight that morning so they could fly back north to Boston for a concert the next night.

Score one for the bodyguard.

I t's none of my business," Wilson said after the plane lifted off and they were settled in first class without so much as a hitch or a second look, "but would you mind telling me something?"

Janey turned her head against the leather headrest and met his gaze. "What do you want to know?"

"Why do you put up with McCoy?"

She couldn't help but smile.

Derek was a prick. For him, getting her into his bed

was an image thing. A personal challenge to make her his latest sexual conquest.

She thought back to that night after the first West Palm concert and realized in retrospect that he'd actually scared her a little. He'd backed off since, so she'd let it pass.

"You don't think much of Derek, do you?" As if she hadn't already figured that out from the dark looks and disgusted head shakes when Baby Blue thought no one was watching.

"Gosh, does it show?" he said deadpan.

She grinned. "Gosh, yeah."

"The guy's a loser."

"True. But he's a helluva drummer."

Jase grunted. "I'm thinkin' good drummers are a dime a dozen."

"You applying for the job?"

"Me? Hell no. I've got a job."

She'd promised herself she wouldn't, but it was time to bait the bodyguard again. It seemed only fair since every time he moved, she got a subtle little whiff of his wonderful scent, which she'd since decided was sage and triggered a few of her pheromones to stand to attention. "And are good bodyguards a dime a dozen, too?"

He didn't hesitate. "Yes, ma'am. They are."

This was something she should be used to by now. Beefcake without ego. Early on, she'd more or less decided she wasn't dealing with the usual suspect here.

"Hasn't anyone ever told you that job security depends on convincing everyone you're the best at what you do?"

"I *am* good at what I do. But so are a lot of others."

She thought about that for a moment. "That's the thing about war, isn't it? Makes for a lot of warriors with skills that transfer to law enforcement or private security.

"*Time* magazine," she explained when he glanced at her

with reluctant interest. "Last week's issue. They had a big piece on it. 'After the War' or something. It was interesting."

He looked thoughtful, then looked away. But not before she saw a glimmer of something . . . she didn't know what, but whatever it was, it made her sad. And it made her wonder what all he'd seen. What all he'd done in those wars that must haunt him yet today.

Not for the first time, she wished she knew more about him.

"How long were you in?"

He was quiet for a long time. She'd about decided that he was going to tell her it was none of her damn business and that small talk wasn't in his job description. But then he surprised her.

"Five years."

Five years? "So, you enlisted right out of high school?"

The look on his face told her he found that question marginally funny. "I went to the U of Iowa and worked on the farm with my dad for four years."

She did the math. And must have looked surprised.

"I'm twenty-seven, if you haven't already figured it out," he said.

"Amazing. You know, if you could somehow isolate that family gene and reproduce it in mass quantities, you'd make a fortune." *Not to mention that wonderful scent,* she thought.

"Yeah, well, it's a pain in the ass that I can't walk into a bar without getting carded."

She laughed. "Must be a guy thing. Most women I know get upset if they don't."

He finally smiled. "Go figure."

"Yeah. Go figure."

She unbuckled her seat belt and turned toward him, folding a leg up onto the seat. She should leave him alone. But she was in a mood to talk. And to pry. And tease a little. Besides, he started it with his question about Derek, so as far as she was concerned, that made him fair game.

For whatever reason, she felt relaxed and comfortable around him. For the first time in days—maybe weeks—she was able to just let the tension go and live in the moment. Have a little fun.

Maybe it was getting away from the tour, distancing herself from the bloodbath by Black's disciples last night that had bothered her more than she'd let on. Maybe it was simply Wilson. He was easy to be around. Whether it was because she'd discovered she actually did feel safer with him at her side or because he was the most normal person in her life of late she didn't know. She just knew she enjoyed his company—she even enjoyed the little sexual sparks flying around, although she still hadn't figured out if she was going to do anything about it.

In the meantime, she wasn't particularly happy to be returning to Tupelo, but she was relieved to be away from NYC. The prying lenses of the press and all the hype that went with a concert date were exhausting. She was grateful for the media coverage—both radio and TV—but relieved the interviews were behind her. She just wasn't up to playing rock star right now.

Most of all, right now she was glad that Baby Blue—she had to quit thinking of him that way or she'd end up saying it out loud someday—was providing a distraction.

"Do you like me, Iowa?" She hadn't intended to ask, but it was out now, so she'd just wait and see what he'd do about it. Was surprised that she really wanted to know.

"Because I like *you,* you know," she added, emboldened now that she'd opened up this line of dialogue. "I didn't want to because I didn't want a bodyguard. But you're okay. And you're not at all what I thought you'd be."

He gave her a leery look. "You were expecting, maybe, the Terminator?"

She laughed. "I was expecting, maybe, the usual muscle head Max hires. You're nothing like them."

He had nothing to say about that. In fact, she got the distinct feeling he felt very uncomfortable talking about himself.

So naturally, she kept it up. "You're a good-looking guy. Okay, a *great*-looking guy. Nice bunchy muscles. Gorgeous baby blues."

He rolled his eyes, blushed. She loved it. And ignored an internal alarm that warned her she might be crossing a line here.

"I had to figure you'd have an ego the size of a refrigerator. But you don't. You're just a nice guy."

He was actually squirming now. "My mother and my old Boy Scout leader would be pleased to hear that."

And the hell with good intentions. Bodyguard baiting had become her favorite new sport.

"So. Do you?"

He let out a deep breath, like he wished to God she'd leave him alone. "Do I what, ma'am?"

Ah. The "ma'am" factor again. She'd finally figured out that he whipped it out whenever he felt a little cornered or uncomfortable. And she kind of liked that she could make him feel that way.

"Do you *like* me?"

He gave her a look that said, *You are such a girl.* "You have a legion of fans who love you. Can't imagine it matters what I think."

"Quit stalling," she insisted, because now she really did want to know. "Just answer the question."

"I like you fine," he said, staring straight ahead after a heavily exhaled breath.

He was placating her. Or he was afraid to tell her exactly

what he thought about her. Which, she was pretty certain by now, was the same way she felt about him. Intrigued. Aware.

Very, very aware.

She propped an elbow on the armrest, dropped her chin into her palm, and studied the way the tips of his ears flushed hot pink. Became fascinated by the smooth, hard line of his jaw, the strong nose and deep set of his eyes. She could see him in uniform. Could see him in special ops mode, focused, able, heroic.

She wondered if she could span his biceps with both hands. Never thought she'd be intrigued by muscle. Maybe it was the gentleness she'd sensed inside all the strength that really mesmerized her.

"Blue," she said, looking at his eyes. "Baby blue."

He slowly turned his head her way. "Excuse me?"

"Um . . . blue. It's my favorite color," she hedged, but found herself grinning when she realized she'd spoken aloud. "What's yours?"

He grunted. "Camo."

He did have a way of making her smile. "Favorite song."

He rolled his eyes. " 'Take Me, Baby.' "

She chuckled when he named her current chart single. "Yeah, right."

"Okay, fine. Anything by Toby Keith," he finally admitted grudgingly.

"Ah. I knew you were a country fan. Don't much like rock, do you?"

He bit his lower lip, like he was biting back the urge to tell her to back the hell off. "Do I lose chow privileges if I say no?"

A funny guy, her bodyguard. "Okay. Forget that question. I can guess the answer anyway. Let's see. Who's been the most influential person in your life?"

He hesitated. Swallowed. And stared straight ahead. "My brother."

There was way more emotion in his answer than two words should have held. More than she thought she wanted to deal with. At least not today. Someday, she'd ask. Maybe. But not today.

"I like to roller-skate. How about you? Ever roller-skated, Wilson?"

"Can't say as I have," he said after a long silence that spoke volumes about what he must be thinking about her mental state.

"Too busy . . . doing what, back in Iowa?"

"Sorting the hayseed out of my pockets, ma'am," he said with such a put-upon scowl that she knew she was driving him nuts.

She hadn't had this much fun in a long time.

"You make me homesick for my dogs. And my cat."

He cocked his head, then shook it.

"Oh . . . no." She laughed at his "what the hell are you talking about" look. "That didn't come out right. Let me try again. I haven't seen them for a while—what with the tour and all. And now I'm thinking—wondering, I guess, how long it's been since you've been home. Wondering if maybe you get homesick for Iowa. And now I realize I'm a little homesick for my guys. The dogs," she clarified when he looked at her like he wished he had a gag.

Okay. It was time to take pity. "Do you play gin?"

Slowly, he shook his head, clearly lost by her mercurial switch of topics. "Do you have A.D.D. or something?"

Real funny guy. "Just letting you off the hook, since you obviously aren't comfortable getting up close and personal."

"I'll ask the flight attendant for a deck of cards," he said, grabbing onto her offer like it was a lifeline.

11

J ase was in a foul mood by the time they made their connection in Memphis for a short flight into Tupelo that afternoon. His concentration was for shit. He'd gotten his sorry butt whipped in three straight games of gin because of it. And losing did *not* set well. He didn't like to lose at anything.

Finally, thank God, she said she was tired, reclined in her seat, and fell asleep.

Jase spent the rest of the four-and-a-half-hour trip in clench-jawed silence, feeling like he'd been rolled over by a Bradley. Here he'd been doing everything in his power to keep from getting up close and personal and she was pumping him about colors and songs and . . . and roller-skating for God's sake.

What the hell was that about?

Maybe she's just lonesome, lunkhead.

Life on the road . . . it was pretty isolating for her. Except for the hour or so she managed to squeeze out for her morning runs, it was pretty much all business, all work, and all at a pace that would give a sprinter fits.

And it wasn't like she had any girlfriends around to help her let off steam. Yeah, Lakesha and Tess dropped by the suite every once in a while, but it was never for long and it was usually to consult on an arrangement or background vocals or costumes. And now Max wasn't even around like he used to be.

Has to be lonely for her, Jase thought again as he waited at the rental-car desk for their ride.

And you begrudge her a little harmless conversation just because you're afraid you can't keep a professional distance.

She looked up from her magazine in the rental-car waiting area when he approached with a set of keys.

She was wearing a pair of faded jeans, a Kid Rock T-shirt with arms long enough to cover her tattoo, and pink discount-store flip-flops that she'd sent out for. And, of course, her cross.

Her hair was tucked up under his Army ball cap. Today, she'd tied a blue and white farmer's bandana around her neck. From the look on her face when she'd met him in the living room of the suite, she'd been as pleased as punch over her getup.

She didn't look anything like a rock star sitting there. The star quality was unmistakable, just the same.

"All set?"

He tossed the keys in the air and caught them. "Let's roll."

"Got us a real hot rod, I'm guessing," she said, her tone saying she figured just the opposite.

"Guess again."

"Boring," she singsonged when he unlocked the passenger door of the white Ford Taurus and helped her in.

"That's the point."

"Even normal people drive sports cars," she pointed out, pulling the strap on her seat belt across her body. "Snazzy red ones. With convertible tops."

"Well, there you go."

She would never come within a Mississippi mile of normal, no matter how much she dressed down and attempted to blend. There was just something about her. Something he needed to quit dwelling on.

Extract your head from your ass and do the job, Wilson.

Just because they'd made it this far without being recognized didn't mean their luck would hold. Or that they'd fooled Grimm, who, Jase was fairly certain, was keeping tabs on her the way a bookie kept tabs on the races at Hialeah.

H er bodyguard covered all the bases; Janey gave him that. When they were within a few blocks of the bank, he called ahead and arranged for the bank president to meet them at the employee entrance.

"No sense taking a risk of you getting made at this point," he explained when she asked him if the term "overkill" meant anything to him.

Talk about overkill. The man did things for a plain white T-shirt and off-the-rack jeans that were downright amazing. She didn't know what he did in his bedroom at night after she turned in, but she had to suspect there might be a heck of a lot of push-ups going on behind that closed door.

When he was in full bodyguard mode—like he was now—she could picture him in a firefight. His cheek flush against a rifle, sighting down the barrel, covering a buddy's back.

He had that lean, mean special-ops look about him when he was like this. All business. All focus. Dangerous . . . in spite of those baby blues and the gentleness of his hand at the small of her back as they walked to the bank's rear entrance.

A middle-aged man in a neat navy suit and power red tie opened the door for them. He was on the short side— maybe five six—with thinning gray hair, silver wire-framed bifocals, and a toothy white smile.

"Ms. Perkins," he said, with an ingratiating smile that she saw all too often when someone wanted something from her. "Robert Haley, the president of Capital Progress. It's a pleasure meeting you. And what good timing. You made it just before closing."

"Mr. Haley," Janey said, taking the hand he offered. Now that they were here, she was officially nervous and wishing she were anywhere else. She wasn't sure she wanted to know what was in her mother's lockbox. Had an unreasonable sense of discomfort just thinking about opening it up. It felt almost ghoulish. Like she was grave robbing or something.

"Jason Wilson." Beside her, Baby Blue extended a hand. "We talked on the phone."

"Wilson," the banker said with a nod, and returned Jase's handshake. "Nice to meet you."

"We need a room where Ms. Perkins can access the lockbox in private."

Well. Nothing like cutting to the chase, Janey thought.

If Haley was put off by Wilson's brusqueness, he didn't show it. "Of course. Yes, of course. Please follow me. And might I add, this is a nice surprise, considering we didn't expect you in person after you'd sent your proxy down this morning."

Janey stopped walking.

Someone came to the bank saying he was my proxy?
She glanced sharply at Wilson, every nerve cell in her
body screaming out a red alert.

He grabbed her arm and pulled her close to his side.

Haley turned with a smile, just then realizing they
weren't following. His smile unfolded into a frown when
he saw their faces.

"What? What's wrong?"

"Miss Perkins didn't send a proxy."

"But . . . Mr. Lemans said you'd sent him as your
representative."

Beside her, Janey could feel Wilson's muscles bunch
with tension. He held up a hand and gave a slight shake of
his head when she opened her mouth to ask him the obvious question: *What in the hell is going on?*

"Is he still here?" he asked Haley.

"Oh dear. I'm sensing something's very wrong," the
banker said with a worried look.

As understatements went, it topped the charts.

"Is he still here?" Wilson repeated more forcefully,
moving in front of Janey and blocking her in between him
and the wall, effectively making a shield with his body.

It was in that moment that all of this became very, very
real. And very, very serious. This man was prepared to
give up his life for her. Yeah, it's what he'd been hired to
do. And she'd accepted that. But that was when they were
talking about a "bodyguard." A nameless, faceless entity.
A body for hire.

Now they were talking about Jason Wilson. Iowa. Baby
Blue. The thought of his blood being spilled for the sake of
hers horrified her, eclipsing the uncertainty of the moment.

"Mr. Haley. I need to know if he's still here," Jase demanded, blasting both her and Mr. Haley out of shock
mode.

"Oh. I'm sorry. No. No, he's gone. I don't know where, but he's not here any longer."

"You're certain."

"Yes. Yes, oh yes. He left . . . let me think. It was shortly before one, I believe. I left him in my office to contact you to verify his authenticity. When I couldn't reach you, I came back to my office and he was gone. I thought it was strange at the time, but, well, I assumed something must have come up and he'd had to leave unexpectedly."

"Something came up all right," Wilson muttered, and let up on the pressure against her body.

Janey's legs felt a little rubbery. And her mind was spinning in circles.

"Do I need to call the police?" Haley's worried gaze flitted from Janey to Wilson.

"We'll get to that. In the meantime, this . . . Lemans . . . what business, specifically, did he say he was here for?"

"Why—to access the lockbox."

Stunned, Janey glanced at Wilson. Saw the same question in his eyes that she was asking herself. *Whoever it was knew about Alice's lockbox?*

"I didn't allow him to, of course. Bank policy clearly prohibits anyone but the owners of the lockboxes from opening them—unless of course we have specific instructions from the owner and verification of the proxy's identity and permissions. Since Mr. Lemans couldn't provide that verification, we were unable to honor his request.

"You know," Haley added, cupping his chin between his thumb and forefinger and adopting the look of an amateur sleuth, "now that I think about it, there was something suspicious about that man from the beginning. And the way he reacted when I told him how surprised I was that Ms. Perkins had sent him in light of the fact that I'd just been notified you were coming—"

"You told him Ms. Perkins was coming to the bank today?"

"Well, yes, I did. I was surprised, of course, and told him as much since I'd thought you were coming."

The word that came out of Baby Blue's mouth was one she'd never associate with babies.

"Oh dear." Haley removed his glasses, wiped at his eyes. "I . . . I thought he'd want to meet her here. Was that . . . was that wrong? I mean, I assumed he works for you." He turned to Janey, his expression stricken.

"Can you tell us what he looked like?" Baby Blue asked.

Medium height. Medium build. Late twenties, maybe early thirties. Dark glasses, so Haley hadn't gotten a look at his eyes. Mustache and beard. Other than that, nothing remarkable.

That's what Mr. Haley remembered about the man. It wasn't much to go on.

"I . . . I know I would recognize him if I saw him again. And I'm sure our security cameras caught him on tape."

"Just like I'm sure he was probably wearing a disguise," Wilson pointed out. "Look, Mr. Haley, could you show us to the lockbox now please? And while we're there, I'd very much appreciate it if you'd pull those tapes, then call the Tupelo police. Ask for Officer Rodman and request that he meet us here."

"Oh. Oh certainly. I can do that. I am so sorry if I've done anything wrong."

"Not your fault. And you did everything right," he assured the distraught banker. "What we need now are the police. And access to that box."

Janey sat at a rectangular wooden table in the middle of a stark ten-by-ten room that smelled of ink and metal and cleaning solution. Her heart knocked around in her chest like a pinball as she stared in absolute shock at the contents of the open lockbox.

"I don't understand," she said on barely a whisper. "Not any of this."

Money. Bundles of it filled Alice Perkins's lockbox in neat, banded stacks.

"Holy God. Looks like there's about ten thousand per stack." Baby Blue's voice came to her from what seemed like a far, far distance.

Standing behind her, he shuffled through the piles of cash, stirring up a slightly musty scent into the room to mix with the scent of her shock. "There must be close to a million bucks in here."

A million dollars. *A million dollars.*

"I don't understand," she repeated. "Why would my mother have this kind of money?"

Unless . . .

"Unless she never spent any of the money I sent her," Janey concluded out loud.

"I'm getting by."

That's what her mother had said that night Janey had called her. *"I'm getting by."*

"You sent her money?"

She nodded, did a quick calculation in her head, and realized that she probably had sent her mother close to a million dollars over the years. "Every month. For several years now."

Wilson rummaged deeper into the lockbox.

"The fact that most or all of it must be here might explain why she lived as modestly as she did. But it doesn't explain why. Why would she keep it? Why wouldn't she spend it?"

"And who would have known about it?" her bodyguard added to the list of questions. "Someone obviously did. They tried to get to it today."

"A tabloid reporter?" she suggested, grasping at straws. "A lot of people have lockboxes. They might have taken a shot in the dark. You know. Trying to get some inside scoop or something not even knowing the money was here."

Wilson had already moved on to something else.

"Look at this." He shoved a piece of paper into her field of vision.

She didn't react at first. She was still thinking about the money. About the "proxy" and wondering what else could possibly happen to complicate her life.

"Janey," he prompted. "Do these names mean anything to you?"

She glanced at the sheet of paper. Recognized her mother's handwriting but not the names.

Kathy (Simpson) Wallace
Candice (Becker) Richards
Lana (Jensen) Fredrickson
Tammy (Quigley) Smith

"No. I don't know. I don't think I know any of those women."

"Your mother must have." He kept digging through the box. "The question is, why would she keep their names under lock and key?"

"The question," Janey said, as she stared at the money, "is what in the hell is going on?"

"Janey . . . this guy look familiar to you?"

She glanced up to see him holding a photograph.

Without a word, he handed it to her. She took it with a shaking hand, sensing on some instinctive level that what she was about to see might change her life forever.

It was an old Polaroid snapshot, faded and cracked and grainy. And as she stared into a face that looked vaguely familiar, into eyes that were deep set, hair that was dark brown, she didn't have a clue who he was.

Or did she?

She closed her eyes as her heart stumbled. Opened them again as her breath stalled while she studied, studied, studied the photograph.

Her fingers felt stiff and cold suddenly. And her face felt flaming hot.

She'd never met her father. Had never known his name.

Could it be . . . could it *possibly be* . . . that after twenty-seven years of knowing nothing about him, she was finally looking at his face?

D o you think it could have been Grimm? The guy at the bank this morning?" Janey clarified when Jase looked across the booth top at her. "Do you think that Lemans was actually Grimm?"

They were sharing a booth in an out-of-the-way mom-and-pop barbeque restaurant on the south side of Tupelo where Jase was certain they hadn't been followed. The place smelled exactly like a rib place should. Of barbeque sauce, wood smoke, and age.

Jase could have used a beer. Instead, he had ordered a Coke for himself, water for her. And two dinner specials.

"It's possible." He studied Janey's face across the worn red oilcloth covering the booth top. Not that it was his job, but he was worried about her. "Hell yeah, it's possible, but . . ." He stopped. Shook his head.

"But what?"

"But why? Grimm's fixation is on you. Getting close to you. Why would he be here? Seems like he'd be in New York. Or on his way to Boston and your next concert."

He scrubbed a hand over his jaw. "Besides, how would he have known about the money?"

She'd been thinking the same thing. He could see that in her troubled eyes.

"Then who?"

He grunted. "Wish I had an answer. All I've got are more questions. Still topping the list is who killed your mother. I know—," he interjected when she would have interrupted. "I know we've been looking at Grimm for that, but this money . . . hell. It puts another motive on the table. Whoever killed her might have been after the cash."

They'd put a lot of spins on things since leaving the bank and checked into a motel to spend the night, since their return flight wasn't until tomorrow morning. They'd talked about everything except that photo Jase had discovered along with the list and the cash in the lockbox.

It was safer for her, he supposed. Safer and easier for her to talk about and think about who had tried to access her mother's lockbox. Safer to think about the $1.3 million Mr. Haley had verified was inside and had already wired to her bank in L.A. than to dwell on the photograph Jase had found.

She had to be thinking the same thing he was. Was it a picture of her father? Why else would Alice Perkins keep the guy's picture in a bank lockbox? He had to have been important to her. So important, she kept the photo under lock and key. Along with the names of the four women. None of whom lived in Tupelo. Or if they did, they had unlisted phone numbers; Jase had already checked the Tupelo phone directory back at their motel, where they'd showered and changed before coming here.

"The four names on the list," she began, her thoughts evidently paralleling his, "what do you think that's about? Do you suppose they were . . . I don't know . . . maybe women in need? Maybe she was planning to give them the money."

Hope was an amazing thing. Hard to explain sometimes, easy to latch onto. It was a little sad that Janey still had hope for her mother. Hope that a woman who had been a helluva drinker but not much of a mother might have had some redeeming quality. Charity. It was a stretch and Jase didn't believe it for a second. But Janey needed to believe it.

"Sure. Yeah. It's possible," he said. "Look, we're not going to find any concrete answers tonight, so why don't you just eat your ribs?"

He nodded toward her plate when he realized she'd done little more than toy with her food. She hadn't eaten anything but fruit at breakfast and she'd eaten damn little of that. "You need fuel. And you need to just not think for a while."

"Oh, right. Not think. I'll get right to work on that," she said, but at least she managed a small smile.

It had been several hours since they'd left the bank with Officer Rodman, who had questioned every employee who might have gotten a look at Lemans. Of course, Jase had no doubt that Lemans wasn't the guy's real name—and as he'd suspected, "Lemans" had been very careful to avoid looking at the security cameras. They'd gotten very little from the tape.

Jase had driven Janey to a budget motel. "You expected the Ritz? In Tupelo?" he'd asked when she'd given him a "you've got to be kidding" look. "We're trying to keep a low profile, remember?"

"Low, lower, lowest," she'd said, glaring at the motel, where the most appealing features were its $29.95 a night rate and free HBO.

"It'll be good for your character."

"If we'd taken my Gulfstream instead of flying commercial, we could have been in Boston by now," she'd pointed out.

"Yeah, and if we'd taken your jet there'd have been an army of sleazebag photographers waiting at the airport when we got here. Think of it as a trade-off."

After they'd checked into adjoining rooms—which were surprisingly neat and clean, if not luxurious—they'd both showered and changed into fresh jeans and T-shirts, continuing the low-profile look. Jase had insisted they go out to eat instead of ordering in.

For one thing, he didn't need to spend any more time than was absolutely necessary in close quarters with her today. Plus, she needed movement. She didn't need to sit in a motel room and brood about all the weird things happening in her life.

Too weird, Jase thought as he dug into his ribs. And she was too wired. He wished she could work up a little more enthusiasm for her own meal. And then it came to him. He was going to be so, so sorry, but he knew exactly how to get her to eat.

"Tell you what," he said, knowing he'd regret it. "I'll make you a deal."

She slumped back in the booth. "What kind of a deal?"

"You were pretty hot to ask me questions on the flight down here. So here's the plan. You can ask me anything you want. But for every question I answer, you have to eat something."

Her eyes brightened marginally. "And if I'm not hungry?" She cocked a brow in challenge.

He lifted a shoulder. "Then you're not hungry."

Hell, she wasn't going to pass up an opportunity to play twenty questions; he knew that. "But my money's on you finishing that plate of ribs before it's all over."

"You think you know me that well?"

He gave her a "get real" look. "No woman I know can resist an open invitation to pry."

She smiled. Not offended. And some of the tension left her shoulders.

"Okay, smart-ass, you're on."

God help him. "Hit me with your best shot."

12

Jase figured she must have had a list already made out in her mind, because she jumped right in.

"So . . . you went to college before the military. What did you study?"

He looked straight ahead. "Law enforcement."

"So why aren't you on a police force somewhere?"

"Same reason I'm not still in the Rangers." He turned to look at her, working hard not to let her see what he was feeling. "Hearing loss—big booms will do that. Just enough that I can't pass the physical."

"I'm sorry," she said, and he realized that she really was.

He shrugged it off. "It happens. Not a big deal."

But it *was*. It was a very big deal.

"How long have you been a bodyguard?"

He grunted. "You might not like the answer."

"Backing out already?"

"Nope. Just warning you. Today's what? The eighteenth?"

She nodded.

"Then it's been twenty-nine days. If you count my three weeks of OJT."

She blinked. Sat up a little straighter. "You mean—"

He cut her off with a wave of his fork. "Unh, unh, unh. Another bite. Then another question."

He liked it that she dove in with her fingers and made quick work of the meat on a rib bone. "You mean you just started?"

"You're my first field assignment," he admitted after she'd swallowed. "Told you that you might not like it," he added, reacting to the shocked look on her face. "Look, if it's the hearing or lack of experience that worries you—"

"No," she cut him off. Shook her head. "No. I'm not worried about any of that. I figure . . . well, I figure what you did in the Middle East more than qualifies you for the job. How long did you say you've been out of the service?"

He glanced pointedly toward her plate. It was either that or get fixated on the little smudge of barbeque sauce clinging to the corner of her mouth—and how tempting it was to lean across the booth and lick it off.

She rolled her eyes but pulled another meaty rib bone off the rack and started munching.

"Six months," he told her when she'd finished it—and dabbed her napkin to the sauce, thank you, Jesus.

He didn't have to prompt her the next time. She ate a forkful of salad. "And for those six months . . . you, what? Trained to be a bodyguard?"

He could lie to her. He probably should lie to her, but what the hell. Lying had never been a part of his MO. He couldn't think of a reason compelling enough to change that now—not even embarrassment.

"I knocked around a month or two. Hung out in a few too many bars. Drank way too much beer. Got in too many fights."

"You don't strike me as the brawling kind—unless you had good reason."

He finished off a rack, considered how much to say. In the end, he just told it like it was. At least like it was for him.

"For five years I'd been part of a rapid deployment team. Wherever there was action, we were there. Always in the hot zones."

He paused, shrugged. "So much adrenaline pumps through your body then . . . it becomes like a drug, you know? You start to . . . I don't know. Crave it. Even after you come home it eats at you. And you look for ways to get a fix. So I drank. And I fought. Then one night I got the shit beat out of me."

"You were hurt?"

Okay. So she looked alarmed. So he liked it that she was concerned for him. Most of all, he liked it that she was loosening up. For a while anyway, her mind wasn't dwelling on all the crap that was happening in her life.

"Mostly my pride," he admitted. "So I quit drinking."

"And fighting," she concluded.

He shook his head, smiled. "Not quite. I just did my fighting sober. And I got paid for it."

Her eyebrows drew together. "Boxing?"

"Nothing that respectable. I joined the WWA."

"WWA?"

"World Wrestling Alliance." When she frowned in puzzlement, he elaborated. "Ever heard of Stone Cold? The Rock? You know—Hulk Hogan types? Grown sweaty men in leopard skins, pounding their chests and flying off the ropes in a ring for money."

Her mouth dropped open.

"Yeah, that's the reaction I got from my mom, too."

"Did you, um, like it?"

"Does Tweety Bird like Sylvester? No. I didn't like it. But I got to beat people around, so I thought I was swimming in champagne."

"Only . . ."

"Only it wasn't my cuppa."

She looked thoughtful. "And security work . . . is *it* your cuppa?"

He leaned forward, forked another rack onto her now empty plate before taking another for himself. "It's honest. It's respectable. So far I haven't had to hit the emergency room after a day's work. That's a plus," he added with a smile.

"But you have to put up with—at least in this case— pushy celebrity types."

She had the barest hint of a dimple in her left cheek when she smiled. He hadn't noticed that before. Wished he hadn't noticed it now.

"You're not so pushy."

"You are, though." He was glad to see a smile when she looked up at him, then down to the ribs in front of her. "Did I ask for another rack?"

"That's a question." He notched his chin toward her plate. "You want an answer to a question, you eat some more ribs."

"You're a pretty stand-up guy, you know that, Iowa?" she said after several moments had passed. She'd evidently taken the time to absorb all the things he'd told her. He hoped to hell it didn't come back to bite him on the ass.

"I mean . . . it's not just that apple-pie and Boy Scout look you've got going on. You're . . . real. I appreciate it . . . you know . . . that you've been up-front with me."

"Yeah, well," he said, telling himself her comments

deserved a reciprocal statement. "You're pretty stand-up, too—for a badass wild-child rocker. Ma'am."

He didn't know why he so liked making her smile, but when she did, he felt sort of pleased with himself. Like he'd done something really good.

"Maybe that's because I'm just a southern girl at heart."

"Maybe," he agreed.

She was Mississippi-born after all. And she'd grown up poor. Probably knew things about poverty and neglect that he'd never know. At least not firsthand.

"So," she said, leaning back and looking, he was glad to see, relaxed and mellow, "did you get to wrestle in a leopard skin?"

He grunted out a laugh at the teasing light in her eyes. "Animal prints were reserved for the stars."

As he'd hoped, that made her smile.

"As ex–Army Ranger Jason Plowboy Wilson, camos and combat boots were my thing. Original, huh?"

"Yeah," she said, giving him a long interested look that had him squirming. "You're an original all right."

He cleared his throat, felt his face go red, and damned his Finnish-Irish ancestry. She was too damn easy to like. Too damn easy on the eyes. Too damn easy to talk to and tease and . . . well. She was just too damn easy.

"Plowboy?" she added as an afterthought. "Guess it doesn't take much to figure that one out."

"Guess not."

She watched him through brown eyes gone all soft and sultry. "So, do I get any more questions?"

Not, he decided, if he wanted to get out of here with one shred of privacy left. "Are you done eating?"

"I'm stuffed."

He thanked Jesus again. "Then I guess the answer would be no. No more questions."

She leaned forward, propped her elbows on the table,

her chin in her folded palms. "Just a couple. Just two itty-bitty little questions."

She was flirting. Which he liked even though he shouldn't. Maybe he'd gotten her too relaxed. Time for a rapid extraction.

"I'll get the check."

She reached across the table. Latched onto his wrist. "Let's look at the dessert menu."

He froze. Looked from her hand, where it felt warm and slight on his wrist, to her eyes. *Devil eyes,* he thought as she made it clear with a wicked, knowing smile that he wasn't off the hot seat yet.

Shit. This wasn't good.

But the two pieces of warm homemade pecan pie topped with melting vanilla ice cream that arrived five minutes later sure was.

She took a bite, swallowed, then hummed with plea-sure. And when she looked over at him with a slumber-ous, seductive look in her eye, he squirmed again.

He lifted his Coke, sipped—

"Boxers or briefs?"

—and damned near spit it across the table.

He grabbed his napkin, wiped his mouth. "Ex*cuse* me?"

She looked way too damned pleased with herself. "Do you wear boxers or briefs?"

He got his coughing under control. "What the hell kind of a question is that?"

"Or do you go commando?" she asked with a little peek under the table.

"Stop that right now," he ordered with a dark look.

"What? Don't like that question, either? Okay. How about this? What do you like best—missionary position or girl on top?"

Then she dug back into her pie like she hadn't just

dropped a MOAB—mother of all bombs—in the middle of the table.

He tossed his napkin on the tabletop. Leaned back and glared. "What are you doing?"

Dancing brown eyes met his with baleful innocence. "Asking questions. Isn't that the game we're playing?"

Okay. That was it. They were out of here. He angled his weight to his right hip, dug his wallet out of his left pocket. "I don't know what game *you're* playing."

Playful changed to sensual in a heartbeat. "Don't you?"

Well, okay. Yeah. He knew exactly what she was up to. And the idea held way too much appeal. Appeal, hell. Try he'd-like-to-clear-the-booth-top-and-take-her-right-there appeal.

He frowned at her over his open wallet. "This is a very, very bad idea."

"Is it?" she asked so quietly, he barely heard her. "Is it really?"

They could not have this discussion. He could not talk to Sweet Baby Jane Perkins about boxers or briefs or favorite positions. He could not talk about it because he couldn't afford to talk about it, not and keep his sanity and his professionalism and his distance from this woman.

This woman . . . who was currently looking at him like she found him cute and amusing and sexy and a very likely substitute for a little nocturnal self-gratification.

Shit.

This was so bad. Because he found *her* cute and amusing and sexy and *damn*, did he want to take care of that particular need for her and satisfy a few of his own.

He couldn't think past the ringing in his ears. Finally realized it was his cell phone and with fingers that felt as thick and clumsy as sausages wrestled it out of the clip on his belt.

"Wilson," he said when he didn't recognize the number on the readout.

"Yeah, Wilson, it's Officer Rodman."

Jase studiously avoided eye contact with the trouble sitting across from him. "What's up?"

"I don't know. But I wanted to run something past you. That car—the one we hauled out of the river?"

The one that hit and killed Alice Perkins. "Yeah?"

"I think I already told you it was stolen from a collector in Jacksonville the day before Ms. Perkins was killed."

"And?" Jase figured there was more. Hell, every time he turned around there was more.

"Well, look, this is a long shot, but can you ask Ms. Perkins if a nineteen-seventy-nine green Pontiac Lemans holds any significance for her?"

A green Pontiac Lemans. Lemans. Like the guy at the bank. Jase didn't like the feel of this.

He hesitated, then held the phone away from his mouth and met her curious eyes. "Seventy-nine Pontiac. Mean anything to you?"

Her expression transitioned from curious to wary—and he knew, he just knew, things had just taken another turn toward weirdville.

"The car that killed your mother. It was a seventy-nine Pontiac."

Pale. She suddenly looked very pale.

"Green," he said after a long moment. "A green Lemans."

She closed her eyes. Folded her hands together on the booth top. Clenched them so tightly her knuckles turned white. "Lemans."

"Yeah." He reached across the booth and covered her

hands, concern taking precedence over his misgivings about touching her.

She looked up at him, her eyes huge and haunted. "Mom had a seventy-nine Pontiac. A green Pontiac Lemans." Her alarmed gaze locked on his. "It was the only car we ever owned."

Janey sat in numb silence as Baby Blue drove them back to the motel and talked on his cell phone to his boss back in West Palm Beach.

Streetlights cast the front seat from darkness to shadows. That was her life these days. Darkness and shadows. She stared straight ahead, weary of feeling numb, weary of feeling weary.

And to think—not more than fifteen minutes ago she'd been flirting with her bodyguard. For a while there, she'd actually forgotten about all the fun and games of murder and mayhem and a million-dollar jackpot that her life had become. Well, she was back on the board now, playing the game whether she wanted to or not.

Damn. It felt like her life had turned into one big blender and she was stuck on the puree cycle.

Whoever had killed her mother knew a lot about her. Right down to the make, model, year, and color of the only car Alice Perkins had owned.

What could that mean? What could that *possibly* mean?

She thought about the photograph she'd tucked into her purse. And didn't know whether to hope she was right or pray she was wrong. Was it a picture of her father? Did she really want to know?

"Here's a list of names," Janey heard Baby Blue say after reviewing with his boss all the bizarre things happening—from Grimm's grisly gifts of raw and bleeding hearts, to the million-plus in her mother's lockbox, to the man trying to pass himself off as her proxy at the bank and using the same name as the car that had been used to kill her mother.

God, her head was spinning.

"See what you can find out about these four women. And start the search in Mississippi. They may be locals. May be women Alice Perkins had known for some time, because she has both their married and maiden names listed."

"Nope, not a clue," he added, apparently in response to a question on the other end. "They don't ring any bells for Janey, either. Don't suppose you have anything for me on the names I gave you the other day?"

He waited a heartbeat, then repeated the names of her band members, backup singers, Neal, Max, and Chris Ramsey.

She kept it together until after he'd hung up. "I don't appreciate that."

He waited for a light to change, tapping his thumbs on the steering wheel. "Which part?"

"You know which part. When did you order background checks on Neal and Max?"

"Right after the break-in. Okay, look, I know you work with those people—"

"I don't just work with them," she interrupted, incensed that he would subject Neal and Max in particular to background checks and Lord knew what else they would do. "Most of *those people* are my friends."

"Then there's nothing to worry about, is there?"

And maybe that's why it upset her so. Maybe there was something to worry about. And maybe she didn't want to know about it if there was. "Why aren't you concentrating on Grimm?"

"I *am* concentrating on Grimm. The *police* are concentrating on him. Everyone's trying to zero in on him," he assured her.

Okay, it was true. Edwin Grimm had been the focus of his long conversation with the boss he referred to as No, who she'd gathered was one of the partners at the security firm that employed him.

"We're both orphans now."

She kept coming back to the message Grimm had left with the hearts in Atlantic City—it still haunted her. And as far as she was concerned, all roads still led back to the crazed stalker. It didn't make sense that he could possibly know about the money in her mother's lockbox, but nothing else made sense, either.

"Look, Janey," Wilson added when she remained silent, "I just want to make certain there isn't something else going on here. What's it going to hurt to cover a few more bases?"

"So what you're thinking is that not only do I have a stalker planning to finish what he started four years ago, but that someone else is out there? Someone who knew about the money in the lockbox?"

"I'm saying," he repeated as they pulled up to the "no tell motel," as Janey had begun to think of it, "I want to cover all the bases. That's all. I'm just doing my job," he reminded her.

"Why the check on my mother?"

He shifted into park and killed the motor. "As far as you know, she didn't work, right?"

"As far as I know," she concurred on a tired sigh.

"And yet, she didn't spend a dime of the money you sent her. So how was she getting by?"

"I'm getting by."

Her mother's words came back to her again. "Maybe she had a boyfriend who paid the bills."

"Maybe," he agreed, opening the door and easing out from behind the wheel. "Maybe not. But she had to be living on something. We need to find out. Make certain there's a logical explanation. And if there was a boyfriend, we need to talk to him. He could shed some light on things."

She let out a weary breath when he came around to her side of the rental car and opened her door for her.

He leaned down in the opening, one hand on the roof, one on the door, unintentionally caging her in. "I'm sorry about all this. And I hate to point it out . . . I mean, I know how hard this must be for you, but we can't lose sight of the fact that someone *did* kill your mother.

"Was it Grimm?" he continued. "Maybe. But maybe it wasn't. The cash changes everything; we need to find out who knew about it. And we need to find out if or how this all affects you."

He was right. She knew it. It was just . . . hell. It had been much simpler when Edwin Grimm was the only likely suspect. Not easy by any stretch, but simpler. And the money *did* put a new slant on things. Added a new element. A new danger. Another level of threat.

She stood when he offered her his hand.

"What do you think it means? That the exact same kind of car we once owned—right down to the color and year—was used to . . . to run down my mother?"

"You keep asking me questions that I've got no answers for." He cupped her elbow as they walked toward the outside, ground-floor entrance to their adjoining rooms.

"Just like you, all I've got are more questions. Like why was the car dumped in the river? I've got to figure it wasn't supposed to be found. But if that's the case, why all the trouble to use that specific car? It took a lot of planning. A lot of effort looking for that particular car and then stealing it."

Janey hadn't thought things out that far. But he was

right. "Why use a car," she continued, picking up on his chain of reason, "that was identical to one my mom used to own when whoever did this never intended for anyone to ever see it? To ever know that specific car was, for all practical purposes, a murder weapon?"

"Exactly. That tells me your mother's murderer knew her. And that the murder was very personal," he added.

"And the car is significant to the murderer, why?"

He shook his head. "Did your mom ever have an accident with that car? Maybe—"

"Run someone down in a drunken stupor?" she speculated, seeing where he was going with this. "It's possible, but I don't know. I . . . just don't know."

They were both silent for a long time. "And it's not a coincidence, is it? That the guy at the bank used the name Lemans?"

"No," he agreed. "It's no coincidence. We find him, we probably find your mother's killer."

It was no coincidence, either, that when Jase unlocked Janey's motel room for her and swung the door open there was a new game prize waiting amid the ruins of a room that had been thoroughly and violently trashed.

13

G et me away from here."
    That's all Janey had to say and Jase had moved into action. As soon as they'd finished dealing with the police and motel management they'd thrown what few things they'd packed in their carry-ons and headed south on Highway 45. Right after he'd stopped at a pawnshop to pick up a handgun.

She didn't like the idea. Jase didn't much care. He was way past concerned. Way past pissed.

Whoever they were dealing with—Grimm or someone else or a combo of both—from this point on, he was packing. If he hadn't been convinced that Janey was in danger after Grimm had broken into her Atlantic City hotel suite, the incident at the bank and the latest break-in had made him a true believer.

Now this deal with the car that had been used to run down her mother—well—someone out there was determined in a very calculated, very sick way to do her harm. Whether the intent was to terrorize, rob, or murder, it didn't matter; at this point it was all the same to him. He needed to protect her. Would do whatever it took to keep her safe. And to do that, he needed firepower.

The gun was within easy reach under the driver's seat of the rented Taurus. He'd have preferred a military-issue M9 Beretta 92F 9mm. He settled for a .38 S & W and was happy as hell that an extra Ben Franklin handled the permit issue.

"This is getting dicey," Jase told Nolan, whom he'd called once they'd been well away from Tupelo.

"No shit," No said on the other end of the line as Jase turned off the highway and pulled into a gas station.

They'd been traveling for a little over half an hour. For the last fifteen minutes, Jase had been filling Nolan in on the latest turn of events, from the precise details about the car that had been used to run down Alice Perkins to another set of bloody hearts that had been prominently displayed in the center of the trashed bedding in Janey's motel room.

"And nothing was stolen?" No asked.

"We're traveling light. Basically there was nothing to steal."

"So you're thinking . . . what? The break-in was supposed to terrorize her?"

"Could be. There was no note this time. Not sure what that means."

"He could have run out of time."

"Yeah. Or he could have been looking for something, gotten angry when he didn't find it."

"The money?"

"Yeah, sure, it's a possibility, but I can't see anyone figuring we'd leave that much cash lying around. And I can't see Grimm knowing about it, either."

"Well, someone does."

"Yeah," Jase agreed, thinking about "Lemans." "Someone sure as hell does."

"So you know, I put Dallas on things full time at this end," No said. "He's already initiated a computer search on the names you gave me earlier."

"Have him do something else for me, would ya? Look up all the available public information on Grimm's trial and conviction. I want to know how much detail was printed on the stalking incidents and how accessible that info still is."

"You got something specific in mind?"

"Yeah. I don't know. Maybe. I can't pinpoint it, but something's off. Grimm's calling card—the two bloody hearts? I've been thinking . . . See if you can find out what kind of birds they came from—and if he always used the same kind of bird. I'm guessing he did."

Beside him, he felt as much as saw Janey shiver as he pulled up to a bank of gas pumps.

"And you want to know if these latest two episodes exactly replicate the ones Grimm pulled three years ago?" No's voice was thoughtful.

"Exactly."

"You're thinking there might be a possibility of a copycat?"

"I don't know what I'm thinking. I'm just . . . I've got a feeling is all."

"Good enough for me."

Jase had been known for his "feelings" in hot zones. More often than not, his "got a bad feeling about this" had been the heads-up their squad had needed and heeded to get them through an explosive situation.

"Anything else?"

"Not that I can think of. Just, well—"

"Just get the lead out and get you something to work with," No supplied what Jase hadn't felt comfortable suggesting to his boss.

"Um . . . yeah. Thanks. *Boss,*" he added with a grin.

No chuckled and disconnected. Jase hung up, wishing he could have had that conversation with No without Janey having to listen to the grisly details.

Couldn't be helped. They needed to move on this. And they needed to move fast. Somehow, some way, Grimm or whoever the hell was doing this seemed to be able to follow Janey everywhere she went. That was also a puzzle. And a big problem.

Unless he was fucking invisible, Jase was having trouble buying the idea that they were being tailed. He'd seen no one, nothing suspicious. And he'd been watchful as hell. And that just added more questions to the mix.

"If it's not Grimm, then who?"

He glanced at Janey as he unbuckled his seat belt and opened the car door. "There you go again," he said, trying to cast light on a very dark situation, "asking me questions I can't answer. And I'm not saying Grimm isn't behind this."

"But you're thinking it may be a copycat," she continued, clearly puzzled and frustrated and needing to think out loud. "Why would anyone copy Grimm? What's the point?"

"Hell, a million-plus could be a mighty big motivator for murder. Grimm could be a convenient scapegoat. We look for him, it throws us off the trail of someone else."

She bit her lower lip. "The names on the list. What do they have to do with anything—*if* they have something to do with what's going on."

He sighed heavily, as frustrated as she was. "Look— there's only one thing I'm certain of right now. Too many coincidences are racking up for them to be coincidences."

Way too many, he thought, getting out of the car and starting the gas pump. A woman was dead. Another appeared to be the next target. *And not just any other woman,* he thought as he topped off the tank. A woman he'd grown to like and respect, and there was no way in hell he was letting anything happen to her.

His mind kept winding back to the million bucks. And that million bucks bumped another question to the top of his list of priorities. He needed to find out how Janey's mother had been living in relative comfort without any means of support and without spending Janey's money. And he needed Alice's motor vehicle record to see if she had ever been in an accident.

Somehow, he felt that an answer to those questions were the key. He wasn't going to get any answers tonight, though. Tonight, the only thing he could do was keep Janey Perkins out of harm's way—and maybe do something about that haunted look in her eyes.

He paid for the gas at the pump and they headed out again. An hour later, certain they didn't have a tail, he pulled into the first motel that popped up along the interstate. She needed sleep and it was up to him to see that she got it.

Okay, hot stuff. Gimme your best shot."
     If anyone had asked her five minutes ago if she was capable of smiling, Janey would have told them with a look and a snarl to get real.

But she was smiling now. It was forced and it was weary, but Wilson had a way about him. And he was employing it to great effect.

He'd checked them into another one of those "we'll leave the light on for ya" motels. He'd booked a suite this time, with two bedrooms and a small living area between them.

She'd watched in curious silence as he'd moved all the furniture to the edges of the living area before it dawned on her what he was up to.

He was offering her a kickboxing match. A chance to work off some of her tension. At this very moment, he stood before her in his jeans, T-shirt, and bare feet. The only other thing he wore was a cocky grin.

Another day, another time, she'd have loved to go a few rounds with him. But this wasn't the time.

Yeah, she'd like to let off a little steam with a good, hard round of physical exertion with an opponent who she strongly suspected could give her a helluva lot better run for her money than a staff trainer at a local gym.

Yeah. She'd like to. But tonight, she was too tense. Too close to the edge. She might end up doing more than fighting. She might end up crying, and she didn't want to do that. Not in front of anyone. Especially not in front of him.

"Look, I know what you're trying to do," she said, putting on her best "I'm fine and dandy" face. "And I appreciate it. But not tonight, okay?"

"What's the matter? Afraid of a little competition?"

He was goading her. It may have been well intended, but it was goading just the same. It ticked her off, but she wasn't going to bite.

"If you want to think so." She turned toward her bedroom, where she knew she'd spend a sleepless night.

Behind her, he made clucking sounds.

She stopped. Clenched her teeth. And slowly turned, working hard to keep her temper from getting the best of her. "Is that how you talked to your dates back home on the farm?"

He raised an eyebrow, his grin broadening. "That's it? That's all you've got? Trash talk? Puny trash talk at that."

Bastard. He was enjoying this just a little too much. "Look, Blue Eyes, when the time is right, I'll drop you like a bag of dirt. But now," she continued, walking slowly toward him, "is not the time."

She struck like a snake. A swift, high, exact kick that caught him off guard and hit him dead center in the breadbasket—just like she'd planned it.

He doubled over with an "umph," gasping for breath and clutching his gut. She took advantage with a sharp kick behind his knees and he landed on his back with a thud.

"On second thought, maybe this *is* the right time," she amended, standing above him with a triumphant smirk.

"Ah," he managed when he caught his breath. "The lady plays dirty. I respect that in a woman."

He held out a hand, which she took. The least she could do was help him up.

Wrong.

The next thing she knew she was flat on her back on the floor beside him after falling for the oldest trick in the book. He'd latched onto her hand, kicked her feet out from under her, and taken her down without so much as a by-your-leave.

"That would fall into the turnabout's fair play category," he said when she turned her head to glare at him.

"Fine. So we've established that we're both cheaters."

"Restores my faith in the all's-fair-in-war theory," he said, his beautiful blue eyes searching hers, she knew, to make certain he hadn't hurt her.

He hadn't. She was fine.

And if she told herself that often enough, she would be. She jerked her gaze away when hot tears stung her eyes.

She was okay. She'd make it be okay. She'd make
the overwhelming sense of vulnerability, the encroaching
sense of catastrophe, go away. She'd make the need to cry
for a mother who'd been a drunk and a father who hadn't
been go away, too. A need that she'd bottled up inside for
more years than she could count. A need that had been
building since she'd been told her mother was dead and
since she'd found a photograph of a man who might be
her father. A need that swelled in her chest, pushed at her
throat, burned behind her eyes . . . and oh, damn.

A huge sob racked her body.

"Hey . . . hey. It's okay. Just let it go. God knows, you
need to let it go."

His voice was soft and soothing. And then his fingertips were there. Just as soft. Just as soothing. Touching
her face, brushing away the tears she'd fought and denied
but spilled over anyway. No matter that she didn't want
them to. No matter that she hated herself for giving in to
the weakness.

"I don't . . . cry," she whispered, her voice clogged
with tears.

"I know. I know you don't. Everyone knows that you're
one tough hombre," he murmured as he gathered her
close against him and held her.

Like she was a child. Like she was fragile. Like her
pain had become his.

And like a child, she turned into him. Snuggled close
to all that warm, male strength and the protective comfort
he offered.

She didn't know how long they lay that way. She didn't
know how long she cried. And she didn't care. He'd been
right. This man who was so not a boy had known exactly
what she'd needed. And he'd given it to her. Selflessly.

His hands on her back were so strong yet so gentle.
His breath in her hair so warm and deep. His body

against hers hard yet giving, his scent a comfort and a distraction.

For the first time in days she felt totally and utterly safe. For the first time in years—yes, *years*—she felt totally and utterly understood.

How had that happened? How had someone she'd known for barely a week come to understand what she needed before she had?

She tipped her head back so she could see his face. His beautiful, concerned face. His eyes were heavy-lidded. His mouth so very close to hers. And the fear and frustration that had finally loosened its hold on her gave way to a slow-building heat, a heat that settled low in her belly and flared to fire when she saw an answering flame in his eyes.

"Love and war," she whispered, unable to resist any longer. She'd wanted to know what it would be like with him since the first time she saw him. Tonight she was finding out.

"All's fair in *love* and war."

And finally, *finally*, Janey did what she'd been wanting to do, what she'd been needing to do, for days now.

She touched her mouth to his. A brief buss of her lips against his. A gentle friction as she brushed her mouth back and forth, soft to supple, warm to hot.

My God. He was so hot. She wanted to lose herself to all that heat. Immerse herself in the power of it, let it take her over, take her under, take her away from the reality of stalkers and murders and the mess her life had become.

"You had it wrong before," she whispered again, loving the feel of all of him against all of her. "All's fair in *love* and war."

His entire body shuddered. He closed his eyes, met her mouth with his, then, on a ragged breath, pulled away. "One doesn't apply here, Janey. And the other . . . the other was just a game."

She wasn't so sure about that anymore. Wasn't sure about anything except that she needed to keep on kissing him. Needed to know what he tasted like deep inside. What he felt like when he was wanting, too.

"Okay." She met his mouth again. And again. Another brush of lips to lips. Not so tentative now. Not so tame. An expedition into foreign territory where they could both be winners if he'd let them.

"Okay. Got it," she whispered, intent on seduction, aching with need. "It's just a game. And we both know the rules up-front. No one gets hurt. No one gets angry."

"Janey." Her name grated out on a low moan when she worked her hand down between their bodies, molded her fingers around the long, thick erection that told her he was as turned on as she was. "We . . . Jesus . . . we can't do this."

"We can." She squeezed, felt his amazing body tense just before he covered his mouth with hers.

His suddenly hungry mouth.

His wildly ravenous mouth that fought hers even as he took her under in a kiss that erupted with passion and fire and a need so sharp and huge it stunned her. She felt his hand in her hair, cried out when he clutched a handful and tipped her head back to scatter openmouthed, biting kisses against her jaw, along her throat, before returning greedily to her mouth and slipping his tongue inside.

An explosion of sensations detonated inside her as he kissed her deeply, not a bit sweetly. She loved it. She craved it. The unchecked need in his assault. The raw desire she tasted on his tongue.

Gripping his powerful shoulders, she rolled to her back and pulled him over on top of her. Then her hands were under his shirt, pulling, tugging, dragging it over his head while he did the same to her T-shirt and made quick work of her bra.

She sucked in her breath on a rush when he released her mouth with a long, eating kiss to find her breast, draw her nipple deep into his mouth, and suck and lave and feast as if she were his last meal. Or his first meal. Or his only meal.

Sharp, exquisite pleasure shot from her nipple and arrowed through her belly where it seared between her thighs. Long. It had been so, so long since she'd felt this electric arousal, this edgy, achy yearning. Maybe she'd never felt it. Not this intensely. Not this desperately.

She was beyond desperate now as she arched toward his mouth and parted her legs, making room for him between them. And lost her breath on a serrated sigh when he pumped his hips against hers fueling the fire, stoking the burn.

His back was so broad, his skin so supple, over hard, ropey muscles. He was so warm beneath her fingers as he rocked his hips against hers, pinning her to the floor with his weight, making her ache with every move. She lowered her hands to his tight buttocks, moaned in protest when he pulled away, then sucked in a breath of urgent shock when he reached between them, worked the snap and zipper on her jeans, and opened them in one swift, wild rush.

He took her mouth again, all hungry suction and greedy tongue, swallowing her gasping moan when he tunneled a strong hand inside her open jeans and cupped her, absorbed her damp heat, then plunged a finger inside.

She jerked against his hand, stunned by the instant, searing pleasure, the breathtaking shock of his invasion. She lost awareness then of the hard floor beneath her. Of anything before this moment. She was aware only of his need and hers. Hyperaware of his touch, of her inner muscles clenching, her body alternately softening and tensing as his finger glided in and out of the damp, delicious heat he created.

"You . . . inside," she managed on a broken rasp, as a restless urgency to feel more, be more, take more, drove every thought. "I need . . . I need . . . Oh, God. I need you inside me."

She lifted her hips, reached down, and pushed and shoved and kicked and scrambled to get out of her jeans. Cried out in complaint when his amazing hand withdrew.

"Please . . . please . . . pleeeaaaazzzze," she begged, clutching at his shoulders, urging him back, then reaching between them to find he'd freed himself from his jeans. Silken heat filled her hand; moisture dampened her palm and she went crazy with her need of him.

"Now. I want you inside me now!"

"God . . . Janey. We . . . Jesus. We can't."

She lifted her head, cut off his words with a deep, carnal kiss of clashing teeth and questing tongue, and guided the tip of his penis to the center of her heat. Damp met damp. Heat met heat. Soft met hard. My God, he was so hard.

On a defeated groan, he gave up the fight. Pushed inside of her with one long, deep stroke that filled her so full she cried out at the pressure. Rich, erotic, amazing. And all she could think was, *More.*

She wanted more of this astounding, electric friction, more of him filling her.

She lifted her hips to his . . . then rocked away. Lifted, rocked, taking all he had to give her, dying a little each time she pulled away. Then he was rocking, too, matching her rhythm, tunneling his hands beneath her hips, and lifting, enhancing the contact to such exquisite depths that everything in her world was reduced to the awareness of the way their bodies connected and rubbed and filled and pleasured.

The friction was combustible. The sensation indefinable and so, so unbearably good as he increased the pace, pounding into her with a frenzy that matched her own need for release that had grown insatiable.

She clutched at him, breathless with the assault of sensations that built and bred and had her clawing his back, biting his shoulder, begging, begging, begging for a release that she wanted and dreaded and finally reached with a breath-stealing explosion of rich, raw pleasure.

"God . . . oh, God." She clung to him, clenched around him, held on for her life as she rode the peak, fiercely clinging to an orgasm so acute and intense she could hardly bear it yet didn't ever want it to end.

Above her, he made one final plunge. One deep, guttural groan and he came on a long, labored breath.

Mindless with sensation, her eyes tearing from the intensity, she held him close, savored the free fall, the weightless sense of floating, and the knowledge that no man had ever taken her this high. Had ever made her feel this safe. Ever earned this much of her trust.

Propped on his elbows above her, his face pressed in the hollow of her shoulder, his back damp with a sheen of sweat, he was silent. For long, endless moments, he was silent.

Too silent.

Devastatingly silent, she realized when her synapses regrouped and finally clicked back into working order.

And for the first time since she'd taken that leap, offered her trust and kissed him, she felt cold.

14

Jase had to move. He had something to do. He had to go shoot himself. Cut off his dick. Clamp his balls in a vise.

Which all fell into the category of closing the barn door after the horse had gotten out.

Stupid! Stupid, stupid, stupid.

He drew in a ragged breath . . . which only served to make his dick twitch, because the movement pressed his chest deeper to her breasts, his belly closer to hers.

He had to move, he told himself again.

And yet he stayed. Flesh to flesh with the sweetest, sexiest, most vulnerable woman. A woman who had taken him by storm, launched a full frontal assault that he hadn't known how to defend himself against.

Like hell.

It was a one-word defense.

"NO!" Capital *N*. Capital *O*. Exclamation point.

Pig simple.

He was about eighty pounds heavier than she was and she'd taken his sorry ass down without a fight.

Some warrior he was.

And some protector. Shit. They hadn't even used a rubber.

"You're awfully quiet up there."

He grunted, lifted his head, and, with every shred of self-control he had, rolled off of her.

He lay on his back beside her, crossed his arms behind his head, and stared at the ceiling. "That's because you're talking to a ghost. Dead men don't talk. And I'm as dead as they get. Or I will be when Max gets wind of this."

"Max doesn't need to get wind of this. No one does. It's just you and me."

He turned his head, looked at her. At her kiss-swollen lips, at her sated brown eyes, at the mess he'd made of her amazing hair.

And wanted her again.

He jerked to a sitting position. Stood. Tucked himself back in his jeans. Didn't trust himself to zip up because his hands were shaking so bad.

"This should not have happened." Hands on hips, his back to her, he shook his head, disgusted with himself. "I apologize. I—"

"Don't." Equal measures of hurt and anger colored her tone. "For God's sake. Do not apologize. Do not second-guess. Do not assume that you own any blame here. I came on to you, remember?"

Jesus, did he remember. She'd been . . . hell . . . she'd been all over him. And he'd loved it. Fought it. Yeah. For all of about a nanosecond.

"I didn't even protect you."

And that ate at him.

So did the rough way he'd handled her. But God. Lord God, the need.

"So you know," she said so quietly, he had to cock an ear to hear her, "I'm healthy. Don't know what you've been reading . . . in the rags and all . . . but I'm healthy. In fact . . . don't laugh, but I've been celibate for two years."

Celibate. Did she say "celibate"?

He jerked his head around, saw the look on her face. Oh man. Oh Lord have mercy on his stupid sorry hide, she *had* said "celibate." For two years. He couldn't even wrap his mind around that. And yet . . . it would explain. It would explain a lot. Her urgency. Her huge, quaking need.

That she'd chosen him. Man. It was a burden he wasn't sure he wanted to carry. And yet it humbled him. He swallowed, turned away from her. Shook his head and confessed his own secret. She deserved to know. "Yeah. Well. That makes two of us. Been a long time for me, too."

Not two years but damn close.

But none of that made what he'd just done right. None of it made what he was going to have to do easier.

"And I'm on the pill," she added. "Ever since Grimm . . . well. As a precaution."

Oh man. The guilt didn't end. She felt the need to protect herself from rape and he reaps the benefits.

He felt lower than low when he heard her stand and walk up behind him. Flinched when he felt her hand on his arm. Fought a groan when her warm breath fanned his bare back. And battled the urge to turn around and see her . . . see every bare inch of her with those sleepy mocha eyes and sexy swollen lips . . . and that wild tangle of hair that he itched to sink his hands into again. See her standing there wearing nothing but that brushed-gold cross, her breasts pink and pouty where he'd sucked them. The curls between her thighs wet from his come and hers.

And then she was pressing herself against his back. Rubbing her little velvety nipples against him, running her tongue along the indentation of his spine, spanning his ribs with her hands. Then gliding them lower, into his open jeans, reaching inside.

He threw back his head, sucked in a fractured breath when she stroked his traitorous, swelling cock, cupped his balls in her small, kneading hand.

"We're both adults here, Iowa."

He groaned out a humorless laugh. "And I'm supposed to be protecting you, not screwing you."

That was mean. He'd known it when he said it. Supposed some ethical part of him wanted to shock her into thinking with her head.

It shocked her all right—but not for long. She tensed momentarily, drew a deep breath, and with her hand still surrounding him slid around to face him.

"You're upset." She pressed a string of kisses to his chest. Flicked her tongue over his erect nipples. Then outlined his eagle with the tip of her tongue.

Lord Jesus God, he was dying here.

"With yourself," she continued, going down on her knees in front of him, freeing him from his jeans as he clutched both hands in her hair.

Help me!

"You think you let me down somehow," she whispered, her breath hot and sweet against him driving him stark raving nuts.

Hell yes, he'd let her down. He'd let himself down. He'd let No down.

"You're wrong," she murmured, and touched the tip of her tongue to the tip of an erection that throbbed and ached and turned his mind to mush. "I needed this. I needed you. I need you again. Please. Please need me, too."

Need her?

Need her?

Need for her was driving him over the line from want to craving. The line he'd drawn dividing right from wrong, ethical from unethical, sane from . . .

"Please," she whispered, and his eyes rolled back in his head when she caressed him with her mouth. "Please need me, too."

Aw God. He'd go to hell tomorrow. Tonight, he wanted heaven. And heaven was on her knees in front of him, begging him, surrounding him with warm, wet suction and a pleasure so wicked and pure, he thought he'd pass out.

On a growl, he lifted her to her feet and walked her backward to the nearest wall. Then he gripped her sweet ass in his hands, wrapped her legs around his waist, her arms around his shoulders, and took her again. Right there against the wall.

The sounds she made. It drove him wild. Kitteny sighs. Breathless, uncontrollable gasps, quivering little screams as he hammered into the tightest, slickest, most mind-bending heat. He caught one of those screams in his mouth, felt it settle to a low, humming note of pleasure and wonder and greed as he sucked on her tongue.

Forever inside her wouldn't have been long enough, yet he shot into her like a cannon, all explosive fire and blinding speed. Groaning her name, he pressed as deep as he could, aware of her hands in his hair, her panting breath on his face, her melting heat pouring around him when she came, convulsing around him, milking him of everything he had before she collapsed against him on a long, keening sigh.

When he came back to himself, it was in a blurry haze.

Amazing. He'd just had the most amazing sex of his life. Twice. Within twenty minutes. With a woman he shouldn't like, shouldn't touch, shouldn't want . . . shouldn't even know in a normal world.

But nothing had been normal since he'd seen her that first night onstage—rocking and rolling—and readjusted his thinking of what he wanted in a woman.

It seemed impossible, but Sara was a distant memory.

This woman . . . this woman was reality. As real as it got.

He lifted his head. Found her ruined and semi-dozing with her head against the wall, her hair falling every which way over her eyes.

He reached up, brushed away a fall of blond silk so he could see her face. Slowly she opened her eyes, reacted to his dark scowl with a sweet, sleepy smile.

"Janey—"

She touched her fingertips to his mouth. It was all he could do not to suck them inside.

"No talking, Iowa. The rest of tonight, no talking, okay?"

She unlocked her ankles, sort of melted off of him as she slid down the wall until her feet touched the floor.

"Just more of this. Just much, much more of this," she murmured, leaning into him and wrapping her arms around his waist. "We can deal with the fallout in the morning."

Fallout. Lord help him would there be fallout. Radioactive fallout.

"Deal?" She tilted her head back. Her hair tumbled over his arms as she met his eyes with such a sweet, searching plea.

So sweet, so searching, he said the only thing he could. "You're going to be the death of me."

Her smile was silky and slow. "Don't worry, country boy. I won't let it come to that."

What could he do? What *could* he do?

Nothing. Nothing but kiss her.

And kiss her and think about kissing her forever.

Finally, he picked her up and carried her to the shower, where he held up his end of the bargain. He didn't think about right. He didn't think about wrong.

He just thought about her. How she looked with the water sluicing down her body. How silky her skin was beneath the tattoo above her breast. Low on her belly.

How she tasted when he went down on his knees and touched the sweet spot between her thighs with his tongue. How she sounded when she came.

But mostly he thought about how he felt when he was inside her. Like he was somewhere he was always supposed to be. Like he was finally the best man he had ever been.

Much later, he lay awake with her sleeping beside him. Her head rested on his shoulder, her hair spilled over his arm. And he knew.

She was going to be the death of him, all right. At least she was going to be the end of his life as he knew it. He was never going to be the same. She'd taken him somewhere he'd never been before. Had never even known existed. He didn't know where it was or what it was; he just knew it was somewhere he'd always want to go.

Was it love? Hell, he didn't know. What did he know about love? All he knew about was war.

He'd thought he'd loved Sara. Thought he'd always love her.

But then there was Janey.

He reached down, lifted a fall of silken hair, rubbed it between his fingers.

Sweet. Sexy. Tough.

And she'd been celibate for two years.

That blew his mind.

Why him? Why *had* she picked him to end the fast?

Maybe . . . shit. He shouldn't even let himself think it.

But as she stirred in her sleep, whispered something that sounded like "Baby Blue" against his shoulder, and snuggled closer, he did think it. Dared to even believe it.

Had tonight been more than sex for her, too? More than an outlet for a tension prompted by terror and fatigue and grief?

Could she . . . was it possible . . . had she picked him because she *did* have feelings for him? Maybe even loved him? Just a little?

He rubbed a hand over his eyes.

Get real, Wilson. You're doing it again. Falling for a woman in trouble. And thinking with your heart instead of your head. Confusing chemistry with happily ever after.

Think, man. That's how it had been with Sara. They'd been friends. Hell, she'd been married. He'd never thought of her as anything but his buddy's wife. And then she'd been a widow. Helpless and hurting. And he'd stepped in, stepped up. And ended up losing his heart.

Sara had never loved him. Not that way. And he knew better than to ever fall into that stupid trap again.

Yet here he was. Thinking about love and . . . and lifetimes . . . and . . . and hell.

Forget about it, Wilson.

You're chasing an impossible dream.

*T*he *next morning, Wednesday, July 19th, West Palm Beach*

"How's it going?"

Dallas Garrett looked up from his laptop at the E.D.E.N. Securities, Inc., office at the sound of his brother Nolan's voice.

"It's going. Ran those names. You'll find this interesting." He handed Nolan a printout of a police report filed in Peoria, Illinois.

"Kathy Wallace." Nolan glanced at the report, then handed it back to Dallas. "She's on the list Jase found in Alice Perkins's lockbox, right?"

"She *was.*"

Nolan's gaze sharpened.

"The woman died two days ago."

"Sonofabitch. How?"

"It's early for the final report, but all indications are it was an accidental electrocution. Hair dryer fell into the bathtub.

"Already on it," Dallas added when he saw that Nolan was gearing up to suggest he dig a little deeper. "I'm waiting for a call back from the Peoria PD. And yeah," he added, figuring he knew exactly what Nolan was thinking. "I'm stepping up the search for the other three women."

"This is way too much of a coincidence, that both Alice Perkins and a woman whose name just happened to appear on a list in her lockbox are dead," Nolan said. "Accidental death or not, I'll be interested as hell in hearing what the officer who handled the case has to say."

"Right. In the meantime," Dallas said, a niggling concern tightening in his gut. "You want to call Jase with this or should I?"

"I'll call him," Nolan said, and left the room.

For the next several hours, Dallas buried himself in online searches. It was where he felt the most comfortable these days. Buried in work.

That way he didn't think about other things. Things like what-ifs and too-bads and where in the hell was she?

His eyes were burning when he leaned back in his desk chair, linked his hands behind his head, and closed his eyes.

But even closed, he could see her.

Amy Walker.

Not a day went by that he didn't think about her. Wonder if she was well. If she was whole. Physically and mentally.

Wonder if he could have done something to make her stay.

And do what, Garrett?

He stared at the ceiling. Damned if he knew.

A month. One full month had passed since she'd left and not a word. Not that he'd really expected one. He'd known her all of what? A week? Two? Didn't matter. They'd shared a lifetime of experience in that short, dangerous snippet of time. It seemed like a dream sometimes. Make that a nightmare. So much of a nightmare he wondered if Jolo had actually happened.

Then he'd take a look at Ethan. His once stoic and unhappy older brother was a changed man. And he was changed because Ethan, Dallas, Nolan, and their buddy Manny Ortega had formed a rogue rescue team and rescued Darcy Prescott from an Abu Sayyaf terrorist cell hiding out on the remote Philippine island. She'd be Darcy Garrett again soon. Ethan and his ex were getting remarried in a couple of months. They were working things out. Working things through.

Yeah. Ethan was a changed man. Dallas was changed, too. After finding Darcy—finding Darcy *and* Amy Walker—in the hands of those scum, they'd all been changed.

Dallas rocked forward in his chair, determined to get back to work. Tried to shake Amy's image from his mind. Tried and failed.

He could still see her when they'd found her a captive of those terrorists. She'd been like a wild animal. Her blond hair filthy and snarled and matted. Her body covered in jungle grime and bruises. Her face flushed with fever from infected cuts and insect bites.

He still had nightmares about what she had to have gone through at the hands of those murdering jackals who hid behind a call to jihad that broke all peace-leaning beliefs of their Muslim brethren.

Yeah, he still had nightmares.

And he still wondered where Amy was.

Told himself he was just concerned was all. It wasn't as if . . . well, it wasn't as if they'd had a future or anything. Christ, she came with more baggage than he could carry in a train of boxcars. He didn't do baggage. So no. It wasn't like they'd had a future.

But damn. He wished he knew where she was.

Right now, though, he had more pressing questions. He agreed with Nolan. Those other three women were in potential danger. And Janey Perkins was in a helluva lot of trouble. His main goal now was to find those women and to give Jase some help to keep the multi-million-dollar franchise alive.

He'd think about Amy Walker later.

And think about her . . . and think about her.

*S*ame *morning, July 19th, Los Angeles*
Max wiped the sweat from his upper lip, dragged deep on his cigarette, and eyed the bar in the corner of his living room. A very nice living room. In a very nice condo with an ocean view. A view that had been paid for thanks to Janey. He owed his living to Janey.

And soon he would owe her his miserable life.

A shot of gin might steady his nerves. And fix exactly nothing.

He was going to betray her . . . all under the grand auspice of keeping her alive.

It was 9:00 a.m. His hand was still shaking. He'd just hung up from talking with Herb Meyers. And the stink of the man he'd just reduced himself to seeped from his pores like toxic waste.

He pressed the heel of his hand against the spot in his chest that never seemed to let up these days. He was officially a thief. Or would be by the end of the week.

It was either steal from Janey or . . . Herb's words came back to haunt him.

"Be a damn shame if something was to happen to little Janey now, too, wouldn't it? . . ."

His gut had been giving him hell ever since Wilson had called yesterday and filled him in on the motel break-in. Yeah, the twin hearts pointed to Grimm. But Max wondered. It would be easy to implicate Grimm—easy for Meyers and the mob he worked for.

Bastards. Meyers couldn't have known about the cash in Alice Perkins's lockbox, though. Hell. Even Janey hadn't known about it, so Max was certain it hadn't been Herb or one of his thugs who'd showed up at the bank.

At the bank, he thought again. Where Janey had found the little windfall that was going to save him.

It was too easy. As her business manager, he handled all of her money. As soon as he'd gotten back to L.A., he'd started the shuffle of funds. In a few days two hundred K would magically disappear from Janey's account and land in an untraceable account in the Caymans. An account Max would empty with a wire of funds to Meyers and his mob.

Jesus. He couldn't think about it now. It had to be done. He'd convinced Herb to give him a few more days. Assured Herb he'd get his damn money. As soon as the transaction was complete.

Max would cover it somehow. He'd repay it. Little by little from his own salary. Or maybe . . . maybe . . .

His cell phone rang.

He jumped. Jumped, for God's sake.

"Yeah," he growled after fishing the phone out of his pocket.

"Max?"

Janey. He took a stab at settling himself. "Hey, snooks. How . . . how's my best girl?"

Okay. *That* was a new low. He was about to steal from her and now he was acting like he didn't have a care in the world.

"I'm okay. How are you? You sound . . . I don't know. Funny."

"Can you blame me? I mean, I let you out of earshot for twenty-four hours and look what happens."

Silence. "You know about last night?"

"Yeah. I talked to Wilson earlier. He filled me in on the break-in at your motel. You sure you're okay?"

"Yeah, I'm fine. Really. I was a little shook, but I'm fine now, so before you suggest it, we are not canceling the Boston show tonight."

"Janey—"

"No. That's why I called. I knew you'd be thinking about it, but it's not going to happen."

"And Wilson's okay with this?"

"Wilson's not calling the shots regarding my career. Look, I've got to go. We'll be back in plenty of time for sound check."

"You're too stubborn for your own good, kid." *And too trusting,* he thought, guilt burning a new hole in his gut.

"Love you, too, Max. I'll see ya later."

"Janey—wait. I won't be in Boston when you get there."

"You won't?"

"I'm already back in L.A. I had to fly back, deal with that one-point-three mil, remember?"

"Oh. Yeah." She paused. "I actually forgot about that for a minute there. You get it handled?"

Yeah, he thought grimly. He was handling it all right. "I'm getting there."

"Okay, well, look—I've got to go. John just gave the warning to kill the cell phones. See you in a few days. I'm looking forward to the downtime."

"Yeah. In a few days," he said, and hung up.

Max stood there for several long moments. Hating himself. Hating his habit.

And wondering what kind of a spread he could get on tonight's Dodgers game.

15

Janey hung up from talking with Max, then turned off her cell phone as her Gulfstream taxied down the tarmac and got in line for takeoff. She was tired, she was grumpy, and she was sore. After the most incredible sex of her life.

And sex, she'd decided, seemed to be all it had been for Jason Baby Blue Wilson. He sat as mute as a stump beside her; his eyes were closed, but she knew he wasn't sleeping. He was faking it. So he wouldn't have to talk to her.

And it had been more than sex for you? she asked herself with an uneasy look out the jet's porthole.

No. It hadn't been more.

She stared at her thumbnail.

Okay. Maybe. Maybe it had been more.

All right. Yeah, she admitted, closing her eyes. Maybe

it had started out as sex. She'd been fascinated by him from the moment she'd first seen him.

But she also understood herself well enough to know that casual sex—no matter how common it was in her circle—wasn't casual to her. Never had been. Never would be. And it hadn't been casual with Baby Blue. It had been something . . . more. Something deeper. An emotional connection. At least it had felt that way.

His eyes. God, he'd be buried deep inside her, and he would look at her with those clear blue need-you eyes and it felt like he was looking into her soul. Seeing her for who she was, not the image she presented onstage or on album covers or in magazines. Seeing her like a man who thought she was someone special, not like a man whose only reason for being with her was because he was being paid to protect her.

He'd been so amazingly sensitive. To her needs. To her pleasure. To how far he could take her until she couldn't take any more. And she'd learned things about him, too—like the answers to several burning questions. He went commando. And he loved it when she was on top.

She fingered the now familiar and somehow comforting weight of her mother's cross and reminded herself of one major factor: All of that was last night. Last night when the only words were urgent whispers and the only world was the one she and Baby Blue created in that motel room. On the floor. In the shower. In the bed.

She clenched her knees together to counter a sharp, electric ache that pulsed through her when she thought of the way he'd touched her. Kissed her. Made dizzying love to her.

Yeah. That was last night. Since he'd awakened her early this morning already showered and dressed and back in bodyguard mode, he hadn't said a word that hadn't had to do with food, transportation, or security.

"I can't take the gun on a commercial flight," he'd said

with a grim scowl when she'd asked him to get her to Boston ASAP. "And I'm no longer sure I can protect you without one."

"Then I guess you've got a problem." Angry and hurt and confused by his cool distance, she'd settled herself into the rental's passenger seat beside him. "Take me to the nearest airport, because we're making that concert and that means we're flying."

In the end, he'd called her pilot, John Cummings, who had flown the Gulfstream to Columbia, Mississippi, to pick them up. The drive to the airport had been silent and tense.

And filled with misgivings.

So. Now she knew what the fallout was like with Baby Blue. After everything they'd shared last night, he couldn't even look her in the eye today, let alone touch her.

Like she was a leper or something.

Or the single biggest mistake of his life.

Maybe if she wasn't so tired—he'd worn her way past out—she would have dug a little deeper. Tried to pin him down on what he was thinking.

Or maybe she didn't want to know. Maybe it was best to just let it be. She'd taken a huge leap of faith last night. Crossed a line she'd drawn between self-esteem and self-gratification.

So you made a mistake, she told herself. Wasn't the first one she'd made where a man was concerned. She'd given herself over to Kevin Larson three years ago, hadn't she?

It had been a match made in music-land heaven—so said the tabloids. The reigning queen of rock and the heir apparent to the king's crown. They'd been the industry's royal couple. And she'd believed she loved him. Believed he loved her.

She'd been wrong. It still burned sometimes. But it no longer hurt.

She heard the landing gear clunk up into place and

settled in for the ride. And a harsh dose of the truth.

Men had fragile egos. Men did things for reasons she'd never understand.

Like leave women.

She thought of the Polaroid from the lockbox that she'd tucked in her purse. Most likely it was a photo of the first man to ever leave her.

And then she thought of Baby Blue and added him to the list of men who had left. At least emotionally. Oh well. Another lesson learned. Trust words. Trust deeds. Don't count on some intangible something she'd thought she'd seen in Baby Blue's eyes last night. Something that *she'd* been feeling at the time. A closeness. A connection. An emotional tug that had been nearly as cataclysmic as the physical pull.

Cataclysmic.

Story of her life lately.

Story of her fricking life.

That night, Boston

"Well, they love her in Beantown, huh?"

Jase kept his eyes on the crowd, not bothering to acknowledge Chris Ramsey's observation but noting just the slightest thread of jealousy in her tone.

He didn't like this woman, and every time he was around her, she gave him another reason not to. She made him edgy as hell. And as he stood in the wings scanning the glut of bodies crowding the stage, the edge grew sharper and keener.

Janey had just started her second set and already house security had had to wrestle half a dozen fans away from the stage. Everyone wanted to get close to her. Everyone wanted to get their hands on her.

Poor bastards. He knew how they felt.

Less than twenty-four hours ago, he'd been as close as a man could get to her. He'd had his hands all over her. And his mouth. And . . . Jesus. He wanted to touch her again.

And that just wasn't going to happen. He had a rule: one out-of-his-mind experience a year.

Arms crossed over his chest, he repeatedly scanned the crowd as JoJo Starbuck's bass guitar throbbed out a hot, heavy rhythm. Inevitably, Jase's gaze strayed back to Janey.

She stood center stage, her whiskey-and-velvet voice belting out "Take Me, Baby." She looked . . . outrageous. And incredible in a black leather bustier and low-riding shorts so short her legs looked a mile long. Four-inch ankle boots made those legs look incredible.

So did the light sheen of perspiration glowing on her skin.

He'd seen her glow like that last night. When he'd gone down on her. When he'd finally tasted that sweet spot between her legs and sent them both soaring.

"Where was a good mind when you needed one," he muttered under his breath, still not believing he'd let himself get so far off track where she was concerned.

He'd screwed up before. But last night—hell. It was the screwup to end all screwups. The mother of all screwups. Shit. It was the world championship of screwups.

There wasn't a damn thing he could do about it now. Except try to forget it ever happened. Try not to notice the hurt he saw in Janey's eyes every time she looked at him. Try not to let himself go to her, apologize—or, worse, tell her she'd been the most incredible, amazing, excellent thing to ever happen to him.

And she had been. Not just the sex—though, sweet, sweet Lord, the sex had been like nothing he'd ever experienced before.

The thing was, it had been more than sex, he admitted

with a defeated breath. Way more than sex. At least it had been for him. But for her—well, she might think it had been more, but he figured he knew what had really happened last night.

She'd needed someone to hold her. Someone to make her forget about all the shit that had been happening in her life.

Always one to volunteer for the tough duty, huh, Wilson?

He jerked his gaze back to the crowd. And forgot all about last night's mistakes when he thought back to the phone call he'd received from No.

He hadn't told Janey—didn't want to hit her with it before she went onstage—but Dallas had discovered that another woman was dead. A woman whose name was on the list with three others they'd found in Alice Perkins's lockbox. Christ. Like No and Dallas, Jase didn't believe for a minute that it was an accident. And like them, he figured the other women were living on borrowed time—if they were still alive.

He scrubbed a hand over his jaw. There was only one thing he was certain of in all this. Janey was not going to die. He was going to make damn sure of it. And to do that, he had to keep his head in the game and his dick in his pants.

The canned spotlights roamed over the audience, from the two tiers of balconies to the floor in front of the stage.

A spike of adrenaline that always foreshadowed trouble shot through his system like a fireball.

Shit. Holy shit, he thought when the light passed a face in the crowd.

There. Just there—row three. Jase squinted, focused, and felt his blood boil.

Grimm. Goddamn, it was Grimm!

The light moved on and Jase lost him in the dark.

Maybe he'd been seeing things. But he could have sworn he just saw Edwin Grimm. Hell, he'd studied the bastard's picture often enough. He knew exactly what Grimm looked like.

Jase grabbed a heavy-duty flashlight and, shining it into the crowd, edged closer to the stage.

Nothing.

Grimm was gone—if he was ever there.

Still, Jase had bumped up to red alert, the hair at the back of his neck standing at attention, that "got a bad feeling" zipping along every nerve ending.

He zeroed his search in on the section where he thought he'd spotted Grimm. Third row, a little left of center. Nothing. If he was there, Jase couldn't spot him in the throng of bodies. They moved together like a monster wave, hands in the air, mouths moving as they sang along, screamed, cried, laughed, and spilled foaming beer.

Okay. Maybe he *had* been seeing things. Maybe—

Fuck.

There he was.

Grimm had maneuvered himself in position directly in front of the stage.

Jase tossed the light and shot out onto the stage like a bullet. He glanced at Janey—and saw in her eyes that she'd just spotted Grimm, too.

"Get off the stage!" Jase yelled on his way, by then launching himself into the crowd and diving straight for Grimm.

I wasn't doing nothin'!" Edwin Grimm yelled.

Jase twisted Grimm's arm behind his back and shoved his wrist between his shoulder blades.

"You got no call to attack me! I paid money! I was just watching the show!"

"Save it for the judge, asshole." Jase steered Grimm around behind the stage area, where he could have a little chat with him before he called the police to come and haul his perverted ass away.

"You're the one goin' to jail, muscle head! I'm going to charge you with assault and battery!"

"Were I you," Jase snarled, shoving Grimm up against a cement wall, "I'd stow it. Because you're starting to piss me off. And you really don't want to see me mad."

"I want a lawyer," Grimm said, some of his bravado waning in the face of Jase's snarl.

"Sit down and shut up."

With a surly glare, Grimm slid quietly to the floor.

"Call the police," Jase said as three or four of the security guards he'd contracted for that night's concert came running. "I'll be right back."

He sprinted for the stage where the band was still rocking and the crowd was still grooving and Sweet Baby Jane had never missed a beat.

Damn, she was something else. And he'd deal with the fact that she hadn't hiked her sweet ass off the stage when he'd ordered her. Later. Right now, he just wanted to make sure she knew the threat was over.

He waited until she moved his way, cut a glance in his direction, and he was able to give her a nod—an all clear.

He caught the flicker of relief in her eyes just before she strutted her stuff back center stage, playing a wicked air guitar, then danced toward the crowd.

Yeah, she was something all right, he thought, and headed back to have a little chat with Edwin Grimm.

• • •

I just came to see the show," Grimm insisted, over and over as the police questioned him in an interrogation room down at the station. "And for the last time, I don't know nothing about Atlantic City or Podunk, Mississippi, and any bleeding hearts. And I'm not answering any more questions until you get me a lawyer."

Standing beside Baby Blue outside the room behind a two-way mirror, Janey stared at the man who had made her life a living hell. She'd finished the concert but skipped the after-show party so she could come down to the station to file a complaint.

"He's not going to change his story, is he?"

Baby Blue shook his head. "Not a chance."

"How long can they keep him?"

"Without hard evidence? Not long."

"We had a restraining order against him before he went to prison. Can't they keep him for violating it?"

"Don't know yet. They're checking on that, but the detective says it was most likely a temporary order—and even if it wasn't, it's probably expired. In the meantime, I've already had them get another one in the works just in case."

"So, most likely, he walks," she concluded, angry at a justice system that seemed to always work toward the criminal's advantage. Angry at Baby Blue, who had to know she could use more than his able protection right about now but kept his distance like a good bodyguard should.

"Janey, look, the PD in Tupelo and Atlantic City are both working the case hard. Now we've got these guys on it. They're working it back at E.D.E.N., too. Something's going to pop to link Grimm to the break-ins. Maybe they'll even be able to tie him to your mother's death. You've got to have some faith that they'll make a case against him eventually."

She turned away from the mirrored glass. Couldn't look at Edwin Grimm any longer. At his pasty prison complexion. At his smug look and disturbing eyes. "Eventually might not be soon enough."

Baby Blue moved in close, touched a hand to her shoulder, quickly let it drop when she looked up at him. Like he'd just realized he'd touched her and was sorry as hell.

"I don't like the idea of him being turned loose any more than you do, but even if he walks, we're going to know where he is this time, okay?"

He paused when she didn't say anything, then explained. "I've already put in a call to Nolan. His brother-in-law used to be a PI. He's going to put us in touch with a friend we can count on to keep track of Grimm. The minute the bastard sets foot on the pavement, our man will be on him. Grimm won't be able to spit without us knowing where and how far.

"Hey." He touched her arm when she didn't respond. "He didn't get to you tonight, did he? Did he?"

She looked up into eyes that had gone hard with determination.

"I promised you I wouldn't let him and I kept that promise. Just like I'm promising you right now that he's not getting close to you again."

She nodded. Yeah. He'd promised. And he'd come through.

"Can we leave?" she asked, trying not to think about other promises. The ones she'd seen in his eyes last night.

Or thought she'd seen.

"Yeah. I need to check in with the detective again; then we can go. Sit tight—and do what I tell you this time. I'll make it quick."

She watched him disappear down a hall after he gave her another stern admonishment to stay exactly where she was.

She stayed. Wishing she were anywhere but here.

For tonight, at least, she was safe from Edwin Grimm. She should feel relieved.

Yet when Jason Wilson, in his dark T-shirt and perfectly fitting worn jeans, walked back down the hall toward her, all she felt was empty.

That's because sometime between landing in Boston and seeing him charge across the stage tonight like an avenging angel, she'd figured something out.

She'd fallen in love with her bodyguard.

You know how to pick 'em, don't you, girl?

She'd fallen in love. Hadn't meant to. Didn't want to. But there it was. She loved him.

And the stern, distanced look on Baby Blue's face as he approached her told her there wasn't a raindrop's chance in the Sahara that he'd want to come within a desert mile of that word.

No. Country boys didn't fall in love with rockers. They just had electric, mind-numbing sex with them.

"I don't want to go back to the hotel," she said when he stopped in front of her.

He frowned. "Janey—it's two in the morning."

"I don't care. Call John and tell him to get the jet ready. I want to get out of here. I want to go home." She hugged her arms tightly around her, drew into herself. "I want to see my dogs."

Bastards. Bastards didn't have shit on him, Edwin thought smugly as he lay on a jail cell cot. They couldn't keep him here. Couldn't pin nothing on him. And as soon as the lawyer his attorney back in California had called arrived, they'd have to turn him loose.

Someone was going to pay for this, he thought as the hollow slam of a cell door made him jump. He hated being caged. Hated what happened after dark.

"Jesus will protect me. Jesus will protect me," he repeated over and over. And tried to think about anything but where he was.

So he thought about Janey. God, she'd looked amazing. She was too good for those trash rockers she ran with. He was good for her, though. She'd see. He just needed to make her see that. But he couldn't get to her. Too many people running interference.

Hell, if he had his way, he'd soon be saying good riddance to a whole shitload of hangers-on—including Derek McCoy. Just thinking about that self-professed cocksman touching her made Edwin see red. And Neal Sanders. The worthless piece of shit sucked onto Janey like a slug now that she'd made the big time.

More than anything, though, Edwin wanted to give that fucking bodyguard what he deserved. Bastard damn near broke his arm. *We'll see who ends up broken next go-round.* When he tied up some loose ends, he'd deal with that baby-faced prick personally.

He thought of Janey's slut of a mother. Was damn glad the bitch was dead. Even Jesus had to say good riddance to that piece of work. His only regret was that he hadn't been personally involved in her death.

They'd be trying to pin that on him, too. For all the good it would do them.

He jerked to a sitting position, then stood when a guard rattled a key in the lock.

"Lawyer's here."

"About damn time," Edwin sputtered, and walked out of the cell.

Yeah. It was about damn time. He had things to do. Things to finish. And he was going to have to step up his game if he was going to get what he wanted.

*S*ame night, Derek McCoy's hotel room

"And you won't quote me, right?"

Chris Ramsey smiled, settled back on the gold brocade sofa, and drew deep on her cigarette. "I keep my word, Derek. I told you that the last time we had a little chat. You can count on that. I just need a little more insight into the 'real' Janey Perkins."

McCoy snorted. "There is no *real* Janey Perkins. She's a flaming robot."

"Stiff as a board in bed, huh?" Chris prompted, knowing the dig would hit home. McCoy considered himself a lady's man of major prowess. "You *have* gotten her into bed, right?"

McCoy sneered and took another toke off his special blend. "You kidding me? She's an ice queen. Damn prick tease is what she is."

Chris loved it. She covered a smile with a conciliatory look. "She does like yanking your chain. I've noticed that."

"Got that right. A major ballbuster, that one."

"I'll bet the right man could put her in her place."

McCoy glared at her through a weed-induced haze. "You saying I'm not man enough?"

"Oh . . . is that how it came out? Sorry. Not what I meant at all. Everyone knows you're the man, Derek. Someone ought to put her in her place, though. Teach her a lesson."

An interested, evil smile tilted the corners of his full lips. "You have something in mind?"

Now they were getting somewhere. "Yeah. I have something in mind."

And after she finished up planting seeds here, she was going to make another attempt at contacting the Reverend Black. The episode with the blood in New York at the Garden was just too juicy to let go.

"Double, double toil and trouble," she singsonged with a grin as she picked up the phone. "Time to stir the pot a little more."

She was taking a chance, yes. Feeding information as to Janey's whereabouts to the religious zealots was risky, but look at the payoff so far. Yeah, the bloodbath was a blast. Chris couldn't help but wonder what they'd do when they found out Janey was home in California.

*T*hursday, July 20th, Malibu, California

Jase stood in the open doorway of Janey's beach house bedroom. It was 10:00 a.m. They'd arrived at LAX around seven this morning. By the time they'd gotten loaded into the waiting limo and they'd made the drive to her beach house, it had been after nine.

A nifty-looking fifty-something housekeeper by the name of Fiona had welcomed Janey home—right after she'd been slobbered over and adored and gifted with about ten pounds of fur from a one-eyed yellow cat named Cat and three of the ugliest mutt dogs Jase had ever seen. As far as he could see, they weren't good for much. They hadn't even barked when he and Janey had arrived.

Nope. Not much in the watchdog department. But very much in the making-Janey-smile department. He'd have to like the ugly mutts for that alone.

She'd sent Fiona for a week off with pay and finally, fully dressed, she'd fallen asleep—God knew she needed to sleep—all three dogs and the cat pig-piled with her on a bed roughly the size and color of a lake.

Jase would like nothing better than to crawl right in there with her. Cover all that warm woman heat and take her someplace where she'd forget about crazed stalkers and murdered mothers and the mystery of who was after the million bucks.

Yeah. That's what he'd like. And that's why he backed quietly out of her bedroom, which was done in dark, rich wood tones and soft, cool blues.

He walked into the main living area. Took it all in— the square footage, the oceanfront view, and the designer décor—and thought, *Whoa.*

So this is "home" for a rock star.

He'd known she made a fortune. But that had been an abstract, nebulous awareness. This was up close and personal. And it was something. He'd heard about places like this. Never thought he'd set foot in one.

Grand. That's what his mom would say about it. Yeah. It was grand.

And if he hadn't already decided there wasn't a beached salmon's chance against a grizzly of anything long-term ever happening between him and Janey, the reality of how far out of his league she truly was would have done it.

Sweet Baby Jane was a superstar. He'd forgotten that during the past few days. He was a workingman. He'd forgotten that, too.

He wasn't likely to forget it again.

And Max Cogan wasn't likely to let him forget that Jase held Janey's life in his hands. Christ. The man was paranoid. He'd called at least three times since they'd arrived in California, sounding more desperate each time with his warnings to stick to Janey like glue. That he'd have Jase's head on a pike if she so much as got a scratch on his watch.

Weary to the bone, Jase walked to a wall of sliders that

opened onto an elevated deck with more square footage than his parents' entire house.

He stepped outside, sank down onto a cushioned chaise under an umbrella that blocked the sun. He breathed in the salt and surf scent of the Pacific and couldn't help but wonder. Five? Six? Ten million for this prime piece of oceanfront property? Easily.

Out of my league.

And he'd been out of his mind to sleep with her.

He closed his eyes, knew he should work up a little more regret for that slippery slide from grace.

Knew he never would.

16

It was after 3:00 p.m. when Janey woke up. She stretched and yawned and hugged and loved on her critters, then headed for the shower.

Dressed in white shorts and a blue bandeau top, she walked barefoot out of her bedroom, running a brush through her hair. Baby Blue was standing at the kitchen island, talking in hushed tones on his cell.

His back was to her and apparently he didn't hear her. Fine. She couldn't deal with him right now anyway. She couldn't deal with seeing him and thinking about walking up and pressing herself against that broad, bare back and suggesting a replay of the night before last in Mississippi—when she'd made the mistake of falling in love.

Turned out she had some pride left, though, because she headed for the sliders instead. She walked outside and down the deck steps, the dogs scrambling along behind her.

She'd missed this more than she'd thought, she realized as the dogs romped and played in the sand. Missed
the scent and sound of the Pacific. Missed the lolling
tongues and wagging tails of her silly little mutts.

For the first time since all of this mess started with
Grimm and the mystery of her mother's death, she drew a
breath that wasn't thick with tension.

One breath. That's all she got before she heard the
whoop, whoop, whoop of distant helicopter rotor blades.

Too quickly, the chopper closed that distance and zeroed in on her, kicking up sand and sending the dogs running and cowering toward the deck steps.

Shielding her eyes with a hand, she looked up at a small
helicopter hovering so close she could see the brand name
on the zoom lens of the camera sticking out the open
cockpit door.

*Was it too much to ask? Twenty-four hours? Twenty-
four freaking hours of peace?*

She thought about giving them the finger, but she followed the dogs to the house instead, just as Baby Blue
came jogging down to hurry her inside.

"Pricks," he said, and hustled her up the deck steps.

"So much for enjoying a leisurely week at the beach,"
she grumbled when he shut the slider behind them.

"I hate to be the bearer of more bad news, but it gets
worse."

That's when she heard the chanting.

*"What would Jesus say? What would Jesus say? Sinner
go away. Sinner go away."*

She hurried over to her front window. "What the hell?"

"They drove up about the same time I heard the
chopper."

When she edged the blinds aside, her heart sank. Twenty to thirty men and women lined the street in front of the house, all of them carrying signs.

Sinner stop singing.
Rock kills morality.
SBJ—Satan's handmaiden.

She was suddenly aware that Baby Blue was looking over her shoulder.

"Nifty friends you've got."

"Welcome to lifestyles of the rich and deviant." She dropped the blinds as a local news van pulled up and a camera crew jumped into the fray. "Who has more fun than me?"

He headed for the door. "I'll get rid of them."

She grabbed his arm. "How? You going to shout them down? Or were you planning to physically remove thirty or so God-fearing, brotherly love and brimstone disciples in front of what's probably a live television feed?"

She shook her head. "I don't think so."

"They can't get by with harassing you like this."

"Oh, I think they can."

To prove her point, she picked up the remote, flicked on the TV, and clicked through the channels until she found what she was looking for. Sure enough, a reporter from a local station was broadcasting, talking over the video footage of the scene in front of her house. The inset in the corner of the screen showed Samuel Black at the pulpit, his heavily made-up, big-haired, bottle-blond wife, Tonya, smiling at his side as if he were the second coming.

"Have a look." Janey tossed the remote aside and sank down onto her sofa.

Standing beside her, a dark scowl on his face, Baby Blue was silent for a moment; then he flipped open his cell.

"I'm getting you out of here," he said, tilting the phone away from his mouth while he waited for his call to connect.

She pushed out a humorless laugh and lifted a hand toward the TV "How? That live newscast is going to bring the crazies out of their caves. The streets will be jammed. In five minutes, we probably won't be able to get past the driveway."

"I said I'm getting you out of here."

"What? You've got connections with Captain Kirk? Is the *Enterprise* going to come swooping down for Scotty to beam us aboard?"

"Something like that. Hey, No. It's Jase," he said when he made a connection. "I need a favor."

W ell, damn." Thirty minutes later Janey watched the sky through the sliders. "Looks like the white hats have arrived. It ain't the *Enterprise,* but it'll do."

She'd dressed in a short pink knit skirt with a single row of ruffles for a hem and a turquoise U-neck shirt that missed meeting the hip-hugger skirt in the middle by a good six inches.

"About damn time." Jase dragged his gaze from all that snug material and bare skin and glanced outside as the chopper closed in on the beach. It was an impressive bird. Big and black and lethal-looking—especially when it swooped low over the beach and muscled the smaller media chopper out to sea.

God, I love this job, he thought, shouldering a pair of duffels. "You ready?"

"As I'll ever be."

He wished he could make it better for her. Felt bad when she dropped down on one knee and hugged each dog good-bye before picking up the cat and cuddling him. All she'd wanted was to get away from things for a while and spend some time with her pets. That wasn't going to happen now.

"I called Fiona, guys," she said, stroking the cat's head. "She'll be here in a couple of hours, okay? Once the crowd thins out."

Jase hated to rush her, but they had to get a move on. "Janey. We've got to go."

She hugged the cat one last time, tossed the dogs treats, and sucked it up. "Let's do it."

"Keep your head down and don't stop until you reach the bird."

With one hand on her elbow and the other on the duffel strap, he raced with her down the deck steps and across the expanse of beach to the waiting bird.

Last time he'd run for a chopper, it had been a Blackhawk and he'd been under fire. He'd gladly have taken some hostile fire today if he could have spared her all of this.

"Welcome aboard, ma'am. Sir." A young man dressed in a flight suit jumped out and onto the sand to help Janey inside. "We'll have you to LAX in no time."

"And where would we be going?" Janey asked once they were airborne and the paparazzi and the Holy Rollers were mere specks as the coastline shrank away.

"Somewhere no one will ever think to look for you," Jase said, and hoped to hell he wasn't making another colossal mistake.

"Oh." She sliced him a skeptical look. "So we're going off planet."

He grinned. "Damn close."

* * *

*S*ame night, Highway 150 near Cedar Rapids

So this is Iowa, Janey thought as she sat in the front seat of a white pickup truck, her legs straddling the gearshift as a July heat and humidity that rivaled any summer day in Mississippi filled the cab through the open windows.

Baby Blue had been right. It was damn close to another world. Iowa—at least this part of it—was green, lush, and littered with rolling hills and beautiful patches of forests.

"You were expecting . . . ?" Baby Blue had asked after she'd remarked a number of times how beautiful it all was.

"Corn. Field after field of corn."

"We've got that, too." He resumed his study of the terrain as it flew past the window.

He sat beside her in the passenger seat, his right arm resting on the door above the open window, his left arm stretched across the back of the seat behind her. Bruce Wilson, the man Baby Blue had introduced as his father but who looked young enough to be his older brother—a very hot older brother—was behind the wheel.

And Janey was still in a state of fascination tinged with surprise. Baby Blue had brought her to his home. They'd landed at the Cedar Rapids airport about an hour ago— eight o'clock Iowa time—and she still hadn't quite wrapped her mind around that fact.

He'd been right about one thing, though. No one would ever think to look for her here. Especially since they'd made it look like a fuel stop and John had flown the Gulfstream on to Atlanta.

"Sorry about the air-conditioning," Bruce said with a shake of his head. "Broke last week and haven't had a chance to get it fixed yet. But then I hadn't figured on having to use the truck for anything but farm business. Mom was still at work with the car when Jase called or I'd have brought it. Man, is she going to be surprised when I pull in the drive with you."

Lots of surprises going around today, Janey thought, giving Bruce a smile. "Don't worry about it. I love the heat. And that scent. What is that?" she asked as they passed a huge open field.

"Hay," Jase supplied. "Just cut."

"Sweet," Janey said. "And fresh."

"Nothing like it." Bruce turned off the four-lane they'd been traveling since leaving the airport. "Cut mine yesterday, too," he added, looking across Janey to his son.

"Guess I know what that means," Baby Blue said.

"What? What does it mean?" she asked when it was obvious neither father nor son felt the need to elaborate.

"I take it you're not a country girl." Bruce shot her a smile. "It means that if it doesn't rain, I'll be putting up hay in the next day or two and since Jase is home—if he's got the time, that is—he'll be getting a good workout."

"I've got the time, Dad," Baby Blue said soberly, and paid undue attention to the fields passing by outside the window.

Janey looked from Bruce to Baby Blue, who was staring straight ahead. The father–son resemblance was stunning. So was the adoration in Bruce's eyes when he'd first spotted Baby Blue at the airport terminal.

Yeah, she could see that there was love and affection all around . . . and yet she sensed something else underlying it all. A cautious tension, maybe. She didn't know. Something was a little off. Both men seemed to carefully guard their words to each other.

"So where you from, Janey? And how'd you meet up with this son of mine?"

"Janey's from Mississippi," Baby Blue said before she

could wonder how she was supposed to respond to Bruce's questions. "We work together."

"Oh," Bruce said thoughtfully. "You a . . . a wrestler, too?" His look clearly said he hoped the hell she wasn't.

"No. I'm not a wrestler." Janey grinned. "Although I do a little kickboxing."

She remembered the last time she'd engaged in kickboxing. A quick glance at Baby Blue told her he was remembering it, too.

Good, she thought. *You remember it well, farm boy. I hope you never forget it.* She knew she never would.

"Not doing that anymore, Dad," Baby Blue said, drawing her away from the memory. "I'm working security now. Out of West Palm Beach. For my old squad leader, Nolan Garrett? You've heard me talk about him."

"Yeah. No-man, right? Well. Your mom will be glad to hear that. About not wrestling anymore, I mean. She was always afraid her baby would get his face messed up," he added with a grin as an aside to Janey as he turned off the blacktop road onto crushed gravel.

"Wouldn't want that to happen." She smiled with Bruce when Baby Blue rolled his eyes.

"So . . . security, huh? What all's that entail?"

Baby Blue drummed his fingers on the window frame. "We design security setups for businesses, test existing security for others, and write recommendations. Sometimes we provide personal security."

"Personal security? You mean like . . . bank guards and night watchmen and such?"

"That, too," he said, and left it at that.

Okay. So she knew the ground rules now. His parents weren't supposed to know who she was and what Baby Blue provided for her. She understood. At least she thought she did.

"So . . . business brings you to Iowa?" Bruce continued

his little fishing expedition when his son didn't elaborate.

"Nope. No business. We just came off a case," Baby Blue lied. "They gave us some downtime. Janey was kind of at loose ends since her parents are vacationing in Europe, so I offered to bring her home with me."

He told the lie so well that she wondered if he'd been working on it for a while or if lying just came easy to him.

"You must have been hard up for something to do." Bruce shot her another of those smiles that so made Janey think of his son.

"I'm easily entertained," she said, finding it just as easy to respond to Bruce Wilson's sense of humor.

"Seems she's never been cow tipping and wanted to give it a try," Baby Blue added with a glance her way.

Bruce laughed. "Well, we can sure make that happen for you, sweetheart."

"Okay. I'll bite." Janey didn't like the evil looks passing between the two of them. "What's cow tipping?"

"Something you need to experience firsthand," Baby Blue said. "You'll just have to wait and see."

"All right. I recognize a setup when I hear one. So if this is some sort of initiation for the farm-impaired, I'll just skip it, thanks, anyway."

Bruce chuckled. "I like her," he said as they approached a lane and turned in. "So much, in fact, that I think you ought to take her snipe hunting, too."

"Maybe," Baby Blue said. "We'll have to see how she handles country life."

"No offense, Mr. Wilson, but you and your son are full of it."

Bruce slapped the wheel and laughed. "Bruce. Just call me Bruce. And you're going to do just fine here, Janey. Just fine."

He might be right, she realized as they drove up to a huge white two-story clapboard house and she felt the oddest sense of coming home. The first gentle shades of twilight were softening the horizon in hues of apricot and gold as she took in a wide set of steps that led up to a wraparound porch. Huge Boston ferns hung from the overhang. A pair of white wicker rockers flanked a low table on one side of the front door; on the other side a swing made for two was suspended from the porch ceiling by chains.

Flowers and shrubs bordered the lattice trim that surrounded the bottom of the porch. Brilliant yellow roses climbed a trellis near a corner porch post where an old border collie roused himself from his nap and, tail wagging lazily, tottered toward them.

"Welcome to Mayberry," Baby Blue said as he got out of the truck and held a hand out to help her down.

No kidding, she thought as she stepped down to the ground. "Just so you know . . . if Aunt Bea comes out of that door wiping her hands on her apron, you've got some 'splainin' to do, Lucy."

*W*hy couldn't she be the spoiled brat of a diva she was supposed to be? Jase thought darkly as he sat at his mother's dinner table across from Janey watching her charm both of his parents.

Why did she have to be sweet and hardworking and humble—with a backbone as hard as steel and a mouth that never failed to make him laugh, or get him hot.

"Jase?"

He looked from Janey to his mother, who was frowning at him. "Sorry, Mom. What?"

"I was telling Janey that you two need to go to the Burke Hoolie tomorrow night."

"Hoolie?" Janey smiled at his mom, who had welcomed Janey like family.

"It's an Irishman's excuse to drink, get drunk, and drink some more," Jase said, wishing his mother hadn't mentioned anything about a party—especially when he saw Janey's eyes light up.

"Don't pay any attention to him, dear. A hoolie is a party—an Irish party. Lots of food, dancing, and fun."

"And lots of drunks," Jase reminded the table at large.

"Spoken like a man who knows from experience," Janey said, grinning at him.

"Never knew you to be one to turn down a chance to drink, son," Bruce said, and suddenly the room grew quiet. Deathly so.

Jase felt his face burn red, felt a shame and an anger he didn't want to own boil up inside him.

He stood abruptly. "Great dinner, Mom. I'm going to get a little air. Excuse me."

And he walked outside. It was either that or make an ass out of himself in front of Janey, piss off his father, and make his mother cry.

It always came to this.

It fucking always came to this.

17

Head buried under the hood of Jeremy's Mustang, Jase tinkered with the carburetor, lost somewhere between brooding over his relationship with his father and concern over the phone call he'd just received from Dallas Garrett.

Jase didn't know how long he'd been out here. An hour. Maybe two. Long enough for Dallas to tell him that (a) Edwin Grimm's hotshot lawyer had gotten him sprung from jail before they'd been able to get a man in place to tail him, and (b) another woman on the list from Alice Perkins's lockbox had recently met with an untimely death, and (c) Grimm had never been picky about the kind of bird hearts he'd used to terrorize Janey. Chicken, pigeon, duck. Nothing with feathers had been safe. It didn't necessarily toss Jase's copycat theory, but it didn't add any particular weight to it, either.

All in all, it had been just a peach of a day. Max's call just before dinner—another warning that reeked of desperation to never let Janey out of his sight—was small potatoes, though, compared to Dallas's news.

He didn't turn around when he heard the machine shed door open and saw the beam of a flashlight cut a path along the rafters.

"Want some company?"

Janey. Better her than the old man, he guessed, and got mad all over. At himself.

A line from an old Jack Nicholson/Tom Cruise movie came to mind: *"You want the truth? You can't handle the truth!"*

Guess he'd proven that again tonight.

"Suit yourself." He went back to tinkering with the carburetor while she bent to pet Tucker, the collie, who had followed him out to the shed.

"Nice car." She walked up beside the hood. "Great color," she added, running her hand along the metallic silver enamel.

"Nineteen sixty-five Mustang. A classic." He'd been surprised as hell when he'd told No about it and found out his former squad leader had one, too. Great minds and all that.

"Yours?"

He straightened, grabbed a grease rag, and wiped his hands. "And my brother's."

She was quiet as he reached up and carefully closed the hood.

"Your mom told me." Her voice was so soft, he figured she knew that she was treading on some very thin ice. "About Jeremy. How . . . how he died. It must have been horrible. For all of you."

Yeah. It had been horrible. One day he'd had a big brother. The next day he didn't. Jeremy had been driving a friend's car—because the friend had been too drunk to drive.

Evidently Jeremy had been too drunk, too. He'd run off the road and headlong into a culvert on the way home from a kegger.

"Yeah. It was bad."

"How old were you when it happened?"

He glanced at her standing there. Looking small and concerned and too much like someone he wanted to confide in.

"Fifteen." Folding his arms over his chest, he settled his hip on the Mustang's fender, crossed his ankles, and stared at his boot tips. "I begged him to let me go to that party with him. But I was just a freshman. The party was for seniors. Otherwise I'd have been in that car with him."

"I told your dad . . . you know. What you told me. That you weren't drinking anymore," she said, after a long silence.

And there it was. The bone of contention between him and his father. At least one of the bones.

"That must have been a hard sell." He pushed away from the fender, opened the passenger door, and motioned for her to get in. "Check it out."

She eased into the passenger seat and he shut the door, aware of her brown eyes watching him as he walked around to the driver's side and settled in behind the wheel.

"He was relieved," she said, turning to him, the white tucked upholstery creaking when she did. "That's all. He was just relieved."

"Yeah. Well, I gave them fits all through high school. Both him and Mom were afraid I'd end up like Jeremy."

And there'd been many times when he'd thought the

same thing. God, he'd been stupid. And young. So damn young. He didn't feel young anymore.

"What was he like? Was he a good big brother?"

Jase didn't think he wanted to talk about this. But he didn't not want to talk about it, either. And the fact of the matter was, no one had ever asked him.

"He was . . ." He stopped, shook his head. "He was something. Great athlete. Great friend. The chicks—man, the chicks went crazy for him. Especially after he got this car."

He ran his hand along the smooth curve of the steering wheel. "I had a real case of hero worship. Wanted to be just like him when I grew up."

"And when he died, you weren't so sure you wanted to grow up," she said with the wisdom of someone who shouldn't know him nearly this well.

He turned his head. Looked at her under the light cast from a bare bulb hanging from a rafter. At that soft, silky hair, at that face he figured he'd see into the afterlife, at those eyes that had misted over. Tears. She was near tears for him.

He looked away because, damn, it would be easy to sink into all that sweet concern. Too easy to pull her into his arms and hold on to this woman who was far too intuitive, and far too tuned in to who he was.

How in the hell had that happened? And why would she even go to the trouble of figuring it out? It wasn't like she didn't have her own troubles to deal with. More trouble than she knew. He wasn't going to lay Dallas's news on her tonight, though. She needed a break.

"Maybe things won't be . . . you know," she said, breaking into his thoughts, "so tense between you and your dad now that he doesn't have to worry about you so much."

Way too intuitive, Jase thought again. And suddenly he was just blurting it out.

"My father and I have what shrinks would probably call a bit of a dysfunctional relationship." He wrapped his hands around the wheel and gripped it tight. "He keeps thinking I'm going to fulfill his expectations and I keep making certain that I let him down. It's kind of an unspoken rule between us. He has hopes—I kill them."

"He loves you."

Jase closed his eyes, let his head drop back to the headrest. "I know. And I can be a real prick sometimes. It's just . . . I'm not Jeremy."

"I highly doubt that he wants you to be."

That much was true. "No. He'd never put that on me. He just wants me to take over the farm someday. That was the plan—with Jeremy. He was going to carry on the tradition. So that leaves me."

"Not wanting to fill that slot," she concluded accurately.

He nodded. "Pretty much sums it up, yeah."

"How you gonna keep 'em down on the farm after they've seen Baghdad, huh?"

He snorted. "More like, I'm not going to live and die on eight hundred acres of Iowa loam when I can see places like Baghdad. Do things like jump out of choppers.

"I'm not a farmer, Janey," he said, feeling defensive and hating himself for it. "He wants me to be. And every time I look at him, it reminds me of how badly I've let him down."

"He's disappointed maybe, but you haven't let him down. He's very proud of you.

"Why do I know that?" she asked when his curiosity got the best of him and he looked at her. "I know because they showed them to me. Yup. Drug out the dreaded family albums after dinner. Your mom got them out—but it was your dad who provided commentary."

He groaned.

"I was particularly taken with the one on the bear rug."

"Oh, God. She didn't."

"She did. And your dad showed me your jock stuff. Lots of track ribbons and medals and wrestling trophies. What the hell is a punt, pass, and kick trophy for anyway?"

He could only shake his head. And smile. Somehow, she'd turned a bitch of a day into something—well— something he hadn't expected it would be.

"It's okay that your dad is disappointed," she said when the silence settled again. "We all have disappointments in life. That doesn't mean you need to feel guilty about your dad's. And it doesn't mean he expects you to."

Yeah. Well. He'd need to think about that. He'd need to think about it a lot.

Just like he'd been thinking about why it had been such a struggle to find his niche after the Rangers. Being rejected by every police department because of his hearing loss—well, it had been tough to take. So he'd floundered and brawled until he'd wised up and joined E.D.E.N. He'd needed to prove that he was still vital . . . still whole . . . still capable for God's sake, despite the hearing problem.

And deep down, he finally realized that a big part of his problem was that he wanted to be the perfect son for his father. And it hurt like hell that he couldn't be.

*F*riday morning, July 21st
     Baby Blue smiled when Janey handed him the Thermos of ice water. "Thanks."

He downed a long, thirst-quenching swallow, then whipped a red bandana out of the hip pocket of his jeans and wiped the sweat and hay chaff off his face and neck.

"So this is what they call making hay while the sun shines," Janey said as they sat side by side on the hayrack,

legs swinging, as the July sun beat down the next morning. A muggy breeze stirred the hair at her nape. "It's
hard work."

"I don't mind the work. Nothing wrong with sweating
for a living. It's in his blood." He nodded toward Bruce
Wilson, who was driving a tractor pulling a full hayrack
toward the barn, where they'd later heave the bales onto a
conveyor and stack them in the mow.

"I can see that." Janey was mesmerized by Baby Blue's
strong, clean profile. She'd never seen a man so sweaty
and dirty look so good.

"For Dad's sake, I wish it was in mine." He glanced at
her, then looked away, a grim expression on his face.

"You can only live your life for yourself," she said,
watching the muscles in his neck and throat work as he
downed another deep swallow of water.

"Is that what you're doing?" He handed the Thermos
back to her.

"Yeah. I am. It's all I've ever wanted to do. Sing," she
clarified. "Most of the rest of it—the glitz, the travel, the
grind—I could do without. But I've always wanted to
sing."

"And what would you do if you weren't traveling?"

His interest both surprised and pleased her. Surprised
because to date, she'd been the only one who'd initiated any
personal questions. Pleased because a part of her wanted to
believe it was more than idle conversation prompting his
questions now.

"We moved around a lot when I was little," she said.
"I've always wanted someplace to call home."

"Malibu isn't someplace?"

She lifted a shoulder, watched a yellow butterfly flit
along the rows of neatly raked hay ready to be baled. "Malibu is a base of operations. Takes more than an address to
make a home."

He reached up, surprising her again, and plucked a piece of hay off the shoulder of the T-shirt she'd borrowed from his mother. The jeans she was wearing were Bev Wilson's, too. A little big, but not much, and covering up, Janey had learned, was a necessary part of making hay.

Not that she'd actually done that much work. She had driven the tractor, though, scared half to death of doing something wrong and proud as hell when she'd actually mastered shifting.

"So how come you haven't hooked up with someone?"

She glanced at him sideways. Intrigued. Well now. A *personal* personal question. She wondered what he'd think if she gave him a *personal* personal answer and decided, what the hell, she'd go for it.

"I did hook up. Once," she confided. "Didn't last, though."

"What happened?"

"Turned out Kevin—Kevin Larson, he's a rocker," she elaborated.

"I know who he is," Baby Blue said, looking a bit disgusted, which was also intriguing, because it was a "what were you doing with a bum like him" kind of disgust.

Looking back, she had the same question. "Turned out he loved his own image more than he loved me. And when my albums started outselling his, it seemed he didn't love me quite so much after all.

"Would have been nice, though," she added on a deep breath, "if I hadn't caught him cheating with someone I thought was a friend. Guess it was his way of saying I wasn't so hot and her way of saying she could have anything she wanted—including something that belonged to me."

When he didn't say anything, she turned to look at him. Saw the muscle in his jaw working and a dark scowl on his face.

"Seems to me you have more than your share of creeps in your life."

She knew he was thinking of Grimm. Maybe even of Neal Sanders. She'd figured out early on that Baby Blue didn't think much of Neal. "Yeah, well, some of us just get lucky."

He grunted, jumped down off the hayrack. He was a sight, this bodyguard of hers. He'd wrapped a blue bandana around his brow do-rag style to absorb the sweat. His white T-shirt was dusty and soaked through. His jeans were as worn as his lace-up leather boots.

And he was gorgeous.

"What about you?" she asked as he headed for the tractor, their break evidently over. "You ever hook up with anyone?"

He hesitated. "Thought I had. Didn't work out, either."

Before she could ask him what happened, he'd jumped up onto the seat, cranked the key, and fired up the tractor. And that was the end of *that* conversation.

By now she knew the drill. She scooted back onto the middle of the rack and hung on as he caught up with the hay baler.

Had some creeps in your life, too, Baby Blue? she wondered. *Or have you just never met the right woman?*

Obviously, he didn't consider her the right one, she thought, as they bounced along through the rough field. After they'd talked in the machine shed last night, she'd hoped that . . . well, she'd hoped that maybe they'd made a connection. One that had opened up more than candid dialogue between them.

She'd hoped for a lot of things last night. As she'd lain in his brother's old bed with Baby Blue in his room down the hall, his parents in their room downstairs, and the house as quiet as a church, she'd actually listened for footsteps in the hall, the turn of the doorknob, the pleasant squeak of a hinge in need of oil.

She'd fallen asleep waiting.

And all day today, she'd wondered.

What if she had gone to him?

The tractor came to a jerky stop, jarring her back to the heat and the hard work yet ahead of them.

"You know, you really don't have to be out here in this heat," Baby Blue said after jumping down from the tractor and rounding the hayrack. "Why don't you head on back to the house? Take the truck."

"Trying to get rid of me?" She eased to the ground and tugged a pair of borrowed work gloves out of her hip pocket.

"Trying to figure out what kind of spin the paparazzi would put on this if they could see the rock star of the decade decked out like Ellie Mae Klampett and getting blisters on her hands."

"Rocker rolls in the hay with hunky bodyguard?" she suggested, then laughed when he shook his head.

"Seriously, Janey. Go on up to the house. Get out of this heat."

"If you can take it, I can take it," she insisted.

"That's not the point."

"Then what is? It's like you said. Nothing wrong with sweating for a living."

When his gaze made a slow, intense sweep of her body—she'd done some sweating, too, and her cotton T-shirt was pretty much molded to her body and transparent—she shivered, despite the blistering heat.

"Suit yourself." He dragged his gaze away. "Just let me know if you need a break."

She needed a break all right, Janey thought, climbing up into the tractor seat. She needed Baby Blue to give her a break and consider thinking about her as something other than someone he needed to take care of.

"Come on," Jase said, opening the screen door after dinner that night. "Let's go for a ride."

"Sounds good." Janey, squeaky clean again, her nose a little sunburned from working out in the sun all day, gamely left the cool air-conditioning of the house and walked outside ahead of him into a sultry summer night.

She'd worked like a dog today. Jase still couldn't get over it. A real trouper, this one. She'd even pitched in and helped his mom with dinner—then dug in like a Ranger who'd lived for a year on MREs.

He should let her rest. But he was inexplicably restless. He needed to get out. Needed some action. Maybe the sight of her dressed in that short little pink shirt with the little-girl ruffle along the bottom again and that band of bare skin between the hip-hugging skirt and midriff-skimming top had something to do with it. If his hands were otherwise occupied on the steering wheel of the Mustang, they wouldn't be so itchy to get ahold of her.

"Hold on." He left her outside and opened the overhead shed door.

Then he climbed behind the wheel, tugged the S & W out from under his shirt, and tucked it under the seat. He hadn't wanted her to see it. She was relaxed for a change and didn't need the reminder that there was still a threat. He didn't expect to need it, but didn't feel comfortable without it, either.

After backing out of the shed, he leaned over, and opened the passenger door, shoving it open for her. "Let's roll."

"Did I mention," she said, easing inside and getting comfy, "that this really is a hot car?"

He grinned. "Couple of times." Then he drove about twenty-five miles per hour on the gravel—as much to irritate her as avoid chipping the paint—before opening the Mustang up when they hit the highway.

"Wow!" Janey laughed as they roared down the blacktop, windows down, radio blasting out rockin' country and the cool night air washing over their skin. "This baby moves. Must be more than a few horses under the hood. Who knew they made cars this fast back then?"

Yeah, who knew? Jase thought as he backed off on the gas when they reached the Clear Creek city limits sign. Who knew that bringing Janey Rock Star Perkins home to Iowa would lead to a positive spin on the relationship with his father that he'd been wrestling to come to terms with for years?

There was something else he was also wrestling with. The way he'd treated Janey after that night—that amazing night—they'd spent together. She hadn't deserved that from him. Just like she didn't deserve that Larson creep cheating on her.

He couldn't do anything about the way Larson had treated her but could apologize for the way *he* had. He was going to do that tonight.

But first he had to work up the guts.

Pathetic. He'd tangled with the best the Taliban had to offer in the mountain wilderness of Afghanistan, faced off with a shitload of heavily armed jihad extremists on a barren stretch of desert, down to his last round of ammo and his squad ten clicks away.

And he couldn't find the balls to tell it right, tell it straight, to one unarmed one-hundred-pound woman.

Some Hooah he was.

◆ ◆ ◆

Janey loved Iowa. From the verdant green timbers and lush pastures dotted with cattle grazing on rolling hillsides to the old-fashioned and original drive-in where Baby Blue treated her to the most decedent turtle sundae she'd ever had.

People waved when Jase and Janey drove down the street. Lifted a finger in greeting when they met them on the road.

"I love it," she said when they cruised out of town past a lit sign:

> You are now leaving Clear Creek, Iowa
> Population two thousand, three hundred wonderful
> people and one grumpy old man.

It *was* Mayberry. But in an updated way. Teens wore pretty much what teens wore in Florida or California. They listened to the same music. The little theater on Main Street played the same movies that the multiplexes played in the cities across America.

Okay, so the news reports on the radio included corn and hog futures along with the rundown on the Dow. It was wonderful. It was . . . special. And so was the man at her side.

She'd never had a car date when she was a teen. The boys she'd known hadn't had money for cars. The life she'd led hadn't left much time for dating.

This must be what it feels like, she thought as they headed back to his parents' farm. *This must be what it feels like to be on a special date with that guy you've been dying to go out with.*

And then she got real. This was no date. This was an

air bubble in time. Some incredible twist of fate had dropped her inside that bubble and floated her to this Midwest summer night. Where she felt safe. Safe from Edwin Grimm. Safe from the reality of her mother's murder and all the unknowns that went with it.

Safe enough, evidently, to let her guard down and start thinking sappy thoughts about her and Baby Blue.

They flew along the blacktop road back toward the Wilson farm; the night smelled of cool dew and new-mown hay. The car smelled of lemon wax and age. An oldies station played a John Cougar song on the radio. And the man behind the wheel—well, the man behind the wheel was as out of reach to her as a father's dream of his only son coming home to run the farm was out of reach to him.

It made her melancholy. It made her sad.

And it made her mad, suddenly, that there didn't seem to be any happily ever afters on the horizon for any of them.

18

It was like the Mustang had a mind of its own, Jase thought when he found himself turning off the blacktop and heading for the gravel pit. Truth was, he wasn't ready to go back to the house yet.

He checked his watch. Almost ten o'clock.

Yep. The Mustang had taken this road before. Most often this time of night. Most often with a pretty girl snuggled up close to his side. And how convenient was it that the local lovers' lane was empty when he pulled up to the edge of the rise overlooking the sand pit lake and killed the motor?

He was out of his mind. He had no business bringing her here. Just like he'd had no business giving her the silent treatment after the night they'd spent together. He'd been an asshole about it for as long as he could stand it.

"Pretty," Janey said quietly beside him.

He looked at her. At this woman who could buy and sell damn near anything she wanted to buy or sell, who had seen the wonders of the world on her tours yet could still look at a gravel pit on a backcountry road and see something pretty.

"It's a gravel pit," he pointed out.

"Really? Hm. Looks like a little lake. And it's still pretty. Look how the moon is shimmering down over the water."

Yeah. Okay. Jase supposed it was pretty. A little. The moon was big and round and . . . and he was letting himself get sidetracked.

"I'm guessing this is a parking spot."

She knew more about country life than she'd let on. "Used to be. Don't know if it is anymore. We used to have parties out here. The landlocked version of going to the beach."

"Bet the girls fell all over you."

Jase didn't know if she was teasing or curious or just making idle conversation. The only thing he knew for certain was that he couldn't stop wondering about her.

"And what about you? You must have driven the Mississippi boys out of their minds."

She gave a little snort. "Not so much, no. I was what you call a late bloomer. Always the smallest one in my class. Skinny as a rail. Didn't need a bra until I was almost sixteen. So, no. The boys didn't pay much attention to me.

"Which was probably a good thing," she added, sounding introspective suddenly. "Some of the 'friends' my mom brought around—well. Let's just say my ugly-duckling looks most likely saved me more than once."

His stomach knotted when he realized what she was talking about. He shifted in the driver's seat until his back was against the door, hooked one arm over the seat back, one over the steering wheel. "God, Janey. I'm . . . sorry."

He could see her perfect profile as the moon illuminated the inside of the Mustang. She shrugged. "Yeah, well, we can't all grow up in Mayberry."

She lowered her head. Shook it. "Sorry. That was—"

"True?" he suggested, hating what she must have lived through as a kid.

"Unnecessary." She shot him a tight, brief smile. "It's not your fault my mom was a drunk. Besides, you had your own things to deal with."

Like Jeremy's death. Yeah. He'd had that. But he'd also had a mother and a father who loved him to help him through it even though they were struggling with their own pain.

"You're . . . you're really something." He searched her eyes when she turned to him. "What you've done. What you've accomplished. What you've overcome."

"Well, you know what they say. What doesn't kill you makes you strong."

Yeah, she was strong. So damn strong.

And he needed to do this. "Janey, about the other night—"

She lifted a hand. "You don't have to say anything. And you *really* don't have to say anything about being sorry, because it's *really* going to tick me off if you do."

She wasn't looking at him anymore. She was staring straight ahead. And she was breathing deep and biting her lower lip.

"I'm not sorry. Not about . . . well, that night. It was one of the most amazing nights of my life."

"Yeah, right. So amazing, you couldn't even talk to me the next day." She shoved open the car door. "So amazing, you couldn't even bear to touch me."

She was out of the seat and slamming the door behind

her so fast that he had to scramble to catch her. She walked toward the edge of the embankment, found a path down the steep slope, and headed down it before he could stop her.

If he hadn't known he'd hurt her before, he sure as hell knew it now.

"Janey—"

"Do people swim in here?" she cut him off when he caught up with her on the tiny spot of sand that passed for a beach.

"Yeah. I guess. Janey, look, I've got some explaining to do."

"Not to me, you don't." She toed off her shoes, then whipped her T-shirt over her head.

He'd known she wasn't wearing a bra. Hell, she hardly ever wore a bra. Didn't need one. She was small, she was firm, and, Lord Jesus God save him, now she was stripping off her short skirt.

When she walked into the water, the only things she was wearing were her cross, a gold hoop in her pierced navel, and a tiny pink thong. Oh—and a scowl that told him she wasn't as mad as she was miserable.

"Janey—"

"Button it, Opie. I don't want to hear anything you have to say on the subject."

Opie? Had she just called him *Opie*?

He felt the start of a slow, roiling boil heat his blood as she disappeared under the water. She wanted to play nasty? He could play nasty. And he was going to have his say.

"Damn woman," he sputtered, and, hopping on one foot, tugged off his boot. The other followed, then his shirt and jeans.

Naked as a jaybird, he waded thigh deep into the water, then made a shallow dive toward the spot where she'd gone under. It was what she'd wanted after all. For him to follow her. Damn if he wasn't going to oblige her.

It didn't take long to find her. The pit wasn't very big. When he broke water, he had an armful of squirming, naked woman. And she was as mad as a cat who'd lost her catnip.

"Let. Me. Go." She fired the words at him like bullets as she raked her hair away from her face, then pushed at his chest.

"How about I just dunk you instead, hothead?"

"How about you just go to hell?"

He pushed her under and held her there for a few seconds while she thrashed and kicked before bobbing up, spitting mad.

"You muscle-bound, immature jerk!" Sucking air and gasping for breath, she popped him in the biceps as water warmed by the heat of the summer day lapped around his chest.

"Immature? *I'm* immature? You're the one who's running away."

"Look, farm boy—"

He dunked her again.

When he let her up, coughing and fuming and clinging to his shoulders so he couldn't shove her under again, she let him have it one more time.

"B- . . . bastard!"

"Brat!" he flung back.

"Coward!" she accused, and tried to break his hold.

Like hell he'd let her go. Even though he knew exactly what kind of a coward she thought he was. The kind that had fallen in love with the most amazing woman he'd ever met and was too much of a coward to trust that she might love him, too.

Bowled over by that revelation, he shoved her away, because hanging on in the face of that news didn't seem like such a great idea after all.

"Fine. I'm a coward."

"Damn straight you are!"

"I said I was, damn it!" he shouted as she waded toward the beach. "What do you want from me?"

"I want you to get over it!" She stopped, turned, her pretty breasts shimmering and glistening wet in the moonlight. "I just . . . want you to . . . to get over it." Her voice wavered. "And damn you, you are not going to make me cry."

No. He wasn't going to make her cry. And he wasn't so ready to let her go after all. He reached for her. Dragged her up against him. With one arm banded around her waist, he gripped her jaw in his other hand when she tried to look away. Then against all reason, against all sense, he did what he'd been dying to do since he'd left her in that lumpy Mississippi motel room bed.

He lowered his mouth and kissed her. And there wasn't anything cowardly about it. Fear wasn't even a distant factor as he slammed his mouth over hers.

He wasn't gentle. He wasn't sweet. He was a marauder. He claimed. He demanded. But most of all he possessed as he slanted his mouth over hers, tunneled his fingers into her wet hair, and held her mouth exactly where he wanted it. Under his. Open and wet. Accepting his tongue. Sighing in surrender. Greedy in defeat.

She wasn't fighting to get away from him anymore. She was fighting to get closer. She wrapped herself around him, knotted her arms around his head, her legs around his waist, and took back as much as he gave.

He skimmed his hands frantically up and down her body, wild for the feel of her. Crazy for the curves of her sweet sexy ass filling his palms, desperate to press between her shoulder blades and rub her breasts against him, experience her diamond-tight nipples sliding against his chest.

He wanted all of her, all at once. And he wanted her yesterday. He lifted her, found a nipple, and sucked. Released. Sucked while she folded her body around him and gave him her other breast, her breath coming in quivering little pants, the cool night air raising goose bumps on her skin.

He lowered her back into the water, reached between them, and, watching her eyes flare, ripped off the delicate thong.

His urgency fueled hers. Her small hands found him, rock hard and huge. Too hard for finesse. Too huge to stop this now. Not at this stage of the game. Not as she positioned herself over the tip of his penis and welcomed him home.

He drove inside her with one fierce, possessive thrust. She sucked in her breath on a gasp, clenched around him, and he damn near sank to his knees. Mindless with pleasure, he clutched her slim hips in his hands and moved her up and down along the length of him.

Jesus. Sweet Lord Jesus, if he died right now, he'd die deliriously happy. And so, judging by the look on her face, would she. Her eyes were closed, her head thrown back, her hair trailing in the water as it slapped against their bodies to a rocking rhythm made all the more intense by the lap of the water around them.

"Janey," he murmured. Just, "Janey," as he drove into her one final time and the top of his head blew off.

She cried out. At least he thought she did. He was so far gone, so far beyond anything he could ever explain, he wasn't sure of anything but sensation. The pleasure consumed him. Fed a craving she'd created and only she could satisfy.

And satisfied, he finally breathed. Breathed in the scent of her wet hair as he cupped her head in his hand and pressed her face into the hollow of his shoulder.

Breathed in the scent of summer and sex and the night that closed in around them.

She wilted against him, exhausted and pliable and ruined. He hugged her close, feeling too damn glad that he was the man who'd made her that way.

Two years. Her confession still obliterated him. She'd been celibate for two years.

Awe. Pride. Amazement. He felt it all. Along with the slowing of his heartbeat and the drain of the adrenaline that had kept him on his feet this long.

Still tucked inside of her, he waded to the beach. He wasn't willing to let her go even as he eased to his knees and laid her down on a makeshift bed of his shirt and jeans.

And he began to move inside her again. Not like a stag in rut this time. Slow. Steady. Aware of the sleek glide of flesh into flesh, the little nuances of body language when she lifted now . . . shifted then . . . sighed and savored as he rubbed her every right way that he knew how.

He leveled himself on an elbow, splayed his hand over her lean belly, bonding with the silk of her skin, the heat of her body, before slipping a finger lower and finding that sensitive nub that he knew would heighten her pleasure.

"Yes?" he whispered, leaning down to suck an earlobe into his mouth. "Here?"

She groaned, shivered. "Yes. There."

High. He was taking her so high. And he wanted to take her higher. He withdrew slowly, sat back on his heels, and tunneled his hands under her hips.

Her eyes glazed over as he lowered his head, lifted her, and touched her with his tongue. Once. Again. Just a taste. Just a tease. Just a promise of more to come before he slipped his tongue between the lips of her vulva. And licked. And laved and sucked until she was bucking against his mouth, clutching at his shoulders, begging for release, sighing out a shivery little scream when he made her come.

Sweet. God, she was sweet. He nuzzled her wet curls, made one last selfish pass with his tongue, then fit himself inside her again and went the same way she did.

Janey didn't know how long they lay on the tiny beach. Couldn't say when he'd rolled to his back and taken her with him, taking her weight, holding her off the ground.

She didn't know what he was thinking, either. He hadn't said a word. He just held her close, one arm banded around her from her shoulders to her hips, the other playing with her hair.

For a man who'd been so determined to have his say, he sure was quiet now, she thought, skimming her hand absently over his chest. And for a woman who'd been mad enough to spit nails, she was feeling pretty mellow. It was an illusion, she knew, but for this small little window in time all felt right with her world.

"Janey . . . we've got to talk about this."

His voice was a low rumble against her cheek.

Yeah. They had to talk. But she'd be damned if she'd be the one to orchestrate the conversation. So she said nothing.

And waited.

Finally, he stirred. "Since we don't seem to get too much talking done without clothes, let's rinse off, then get dressed."

"Sure. Fine," she said, and eased to a sitting position beside him.

She started to stand, but he stopped her with a hand on her arm. He leaned up on an elbow, stretched to kiss her.

The sweetest, most tender kiss, which made her heart ache.

He pulled slowly away, searching her face.

"What?" He wanted to say something, she could tell.

"Nothing. I . . . I just needed to kiss you."

Then he stood and walked into the water.

Magnificent, she thought as she watched the moonlight play over the broad expanse of his shoulders, along his slim waist and the tight, taut muscles of his very superior ass.

She sighed and followed him, carefully keeping her distance as she sank down into the water and rubbed the sand off her legs and anywhere else it had gotten attached. Distance, something told her, was crucial at this juncture in their . . . their what? Relationship? Not quite. But not quite not. Whatever it was, it was fragile.

As fragile as she felt when she waded back to shore, pulled her skirt up over her hips, and slipped into her shirt. Her thong was lost forever, sunk to the bottom of the sand pit. At least she hoped it was at the bottom, not floating somewhere where someone would find it and have a good laugh.

She kept her back to him when she heard him wade back toward the beach. Didn't think she could bear to watch him rise up out of the lake like some water warrior, naked and splendid and wanting to . . . talk, she thought morosely.

"Sit," he said, when she headed for the embankment. "Let's just sit a minute, okay?"

He was dressed again, wearing his T-shirt and jeans and tugging on his boots when she turned to look at him. His expression was sober as he sat in the sand, his knees raised, his forearms draped across them, his hands clasped.

She almost felt sorry for him as she eased down on a thick stump he'd pulled up for her to sit on. Might have reached down and smoothed the worry off his brow if she wasn't so wary of what came next.

"You know," he finally began, "you know this can't go anywhere."

Her heart sank. And her disappointment sent her anger simmering to life again.

"This," she repeated. "What is *this* exactly? You say we have to talk about *this*. *This* can't go anywhere. Spell it out for me, would you please, because I want to make certain I know exactly what *this* is."

"Now you're being obtuse," he said with a weary sigh.

"Obtuse? Oh my, that's a big word for a country boy. And you're pointing that finger the wrong way. *You're* the one who's obtuse. And dull witted. And thickheaded. And . . . and stupid and slow."

He tipped his head back, looked at the night sky, and blew out a breath through puffed cheeks. "Don't hold back. Tell me what you *really* think."

She snorted. He wanted to hear it? Fine. "I already told you what I think. I think you're a coward. I think you're so afraid there's something good going on between us that you're determined to shoot it down before we have a chance to figure out what's happening."

"What's *happening*," he countered grimly, "is that I can't look at you without wanting to rip your clothes off and lay you down on the closest flat surface."

"And this is bad because?"

"Jesus, Janey." He clenched his hands together, glanced toward the sky like he was appealing for patience before pinning her with a hard look. "You know why it's bad. I'm supposed to be taking care of you."

"You took care of me just fine," she said, hurting even more and feeling nasty with it.

"You know what I mean."

"This is what I know," she said, deciding to risk it all. "I know that when I'm with you, I feel . . . alive. And I'm not just talking about the sex. I'm talking about how you make me feel. As a person."

He looked up at her, his blue eyes troubled and curious and, if she read him right, a little bit hopeful.

"Why do you have to make this so hard?" She knew it came out sounding like a plea. She didn't care. She was past pride. "It doesn't have to be. Can't we just let things take their course? See if what we're feeling isn't something worth hanging on to?"

"What we're feeling?" he repeated with a weary frown. "Janey, you can't possibly *know* what you're feeling right now. You've got a convicted stalker terrorizing you. Your mother has been murdered and we still don't have a bead on who did it—only a million dollars as a probable reason why but no clue who knows about it."

He shifted so he could look directly at her. "Your life is one big, ugly, dangerous puzzle with a million missing pieces. How can you know what you're feeling other than shock and fear and uncertainty?"

"Look, Dr. Freud, my life—regardless of stalkers and murders and mysteries—is *always* one big sloppy mess. Concerts, photo shoots, celeb appearances . . . hell. Pick something. It's probably on the agenda. Give me some credit here. You think I can't sort the dimes from the dollars? You think, after six years of organized chaos, that I haven't learned to cope? Can't see what's good for me?

"It's called compartmentalizing," she added, trying to drive her point home. "It's called multitasking. And I'm damn good at it."

When he looked unconvinced, she shook her head. "You're the one who can't get a handle on your feelings, Baby Blue. Don't lay that trip on me."

He blinked. Blinked again. "What'd you call me?"

She scowled at him. "What? When?"

"Just now. Baby Blue, was it?"

She rolled her eyes, gave a dismissive shrug. "Yeah. So what? You called me a brat. Earlier," she clarified when his puzzled look intensified.

"Well, you called me Opie."

"Oh for God's sake. What does that have to do with anything?"

"I don't know," he said, frowning. "I haven't figured it out yet. I haven't figured any of this out."

She stood, brushed off her butt. "Tell you what. When you do, we'll have another little chat . . . about . . . *this*. We can even talk about *that* if you want to," she said sourly. "Until then, I don't want to talk about *this* again. I just want to—"

She jumped, startled when a ping of a sound had the sand a few feet away flying in a showering spray.

"What the—"

The sand flew again. So close to her feet this time that it stung.

"Jesus." He scrambled to his feet, grabbed her arm, and pushed her behind him. "Some crazy sonofabitch is shooting.

"Hey, dickhead!" he yelled into the dark. "There are people down here. Do your target practice somewhere else."

A rapid succession of pings zipped into the night, making the earth jump and dirt spray all around them.

"Shit! Crazy bastard must be drunk. Come on. We're getting out of here."

He grabbed her hand and ran, pulling her along behind him. Her heart pounded like crazy as he tugged her up the steep embankment like their lives depended on it. It wasn't until she felt a warm, sticky wetness seep between their joined hands that it really hit home that their lives did depend on getting out of the line of fire.

Blood.

Blood ran down his arm like a river.

"You've been hit," she cried.

"Get in the car." He shoved her through the driver's door, then piled in behind her.

She scrambled over the center console, banged her knee on the gearshift, and fell face-first onto the floor. She was in the process of righting herself when he turned the key, revved the motor, and shoved the Mustang into gear. Tires squealed and gravel shot in a rooster tail behind them as he floored the accelerator and tore down the gravel road.

"You okay?" he asked as she turned herself around so her bare butt was on the floorboard. She lifted her hand to grip the passenger seat—and met with more blood. Not warm this time. It was cold. Cold blood.

She jerked her hand away and stared.

There, in the middle of the pristine white upholstery, two tiny, lifeless hearts lay in the middle of a bloodred cloth.

19

Grimm." Jase pounded the steering wheel as they flew down the gravel road, kicking up dust in their wake. "How in the *hell* did he find us here?"

Beside him, Janey scooped up the cloth with the hearts and chucked them out the window. "You're bleeding," she said for about the tenth time.

For the tenth time, he told her he was fine, yet she got busy trying to rip a piece of the pink ruffle from her skirt to use as a bandage.

"Forget about that." He glanced in the rearview mirror and spotted headlights bearing down on them. "And buckle up. We've got company."

She twisted around in the seat and saw the lights. "Oh, God."

"Buckle up," he repeated in a cold, steely voice, and laid on the gas.

The Mustang responded, roaring down the gravel road like the muscle machine it was, all 360 horses running at checkered-flag speed.

He'd like nothing better than to face off with the sick bastard—and he would. But not yet. Not until he had the advantage. He couldn't risk something happening to Janey until he did.

Behind them, the headlights closed in. Jase braked, whipped the Mustang around a curve, and damn near spun into the ditch when the car fishtailed.

He gunned it, righted them, and glanced at the tach needle as it spun to the top of the dial.

He swore after another quick glance in the rearview mirror confirmed his fears. "He's gaining on us."

Janey, bless her, had to be good and scared, but she didn't scream, didn't cry, when he came to another four-corner crossroad and took the corner on two wheels.

He cut the lights. That finally made her gasp.

"It's okay. I know these roads. Grimm doesn't. And there's enough moonlight that I can see where I'm going. Hang on."

They sailed up over a rise, caught some air before all four wheels kissed the gravel again. He headed for the county park just a few miles up the road.

"I'm going to try to ditch him in the woods," he told her when he swung hard left and headed up the road to Clear Creek Recreation Center.

The forest was thickest at the opening to the park. He took advantage of the dark and his knowledge of the snowmobile trails he used to ride every winter. He headed straight for the Shimmac Trail. It was winding and narrow and, if he remembered right, had several little tributary routes closed in tight with scrub brush and sumac.

Still running without headlights, he turned onto the trail, drove for a quarter of a mile or so, then stopped and backed into an opening in the undergrowth just big enough to shelter the Mustang.

Then he cut the motor. And listened.

In the far distance, he could hear the engine of what he suspected was an SUV. Far enough distant to know that Grimm had lost them but hadn't given up.

Jase drew his first deep breath since the first shot was fired. "You okay?"

Janey stared straight ahead, one hand clamped on the dash, one on the console between them. "I'd pee my pants if I had any on."

Christ. That was so not the picture he needed right now.

But then she looked at him, all small and wild-eyed. "That was supposed to cut the tension." She gave him her gamest smile.

He groaned as much as laughed. "Mission accomplished."

He followed her gaze to his arm. A thick trail of blood ran down his right biceps in a slow, steady trickle.

"It's just a flesh wound," he assured her after checking it, even though the adrenaline had let down enough that it was starting to burn like hell.

"Call me crazy, but in my mind 'just' isn't a good fit in the same sentence with 'flesh' and 'wound.' My God. You're bleeding like crazy."

Not that much really, but when she went back to work on her skirt, getting nowhere on her attempt to rip the ruffle off for a bandage while he fished in his jeans for his pocketknife.

"Try this." He handed her the knife, then had second

thoughts when she held out trembling fingers. "Never mind. I'll do it."

He set the knife to the pink cotton and made the first slice. She was able to pull the ruffle off after that, so he sat in silence as she busied herself bandaging his arm with it.

"Shh." He lifted a finger to his mouth when the sound of an engine grow closer. Then he saw the headlights bouncing down the trail in their direction.

He reached under the seat for his gun.

Gone. *Fuck.*

The bastard must have taken it when he planted the hearts. That only left one option.

"Hang on. We're going to turn the tables on this creep."

The car drew closer. Jase was confident the Mustang was well hidden. Ninety percent confident anyway. Still his hands were sweating on the wheel when a late-model four-wheel-drive SUV idled slowly by.

"He didn't see us." She sounded breathless with relief.

"Nope. But the sonofabitch is gonna see us now."

He turned the key and slammed the Mustang into gear. They roared up out of the thicket and burst back onto the snowmobile trail—right on the tail of the SUV.

"What are you doing?"

"Letting him know that two can play this game."

He hit the lights, flooding the back of the vehicle like a spotlight. After a moment of shock on Grimm's part, the SUV took off.

Jase stuck to his taillights like white on rice. "There's a pen in the glove box. Get the license number."

"Got it." She scribbled frantically on the back of her hand. "Now what?" she asked as they bounced along the uneven path.

"Now we hope I can bump him hard enough that he'll run off the road."

"You're not serious."

"As a heart attack," he said, just as the SUV reached one of the access roads. Leaving a trail of dust, his tires spun off the shoulder into the gravel and he sped off down the blacktop.

"And the race is on." Jase put the hammer down and they roared onto the road in hot pursuit.

"Would now be a good time to point out that you don't have a gun?"

"There you go. Looking on the downside."

Speaking of guns. Jase saw the flash of fire just as it registered that Grimm had stuck the barrel of one out the driver's window.

"Get down!" He shoved Janey's head below dash level.

One of his headlights went dark; glass fragments flew against the windshield and a tire blew. He slammed on the brakes, fighting to keep the Mustang under control as the SUV sped off, dust hanging in its wake like a jet trail.

Finally, Jase managed to ease the car to a stop. Engine idling, he shifted into park and turned to Janey. "Are you hurt?"

She shook her head, raked her hair away from her face, then shook her head again. "Fine. I'm . . . fine."

Yeah. She was fine all right, Jase thought as the dust settled and the SUV's taillights gradually faded to small pink dots. As fine as any woman could be after someone had just tried to kill her.

B astard shot out a tire." Jase climbed back into the Mustang after inspecting the damage. "We've got to get out of here before he decides to come back."

Janey thought that was a damn fine idea. Would have

said so if she hadn't looked up. Headlights. Bearing down. Fast.

"Too late," she said, transfixed by the twin yellow gold and glowing lights heading toward them.

Baby Blue swore and shoved the Mustang into reverse. He cranked the wheel hard right, shifted back to drive, and headed back down the road and away from the rapidly oncoming car.

"What are the chances it's not him?" She twisted in the seat and looked over her shoulder.

"Same as me winning the lottery," Jase said, eyes dead ahead.

"I think he's gaining on us."

"We can't outrun him. Not on three tires."

"What are we going to do?"

"I can't lead him back to my parents." He glanced in the rearview again. She didn't have to turn around to know what he saw. Grimm wasn't more than a football field away.

"And it's time I call this asshole out. He's obviously done playing around. He means business now."

They took a corner on two good wheels.

Jase glanced around at the hilly terrain cast in night shadows by a low-hanging moon. "Can you run in those shoes?"

Her sandals were little more than flat soles and a few crisscrosses of leather. The Italian designer hadn't had running in mind when he'd crafted them. She hadn't had running for her life in mind when she'd put them on.

The headlights grew even closer.

"I can run." She'd run barefoot over broken glass if she had to.

"We're near the Cochran Caves," he said as they raced along on the blown-out tire; the stench of burned rubber permeated the air.

"Caves?" Oh, God. Caves meant dark and damp and bats. Bats. Ever since she was a little girl and a bat had found its way into their trailer, she'd had an unnatural and unreasonable fear of bats.

She swallowed back an "ohmygod" that would have come out as a scream. He didn't need hysterics. And she needed a drink.

"We used to play in the caves when we were kids. I think I can still find my way through them. You up for it?"

Janey closed her eyes, swallowed thickly, and managed a nod. "Yeah. I . . . I can do it."

God, help me do it.

"If there were any other way—if I could get you out of the mix—I would."

She actually found herself laughing. "Out of the mix? My God. I'm the reason you're hurt and your life is in danger. I *am* the mix."

"Okay. Here's the plan. When I stop, you haul ass out of the car."

"And then what?"

He roared up the hill, battling to keep the crippled Mustang out of the ditch. "Then we run like hell."

He glanced around, like he was looking for a landmark, then slammed on the brakes and skidded to the side of the road. "Now," he said, unbuckling as he killed the motor.

Janey followed his lead, then took his hand. When they cleared the car, she did as she was told. She ran like hell, far too aware that Grimm would catch up with the Mustang in seconds.

Has to be adrenaline, she thought as she and Jase raced up a grass and limestone hillside. That's the only way she could keep up with him. Adrenaline and the knowledge that Grimm had pulled up behind the Mustang.

She heard a car door slam. And she kept running, kept her hand clasped in Baby Blue's.

The sharp crack of a rifle shot ripped into the night. The limestone at their feet exploded. She gasped as shards of rock peppered her ankle. The pain was instant and biting and she almost went down.

Baby Blue kept running, pulling her along when she stumbled, zigzagging his way up the side of a hill that grew steeper and rockier.

Just when she thought she couldn't go any farther, the limestone at shoulder level detonated. He jerked her up against him, made a shield of his body, and pressed her into the side of an outcropping of stone and tree roots.

She'd hardly drawn a breath when he was on the move again, scrambling higher, dragging her around a curve in the hillside—and into the deepest, most absolute dark she'd ever known.

"How do you do with dark?" Baby Blue whispered beside her.

"Love it. Can't get enough of it," she lied, and tried to keep her teeth from chattering.

"That scared, huh?"

"Oh yeah."

"You just hang on to me."

Like epoxy.

She could see exactly nothing. *Nothing* as he took her hands, maneuvered her behind him, then wrapped her arms around his waist. "I know these caves, Janey. That's all you need to think about. Just trust me. When I take a step, you take a step. Just like dancing, okay?"

"Dancing in the dark. Got it."

"Good girl. Hang on. Here we go."

She almost laughed when she realized she'd pinched her eyes closed tight. As if avoiding opening them and seeing that she couldn't see a thing—not even his broad back, which was one inch from her nose—would make this all go away.

Inch by inch, Baby Blue led them deeper into the cave.

"Head down," he warned in a whisper. "The ceiling drops to about four and a half feet here."

She ducked, then stopped, midstep.

"What?"

"I . . . think I heard something behind us."

In the next second a beam from a flashlight confirmed it.

"It's okay. We're almost to a switchback. We'll wait for him there."

"And do what?"

"He may have the gun, but I have the advantage. He doesn't know where he's going; I do. And the dark is on my side. You still with me?"

If she could draw a full breath, she would have whimpered. Her ankle throbbed and burned like fire where the rock fragments had nailed her. Blood ran into the sole of her sandal, making her foot slide on the leather and walking tricky. And God help them both, if a bat dive-bombed her, she'd probably faint dead away. But she was still with him.

"Where else would I be?"

He covered the fingers she'd linked together around his waist like a set of locks, squeezed in reassurance. Then he made a sharp left, swung around in a 180, and stopped, taking them out of the approaching flashlight's range and plunging them into darkness again.

"Not a sound," he whispered against her ear. "It's going to end here." He pressed her a little deeper into the unrelenting blackness. "Don't move. No matter what happens. Don't move."

Then his solid warmth and protection left her. She bit her lower lip. Reached out into the void in front of her and felt only air. Cold, damp, dank-smelling air. Beside her, her right hand encountered rock. Because it was the only thing tangible, she moved into it for support, wishing the unyielding stone felt as comforting as Baby Blue's warm back against her cheek.

Please, God, don't let anything happen to him.

Then she heard it. The sound of footsteps. She held her breath as the faint beam of a flashlight cut into the absolute dark. Made herself breathe when Baby Blue's silhouette took shape a yard ahead of her where he crouched at the edge of a wall of rock. Waiting for Edwin Grimm and his gun.

Waiting with what looked like a knife.

She felt her first inkling of relief. He was armed. But as the light grew closer, casting an eerie, shifting glow on the wall facing them, she could see that it wasn't a knife at all. It was a rock. Long and narrow and marginally tapered.

God. He was going to fight a man wielding an automatic rifle with a rock. A dozen deadly conclusions to that scenario formed in her mind when a narrow beam of light bent around the corner.

This was it. One way or the other, this was all going to be over soon.

Heart hammering, she waited, waited, waited for an eternity of seconds. The silence suddenly became as thick as the darkness of moments ago.

Grimm was waiting, too. Considering. Deciding if he was walking into a trap. Just when she thought she'd die from the suspense, both the light and the nose of a rifle poked around the corner, not six inches from Baby Blue's face.

It was the moment he'd been waiting for. With an echoing growl, he stood, chopped at the gun barrel with a swift, downward hack.

A burst of blinding light was followed instantly by the ear-splitting report of a rifle. Her eyes were still traumatized by the fire flash and her ears still ringing when she heard a groan, the thud of a body connecting with the cave floor.

Adrenaline pumped through her blood at the speed
of sound—she could hear it in her ears along with the
ringing, feel it in her throat. Finally, her pupils dilated and
she could make out the faint glow of the flashlight, its beam
cocked at an unnatural angle toward the ceiling of the cave.

Where hundred of bats hung upside down and had
started to stir.

Oh, God.

She dropped to her knees, shrinking herself as small as
possible. She wanted to call out to Baby Blue. She wanted
to run toward the light—and that's when she realized the
flashlight was less than three feet away.

Holding her breath, she inched slowly forward on her
hands and knees. Six inches. She could almost touch it.
And she almost did. At the last moment, she pulled her
hand back, followed the wide swath of the beam where it
flared downward—and saw Grimm's dark silhouette standing over Baby Blue, rifle in hand, ready to fire.

She forgot all about the bats; she forgot about her fear
of the dark. With a roar, she shot to her feet. Startled,
Grimm swung toward her, but she was already in motion.
She kicked high and hard, clipping him in the jaw.

He screamed in pain, dropped to his knees, and the rifle went flying. Sheer instinct had her scrambling for the
weapon when it skittered toward her. She grabbed it and
drew it to her shoulder.

"Don't move." Terrified, she hardly recognized her
own voice. He stood and took a step toward her. "I said
don't move," she shouted, near panic.

When he stopped and held his hands up above his
head, her breath came out in a series of ragged hitches.
She couldn't see his face in the dark. Couldn't distinguish
anything but his hulking silhouette. She didn't have to see
him. His face had fueled nightmares for four years; she
remembered every inch of it.

And now she had another nightmare to thank him for. Baby Blue lay lifeless at her feet.

Be alive; be alive, she begged him. Just as she knelt to check, Grimm lurched forward. She raised the gun to her shoulder, fired wildly. The recoil knocked her backward, set her on her ass. She fired again.

Her ears were still ringing, her eyes still blinded by the fire flash, when she looked up, struggling to find Grimm, and fire again if she had to. But she couldn't see anything. And all she could hear was the horrible ringing in her ears. All she could feel was Jason Wilson's lifeless form beside her.

Long moments passed before she realized they were alone in the cave. Alone with the bats. Finally, her sight adjusted. And her mind clicked out of panic mode when she heard the distant roar of an engine.

She rose to her knees, bent over Baby Blue—and almost wept when she felt his breath against her face, his pulse against her fingertips.

She lifted his head and cradled it in her lap. It didn't take long to find the bump on his temple. But it took what felt like forever for her to rouse him.

"Grimm?" he mumbled.

"Gone," she said.

Then and only then did she cry. And curse. And laugh until she started crying again.

He lifted a hand, cupped her head, and shushed her.

"I'm okay. I'm okay, babe."

She'd thought he was dead. Because of her.

She'd thought they were both going to end up dead.

But they were alive.

Thank you, God, they were alive.

That was the good news.

The bad news: Somewhere out there, Grimm was still alive, too.

20

One thirty a.m., Saturday, July 22nd

"I wish to hell I knew," Jase told No as he tossed his duffel on the bed in his old bedroom on the second floor of his parents' house.

His head throbbed like a bitch. But he wasn't seeing stars anymore, so that was a plus.

In Jeremy's room, Janey was also packing her things. Damn, was she something. He'd been out cold for the grand finale. Must have hit his head on a rock when he'd tackled Grimm.

That was the last thing he remembered. If Janey hadn't kept her head and gotten Grimm's assault rifle, they'd both be dead now. He'd deal with the ego hit later. Right now, he had to get her out of here.

"Somehow, some way, Grimm is tracking her," Jase told No. "And the sonofabitch has stepped up his game."

He wedged his cell between his shoulder and ear, checked the cylinder on the Ruger that his dad kept around to chase off coyotes.

"Her cell phone?" No suggested.

"I checked it. It's clean. Hell, I've checked everything I can think of. Her clothes. Her purse. Makeup. Nothing. It's spooky as hell."

"So is Dallas's latest find." No's voice was stone-cold.

Jase felt his stomach, which was still queasy from the blow to his head, sink like a stone. "Don't tell me we've lost another woman on the list."

"Make that two more. One in Florida and one in Texas. With Alice Perkins and the woman in Illinois, that makes four—all within a few days of each other."

Jase tucked the gun into his jeans at the small of his back and shouldered the duffel. "Still nothing to tie them together?"

"Actually, there is. We've traced them all back to Mississippi. They all lived within thirty miles of Alice Perkins about twenty-seven, twenty-eight years ago."

"So she might have known them. Anything else?"

"Yeah—Dallas has a lead on the fourth woman. In South Dakota of all places. He's catching a plane in the morning—with some luck, she'll be able to fill in some blanks for us."

"Okay, look." Jase checked his watch—it was almost one-forty-five—and zipped up his duffel. "I'm getting Janey out of here. I didn't have much choice but to fill my old man in a few minutes ago. He can handle himself if Grimm shows up after we leave, but I don't think that's going to happen. The bastard wants Janey. He backed off tonight, but I have no doubt that he'll come after her again."

"Where are you going?"

Jase grunted. "People keep asking me questions I don't have answers for. All I know is I've got to get her out of here and away from my parents. I don't want them caught in the middle of this."

"I've got an idea," No said.

"I'm all ears, man."

"How far are you from Chicago?"

"Three, three and a half hours with a tailwind."

"Head for O'Hare. Grimm wouldn't dare make a move with airport security as tight as it is."

"Which means I'll have to ditch my piece."

"Don't worry; where you're going, there will be plenty of weaponry and ammo."

"And where might that be?"

"On the off chance Grimm's got a line on this conversation, let's just keep that part a surprise for now."

"Let's keep something else a surprise, too," Jase said, in complete agreement with No. "Our mode of transportation. I'm beginning to think there might be a GPS transmitter planted on Janey's jet."

"Fine. You'll fly commercial. I'll arrange to have tickets waiting when you get there. When you get to O'Hare, call. I'll let you know what airline. You'll be long gone before Grimm can catch up."

"Roger that." Ignoring the headache, Jase shouldered the duffel, and headed out the door toward Jeremy's room.

"Jase—there are a couple of other things."

"Of course there are," he said wearily, and sagged against the wall in the hallway. Something told him he didn't want Janey to hear all of this. "Okay. Shoot."

"Has Janey ever said anything about Max Cogan having a gambling problem?"

That stopped Jase cold. "Whoa. Max? No. She's never mentioned it. I'm not sure she would though, even if she knew. She's pretty loyal. Come to think of it, I did notice that Max hit the casinos pretty hard when we were in Atlantic City."

"Yeah, well, he likes the horses, too. And sports bets. Word is he dropped a bundle a few weeks back and some not-so-nice guys have been leaning on him pretty hard to pay up."

Just what Janey needed. To find Max floating facedown in a river somewhere. No wonder Jase had sensed Max was off his game lately. And Max had been eating antacids like they were candy.

"Max loves Janey," Jase said aloud. "I can't see him putting her in the middle of his problems."

"Maybe he didn't have a choice. According to his bank records, he's tapped out. His condo is mortgaged to the hilt and his credit is for shit. The big boys might figure Janey is Max's ticket to pay them off."

"Christ." Jase felt weary to the bone suddenly. "I don't like the direction this is going."

"Then you're not going to like this, either. Janey's friend? Neal Sanders?"

"Yeah?"

"As of last night, Sanders is missing."

M issing?" Janey felt marginally better after she had taken a very quick shower and dressed in clean jeans and a tank top. At least she *had* felt better until Wilson had made his announcement about Neal.

"What does that mean? Everybody scattered after Boston to take advantage of the two-week break. I think Neal said he was heading back to NYC."

She ran a pick through her damp hair as she sat beside Baby Blue in Bruce Wilson's borrowed truck. The Mustang wasn't drivable—something, Baby Blue had announced with a dark scowl, that Grimm was going to pay for, big-time.

He checked his rearview mirror and pulled out onto I-80 heading east. In the pale light of the truck's cab, she could see the bump on his temple. A reddish-purple bruise covered a knot the size of a quarter and radiated down to his eye. After fussing over his arm and head injury, Bev Wilson had helped Janey clean and dress the cuts on her ankle.

"Yeah. Well, he didn't show. Didn't make his flight. Never checked into the hotel he'd booked."

"So he had a change of plans. He does that sometimes."

"Janey—he never checked out of the hotel in Boston, yet all of his things were left in his room. The maid alerted management when she went to clean, because he was supposed to have checked out."

It was easier, sometimes, to avoid the truth than to deal with it. "He's probably holed up with his woman of the week somewhere." But even as she said it, she knew she was reaching.

Jase shook his head. "Apparently the room was trashed—and not just because Sanders is a slob. Seems there might have been a little scuffle. It's starting to look like maybe he didn't leave willingly. He left his wallet behind, his stash of weed, all of his clothes."

She closed her eyes, dropped her head into her hand. "So you're thinking what? That someone abducted Neal? That's crazy."

He was quiet for a while, then glanced her way. "Okay, I know you don't see this, probably don't want to hear it, either, but Sanders isn't a very nice guy."

"I'll admit that he's changed some lately," Janey said reluctantly. "And not for the good. But he was my friend when I needed one most. I'm not going to forget that.

Besides, you don't understand him," she said, automatically coming to Neal's defense.

"What I understand is that he's a leech."

She knew Jase was right but didn't want to fully embrace the truth. "He's insecure."

"He's a prick."

"Who might be in some trouble," she pointed out angrily.

He let out a deep breath. "Who might be in some trouble," he finally concurred.

Janey looked out the window. Frustrated. Exhausted. Done in. "Okay, this is going to stop sometime, right?" An overwhelming sense of helplessness coupled with fatigue and threatened to overtake her. "I'm going to wake up in the morning and all of this is going to be like some Ex-induced dream and I'll be back in charge of my life again."

Didn't matter that she'd never done drugs and never would; she had to figure that this was what it must feel like to live through a bad trip.

"I mean . . . it's too much. On top of everything else, this is just too much."

"Yeah," he agreed softly, then surprised her by reaching out and covering her hand with his. "It's way too much.

"And so," he added with a meaningful squeeze, "are you. You were really something . . . you saved my sorry hide in that cave."

Yeah. She had. And she was still amazed that she'd kept it together, because when she thought about it she came damn close to falling apart.

"I . . . I can still see him . . . standing over you. He . . . he was going to shoot you."

"Hey—don't think about it, okay? It's over. And so is his little reign of terror. There was a trail of blood leading out of that cave. Too much blood to have come from your ankle. You got him, babe. Put him in a world of hurt."

She knew it had been a shoot-or-be-shot situation, but still the idea of hurting another human being—even an animal like Grimm—well, it was hard to think about.

"Nolan notified all the police departments involved. There's a nationwide APB out for Grimm now. Sooner or later, he's got to come up for air—he's probably already on his way to an ER somewhere. And if not now, he'll show up in one soon. Then they'll get him. And this will all be over."

Over. Yeah. More than anything in the world, she wanted this to be over. She wished she could believe he was right. Just like she wished she was right about Neal. That he'd show up soon.

Somehow, though, she had a feeling that maybe she'd gotten all the wishes she'd been allotted for one life. Wishes *and* prayers, both of which had been answered when Baby Blue had opened his eyes in that cave—a little battered, a lot bruised, but alive.

*N**ear sundown, same day, outside of Jackson Hole, Wyoming*

"Who did you say this place belonged to?" Janey asked as they pulled up to the mountain retreat a few miles north of Jackson Hole.

"No's wife, Jillian. It's her parents'. Guess the Kincaids rarely use it," Jase said as he got out of the rented SUV. "Man. I'd be here fifty-three weeks a year if I owned a place like this."

Which he never would, he reminded himself as he opened the rear door of the SUV and lifted out their duffels. Just one more reason to remember that wealth on the scale of publishing moguls like Jillian's father, Darin Kincaid, and rock stars like Sweet Baby Jane separated them from the working class.

Of which he was a card-carrying lifetime member.

"Wow. This is gorgeous." Janey stepped out of the SUV and joined him on the path of natural stone that led to the massive house constructed of log, stone, and glass. The house appeared to be one with its surroundings of aspen and evergreen and rock.

"It's damn remote," Jase said, knowing from his field experience that the location could be a good or a bad thing from a defensive standpoint.

Good because anyone looking for them was going to have a damn hard time finding them out here. Bad because if they were found, there wasn't a cavalry in the world that could charge in here in time to save the day. And while he'd tried to whitewash the Grimm situation for Janey—Lord knew she needed a little relief from it— he wasn't taking any chances. The bastard kept showing up when there was no way in hell he should have found them.

If he turned up here, Jase was going to be ready.

Dusk was fast approaching and a low-hanging sun glinted off a twenty-foot wall of windows. As they walked toward the house, Jase realized that the past twenty-four hours were catching up with him. They'd caught a 4:45 a.m. flight out of Chicago to Atlanta. In an attempt to throw Grimm off their trail, they'd hopped on a last-minute flight from Atlanta to Minneapolis, then on to Salt Lake City before connecting with their final flight to Jackson Hole. Damn near twelve hours in the air or at an airport.

Try and find us now, you sick fuck.

Frankly, Jase would like nothing better than to make a stand, call Grimm out, and get Janey out from under his reign of terror. He wanted to be the one to take Grimm down—especially after last night. He touched a hand to the lump on his temple. Grimm had some payback coming.

If it were a case of mano a mano, that would be Jase's choice. A one-on-one showdown. Let the bastard come. He'd enjoy the hell out of taking him down.

But that wasn't the case. Janey's life was still on the line. And then there was the trail of dead bodies from Illinois to Florida to add to the mix. He still couldn't figure tagging Grimm for those deaths. And that left one more level of threat to deal with and figure out.

"Come on." Once they'd cleared the steps leading to a massive porch that ran the width of the house. He hitched his chin in the direction of a double front door. "Let's get inside."

As little as Janey was, she made way too big of a target for someone with a rifle and a scope. And Jase had a damn bad feeling that no matter how well they'd covered their tracks, they were going to have company of the badass variety.

He punched the security code No had given him into the keypad and let them inside.

"Fridge is full," he announced after checking out the kitchen. No had told him the Kincaids' caretaker, who lived in Jackson Hole, would stock the place for them, then make himself scarce.

"Your boss came through."

"No always comes through," Jase said, then stopped long enough to look at her.

She looked beat. And in spite of that, she looked beautiful. Damn, she looked beautiful. Too beautiful for him to be tucked away with her in a remote mountain retreat. She was also about ready to drop.

"You need to catch some sleep."

"And you should have seen a doctor for your arm and your head."

"I told you, I'm fine. And I need to do a little recon." He went in search of the gun cabinet No had told him was hidden in a closet down the hall off the kitchen.

"Jackpot," he murmured when he found it. While he'd have preferred an M4 or an M16, the .300 Weatherbee bolt-action rifle would do. He shouldered the weapon, sighted through the scope. "Nice."

So was the Ruger Magnum. Shoving the handgun into the waistband of his jeans, he grabbed ammo for both pieces and headed back to the main living area.

And found Janey sound asleep on the sofa.

As he stood there, armed to the teeth with enough firepower to incite a minor coup, he felt a tenderness that damn near took him to his knees.

God, look at her. For the first time in his life, he understood why men had fought over and fought for their women since the dawn of time.

It wasn't about testosterone. It wasn't about possession. It was about knowing, deep down inside on a level buried under pride and posturing and the need to provide, that without woman, without *the* woman, man was nothing. And life was not complete.

Talk about your life-altering moments. Jase set the rifle aside and carefully covered her with a colorful woven throw he tugged from the back of the sofa. *Talk about your moments of truth.*

He understood something else now, too. He finally understood what had been confusing him from the first time he'd set eyes on Janey Perkins. He had loved Sara, yes. Because she'd needed him. Because he was a giver and she'd filled his need to give.

But he loved Janey for an entirely different reason. He loved Janey because *he* needed *her.* It didn't get more simple than that.

"Why do you have to make this so hard?"

He could still see the frustration and hurt in her brown eyes last night at the sand pit. After they'd made love. After he'd been determined to make her understand that since hell hadn't frozen over and the sky hadn't fallen he didn't see the two of them making things work together as happening, either.

"And why, exactly, is that?" he asked himself as, still watching her, he sank down in a plump, overstuffed leather side chair.

He propped his elbow on the arm of the chair, stroked his chin, and tried to dredge up all those damn good reasons why it wouldn't work.

And they didn't seem so damn good anymore.

"When this is over," he whispered, watching this woman who had so changed his life sleep, "we'll see. We'll see what happens."

But first, he had to get her through this. He stood, then had to wait for his head to quit spinning because he'd moved too fast. Marginally level again, he stretched out the kinks and, grabbing the rifle, headed outside to take a look around.

He could sleep later. Right now, he needed to scout the lay of the land and check in with No.

"Jesus," he said after he'd hung up half an hour later; his mind reeled with Dallas Garrett's latest update. "Jesus. What in the hell is going on?"

21

I t was dark when Janey woke up. She stretched and rolled to her back, opening her eyes to the soft glow of the table lamp at the end of the sofa and to the wonderful scent of something cooking.

Yawning hugely, she sat for a moment, waited for the fog of sleep to dissipate, then rose and walked barefoot toward the kitchen. The delicious scents that greeted her sent her stomach growling.

"Wilson?" she said softly when she didn't find him in the kitchen area of the open and spacious house constructed of interior log walls, open beamed ceilings, a huge stone fireplace, and acres of glass.

She flicked on a light switch. Honey-gold wood flooring shined beneath her feet. Unable to resist, she peeked inside the oven; it was filled with crisp bacon and a fluffy cheese omelet.

"And he cooks," she said with a smile, and, because she was suddenly ravenous, helped herself to a piece of bacon.

"Thought we'd already established that," a dark voice said from behind her.

She turned around, more stunned by his words than by surprise when she saw him standing just inside the back door, a rifle cradled in his arms.

She wasn't sure which affected her the most. His obvious decision that he needed to carry that much firepower or what he'd said. And the way he'd said it.

"Thought we'd already established that."

Flirting? Was he actually flirting? Maybe his head injury was worse than she'd thought.

"We absolutely have," she agreed when she found his eyes were clear and alert.

She was intrigued all over again by the sudden flush that stained his cheeks, a flush that told her they were both thinking about the cookin' they'd done together in a little pool of water and on a tiny sand beach back in Iowa.

God. Had that really been just last night?

"There's fruit in the fridge," he said, breaking eye contact. He walked across the kitchen and set the rifle in the corner within easy reach of the table.

"You've been busy," she said, choosing to dwell on the idea of him loosening up enough to flirt instead of dwelling on all the implications of the rifle. Could it be that Baby Blue had been thinking things over?

"Help yourself." He dusted off his hands, then joined her. "Catch up on your sleep some?"

"Some. Obviously you didn't. How's the head? And your arm? Maybe I should take a look at it." His mother, horrified by the blood and the real story that Jase had been forced to tell his parents, had dressed it properly before they'd left for Chicago.

"For the last time, the head is fine. The arm is fine. The dressing is fine," he insisted. "I'm fine."

"Yeah, well, don't take this wrong, but you don't look so fine." Actually, he looked like he always did. Delicious, decidedly conflicted, and dead beat. "Why haven't you slept?"

"I'll sleep tonight." He nodded toward the table. "Let's eat. Then we have to talk."

"About?" she asked carefully.

"I spoke with Dallas a while ago."

She studied his face, then felt her stomach knot before he turned to the cupboard and pulled out a pair of plates. "I know that look. That's the 'other shoe is about to fall' look."

The grim set of his mouth when he turned back and set the plates on what appeared to be a hand-carved table confirmed it.

All of her good spirits deflated. "What's happened now?"

"After you eat," he said, looking very domestic wielding an oven mitt as he set the plates of food on the table. "That'll be soon enough."

"Afraid I'm not going to have much of an appetite after I hear what you've got to tell me?"

He didn't say a word. He just dug into his food like it was a job that needed doing. Which told her she was right. The other shoe was about to drop—and the weight of it was probably going to crush her.

O kay. Let's have it," Janey said after they'd cleaned up the kitchen and settled in the living room.

She curled a leg up under her on a corner of a chocolate leather sofa that matched two overstuffed side chairs.

Jase sat in one of those chairs instead of sitting down beside her. It had been hard enough being so close to her in the kitchen. He needed his head on straight while they talked through Dallas's news. Somehow, they had to make sense of it.

And somehow, he had to break it to her—without breaking her.

"Dallas did some checking on your mom's financial situation," he said, biting the bullet. "Seems that from the time you were little, she never had a steady job. Did you know that?"

She shrugged. "More or less. I reached a certain age and figured out we were probably living off welfare."

"Well, that's the thing. Dallas checked on that, too. He couldn't find any evidence of that in the public records. What he did find," Jase continued when her delicate eyebrows drew together, "was that right up until the time she was killed, someone was making deposits into her bank account. Every month, just like clockwork."

He watched as she sat up a little straighter, gave a little shake of her head—like she was trying to make sense of this news. "From who?"

"That he couldn't find out. Whoever was making the deposits buried the paper trail deep and wide. Dallas ran into one dead end after another."

"So," she said after a long thoughtful pause, "someone was keeping my mother."

"Yeah," Jase agreed, hating the barren look on her face. "It looks that way."

"Someone who didn't want to be traced."

"So it would seem."

"Lemans?" she suggested after a moment. "Or whoever the hell that was at the bank?"

He nodded. "Possibly. And to add to the mix, the payments had increased substantially over the last six months."

"How substantially?"

"Doubled."

She shifted her weight, set her feet on the floor. "And you're thinking?"

He lifted a shoulder. "Maybe she convinced whoever it was that it would be in their best interest if they upped the ante."

He felt bad for Janey when she put it together. "You think she was blackmailing someone?"

"If I had to guess—and guesses are pretty much all we've got at the moment—yeah, blackmail's at the top of the list. It's one of the oldest motives for murder on the books."

Still absorbing and sorting, she ran a hand through her hair. "What about the car? Did he find out anything about her driving record?"

"Nothing. She was never involved in a vehicle-related accident."

She sniffed, sat back. "So, there goes the notion that someone might have used a Pontiac Lemans for retaliation."

"Pretty much, yeah. Look, Janey," he said, reluctant but determined it was time to tell her the rest. "There's more.

"It's bad," he added, and watched her physically brace herself. "Those names . . . the four women on the list?"

"You found them?"

"Dallas found them." He'd located the fourth woman just this morning. Jase met her eyes. "They're dead. All four of them."

Her face drained of all color. "Oh, God. When?"

"Within a couple days of your mother."

She swallowed, closed her eyes. "H- . . . how?"

"At first glance it appears they were all accidents. But like I said last night, there's no such thing as coincidence. We figure there's a good chance they were murdered."

"Like my mother." Her voice was so soft he barely heard her.

She rose, hugging herself, and walked toward the dormant fireplace as if she were turning toward it for heat despite the July night. "Jesus. *Jesus.* What kind of an animal goes around killing people at will?"

It killed him to see her so tormented. And he wasn't finished with his grisly revelations yet. He rose. Went to her. Turned her into his arms.

"You need to be strong, now. Because it gets worse."

She stiffened, stopped breathing.

There was nothing for it but for him to tell her.

"Janey . . . they found Sanders. I'm sorry. I'm so sorry, sweetheart." He hugged her hard against him. "He's dead."

When Jase woke up, it was dead-of-night black. He was stretched out on his side on the leather sofa. Janey was wrapped in his arms.

And he knew instinctively that he was the only one who'd been sleeping. He kissed her temple, then pressed his forehead there. "How you doing?"

"I'm okay," she whispered. "Go back to sleep."

He yawned, stifled a whole body stretch, and shook the cobwebs out of his head. "I'm good. Just needed a little combat nap."

And she was going to need a shrink before this was all over, Jase thought when she turned onto her side to face him, wedging her knee between his thighs and snuggling close.

Her knees had buckled after he'd told her about Sanders. That was how they'd ended up on the sofa. He'd laid her down and wrapped himself around her, then reluctantly answered the rest of her questions.

Sanders's body had been found in an alley not far from the hotel. His throat had been cut.

If she had cried, Jase wouldn't have been as worried about her as he was. But she hadn't cried. Not one tear. She'd just started trembling. Trembling so hard he'd been afraid she'd splinter into a million little pieces.

So he'd held her. Just held her. And then he'd had the balls to fall asleep. While she'd been wide awake hurting.

Some hero he was.

"It's okay to cry, Janey," he said, stroking her hair.

"It won't solve anything. It won't bring my mom back. Or Neal. And it won't make this all go away."

"No. But the release might do you good."

"This is doing me good." She tilted her head back so he could see her face. "Feeling you. Being held by you."

How did a man fight words like that? How did a man deny the implied request? How did he resist the "please make love to me" look in her somber brown eyes?

Maybe a better man could. This one couldn't. This one didn't want to.

He lowered his head to hers. Kissed her. With less fire than feeling. With more emotion than need.

He undressed her slowly then. Learned things about her body in the candlelight that he hadn't taken time to appreciate in the dark.

Learned with his lips that the twin dimples on her lower back were sensitive, that licking her there made her shiver. Learned that the skin on the inside of her upper arm was baby soft, that the tiny strawberry birthmark on the inside of her thigh tasted sweet.

He kissed her face. Kissed her throat. Kissed every part

of her that needed special attention. Beneath her eyes. Between her breasts. Around the bruises on her ankle.

And then he made love to her with his mouth. Soft and gentle. Easy and slow. Building her pleasure with each calculated glide of his tongue over her clitoris. Heightening her sensation with finesse instead of speed, with giving instead of greed. He took his time with her, made it all about her as he guided her over the top in a slow and sensual ride that had her melting into his mouth and destroying him with the sensual abandon in which she let him take her.

So. This really was love, he thought as he held her afterward and her heart beat like crazy against his chest.

This was love.

Now he just had to figure out what to do about it.

Sunday, July 23rd

Janey woke up in bed. Alone. Feeling relaxed and limp as a noodle and a little sore between her legs.

Blissfully sore, she thought with a dreamy smile, remembering the way Baby Blue had made love to her last night.

Remembering and aching to have him love her that way again. And knowing what had provoked him to be the way he'd been. So tender and giving. So unrelentingly determined to destroy her with the most exquisite pleasure she'd ever experienced.

Just sex?

"I don't think so, Baby Blue," she said aloud as she tossed back the covers and headed for the shower in the master bath.

Time, she told herself, would tell. He wasn't much for words, this man who was determined to keep his distance but just couldn't seem to make that happen. He cared about her. Had reached out to her when she'd been hurting—over Neal's death. Over the disaster that was suddenly her life.

In the meantime, she could wait him out. Wait for him to figure out what she already knew. He loved her. He couldn't make love to her like that if he didn't. Yeah, she could wait. And think about all the things he made her feel.

It beat thinking about Grimm, she thought as the hot water stung the cuts on her ankle.

But think about him she did as she dressed and headed downstairs, tensing up again over the prospect of what disaster this day had in store for them.

H e bellied down on the rise overlooking the log lodge and focused the binocs.

First-class digs, he thought, ignoring the biting pain in his shoulder. Ignoring the blood that had started seeping from the dressing.

He still couldn't believe that the bitch had shot him. Couldn't fucking believe it. She wasn't what he'd thought she was. He'd thought she was as soft as her name. Sweet Baby Jane.

But she wasn't. Wasn't anything like what he'd thought. And she shouldn't have shot him. It was a humiliation.

And it was going to be the end of her.

Yeah, the game had changed that night in the cave. And what he'd wanted from her before was a far cry from what he wanted now.

Now, he just wanted her dead.

By midnight, she would be. Her and her guard dog.

A fly buzzed around his head. He ignored it, concentrated on committing the lay of the land to memory. He did his best work at night. And when he got done with them tonight, there wouldn't be a body part big enough to identify.

He was saving his best work for last. He rubbed absently at his shoulder where the round from his own weapon had ripped open his flesh. Yeah. He had something special in mind for Janey Perkins. Something that had been a long time coming.

On elbows and knees, he backed away from the ridge. He needed to get somewhere and stop the bleeding. Needed something to stall the infection he felt building inside him and ripping through his body like shards of glass.

Then he'd be back. After dark. After he'd rested. After he'd worked out his plan of action.

There were a number of ways he could take both of them out. He just had to figure out the most satisfying. By nightfall he would. And then it would be all over but the headlines after the remains of their lifeless bodies were found.

Jase stood by the wall of glass windows making up the front of the lodge, looking through a pair of binocs. He scanned the rock-and-aspen-lined ridge about 150 yards from the lodge, searching for a flash of light. The one he'd seen moments ago—like sun glinting off glass.

Nothing. There was nothing there now. Maybe it had been a play of light and shadows. And maybe someone was up there.

"Hey," Janey said behind him.

He lowered the binocs, turned at the sound of her

voice—totally unprepared for the emotions that slammed through him at the look of her standing at the foot of a staircase crafted of mountain pine.

She looked as bright and clean as a shiny penny. Her hair was damp from a shower; she'd pulled it back into a long tail at her nape. Her face glowed all pink and pretty against an emerald-green top that she'd tucked into snug jeans. Her feet were bare. Everything about her shouted vitality and verve and unembellished confidence.

Everything but her eyes. Her eyes gave away what she was feeling. A shy hesitance. A reluctant uncertainty.

And he felt a stab of guilt. He'd put that look in her eyes. He'd turned away from her after the first time they'd made love. Had told her they had no future after the second.

He still didn't know if they had a future but no way could he keep his distance this morning.

"Come here," he said gruffly. When she lingered on the bottom step, he went to her instead.

And held her. Just held her, wallowing in the mountain-stream scent of her hair, in the warmth of her incredible, responsive body, reveling in the way she clung to him.

And for the moment, it was enough. Enough that she understood she was more to him than hot sex and an assignment. Enough that when he pulled away and looked into her eyes, she understood he was in far deeper than he wanted to be. Enough that she knew they were closer to a beginning than they were to an end—but that he had a lot of sorting to do. A lot of thinking—once he got her out of this alive.

"How are you?" He touched the back of his knuckles to the delicate rise of her cheekbone.

"Good. I'm good."

Her mother was dead. A friend was dead. Max Cogan

was in debt up to his eyeballs with the mob—Jase hadn't broken that news yet—and there was a trail of bodies that he suspected would eventually lead to her.

But she was good. Sure she was.

He let it pass. No good would come from pointing out the obvious.

Arm around her shoulders, he walked her toward the kitchen. Sat her down at the table and fed her again. He really liked feeding her.

"Other than in the cave," he began, swinging a chair around so the back faced the table, then straddling it, "have you ever shot a gun?"

"That would be a no," she admitted after swallowing a bite of strawberry. The cross hanging just above her cleavage caught the sunlight shining through the window. "Are we going to need to change that?"

"Grimm hasn't shown up anywhere," he said, passing on information No had given him in an early-morning phone call. "That means one of three things. He's dead, holed up somewhere licking his wounds, or on the move."

Her face drained to pale. "Dead?"

He knew what she was thinking. The same thing he'd thought the first time he'd pulled a trigger and a heart had stopped beating.

"Janey—he was going to kill you. He would have killed me, too. You don't have to justify. You don't have to second-guess. If he's dead, it was his doing, not yours."

She nodded, but her eyes told the tale. The thought of taking a life horrified her.

"How did you do it?" Huge brown eyes turned on his. "How did you go to war? How do you—"

"Live with myself knowing that people are dead because of me?"

She swallowed. Nodded.

"The world is full of bad guys. Whether they're terrorists, jihadists, psychopaths . . . doesn't matter. If we don't
kill them, they won't think twice about killing us. It's a
job. It has to be done."

"And you . . . get used to it?"

"Never. But you deal with it. And you move on."

At least you tried. He knew of guys. Guys who had
come back, couldn't cope, couldn't compartmentalize.
Some of them ended up dead. Some were drunks. Some
were twisted.

He'd come close on all counts. And he thanked God
every day that he'd pulled out of the abyss.

22

They spent a better part of the day doing target practice. Janey had proven to be a pretty good shot. Then, rifles in hand, they'd hiked up the rise to the spot where Jase thought he'd seen that flash of light.

"What do you think?" Janey asked as he searched the area.

"Someone was definitely here. Could have been a hiker or a hunter." He squatted down on his heels to touch the scrub grass, study the indentation that could have been made by a man lying on his belly watching them through a pair of binocs—or a rifle scope.

"Or it could have been Grimm," she finished what Jase hadn't wanted to say.

He shook his head. "I still can't figure it. How he keeps finding you."

She looked up at him, squinting against the sunlight that glinted off her cross.

And that's when it hit him.

Man. Oh man. How the hell did I miss it?

He grabbed her hand. "Come on. We need to get back to the lodge. There's something I want to check out."

Fifteen minutes later, they stood under the canned lighting in the well-lit kitchen.

He reached out, lifted the cross away from chest. "You started wearing this . . . when? After your mother died, right?"

She nodded, looking confused.

"Ever take it off?"

"No. Not since I found it."

His mind flashed back to another sunny day.

"That day in Atlantic City. The day we ran on the beach. You didn't wear it then."

She frowned, then followed his gaze downward to the cross. "That's right. You made me take it off along with the rest of—"

"Of the bling," he finished. "And when we came back, Grimm had been in your room.

"Take it off," he said.

Sensing his urgency, she reached behind her and unclasped the chain.

"Fuck," he muttered after he'd inspected the cross.

"What?"

"See this?" He held the piece of fake gold jewelry on its side. A seam was clearly visible. "I'm guessing if we pop this apart, a transmitter is going to fall out."

"Transmitter?"

"A receiver for a tracking device," he clarified. "I need to check it out, Janey."

"Christ," he said a few minutes later. He'd carefully pried the two halves of the cross apart and now held a tiny piece of metal on the tip of his finger. "No wonder the bastard shows up everywhere you do. When he broke into your suite that day, he must have planted this in the necklace. He's been tracking you every step of the way since."

"Which means he could be watching us right now," Janey said, her gaze locked on his.

"Yeah. That's exactly what it means."

*I*t *was too easy. Like catching fish in a barrel,* he thought as he lowered the black ski mask over his face and crept through the midnight dark to the log lodge.

There he waited, his back plastered against an exterior wall. And he listened. Silence. Nothing but silence.

He felt strong again. Rested. The bleeding had stopped. The antibiotics had started to kick in. It never ceased to amaze him that local yokels who ran businesses in these Podunk cowboy towns thought a locked door meant protection. The back door to the pharmacy was wood, for God's sake. He could have busted it down with one kick. A pick kit had been just as effective—and quieter.

The two of them—*Janey and her bodyguard,* he thought with disdain—were asleep inside. He was 99 percent certain of it. He'd watched from the ridge for several hours as they'd moved through the house—cozy as hell— before darkness fell and they finally walked up the stairs. A light had come on in an upper-story window—in a bedroom where they had probably fucked like rabbits.

There weren't any lights on now. Hadn't been for two hours. He hadn't minded the wait. Not after biding his time this long.

He pulled the Glock out of his belt. He wasn't messing with a rifle this time. Too cumbersome. The Glock wasn't his weapon of choice, but it would do. And the knife tucked into the sheath in his boot would provide entertainment after.

Quiet as a cat, he moved to the rear of the lodge and what he'd determined was the kitchen door. It was locked. He'd expected it to be. Just as he'd expected the electronic security system. He took care of that with a quick snip of wire cutters to the electrical box hidden behind a network of vines.

Then he took out the electricity and phone, halfway wishing for more of a challenge. Rich people. They paid thousands for security systems, then relied on the local Barneys to come to their rescue when a system was breached.

He'd be long gone before the Jackson Hole police department responded to the silent alarm. And Janey Perkins and her "bodyguard" would be long dead.

His heart was pumping—a nice adrenaline rush—by the time he slipped inside. Waited. Listened. Then proceeded toward the stairs.

At the top of the landing he stopped again. Waited again. Listened again. Dead quiet. Exactly the way he wanted it.

They were exactly where he wanted them, too, as he slowly eased open the bedroom door with the barrel of the Glock and slipped inside.

He could just make out the outline of two figures huddled together beneath a snow-white comforter. And if he acted now, he'd be on a flight out of here in forty-five minutes.

He lifted the gun, mouthed a silent, *Adios, suckers*, and squeezed off six rounds without batting an eye.

His shoulder was still vibrating from the recoil and the acid scent of gunpowder permeated the air when he slipped a penlight out of his breast pocket. He walked to the bed and whipped back the covers.

"What the—"

"Drop the gun."

He whipped around, aimed the Glock toward the direction of the voice—and heard, more than felt, the report of the rifle that was pointed dead center at his chest.

The pain was a vague, nebulous sensation as he lifted his hand and felt the wet, gaping hole directly over his heart. The cold, however, was dramatic and intense as he felt his legs buckle and he crumpled to the floor.

The darkness, when it came, was cavernous and vast.

He was a dead man. After all he'd been. After all he'd done. He was a dead man.

And the bitch of it was, he hadn't even seen it coming.

I t wasn't Grimm.
It wasn't Grimm.

Janey couldn't believe it. Could hardly believe the man who had been trying to kill her was dead—and that they were alive. If it hadn't been for Wilson's intuition and planning, they probably wouldn't be.

"Got a feelin'," he'd said shortly after he'd discovered the tracking device in her cross.

And then he'd told her what he planned to do.

"He's not going to strike in the daylight. If he'd planned to, he'd have done it today. He's going to come after us after dark—like the night viper he is."

He'd kept her calm through the rest of the afternoon. Made certain they were just visible enough, just long enough, that if anyone had been watching them, he'd never get a clear shot through the windows. Made sure he was always close beside her, always between her and a possible bullet.

The two hours they'd spent in the dark in the upstairs bedroom behind the door had felt like two decades.

"If you hear anything—anything at all," Baby Blue had whispered close to her ear, "tell me."

She'd understood then how concerned he was about his hearing loss. Turned out, he didn't have to worry. She'd actually dozed off—amazing—and he'd awakened her with a finger to her lips and a nod toward the door.

That was when she'd heard it. Above the frantic beat of her heart, she'd heard the faint sound of footsteps on the floor outside the bedroom door.

She'd heard the shots all right. Flinched and bit her lip to keep from crying out when the gunman had stood just inside the door they were hiding behind and, cold and calculating, killed the hell out of their pillows.

She shivered and snuggled closer to Baby Blue, who was on his cell phone filling Nolan in.

"No," he told Nolan again. "It wasn't Grimm. No. She's never seen this guy before. The detective on scene is going to fax a photo to Boston and Atlantic City and Tupelo. I've already called Rodman and told him he'd be hearing from you. He's agreed to fax you a copy."

She stared out the window as the last of the police cars and the hearse carrying the county ME and the shooter's body drove down the lane and out of sight. Nolan said something on the other end that she couldn't hear.

"Yeah. The receiver was on him. I'll be overnighting the transmitter to you in the morning so you can check it out. . . . Yeah, well, I thought you could do more with it than the local police. It'll be a big oops on my part if it comes to an obstruction charge, but since the guy is dead, I don't see the problem."

He hung up shortly after that.

"How you doing?" He cupped her shoulders in his hands and turned her to face him. The electricity was out, but she'd found several candles and busied herself lighting them all over the living area while he'd talked to the police.

"I don't know," she admitted. "I should feel relief. And I do . . . to a degree."

"But all this time you've been expecting Grimm," he concluded accurately.

"You think . . . you think maybe this guy . . . maybe he was the one who murdered my mother? And those women?"

"Yeah. That's what I'm thinking. Whether the police can ever tie him to any of those deaths . . . that's a different matter."

She leaned into him when he pulled her against him, kissed the top of her head. "And where does that leave Grimm in the mix?"

He squeezed her harder. "Got me, babe. But we'll get there. We'll get to the bottom of all of this. In the meantime—"

"The worst is over," she said, and prayed to God she was right.

His cell phone rang. "Wilson," he said, after fishing it out of his hip pocket.

Lost in thought, she tuned out of the one-sided conversation until she realized he'd hung up. And that he'd become very quiet.

She pulled back. Looked up and into his face. His ashen face.

"Oh, God. What now?"

"It's Max. He's in the hospital. He's had a heart attack."

*M*onday evening, July 24th, CCU waiting area, Cedars-Sinai Hospital, Los Angeles

"Janey, you're not going to do him any good if you drop from exhaustion."

Jase was worried about her. He sat on a small vinyl sofa on Janey's left. Lakesha Jones sat on her right.

"He's right, Janey. You should go home. Or go to a hotel. Get some rest."

"I'm staying," she said stubbornly, and Lakesha rolled her eyes over Janey's head.

Janey hadn't even had time to process that a man who had tried to kill her was dead, that she could have died, and that Grimm was still alive.

And now she had to deal with Max's condition.

A condition that wasn't good.

He'd had a major heart attack around ten o'clock last night following dinner with a rep from the label. The only reason Max was still alive was because they hadn't yet left the restaurant when it had happened. The maître d' had performed CPR.

Max Cogan was alive by the grace of God, it seemed. Once they'd stabilized him, they found five blocked arteries. All of which they'd fix—when and if he survived the heart attack.

If he made it through the first twenty-four hours, he might have a chance. Until then, it was heartbeat by heartbeat.

"Janey," Jase said again, and when she finally looked up at him, his heart broke.

Her face was swollen from crying. Her eyes windows of despair.

"I can't leave him. He . . . he might wake up. He'll need someone. Someone who cares about him."

Jase understood. Max was family. The only family she had now. And there was no way in hell she was going to let Jase pry her away from his side.

"Okay. Fine," he murmured with a gentleness that he hadn't known he had in him. "But you're going to eat something. And then you're going to sleep. The staff knows to wake you if he comes around."

"I'll run down to the cafeteria and get something for both of you," Lakesha offered.

Jase nodded his thanks and pulled Janey back against him, pushing her head down onto his shoulder as if he could will her to sleep.

"What about you?" She leaned back against him as another couple entered the waiting area, their eyes just as strained, their hearts just as heavy. There was only one reason anyone sat in this room done in subdued colors of blue, rose, and gray.

They were waiting for someone to live. Or waiting for someone to die.

"I'm fine. I'm a big, tough bodyguard type, remember?"

"Yeah," she said, and he finally felt her relax against him. "I remember."

They sat in silence for a long time. Neither of them had slept in over twenty-four hours. Jase knew she was running on fumes. His tank wasn't exactly full, either, but he'd trained for this in the Rangers. He was used to it. She wasn't. And she was almost asleep when a nurse came out. The shift had changed an hour ago, so Jase didn't recognize her.

"Is there anyone here for Max Cogan?"

Janey shot awake. Jase stood when she did. "We are," Janey said.

"Janey Perkins," Jase said, introducing her to the nurse. "I'm Jason Wilson."

"I'm Shelly. And I've got good news. He's awake," she said cheerily. "And he's asking for you."

Janey rushed toward the CCU door.

"I'm sorry." The nurse stopped her with a hand on her arm and a sympathetic look. "He's asking for Mr. Wilson."

Janey stopped, stricken. Hugged her arms around her ribs.

Jase squeezed her arm. Smiled in reassurance, although he was as puzzled as she was as to why Max had summoned him and not her.

"You'd better hurry," Shelly said. "He may not be awake and alert for long."

He was awake long enough, Jase thought with a grim set to his mouth when he left Max five minutes later. He'd been awake long enough to turn Janey's world upside down again.

Desperate. Max Cogan was desperate. And he'd made Jase the designated proxy to level the blow of just how desperate Max was.

As Jase walked back into the waiting room and saw the concerned, expectant look on her face, he only hoped she was strong enough to keep it from knocking her down.

G ambling?" Janey looked stunned as she sat on her leather sofa, the dogs lying contentedly at her feet, the cat purring on her lap.

They'd returned to her Malibu beachhouse a couple of hours after Max had come clean to Jase.

"Max has a gambling problem?"

"Apparently a big one," Jase said, wondering how much more she could possibly take.

He handed her a bottle of water that he'd just pulled out of the fridge, thinking he was glad that he'd kept his mouth shut when No had called him in Iowa. Glad he'd withheld the info about Max and his gambling issues. It was hurting Janey bad enough to hear it now in the form of a confession from Max. It would have hurt more if Max hadn't been the one to spill the beans on himself.

Jase hadn't wanted to talk about Max's confession at the hospital. Not with Lakesha there. Not until he had

Janey where she could have some privacy to absorb this latest twist. And until the doctor had come out later with the announcement that Max had made it past the critical hour and it looked like he was on track to recovery, Jase hadn't been able to budge her from the hospital.

"Why didn't I know this? How could I not have known?"

"Shame motivates. Max is ashamed of his habit. He hid it well because of that. He never intended for you to know."

"And he was making what he thought was a deathbed confession?"

"He was trying to save your life."

She blinked up at him.

He let out a deep breath and sat down on the arm of the sofa. She looked small and breakable and ruined as he related the story Max had told him. How he'd gotten in deep with a bookie by the name of Herb Meyers—how Herb turned out to be mob-connected and how Max had gotten into them for two hundred thousand dollars. And the hard part, how Max had planned to "borrow" the money from Janey and hope she never found out.

"Only Max had a change of heart," Jase told her, watching her face, wishing he could fix all the things that were so very wrong in her life. "In the end, he couldn't do it. He couldn't steal from you. So this Meyers guy came after him again—Max spotted him at the restaurant. That's what prompted the heart attack."

"Why didn't Max come to me? Why didn't he ask me for the money? I would have given it to him. He knows I would have given it to him."

"He loves you," Jase said simply. "He didn't want to let you down—like your mother let you down, he said."

"So he figured stealing from me was the way to go?" Anger bled into the hurt and confusion.

Jase understood. And sympathized. "It's hard to see any good in this, but remember, he couldn't do it. And the only reason he felt desperate enough to even consider it was because Meyers had made threats—threats involving your life. That's why Max called me so often. He'd never give me any specifics—but I sensed that he was desperate. Now I know why he didn't want to talk about it over the phone."

"So . . . so you're thinking the man . . . the man who tried to kill us at the lodge . . . that this Meyers person sent him?"

"When I told Max about it, he seemed to think so, yes. As payback for Max not coming through."

"That's our answer then?" Her eyes looked dead. "Meyers hired an assassin to kill me because Max didn't pay up?"

"I'd like to think so," Jase said, wishing he could work up some enthusiasm for the idea. "It would put a period to this sentence."

"And to make certain Meyers doesn't send someone else, the simple answer would be that I just pay off Max's debt and the story is over."

Jase looked at her carefully. And knew she didn't buy that idea any more than he did.

"Or it would be," she continued, "if Neal wasn't dead. If Grimm weren't still on the loose. If there weren't four dead women whose names just happened to be on a list in my mother's lockbox."

Her mother, who was also dead, Jase thought, knowing she was thinking the same thing.

Jesus, what a mess. What a fucked-up, deadly mess.

He watched as she sank deeper into her sofa, hugging Cat to her breast . . . and all the while, his "got a bad feeling" feeling ramping up about one hundred clicks.

23

Same day, Sioux Falls, South Dakota

Dallas checked the address, parked his rental car, and walked up the sidewalk toward the neat little ranch house on the south end of the city.

A petite dark-haired woman answered the door. He saw the resemblance to her mother immediately. Emma Richards looked very much like the photograph Dallas had found of Candice Richards—the second woman on Alice Perkins's list.

The woman he'd been too late to save. She'd died three days ago. In her own garage, of an apparent accidental carbon monoxide poisoning.

"Can I help you?"

"Miss Richards? I'm Dallas Garrett. I called earlier. About your mother?"

"Of course. Please." She stepped aside, hesitant but still inviting him in. "Come in. Although I really don't know how I can help you, Mr. Garrett."

She offered a hand toward a chair, an indication for Dallas to sit down.

"I appreciate your time. And I'm truly sorry about your mother."

Tears formed in her eyes as she sat opposite him on a delicate floral sofa done in pinks and greens. "It's . . . such a shock, you know."

Yeah. He knew. "I'm sure it is. And believe me, I wouldn't intrude at a time like this if it wasn't important."

"What is it that you think I can help you with?"

Since all of the women on the list were dead, Dallas had decided to question their children. Emma Richards was the first. He fished the list of names out of his pocket. "Do any of these names mean anything to you?"

She studied the list, her brows furrowed over deep brown eyes. "No," she said, shaking her head. "I don't . . ." She paused, frowned. "Wait. Maybe. I'm thinking my mother may have mentioned—" Her eyes widened in alarm and she cut herself off.

"Your mother may have mentioned what?"

She tucked her lower lip between her teeth, handed him back the list. "I'm sorry, Mr. Garrett. I don't think I can help you."

Dallas felt all of his antennae rise to attention. *Jackpot.* This woman knew something. The trick was going to be convincing her she needed to tell him.

"I think you can," he said gently. "I think you need to. I arrived too late to save your mother, but—"

"Wait. What . . . what do you mean? Too late to save my mother?"

He met her dazed frown. "I don't think your mother's death was an accident, Miss Richards. I think she was murdered. Just like the other women on this list. And if we don't act fast, yet another woman may die."

All the color drained from her face.

"And I think," he added when it was clear the urgency of the situation had set in, "that you might have some information that could keep her alive."

S ame night, New York City, Marriott
     McCoy was such a prick, Chris Ramsey thought as she rode the elevator to the tenth floor for their eight o'clock meeting.

She'd been pimping McCoy for days, trying to work him into a lather that would push him over the edge so he'd do something stupid—stupid and sensational—to Janey.

Like call her out in public. Make a big scene by telling her what a bitch she was.

She was getting there, Chris thought with a smug grin as the elevator doors opened. Yeah. She was getting there. By the time the tour started up again in a little over a week, she'd have McCoy at a boiling point.

And she was going to catch it all on tape. The price for her film would skyrocket. *Ka-ching.* If McCoy actually got rough with Janey, well—she grinned, just thinking about it—all the better.

She stepped out of the elevator cab—and was almost knocked down. She felt a sharp pain in her ribs from the blow.

"Hey! Watch where you're going, creep!" she sputtered, and glared up at the asshole who'd run into her.

The crazed venom in the man's eyes stole her breath. She stumbled backward, punched in the gut by sheer, instant terror.

For the first time in her adult life, she wondered what it would feel like to die. Just when she thought she was going to find out, he took off down the hall, disappeared through an exit stairwell door.

"Christ," she said, working to catch her breath as an unprecedented weakness threatened to buckle her knees. "Jesus H. Christ."

His eyes. She'd never seen such rage.

And that's when it hit her. She recognized him.

Holy fuck. He was Janey Perkins's stalker. After the incident in Atlantic City, the cute little bodyguard had had Edwin Grimm's picture circulated to everyone who had contact with Janey.

Still reeling with that knowledge, wondering what in the hell Grimm was doing here, Chris stumbled toward McCoy's room.

Then she felt her heart kick up about a hundred beats per when she reached the door. And found it ajar.

Wrong. Everything was wrong. Grimm. The open door. The catch of her breath. The jerk, crash, jerk of her heartbeat. The stabbing pain in her side.

"McCoy?"

Even before she pushed the door all the way open, she knew he wasn't going to answer. Derek McCoy lay prone on his back on the floor, a brilliant red stain bleeding from his throat onto the plush white carpet.

Dead, she thought, mesmerized by the blood flowing from McCoy's throat . . . suddenly aware of the blood dripping to pool at her feet.

In a dazed sort of comprehension, she looked down at the hand she hadn't even realized she held against her ribs.

It was covered in blood. Her blood.

"Bastard," she swore, and, stumbling into the room, crashed against the desk. "That bastard is not going to kill me, too."

She reached for the phone. Fumbled with the receiver, followed it down when it fell to the floor.

She dragged the base of the phone down with her. Punched zero.

And begged them to come for her. To not let her die like this.

*T*he next night, Janey's Malibu beachhouse
      Janey stared solemnly at the TV, petting Cat, the dogs sleeping at her feet, still feeling marginally dazed over the news about Max. It hurt. Hurt to know that someone she loved had been about to betray her. Hurt more to know that Max had almost died.

Too many deaths. Too much drama. Still too many unknowns. Like was she out of danger now that the assassin was dead?

Assassin. Lord. Max's loan sharks had sent an assassin to kill her.

"His name is Alex Marshall," Baby Blue had told her after he'd received a report from the police. "He's a known gun for hire. Had been on the FBI's most wanted for four years."

He was also an ex-cop.

"How does that happen?" she'd asked Jase. "How does someone who protected and served . . ."

"Turn rogue?" he'd finished for her when she'd found herself at a loss to comprehend. "Who knows. Something must have clicked off inside him," he'd offered, and they'd left it at that.

"The main thing is," he'd continued, "that he's not a threat to you anymore."

"And as soon as they know I'm going to pay Max's debt, Meyers and his pals are out of the picture, too, right?"

"Right," he'd said, but something in his eyes hadn't been all that reassuring.

That's why she was sitting here. Watching a plastic-faced and polished reporter stare earnestly into the camera, her long sable hair perfectly coiffed, her makeup flawless.

"In our top news story tonight, we'll take you to Santa Monica, where one of the biggest news makers of the year, the Reverend Samuel Black, is staging the latest and, might I add, largest revival service in the history of his ministry."

"Why are you watching that crap?"

Janey looked up over her shoulder as Baby Blue came into the room.

"I'm turning over a new leaf. As long as my life is in the crapper, I've decided to become a narcissist."

"Not funny," he said with a concerned look.

"Sorry. It's the best I can do."

She watched him walk across the living area to the kitchen. He'd just showered. His chest was still wet. He was barefoot and wearing only a pair of faded jeans.

But even the sight of his lean hips and broad bare back couldn't rouse her out of her funk. She barely smiled when he handed her a bottle of water and popped the top on his can of Coke.

"Charles Crocker is in Santa Monica now to bring us that story," the reporter went on with a practiced smile. "Charles, what's happening there?"

"Well, Shawna, as you can hear in the background, it's a night for an old-fashioned revival. The tents are up, the choir is singing, and the Reverend Black is breaking records with his 'take it to the people' crusade. Have a listen to this interview we taped with him earlier today."

Janey sipped from her water bottle, aware of Baby Blue easing a hip onto the arm of the sofa beside her as the camera cut to a pristine white backdrop upon which hung a slim gold cross. The Reverend Samuel Black, in all of his spiritual glory, entered the shot, his salt-and-pepper hair groomed to perfection, his smile benevolent and serene, his manner godly in his black robe.

"You've got quite a gathering here tonight, Reverend," a reporter stated off camera. "To what do you attribute your ever-increasing popularity?"

"I am but a shepherd," the reverend said modestly. "It's my responsibility to lead my flock—and they have been looking for leadership for a very long time."

"You've expressed very definitive views on everything from politics to music," Charles prompted.

"I have indeed. We are in the midst of a moral decline, much of which I fully attribute to the music the young people are forced to listen to today."

Here it comes, Janey thought. *He's going to let me have it.*

"You've been a vocal critic of rock. To the point of singling out certain artists."

"Sweet Baby Jane and her ilk are not artists. They are the devil's spawn. They will know retribution someday. In the meantime I merely attempt to steer my flock back to the right path."

The shot flipped back to the studio. "Thank you, Charles. And thank you, Reverend Black, for your insights."

"Pious bastard."

Janey glanced up as Jase touched a hand to her hair. "You okay?"

"It's funny. I've had a lot of time to think lately . . . you know. Childhood stuff. Anyway, it's ironic that Black decided to single me out because I remember how my mom used to watch him on TV on Sunday mornings. How she used to watch him and cry."

She lifted a shoulder, let it drop. "Sunday morning penance for a drunk Saturday night. I think she always wanted to be a better person and when she listened to him, it made her realize how . . . well, how far she was from the person she wanted to be. I even remember that once, she took me with her to one of his tent revivals."

Janey laughed, but there was no humor in it. "She even tried to get backstage to see him. Funny, huh? That she was a follower—and he considers me evil."

She was beyond anger. Beyond reaction. Or at least she thought she was.

Shawna's voice cut into her thoughts. "And now to a breaking story that's just come across the wire. Ironically, it's about Sweet Baby Jane's drummer, Derek McCoy."

Janey froze, her attention drawn back to the TV at the mention of Derek's name.

"Word out of New York is that McCoy was found with his throat cut in a Times Square hotel earlier tonight. Christine Ramsey, another intended victim of McCoy's murderer, discovered the body and was herself stabbed in the process."

Janey couldn't believe what she was hearing. Beside her, Baby Blue swore.

"Ms. Ramsey is resting in satisfactory condition in the hospital after identifying her attacker and McCoy's killer as one Edwin Grimm, an ex-convict who had been recently released from prison where he'd served time for stalking rocker Sweet Baby Jane.

"We have it from a source on the NYPD that Grimm has been apprehended and freely confessed to not only the murder of Derek McCoy and his attempted murder of Chris Ramsey but also the murder earlier this week of Neal Sanders, another member of Ms. Perkins's entourage. In addition, Grimm produced a list of individuals he had targeted for murder, stating that they all stood in

the way of a relationship with Ms. Perkins—a relationship that Grimm maintains Jesus had ordained.

"One wonders what the Reverend Black might have to
say on this turn of events," Shawna added with a veiled
smile. "And now, on to other news . . ."

J ase was worried about her. Since the news report
had aired on Derek McCoy's death, Janey had been
quiet. Too quiet except for several guilt-ridden statements.

"Derek . . . he was a bastard sometimes, but he didn't
deserve to die. Not on my account."

Jase understood why she was blaming herself. What he
couldn't comprehend was how to convince her that she
was blameless. It was a hard sell.

"Not my fault? Both Neal and Derek are dead," she'd
countered when he tried. "Chris Ramsey is in serious
condition."

"And as I've told you before, you have no control over
the workings of a madman's mind."

She'd just curled into herself on the sofa and closed
her eyes. That had been an hour ago. Even the news from
the hospital that Max was rallying and they were very en-
couraged hadn't roused her.

Time, Jase thought. She just needed some time. To
rest. To heal. To accept that her nightmare was officially
over.

And then his phone rang—and the news Dallas Garrett
fed him jarred him right out of that little fantasy with the
impact of a gut punch. If Dallas was right about his conclusions, not only wasn't the nightmare over, but it had
just begun.

♦ ♦ ♦

Five minutes later, Jase ripped the fax that Dallas had sent free of the machine.

"Jesus," he muttered, dragged a hand over his face and walked toward the living room, where Janey was still curled up on the sofa with her cat.

"Who called?"

He looked up. Breathed deep. "It was a fax. From Dallas."

Jase watched as she slowly sat up. Watched her stretch and shake the sleep from her stiff limbs.

"More news of madness and mayhem?"

He looked at her long and hard. Long enough and hard enough that she slowly shook her head. "God," she said, comprehending. "That was supposed to be a joke."

Jase folded the faxed page in his hand, walked around the sofa, and sat down beside her.

"I need you to bounce one more time, babe," he told her.

"Nope." She shook her head. "I'm all bounced out."

"Wish I could give you that, but you need to hear this."

She leaned back against the cushions, drew her knees to her chest, and hugged them. "I reserve the right to tune out whenever I want to."

He'd give anything to spare her this. "Dallas called while you were asleep. He finally connected the dots on the list. Long story short, he talked to the daughter of one of the victims and found some links."

"Such as," she said, lifting her head.

"Such as, he'd already figured out that all of the women had children. All of them about your age. All of them spread across the country. But the mothers all lived in Mississippi at the time of conception."

When she frowned, he continued. "When he dug deeper, Dallas found that all of these children were illegitimate, fathers unknown."

"And now all of their mothers are dead. Which leads you to what conclusion?" she asked warily.

"That they shared the same father."

He waited for that to settle.

"A father," he continued when she'd latched on, "who has apparently gone to great lengths to ensure his ID wasn't discovered."

"By having the mothers all killed," she concluded. "Jesus. What kind of a monster would do that?"

"Someone who has a lot to lose if he's identified. Someone your mother may have been blackmailing to guarantee her silence."

Janey stared into space. Sifting, digesting. "So . . . the money in her lockbox? And Lemans?"

"I have to eat a few words, but it's looking like that was coincidental. The real target wasn't the money, but the list."

She shook her head. "To what end? He obviously knew who they were? He killed them."

"Maybe the list was your mother's bargaining chip. Maybe she was threatening to make it public. After he had her killed, he might have decided to make certain that the list never saw the light of day. I mean—think about it. Every single one of those deaths was made to look like an accident—including your mother's."

"So . . . it wasn't the loan sharks after all? I became a target because . . . because my own father was willing to kill me for a list of names?"

He couldn't imagine the pain she was going through. "Yeah," he said gently. "Yeah, it looks that way."

She dragged both hands through her hair. "Who is he? God or something? A senator?" she speculated, glancing his way for answers. "The governor?"

Jase exhaled, unfolded the fax. "You were closer the first time. This is a picture one of the children remembered her mother kept. A picture her mother had always told her was her father." He held it out to her.

She took it with a trembling hand. Stared, then went pale.

It wasn't as old as the photo they'd found in Alice Perkins's lockbox. In fact, it was fairly recent, but the resemblance was there. Unmistakable, at least to Jase.

He saw the moment recognition dawned on Janey, too.

"Oh, God." She looked up from the photo, disbelief warring with the heartbreaking acceptance in her eyes. "It's Black."

Yeah. The Reverend Samuel Black.

"IIe's my father?"

"So it would seem." Just as it seemed Black wanted her dead.

A single tear trickled down her cheek as Jase pulled her into his arms. "Guess it wouldn't be too good for a man of God's public image if the world found out that the rocker he's been touting as the spawn of Satan turned out to be his daughter, would it?"

"I'm so sorry, babe," he murmured against the top of her head.

He was still holding her when the hair on the back of his neck stood at attention and he realized they were no longer alone.

24

I'm touched."

Jase whipped his head around—expecting to see Black standing there.

But it wasn't Black. It was his devoted, devout wife, Tonya, who stood just inside the sliders, the business end of a revolver pointed directly at Janey's head.

"Don't try to save her," Tonya cautioned when Jase moved to shove Janey behind him and the "guard" dogs lifted their heads and wagged their tails in welcome. "It's preordained, you know. She must die."

Jase froze as Tonya Black stepped fully into the room and without turning around closed the slider behind her.

The gun never wavered. Tonya Black's lacquered blond hair never moved. And the look of undiluted madness in her heavily made-up eyes told him she'd shoot them both without provocation if he made the wrong move.

"Preordained?" Jase asked carefully, all the while inching slightly forward, easing Janey back behind him.

"It truly is touching," Tonya repeated with a sad shake of her head. "But your loyalty is misplaced, young man. God's will must be done."

"I understand," Jase said, working to keep his voice supplicating, non-confrontational. "I understand why God might want Alice Perkins dead—"

"Who wouldn't understand?" Tonya interrupted, her face flaming the brilliant red of righteousness. "She was a fornicator and a whore. She was the devil's instrument. She lured and tempted and dragged Samuel down in the slime with her."

Jase felt Janey coil as tight as a spring beside him. He squeezed her leg. A caution. A plea to be quiet. To not do something stupid.

"So you hired Alex Marshall to kill her," he concluded with what he hoped passed for an appreciative nod of his head. "And to kill the others, too."

Tonya smiled. "I knew you'd figure it out eventually. You're a smart young man."

"Not smart enough to figure out why you would hire a murderer to do God's will." *Chew on that one, sister.*

As he'd hoped, his conclusion shook her. At least momentarily. "Alex Marshall was my instrument. My instrument through which I dealt the Lord's will."

"God's will?" Jase shook his head. "I've always thought God was benevolent."

She didn't much like that. The narrowing of her eyes on him told him so.

Yeah, that's the ticket. Get pissed at me, you sick old bitch. Point that gun at me.

"The Lord works in mysterious ways. Presents Himself to us mortals in varying forms—takes various forms of retribution. Alice Perkins needed to die because she had been making noises about revealing Janey's paternity. She'd been demanding more money of my husband."

"Ah. So your husband had been paying her bills."

Her face grew dark. Hatred spewed with each word. "For too long. Ever since she approached him at the revival in Tupelo years ago, he'd been depositing money in her account. You were so spoiled, child."

She glared at Janey, her attention once again devoted to her. "But you probably didn't appreciate how much better your life became once your whore of a mother started blackmailing Samuel.

"For that alone, your mother deserved to die. But when she started hinting that she knew about the other children my husband, the great prophet, had sired—well. I simply could not let that happen."

Jase had to divert Tonya's attention back his way somehow. When that gun went off, he didn't want it aimed in Janey's direction. "So where's your husband's blame here, Tonya? Why isn't the great Samuel Black on the block? Why does all the blame fall on the women?"

She cut a murderous gaze back to Jase.

That's it. That's a good old bitch. Stay pissed at me.

"My husband is subjected to horrific temptation on a daily basis. Legions of devils work on him relentlessly. They seduced him into fornicating with those pitiful, hope-starved women and producing the devil's children."

"That's why they were all killed?" Janey said, disbelieving. "Because your husband slept with them?"

"Because I could not take the chance that they would decide to talk."

"Ah," Jase nodded, "and that's because if anyone found

out that your husband is a womanizer who abandons his own children, the money might quit flowing into the ministry, right?"

Murderous transitioned to snide in the blink of an eye. "Why, yes, there is that," Tonya agreed.

"Well, you had us all fooled," Jase said, drawing her attention back to him again. "We thought it was Edwin Grimm. But you had the hearts planted, didn't you? And the note—'We're both orphans now.' The Lord must truly be on your side."

"Because I am on the side of right. And because I was smart enough to hire someone to plant those horrible bloody hearts. And yes. The note was clever."

"Very clever. But answer me something. Why didn't you just have Marshall kill Janey right away? Why the elaborate production? And why the nineteen-seventy-nine Pontiac Lemans?"

"Ah. The Lemans. It was only fitting. You were conceived in the backseat of a Pontiac Lemans; did you know that?" She averted her gaze to Janey again. "It wasn't supposed to be found. That was to be my little secret. My little private revenge."

"And Janey?" Jase asked, and repeated his question to regain Tonya's attention. "Why not kill her right away?"

"Because, young man, I didn't know where Alice Perkins's list was. And yes, she threatened my husband that she'd make it public. Until I knew whether Janey had recovered it, I had to keep her alive."

"So that was your man again in Tupelo."

"Marshall? No. Just someone I hired to do some investigating."

"And when he didn't find the list for you," Jase speculated, "you decided the path of least resistance was to kill the other women. They were, after all, expendable."

"One must do what one has to do in the cause of right."

"How is Janey on the side of wrong? She's an innocent in all of this."

"Innocent? How can the devil's spawn be innocent? Her evil comes out in her blasphemous music. Even Samuel recognizes that. He's watched Satan's words spew out of her mouth over the years. And he's known that eventually she'd have to be sent to hell, where she belongs."

"So why isn't my father here?" Janey asked defiantly.

Jase swore under his breath, and shot Janey a *Be quiet* look.

She ignored him. "Why isn't Samuel Black holding the gun? Why did he send you to do his dirty work?"

"There is nothing dirty about my work. My work is the Lord's work. In this mission, I am His instrument. And I grow weary of all this talk.

"You must die, too, of course," she said, glancing at Jase. "Pity. You're such a pretty young man."

"It will hurt my mother," he said, grasping at straws to buy some more time. "To see me die. As a mother yourself, you must know that. Must sympathize."

She drew back her shoulders, lifted her chin. "I have no children."

"No? How sad. A God-fearing woman like you. Why would the Lord deprive you of children?"

"I was . . . I was barren."

Liar. Oh yeah, I have her number now.

"Barren? Or frigid?"

Pay dirt. She glared at him, all of her attention focused in a mad, intent stare.

"Yeah, I think I'm getting the full picture here now," Jase goaded. "Couldn't be a real wife to Samuel, could you? So he had to go to other women because you wouldn't let him in your bed."

"I . . . I was not . . . frigid. I have been a good wife. A good wife."

A tear streamed down her face, leaving a macabre black track of mascara in its wake.

She lifted a hand to wipe it away—and that was when Jase made his move.

He leaped off the couch, used the coffee table for a springboard, and launched himself at Tonya. They both went down in with a crash. He heard more than felt the gun go off against his side before he reared back and did something he'd promised his mother he'd never do: He hit a woman. Hauled back and delivered a solid right hook to Tonya Black's glass jaw.

She went out like a light.

And when he rolled to his back, heard his breath whistle through the hole in his lung, it was lights-out for him, too.

The next time Jase opened his eyes, it was two days later.

"Hey," an angel said softly. An angel with brimming brown eyes and long blond hair.

"Hey," he whispered, swallowed what felt like a bucket of sand, and tried again. "Hi."

"I'm getting tired of you making me cry, Iowa."

"Not . . . worth . . . the . . . effort," he managed.

"You're going to be all right," he heard her whisper, and felt the moisture from her tears on his face before he let the darkness take him under again.

Two weeks later
"She *what*?"

Jase shoved aside the hospital sheet and was halfway out of bed before he realized he was wearing one of those ego-deflating hospital gowns that left his ass bare for the world to see.

"She canceled the rest of the tour," Max said, grinning at the sight of this burly, albeit beat-up, bodyguard grumbling about Janey's decision.

"She can't cancel. She never cancels. Not for anything."

"Never had a good reason to cancel before."

Jase looked up, saw her standing in the hospital doorway, grinning, her arms full of flowers.

"And don't you look yummy, with that incredible tush just . . . out there for the nurses to see."

"I've seen better." The day nurse—a sixty-something matron with a big laugh and a wicked gleam in her eye—followed Janey into the room. "'Course, it's been a while."

"Why did you cancel the tour?" Jase blustered after the nurse had made certain he'd swallowed his pills, and left the room.

"I thought we'd established it was because I had a good reason."

"Me?"

"You."

He fell back onto the bed with a huff. "Janey. We're talking about your career."

"My career can hold. You can't."

"I figured it was that way with you two," Max said as he stood and headed for the door. "Three's a crowd, so I'll just let you duke this out without an audience. Don't beat him up too bad, snooks. After all, he did save your life."

"You don't have to leave," Janey insisted. "We might need a referee."

"I have a feeling you'll do just fine. Besides, got a meeting to go to. I'm expected."

Jase glared at the door after Max left; then he glared at Janey.

"I'm proud of him," she said, adding the bouquet to

the dozens that already filled the hospital room. "He hasn't missed a Gamblers Anonymous meeting since he joined."

"Okay, yeah, fine. I'm happy for him. Happy that his ticker is on the mend. I'm not happy with you."

"Guess what? I don't care. Now, did you eat your dinner?"

"Hell no. The food is crap. It's like they lost the salt-shaker or something."

"Poor baby. They've abused you terribly in here, haven't they?"

"Damn straight," he grumbled. He hated this. Really, really hated being an invalid. Two weeks in a hospital bed was two damn weeks too long.

"Word on the street," she said, easing a hip onto the side of his bed, "is that if you're a real good boy, you might get sprung tomorrow."

"Then there isn't a need for you to hang around another day and play nursemaid, is there?"

An evil and intimate smile tilted her beautiful lips. "I thought you liked it when I played nursemaid."

Oh, God, did he. Just last night, she'd shown up wearing a nurse's uniform and nothing else under her long jacket. Then she'd proceeded to crawl up onto the bed, straddle him, and administer a little first aid of the mind-numbing variety.

"Janey, we have to talk."

She rolled her eyes. "Here we go with the talking again."

"You refuse to take me seriously."

"What I refuse to do is let you talk me into believing what that pea-sized brain of yours has convinced you is the right thing to do."

He let his head fall back. Closed his eyes.

"What are you so afraid of?" So much confusion, so much frustration, so much everything, colored her tone that he realized it was past time he was straight with her.

Straight with himself. He'd had a lot of think time in here. And he'd finally figured things out.

"Okay, listen. Just listen. And give me a minute to get this out."

"I've got all the time in the world," she said gently.

"It's going to sound . . . whiny."

"I don't care what it sounds like. I just want to know."

He let out a deep breath. Winced when it burned like hell and got it together. "Look . . . things don't work out for me."

"Don't work out how?"

"No questions. Just let me do this in my own time."

She lowered her head, nodded.

"Okay. It's just . . . I let people down, you know. Not just people. Important people. I don't mean to. It just . . . happens. I let No down—when I first got out of the Rangers. He wanted me to come work for him then. But I walked away.

"I always walk away. My old man. I let him down, too." He felt tears burn his eyes. He angrily wiped them away.

"And you," he continued, determined to get this out. "You're . . . important. Real important. I . . . I can't take the chance." He looked up into her beautiful brown eyes and felt his heart swell and burn. "I can't take the chance of letting you down, too."

She was silent for a long time. Thought for a long time.

"That's it?" she finally asked, sounding dumbfounded.

"Janey," he said with a measure of desperation, "did you hear what I said?"

"I heard. And I understand. I do. You're scared."

Damn straight. His big bad self was scared to death.

"So let me ask you a question."

He looked at her beautiful face. Waited.

"What scares you more, Baby Blue? The idea of letting me walk away without ever giving us a chance, or the idea of taking what we've got to the limit, risking it all on the possibility that I'm the one who's going to break your streak?"

She searched his face, waited. And he couldn't, just couldn't, make himself say what she wanted to hear. Finally, she eased off the bed and walked out the door.

And didn't come back.

Not that night.

Not the next day when they released him.

It was for the best, he told himself as he hailed a cab to take him to the airport. Break it clean. Break it now.

"Where to?" the cabbie asked.

"LAX."

"You got it."

Yeah. He got it. He got it right this time.

And getting it right hurt like hell.

When her doorbell rang, Janey told herself to get over it. Told her heart to stop with the *clank, clank, clank* already. Told her hands to stop sweating.

It wasn't him. He wasn't coming.

Making herself breathe deep, she walked to the door, flung it open.

And almost launched herself into the arms of the man looking uncertain and miserable and like he was about to leap out of a plane without a parachute.

"I was going to leave," Baby Blue grumbled, shouldering past her and into the house.

She closed the door, resisted the urge to lock it. "But you didn't."

His scowl was as black as a thundercloud. "I should have."

"Maybe."

He turned toward her, his expression grim. "You called me a pea brain."

Oh, God. Leave it to him to avoid the main issue. She shouldn't, but she grinned. "I may have, yes."

He glared at her. "Take it back."

Poor, poor baby, she thought, fighting the urge to go to him, take him in her arms, and promise him it was all going to be okay. But this was a fight he had to fight himself.

She squared her shoulders. "Give me a reason."

He looked antsy and itchy as he paced to the sliders and looked out over the ocean. "You're taking a big chance on me."

There it was. Surrender. Joy scored a direct hit to her heart. "I live for danger."

He expelled a heavy breath. "You know that I love you."

So it was true. A heart could actually swell. Hers filled her chest. "I do."

"Well?"

"Well?" She drew out the word, savoring the moment.

"I could stand to hear it, too, you know."

So much joy. So much relief. So much love embraced her as she walked to him. Framed his beautiful face between her palms and searched those baby blue eyes. "I love you, Iowa. Don't you ever doubt it."

Epilogue

West Palm Beach, two weeks later, Wes Gar-rett's backyard

Jase had heard about the Garretts' ongoing competition that they waged at family get-togethers—but until he'd been dragged into one, he hadn't believed the stories.

Cutthroat croquet. Lord Jesus God. It was one for the books.

"So, the indictments are coming down on the Blacks next week, right?"

Beside him, No held his newborn son, Conner Wesley Garrett, in one arm, a mallet in the other.

"Last I heard," Jase said. "They'll never see the light of day. Neither will Grimm."

"Ought to get the death penalty for ruining that Mustang alone," No mumbled. He'd almost cried when Jase had told him what shape it was in. "How's that videographer doing?"

"Chris Ramsey?" Jase grunted. "She's going to be fine. She finally came clean that she'd been trying to stir up trouble with McCoy."

"Yeah?"

"Yeah. But only after her conscience had gotten the best of her. She also confessed to feeding Black's camp information about Janey's schedule."

"She being charged, too?"

Jase shook his head. "No. She had no idea that Black and his wife had targeted Janey for murder. She'd just been doing her damnedest to create drama for her video."

"Which will never see the light of day," Janey added as she walked up behind Jase.

Small concession for what Ramsey had done, in Jase's mind, but at least she wasn't going to profit from her own subterfuge.

"Hey. What am I supposed to do with this?" Jase asked with a rising panic when No unceremoniously handed him the baby.

"Just hold on," Janey said, grinning. "Just hold on."

Jase smiled down at this woman who had become his life. "I plan to," he whispered, and bent to kiss her. "I plan to."

"Okay, no kissy face on the court." This from Eve, who was the reigning croquet champion and never let an opportunity pass to remind her brothers and her husband.

"She's a die-hard," Tyler "Mac" McClain said in an aside. "Leave 'em be, lady. You remember what it's like to be young and in love."

"Remind me again. When was that?"

McClain grabbed Eve around the waist, spun her toward him, and planted her with a huge, smacking kiss.

"Oh yeah," Eve said, looking dazed. "It's all coming back to me. Wait," she sputtered when McClain set her aside, then knocked her ball into the rough. "You just did that to distract me."

"Like putty in my hands," McClain announced to the group at large, which had his lovely wife calling him names that would make a Ranger blush.

"I like these people," Janey said, taking the baby from Jase when Ethan, the oldest of the Garretts, announced that it was Jase's turn.

"Don't hold up the game and you'll stay on our good side," Ethan said, and promptly scooped the baby out of Janey's arms. "Your turn, sunshine."

"For heaven's sake," Susan Garrett, the mother of this amazing group of competitors, eased the baby into her arms, "have a care with this child. You can't just pass this sweet boy off like he's a football."

"But it's croquet," all four Garretts pointed out in unison.

Susan, an older and just as beautiful version of her daughter, shook her head, then walked off with the baby, cooing her way across the yard to Wes, who was busily grilling hot dogs and burgers.

Ethan's soon-to-be wife, Darcy, and Nolan's wife, Jillian, had draped their beautiful selves in twin chaise longues. They sat with their heads together sipping lemonade and grinning at their guys.

"They are both so beautiful," Janey said, standing under the shade of a palm tree with Jase.

"That would be one of the reasons you fit right in."

"You think? You think I fit in?"

He pulled a face. "You can't be serious. Eve did everything but drool over you. And Jillian and Darcy—well, it's obvious they think you're great."

The Garretts had all accepted both Jase and Janey like they were part of the family. "It's all a bit . . . noisy, isn't it?"

"By 'it,' you mean the Garretts?"

She grinned. "Yeah. I guess I do. They're so full of life. Well, all except Dallas. He seems pretty quiet."

Jase looked Dallas's way. He was in the thick of the game, but Janey was right. Dallas was quiet. "You know that mission I told you about? The one where the three of them and Manny Ortega rescued Darcy?"

She nodded and, as she had when Jase had first told her the story of Darcy's rescue, remarked on how amazing it was.

"Well, something happened between Dallas and the other captive."

"Amy, right?"

"Yeah. She more or less disappeared after they got her back to the States. No says Dallas has been brooding ever since."

"You think he has a thing for her?"

Jase shrugged. "Yeah. Maybe."

"Sad," she said with a thoughtful sigh. "And Manny. Where is he?"

"Boston. He's a detective on the police force there. At least he was. Ethan said he called the other day, though. Kind of got the sense that Manny might have been feeling him out about the possibility of coming on board with E.D.E.N."

"Really?"

Again, Jase shrugged. "Guess time will tell."

"Speaking of time," he leaned down and nuzzled her neck, "do you know how long it's been since I made love to you?"

Her eyes flared with fire. "You make our excuses. I'll go kiss the baby good-bye."

"Hey, everyone. Thanks for the great party. We're going to split and go have wild monkey sex."

"You call that an excuse?" Janey sputtered when Jase led her out of the backyard toward the car.

"No. I call that taking a chance. You wanna make something of it?"

She snagged his hand and pulled him to a stop. "Yeah," she said and kissed him until his knees damn near buckled. "I'm going to make it darn hard for you to get home."

I could get used to this," Janey said as she stretched and snuggled deeper into the king-sized bed of the master bedroom of their rented condo overlooking Lake Worth.

Yeah, she could get used to waking up rubber-limbed and wasted from great sex and the memory of a hard warm body holding her through the night. A hard body that was currently standing in the bedroom doorway holding a breakfast tray and wearing only boxers and a slow smile.

She liked that smile. She *loved* that smile. It was spontaneous. Unguarded. Didn't set limits. Was open to possibilities. Ready to take chances.

And the list went on and on. They'd decided they needed a place in Florida, too, so Jase could be close to his job. A job he loved and intended to keep even though she had no immediate plans to renew her tour.

She found an amazing sense of peace with that decision. She wanted to write. She wanted to produce. The new home under construction would include a studio to provide those options. She planned to use the money from her mother's lockbox. Had even let herself take some comfort in concluding that her mother may have intended the money as a gift, a form of apology for what she hadn't been able to be for her.

She sat up, stretched her arms above her head, knowing full well that the sheet had dropped to her waist and she was giving Baby Blue an eyeful.

"Hey, cowboy," she purred when his eyes glazed over. "Wanna get lucky?"

His grin was cocky and slow. "Are we going to play Marshal Dillon and Miss Kitty again?"

"Yeah, and to show you what a sport I am, this time I'll let you play the marshal."

Eyes dancing, he walked toward the bed. "You're trouble, you know that?"

She snatched a slice of melon off the tray when he set it in the middle of the mattress, aware of his gaze on her breasts. "No trouble at all," she assured him, rose to her knees, and leaned over to tuck a piece of melon in his mouth.

His gaze on her, he chewed, swallowed, and opened his mouth when she leaned closer to kiss him.

"Umm. Sweet," she murmured, and slipped her tongue inside his mouth. "Fruity."

"Bite your tongue," he said with a laugh.

"I'd rather bite yours."

He pulled away, looking pleased and smug. "Stockpiled a lot of energy the last two years, haven't you?"

She laughed. "So it would seem. Am I wearing you out?"

"Never happen."

And then he proved it by taking her to the moon and back with the slow sweep of his hands, the warm glide of his body into hers.

Later, while she lay drifting, he propped himself up on an elbow, touched his fingertips to the tattoo on her biceps. "Why 'Crazy Force'?"

"Hm?"

"Why did you have 'Crazy Force' tattooed here?"

Her eyes popped open. " 'Mad Power.' It says 'Mad Power.' "

He chuckled. "Umm . . . sorry. I checked it out. Those are kanji symbols for 'Crazy Force.' And this one." He swirled a fingertip over the tattoo on her neck.

" 'Naughty Girl,' " she said, looking defensive when he laughed. "What? What's so funny?"

" 'Closed-minded woman.' "

"No," she fumed.

" 'Fraid so. Fits somehow though," he said, then grunted when she punched him in the ribs.

"I suppose you're going to tell me this one," she touched the tattoo above her right breast and looked like she was heading for a deep pout, "doesn't mean 'Soul.' "

"No," he said softly. "That one's right on the money. You have more fire and more soul than any other woman I know."

She touched his face. Cupped his cheek. "So. All this risk taking. How's this all working out for you?"

He knew what she meant. He knew exactly what she meant. "Been a bit of a letdown."

When she slugged him, he rolled her beneath him with a laugh that made her eyes shoot a different kind of fire his way.

"It's working out fine," he said, kissing her. Loving the way she softened and moved and melted underneath him. "It's working out just fine."

*Turn the page for a sneak peek at the next stunning novel
in the Bodyguards series*

UNDER THE WIRE

Coming from St. Martin's Paperbacks
in Fall 2006

Managua, Nicaragua, 17 years ago.

M anny Ortega awoke from a dead sleep. Fully alert.
All senses vibrating with awareness.

The sharp crack of breaking wood splintered the night
silence like a gunshot. A blinding light pierced his eyes.
Then the glint of a gun barrel pointed directly at his chest.

Four Sandinista soldiers stood over his bed, guns
drawn. General Jorge Poveda's men, he was certain.
Which meant he was in deep, deep trouble.

Yet Manny's first thought was to protect his lover. But
Lily was gone. He was alone in the bed. And the tangled
sheets beside him and under his palm were cold. All of
that registered peripherally as a hard boot hit him mid-
thigh.

"Get up, traitorous dog, or we will kill you where you
lay."

Manny shifted from shock to self-preservation mode. He raised his hands, smiled and did what he did best. He lied through his teeth. "Traitor? Amigos. You've got the wrong man. I'm one of you." He nodded toward their Sandinista uniforms—it was the same uniform he wore although his reason for wearing it was much different from theirs. "I am Manolo Ortega. Lieutenant Ortega."

"We know who you are, Contra pig." The butt of a rifle connected with his gut and doubled him over. "So does the General. Your American puta, she spread her legs for you, eh? And you tell her everything."

As he gasped for breath and fought the pain, Manny knew who he was, too. And he was a dead man. And he was a fool.

They let him pull on his pants then dragged him at gunpoint from the apartment. During the long walk down the stairs, he knew something else. He was betrayed.

No torture Poveda could inflict now that he knew Manny was a spy for the freedom fighters would be as painful as that truth.

Your American puta.

Lily.

They could only be talking of Lily Campora of the diamond black eyes and beautiful breasts.

He didn't want to believe them.

The sheets beside him had been cold.

Lily was gone. As if she had known they were coming for him.

Betrayed.

Tears of anger stung his eyes. No. They had to be lying. He could not bear to think that the woman he loved could have turned him in. But why else—*how* else—would Poveda have found a reason to send his squad of thugs for Manny and brand him as a traitor?

The things Manny had told Lily in this bed, he'd told no one else. So what other explanation could there be?

He couldn't think of that now. If he wanted to live, he could not think of *her* now. He had to figure out how to get out of this. Then he would deal with Lily Campora.

Anger rolled over his heartbreak. Resolve kicked him into survival mode. Talking himself free was not an option. Poveda's soldiers did not want to hear anything he had to say. He was on his way to prison—if he made it that far.

The Managua streets were midnight dark and deserted as a ghost town. The soldiers hauled him roughly to an open Jeep then took off down the pocked streets.

They'd tied his hands behind his back. The rope cut into his wrists and already he could feel the loss of circulation in his fingers. He was shirtless and his feet were bare. The business end of an AK-47 was trained dead center at his heart and he was running out of time.

He glanced at the soldier riding shotgun in the front seat. Recognized him, though he'd never met him. Garcia. He was Poveda's hatchet man. Specialized, it was said, with a stiletto and he had a penchant for using electricity to make his victims talk. He particularly loved to use it on freedom fighters.

Manny didn't recognize the driver but in the seat beside him, a young corporal watched him like a hawk, his eyes narrowed and intent on Manny's face.

Well-trained, Manny thought. Always watch a man's eyes. They were telegraphs to his thoughts. For that reason, Manny kept his eyes as blank as white paper. Didn't let on as the Jeep headed toward the outskirts of the city on the Lago Managua road that he'd figured out where they were taking him.

He'd heard of the torture camp in the jungles outside

of the city. And he knew of no one who survived it.

Miles and maybe an hour went by. The city lights grew distant. Up ahead, he saw the glimmer of moonlight off water and realized they were approaching the Rio Tipitapa bridge.

He didn't so much as glance ahead or to the side. He sat. He waited. Silent. Hunched as if still in pain from the blow to his gut and resigned to his fate. They would soon find out he was far from it.

The city lights were a memory as the Jeep hit a slight incline leading to the narrow bridge he had known was coming up. Manny counted to five then made his move.

With a sharp kick at his guard's chest, he dislodged the rifle long enough to sway the barrel away from him. It discharged wildly into the air as he stood and leaped from the moving vehicle.

He landed on the cracked pavement with a bone-jarring jolt then rolled like a square, wooden wheel. His shoulder and hip screamed in pain. He forced himself to his feet to the sound of squealing tires and guttural shouts.

He didn't wait to see if the soldiers had drawn on him. Off balance with his hands tied, he vaulted to the stone rail of the bridge. Without a backward glance, he launched himself toward the Tipitapa, flowing fifteen feet below.

The night exploded in a hail of gunfire just before he hit the surface of the rapidly running river. The cold and the current sucked him under and he shot toward the riverbed like a bullet.

He sank like a stone, found the silty bottom with his feet and praying he had the lung power, pushed off.

He surfaced on a gasping breath. Shook the water from his eyes and for the first time since Poveda's men had shattered his sleep and his illusions about Lily, he found something to smile about. The swift running current had already carried him fifty yards downriver from the bridge. There was no way they could spot him in the inky black night.

His smile was short-lived. The current sucked him under in a vortex of speed and darkness. Without the use of his arms, the river rolled him like a deadhead—a water logged stump—spinning him out of control. The harder he fought, the deeper the river took him.

He forced himself to relax, to sink to the bottom again then he pushed off with a prayer. He broke the surface with a gasp, coughing muddy water and sucking air. He was a good hundred yards downriver now and the jungle had thickened, closing in on the meandering river as the current flowed toward Lago, Nicaragua, a hundred miles down stream.

It wasn't until his third trip down that he figured out what to do. The only way to fight the current and gravity was to go with it. When he surfaced, he spread his legs, used them as rudders and rode the river.

With concentrated effort, he let himself be a log instead of fighting that fact that he was one. Logs float. So he floated. Coughing and spitting and gasping for air. Sometimes on his back. Sometimes on his belly. However the Tipitapa wanted him. But always with an eye toward the shore and an opportunity to beach himself.

He didn't know how long he drifted like that. Long enough that his strength was fading fast. And he suspected he knew the reason why.

One of the soldiers had gotten lucky. As Manny was freefalling off the bridge, he'd felt the round connect with his shoulder. Felt the slice and the burn.

And now he felt the effect of the blood loss.

Light-headedness. Fatigue. And for the first time, disorientation.

A wave of darkness hit him and he went under again. He battled the urge to fight it. Slowly let himself surface and grabbed the breath he desperately needed. He fought to stay conscious. Fought the chills that overtook him. Made himself stay relaxed so he wouldn't sink like a stone again.

And then he was fighting something that snagged at his legs. Grabbed at his feet.

Panic hit before understanding. The Tipitapa was home to any number of night stalkers—including bull sharks, the only freshwater sharks in the world. And if the sharks didn't get him, there was a good chance a bushmaster would. He'd never tangled with the large pit viper whose venomous bit could kill a man in minutes. He prayed to God he wouldn't have to now. It was a battle he could never win.

He kicked for his life and managed only to become more entangled. And that's when it hit him. Brush. He'd hid a patch of brush. Which could mean shore. Or a downed tree.

A tree he decided. It was branches, not a shark or a snake that had latched onto his pant legs and ended his free float down the river.

He was saved. And yet this saving grace could kill him. If he couldn't figure a way to break free, yet use the tree to keep him from floating away, he'd eventually be sucked under again. Each time he'd gone down, it had become harder to come up. He strongly suspected he had very few resurrections left in him.

Drawing from the last of his reservoir of strength, he dug deep and threw a leg over what felt like a stout arm of the tree. When he felt a connection, he clamped his thighs together like a vice and put his weight into righting himself.

He teetered precariously, the river flowing around his hips, strong and determined to knock him from his perch.

But he hung on.

Panting for breath.

Fighting the pain that screamed through his arm.

Clinging to consciousness.

Determined not to fall.

No way was he going back into that spin cycle. This, he understood, was his last chance. If he fell back into the water, he was done.

He shook his head, cleared the cobwebs. Struggling with balance as he straddled the tree, he tried to orient himself to his position. The night was dark but a sliver of a moon shined across the rippling water. He could actually see the riverbank. See the roots of the downed madrono tree that held him, the base of the trunk as it disappeared into the water some thirty feet away.

Thirty feet that separated him from drowning.

On a bracing breath, he leaned back, just far enough so he could reach the tree with his hands, gain a measure of balance. Now, if he could only feel his hands.

Inch by cautious inch, he pushed forward, his eyes on the bank, his mind blank of anything but reaching his goal.

He didn't think of the pain. He didn't think about falling. He didn't think about the heat of the night—and yet he was shivering. Shock, most likely. Blood loss.

Most of all, he didn't think about Lily. To think of her would make him weak. To think of her betrayal would make him want to die.

So he pressed forward at a snail's pace. It felt like years. A century passed as mosquitoes bit him incessantly and night creatures slithered along the bank and brushed against his bare feet.

Finally, his toes touched mud.

Thank God. He'd reached the bank. Barely conscious now, propelled by muscle memory and guts he threw his leg over the log—and fell up to his chest in water and muck.

He sucked in a gasping breath when the cool water rushed over the inside thighs scraped raw from grating across the madrono bark. His arm throbbed and ached like someone had nailed him with a branding iron.

He had no feeling in his hands. No real conception of how he'd gotten there as he half-stumbled, half-crawled his way out of the water and up the muddy bank.

Where he collapsed. Facedown. Covered in muck.

He passed out cold—and dreamed fitful dreams of Lily. Of the first time he'd seen her beautiful, treacherous face. The first time they'd made love.